Secrets of the Sword I

Death Before Dragons, Book 7

by Lindsay Buroker

Copyright © Lindsay Buroker 2020

Illustration by Luisa Preissler

No part of this book may be reproduced, scanned, or distributed in any printed or electronic form without permission. Please do not participate in or encourage piracy of copyrighted materials in violation of the author's rights. Thank you for respecting the hard work of this author.

This is a work of fiction. Names, characters, places, and incidents either are the product of the author's imagination or are used fictitiously, and any resemblance to locales, events, business establishments, or actual persons—living or dead—is entirely coincidental.

DEATH BEFORE DRAGONS

SECRETS OF THE SWORD I

LINDSAY BUROKER

CHAPTER 1

DRIZZLE SPAT FROM THE GRAY sky as I grabbed my weapons, climbed out of the Jeep, and looked for the mysterious magical artifact that plucked at my half-elven senses.

A bog stretched away from the gravel parking area, white and red cranberries floating on the surface, smoke hazing the air above them. That air smelled of the Pacific Ocean, decomposing leaf litter, and a barbecue gone terribly wrong.

I wrinkled my nose and spotted a fire smoldering near a manufactured home overlooking the bog. Animal carcasses were piled beside it, hooves and antlers jutting out of the tangle.

"Cozy place," I muttered.

A grizzled man in a yellow raincoat came out of the house—the farmer who'd called my boss and requested my presence? He carried a rifle instead of a hoe or rake or whatever one used for collecting the harvest.

The man didn't point his rifle toward me, but he squinted suspiciously, and his knuckles were tight around it. If I hadn't sensed magic out in the water, I would have wondered if I'd gotten the wrong bog.

I let my fingers rest on the hilt of Fezzik, the compact submachine pistol in my thigh holster, though he was a full-blooded human and likely couldn't see it or Chopper, the sword in a harness on my back. Both weapons were magical and difficult for the mundane to see.

"Are you Gene?" I asked.

"Yup. You Val Thorvald? The assassin, great warrior, and expert in kooky magical shit?" He eyed my jeans, combat boots, leather duster, tank top, and finally my long braid of blonde hair draping down to my boobs. The latter prompted a lip curl instead of the more typical masculine interest.

I flicked the braid over my shoulder. "That's more or less what my business card says."

"I was expecting a guy."

"You thought Val was a man's name?"

"I hoped. Knew a big German guy named Valentin once."

"Well, you got a six-foot-tall Norse gal named Valmeyjar. It means corpse maiden if that makes you feel better about my abilities."

"Not really. Here." Gene tossed a pair of muddy hip waders onto the damp grass in front of me. "These are for you."

"I'm honored. I didn't know I'd receive gifts on this gig."

"You can borrow them. I assume you're going in. The *thing* is out about there." Gene pointed his rifle toward the center of the expansive bog—there had to be twenty acres underwater. "You can see it glowing at night."

"A shame I didn't come later. I assume you didn't put it out there?"

He gave me a scathing look. "Of course not. It just appeared, somehow rooted down to the ground. It happened three nights ago, right after I flooded the bog for the harvest."

"Can you *unflood* it?"

Whatever it was would be easier to remove if it wasn't underwater.

"Not until the berries are harvested." Gene's expression shifted from scathing to pitying, as if I were a slow city simpleton. "I'm sure you can find the *thing*. Look around the property first, if you want. There are dead animals everywhere, dying faster than I can burn them." He shifted his rifle toward deciduous and evergreen trees to the sides of the bog, fall leaves matted into the grass underneath them, creating a soggy red and orange carpet. "I trust you're not squeamish, *Corpse Maiden*."

"I'm not, and you can call me Val. You think this artifact is killing the animals?"

"Artifact?" His forehead wrinkled. "This isn't some archaeological find. It's a weird glowing bundle of balls that you can't get out of the water. If you touch it, it'll zap you. If you shoot it, the bullets bounce off. Which I guess you won't be doing since you don't have a gun. I thought a *great warrior* would have a weapon."

I drew Chopper, plunged the longsword into the ground, and released the hilt.

He jumped back as it seemed to appear out of thin air to him. The sword's magic only camouflaged it when I carried it. In the dim afternoon daylight, the blue glow of Chopper's blade was noticeable, and Gene gaped at it.

"Hopefully, that'll do." I pulled Chopper out of the ground, silently apologized for sticking it in the dirt, and wiped it with my cleaning cloth. The magical blade never dulled, and I'd used it to pry and dig my way out of everything from wrecked cars to cave-ins without harming it, but I still felt guilty over improper use.

I grabbed the bog boots and stalked away, wanting to finish this task as soon as possible. The clouds promised more serious rain, and the scent of burning carcasses was turning my stomach.

"Where'd you get that sword?" Gene called after me, reverence replacing the sarcasm in his voice.

"Killed a zombie lord ten years back. He didn't tell me where *he* got it before he died."

A shame because it would be nice to know. I'd come across magical beings from other realms who had accused me of stealing the sword. Only recently, I'd learned that Chopper—I had no idea what its real name was—had many more powers than I'd suspected.

With luck, it would shatter an animal-slaying magical artifact if need be.

I headed around the bog toward the far side, less because I wanted to see the promised dead animals and more out of a reluctance to put on hip-high rubber boots for the first time in front of a stranger. My elven blood gave me more balance than the average human, but that was no guarantee of finesse in dressing.

My phone beeped with an incoming text message from my daughter, Amber.

I can't practice swords this weekend. Too much homework.

I paused to stare bleakly at the words. It was her third time canceling this month.

This past summer, after a run-in with a dragon, she'd asked me to teach her how to defend herself, and I'd even finagled a magical short sword from Colonel Willard for her, but Amber had been extremely busy since school started up again. Or so she'd told me.

I believed her, but I couldn't help but feel rejected. She lived with my ex-husband, and the weekend sword practices were the only excuse I had for coming by, so every time she canceled meant I didn't see her that week. Maybe she'd decided she preferred it that way.

Sighing, I put the phone away. *Great warriors* weren't supposed to feel sorry for themselves. Besides, I had a mission to focus on.

At first, I passed only dead crows and seagulls, but a couple of coyotes had collapsed in a thicket at the edge of the trees. They weren't gaunt, aged, or visibly injured. Just dead. Poisoned by the proximity of the artifact's magic? If so, why hadn't the farmer who lived bog-adjacent been affected?

I rubbed a cat-shaped charm on a leather thong around my neck, one of many magical trinkets I'd found, purchased, or won in battle over the years. A silver mist formed at my side, and Sindari, a seven-hundred-pound silver tiger, solidified with the top of his head almost level with my shoulder.

You went into battle without me? Sindari asked telepathically, his green eyes accusing.

"Nope. These seagulls and coyotes were dead when I got here."

He gazed around, nostrils twitching. *I suppose that is acceptable. They would not have been formidable foes. I sense something magical in that water.*

"That's what I'm here for. I'm going to go check it out. Can you sniff around and let me know if you smell or sense anything else unusual in the area?"

Other than a dozen dead animals?

"Yeah. Also, have you heard of any artifacts designed to kill animals but not people?"

In many realms, humans, with their utter lack of magical senses and abilities, are considered animals.

"As a half-human who grew up in Seattle, I'll try not to find that offensive." I tugged on the first of the tall rubber boots—it was as awkward as I thought it would be.

I am simply saying that I do not know why an elf or dragon or other enchanter of artifacts would bother excluding humans from a creation designed to kill animals. Sindari wandered off, sniffing the ground and air as he continued to speak telepathically with me. *I am also not aware of many artifacts that are designed to kill animals, unless it is a booby trap that is protecting something.*

"If a dragon made it, I'm sure it wasn't put here to guard the cranberries. Zav complains if there's even ketchup on his hamburger patty." As I'd found out recently when taking my dragon mate to Dick's Drive-in for a late-night snack in Wallingford. The cook had left the buns off our order of twenty burgers—even in human form, dragons had ravenous appetites—but he'd refused to believe that anyone would want the meat without condiments. "I'm positive he wouldn't want cranberry sauce on a turkey drumstick."

Dragons are carnivores, as are all apex predators. Magnificent predators would not have fangs if they were meant to eat berries.

"Why do I have a feeling you're talking about yourself more than Zav?" Once I'd gotten the boots on, attached the straps to my ammo belt, and removed my thigh holster so Fezzik wouldn't get wet, I waded out into the chilly water. A nippy wind gusted in from the ocean, salty and cold and promising a storm.

Because you know I am magnificent. I am going into the woods.

Let me know if you feel woozy from the artifact's magic. I switched to telepathy as we moved farther away from each other. My boots bumped against underwater cranberry bushes with every step, making the passage arduous. *I'd hate for such a magnificent predator to keel over like a poisoned coyote.*

I detect nothing deleterious in the air. Perhaps the water is tainted, and the animals were drinking it.

The words made me pause and eye the water halfway up my thighs. Coming out here might not be wise, but what choice did I have?

"Let's hope rubber repels magical poison," I muttered and waded onward, floating cranberries bumping off my thighs.

Though I still couldn't see it, my senses tingled as I drew closer to the artifact. They guided me until a faint white glow grew visible, emanating from under a raft of cranberries. Whatever the artifact was, it was fully submerged.

Wishing I'd thought to bring a rake, I used my hands and legs to make waves to drive the berries away so I could see under the water. It only partially worked, but it was enough for me to make out what reminded me of a bouquet of balloons. Balloons emanating magic.

My chest grew tighter, a telltale sign of the asthma I'd developed in the last year rearing its head. It tended to get worse in stressful or emotional situations—and also if the air was polluted with such noxious things as woodsmoke or mold spores.

I eyed the distant bonfire—no, the *funeral* pyre—burning near the house, but this probably had more to do with concern about what this weird artifact might do to me. Surreptitiously, I dug out my inhaler, put my back to the farmer—he was standing on the shoreline and watching me—and took a puff.

My new vantage point let me see Sindari, his silver fur visible as he skulked through the trees. No, he'd stopped skulking and had his nose to the leaf-littered ground.

I have found a fairy ring, he informed me.

Like a circle of mushrooms? I'd heard the stories that they marked doorways into the fae realm, but I'd never seen such a doorway, so I didn't know how much stock to put in rumors. I'd encountered people with fae blood before, but I'd never run into a full-blooded representative of the race. Elves and dwarves had once lived in hidden colonies on Earth, but I'd never heard suggestions that the fae did anything but visit and kidnap fair maidens.

Indeed. There are footprints around the mushrooms. Unlike the tracks around the bog, I do not believe they belong to the farmer or his family.

Do they belong to whoever planted this artifact? Perhaps unwisely, I stuck my finger in the water to touch one of the balloons to see if the farmer had been telling the truth about being zapped. A mere brush sent an electrical shock up my arm that reverberated through my torso and made me gasp and jerk back.

I cannot tell that. They were made a few days ago.

The farmer said this artifact appeared three days ago.

Few lingering scents remain, but I believe… Yes, fae or someone traveling from the fae realm may have been here. I detect an otherworldly smell.

What constitutes an otherworldly smell to my otherworldly tiger? I poked my sword into the water under the balloons, trying to locate whatever bound them together and to the bottom, and hoped the electrical charge couldn't travel through my blade to me.

The dirt and foliage of their realm has a distinctive smell. All of the fae lands were crafted by magic.

My sword hit something. Not a chain or a rope or anything with give. I poked around it with the blade. A stem? No, more like a trunk. I probed to the bottom and pushed the tip into the mud.

"Sorry, Chopper. I'll give you a nice oiling later."

Unlike Sindari, the magical sword didn't communicate with me, but it pulsed a brighter blue as if to acknowledge the comment. Odd. In the ten years I'd had the blade, I couldn't remember it doing that. Usually, if it glowed a brighter blue, that meant an enemy was near and we were about to charge into battle.

I scanned the shoreline of the bog again. Though I didn't see anyone but the farmer, the sensation of being watched crept over me.

One of my necklace charms allowed me to turn invisible, and I'd encountered others with similar trinkets or innate magic, so not seeing anyone didn't mean that nobody was there.

The hair on the back of my neck stood up. *You're* sure *those tracks are three days old, Sindari?*

They are not fresh.

A *thwump* came from the farmer's bonfire, and the flames leaped ten feet into the air. He charged over to check on it.

I didn't sense anything in that direction, but that hadn't appeared natural. I still had the feeling of being watched.

"This place is giving me the creeps." Not wanting to hang around in the water any longer, I angled Chopper so that I could saw at the trunk under the balloons.

The tough fibrous material gave but surprisingly slowly. Chopper had an edge sharper than any mundane blade, and I could have cut down a redwood with it, but the sword struggled to make progress on this.

I switched to hacking instead of sawing, but the water made the cuts less effective. My arm brushed one of the balloons, and it zapped me through my sleeve.

Pain and irritation swept through me, and without thinking of the consequences, I lifted Chopper and smashed it into the artifact. The balloon didn't pop, but it shattered, spewing out a puff of glowing white mist and glass-like shards. One gouged my hand as I skittered away from the tainted air.

"Good move, Val." I eyed the glowing mist and scooted back farther, almost tripping over a submerged bush but hardly caring. Whatever that mist was, I didn't want to breathe it in.

My thoughtless bashing of the balloon had destroyed it—the remaining shell had gone dark—and the artifact oozed slightly less magic. The mist faded and nothing untoward happened to me. That didn't keep me from wishing that I had a hazmat suit in the Jeep that I could have donned. For good or ill, I was being paid to take care of this and had to finish the job.

Do you know of any possible side effects from destroying fae artifacts, Sindari? Assuming this is *a fae artifact.*

Aside from irritating the fae who placed it there?

Yeah. Irritating people is my job. I'm not that worried about that.

Like elves and dragons, the fae have numerous kinds of magic. There are thousands of things that artifact might do. Side effects, as you call them, could be copious.

Fabulous.

A pair of deer had come out of the woods while we were communicating. I didn't notice them until they reached the water and bent their necks to lap at it.

"Beat it, deer!" I yelled, waving my sword.

They skittered back to the trees and stopped to stare at me. The farmer was also looking over from the fire. It had returned to normal, but he shook his head slowly, as if to say the trouble was only beginning.

The deer must have gotten some of the water. One wobbled, took a few faltering steps, then crumpled to the ground.

I swore. What kind of poison worked so quickly?

The other deer fled back into the woods, but its gait was ataxic, and I feared it wouldn't make it far. I eyed my hand, blood now welling from a cut between my thumb and forefinger, and wondered if I'd just screwed myself. Another perk of my mixed blood was that I healed faster than normal humans, and I'd survived injuries that would have killed someone else, but I wasn't bulletproof.

I'm destroying it, Sindari. Jaw set, I turned back to the artifact.

I understand.

This time, I was more careful. I angled my slashes carefully so the shards from the broken balloons flew in the opposite direction. Even the water worried me, so I did my best to keep it from splashing me.

"Hazmat suit," I muttered as a droplet hit my jaw anyway. "I'm buying a hazmat suit and keeping it in the Jeep for all future road trips."

Chopper shattered the last of the glass balloons, and I backed away again. Faintly glowing white mist hung in the air above the destruction, but the magic faded from my senses.

Despite my care, a shard had landed on my shoulder—or maybe that had happened on the first strike. I lifted a hand to knock it away but paused. Just because I'd destroyed the artifact didn't mean the mystery was solved or that we'd never have to deal with it again. What if these bundles of balloons started popping up on farms all over Washington?

I gingerly plucked up the shard and slid it into my duster pocket. Willard's people could go over it.

The deer are dead, Sindari reported as I waded toward the shoreline, Chopper resting on my shoulder. I would dry the blade before putting it away.

I'll tell the farmer to drain the field. He better get rid of this harvest—it could be as tainted as the water.

Val? Sindari sat on the shoreline, his head tilted as he gazed at me, his telepathic voice carrying an odd note.

Yes? I grunted as my boot snagged on another bush.

What's wrong with your sword?

As I climbed onto the shoreline, I pulled Chopper off my shoulder for a look, expecting half a cranberry bush to be dangling from the tip.

But the tip wasn't the problem—the entire blade was glowing with pulsing white energy.

Sindari scrutinized it. *It's sending out a wave of magic with each pulse. Like a beacon.*

A beacon that will let my enemies know exactly where I am?

A beacon that will let everyone *know exactly where you are.*

Hell.

CHAPTER 2

I DRIED OFF CHOPPER, HOPING THE sword would stop pulsing once the contaminated water was removed. It didn't.

I laid the blade in the grass and backed up a few steps. Immediately, I sensed the waves of magical energy emanating from it, as Sindari had promised. Strange that I hadn't felt anything apart from its usual aura when I'd been holding it. It was like the difference between being under the water when a wave surged to shore versus being caught on the surface.

Backing a few dozen steps away did nothing to diminish the pulses of energy that washed over me. A beacon was right. How far away could the waves be sensed?

"This would be less concerning if there weren't a few hundred ogres, orcs, trolls, and other aggressive species in the Pacific Northwest who want me dead." Whether working for the government or as a freelancer, I only assassinated magical bad guys who *really* deserved it—primarily murderers—but that didn't keep their friends and family members from detesting me and wanting revenge. "And if people hadn't already tried to steal this sword from me in the past."

Magical swords were hard to come by on Earth, and as I'd learned of late, Chopper was one of the more badass weapons around. Someone from another realm had told me it was called a dragon blade, and I knew from experience that it could cut through their armored scales when few other weapons could hurt them. A dwarf had told me it was ten thousand years old and made by an ancient dwarven master enchanter.

All I knew for sure was that it made my job a lot easier, and I didn't want to lose it. Fezzik, which had been made by my weapons-crafting friend Nin, could mow down people who weren't protected by magic, but not everyone fell into that category.

You do have cause for concern. Sindari still sat on his haunches by the blade, but he gazed into the woods, as if potential thieves might even now be creeping up on us.

I walked back over, picked up Chopper, and wiped it down again, still vainly hoping that somehow cleaning it was the answer. "Will you show me the fairy ring?"

Certainly.

Before I'd taken more than a few steps after Sindari, my phone buzzed in my pocket, startling me. It was Dimitri, one of my roommates and the majority owner of the Sable Dragon, a quirky coffee, potion, and enchanted-yard-art shop in Fremont. In a fit of dubious wisdom, I'd volunteered to become a ten-percent owner in the establishment, so his problems were my problems. As if I didn't have enough problems of my own.

"Yeah?" I answered warily, expecting news about a fight between ogres or goblins or some other patrons of the coffee shop—for some reason, it attracted full- and partial-blooded magical beings like flames attracted moths.

"Are you at the beach?" He'd seen me off that morning and knew about the trip.

"A cranberry bog that's beach-adjacent."

Technically, we were leaving the bog and heading into the woods. Sindari weaved through the trees, and I stepped over soggy logs and moss-draped boulders as the rain picked up, spattering off the top of my head.

"I mentioned to Zoltan that you were going to Long Beach, and he wants you to pick up some things."

"I'm not his personal shopper."

Dimitri paid rent to live in the old Victorian house in Green Lake that we shared. Zoltan, the alchemist vampire who lived in the basement, did not. That left me disinclined to run errands for him.

"He said he'd give you a discount the next time you need his services."

I almost told him to stuff it—no, to tell *Zoltan* to stuff it—but then I thought of the shard in my pocket and my glowing sword. Willard had people who could research magical items, but Zoltan had a lab full of equipment in the basement. He'd proven useful more than once—as the ridiculously overpriced invoices he sent me attested.

"What does he want?"

"Devil's club and hairy manzanita."

"Those don't sound like things I can pick up at the gas station." I vaguely knew what manzanita looked like, but *hairy* manzanita? And I had no idea what devil's club was. Why couldn't alchemists ask for *normal* ingredients? Like eggs and flour?

"He says they grow wild in abundance out near the coast."

"Uh huh. I'm not foraging for plants in the rain. Use your Google-fu powers to find out where I can buy some, and I'll pick them up on the way out of town." I eyed my glowing and pulsing sword. "Make it quick. I'm leaving soon. *Very* soon."

"Uh, all right. Can you get *me* something?"

"What?" I asked, wariness returning as I stopped in a grassy clearing beside Sindari. "I'm not piling driftwood, nets, and glass fishing floats in the back of the Jeep for your art projects."

Sindari pointed his feline nose toward a rough circle of three- to four-inch-wide mushrooms protruding from the grass and leaf litter. I didn't sense anything magical about them, and they didn't look any different from other forest mushrooms. From time to time, I'd encountered rings of them, and I'd never seen any magical beings pop out of them.

"Good to know," Dimitri said, "but I was going to ask for cranberry fudge. I've only ever seen it at the coast. It's *amazing*."

"Sorry, buddy, but I've got a bigger problem. I'm not going souvenir shopping." More than one problem. The cut on my hand stung—was it my imagination that it was throbbing in sync with my sword?

Not deterred, Dimitri said, "I can send you the address. There's a quilt shop in town that sells fudge."

"The *quilt shop* sells candy?" Maybe they had manzanita too.

"Yup. The last time I was there, they had three kinds of the cranberry. Did I mention that it's amazing? Get the chocolate version, please. With walnuts."

"I'm hanging up now."

"*Val*, just a little? I'll make you something."

I said goodbye and stuck my phone back in my pocket.

Here are the footprints. Sindari pointed one of his big paws to what looked like, to my unsophisticated tracker's eye, slightly flattened grass.

They head in the direction of the bog. I followed them to the best of my ability, but as I said, the trail is several days old.

"I guess I should have brought Rocket," I said, naming my mother's golden retriever. Rocket adored Sindari—he adored *everybody*—but Sindari found him overly boisterous and couldn't forgive all the whaps in the face he'd received from Rocket's tail. "He's an expert tracker."

Sindari's green eyes turned toward me, cool as a glacier-fed mountain lake. *That bumbling canine can barely find his own tail. He would have no better luck than I. He would have flung himself into the bog to retrieve a stick as soon as we arrived.* Sindari issued the tiger equivalent of a haughty sniff. *It is likely he wouldn't have found the fairy ring at all.*

"What a shame that would have been." I used Chopper to poke a couple of the mushrooms, hoping to elicit a magical response, but despite Sindari's promise that someone otherworldly had traveled this way, I suspected these were random and mundane toadstools. Still, in case there *was* a hidden door, I gripped my lock-picking charm—its primary purpose was to open enchanted doorways, after all—and willed it to open the hypothetical magical passageway. Nothing happened. "Any other clues that might be useful?"

I have found nothing else. Your mother's hound would have found even less.

"Uh huh. Maybe you two need to have a tracking contest the next time you meet. Rocket finds missing people for a living, you know."

I thought he played with balls for a living.

"That's just a hobby."

We headed back to the manufactured home, where Gene waited with his rifle. He gaped at Sindari walking at my side.

"What is *that*?" the farmer whispered, pointing at him as we approached.

"A tiger. Hey, I think the water was tainted by that thing. And by tainted, I mean poisoned. You better drain the field and get rid of your crop." I eyed his house, the yard, and the bonfire—it had returned to burning normally. My instincts still suggested that someone—or something—was watching me, but Gene was the only one in sight.

He rocked back on his feet. "That would bankrupt me. I called your boss so I wouldn't *have* to get rid of the crop."

"I assumed you were just tired of burning animal bodies."

"That's a fortune in cranberries." Gene waved toward the bog.

"Now it's a poisoned fortune." I eyed the water, wondering where it would be drained *to* and if more wildlife might die if it was dumped in a river or the ocean. Most likely, it would be diluted enough that it wouldn't make a difference, but I had better check with Willard. "On second thought, don't drain it until I talk to my boss. Maybe artifact-tainted water needs to be professionally remediated."

"Remedi-what?"

Val? Sindari faced north, looking across the berry-covered water and out into the forest. Or *above* the forest. *I sense a magical creature flying this way. Two of them.*

Not dragons, I hope. My senses extended a couple of miles—I'd been practicing broadening my range—but Sindari still detected those with magical auras sooner.

I believe they are rocs. They're flying directly toward us.

I grimaced. I'd battled the quasi-intelligent magical birds before. Some of them were smart enough to know there would be repercussions if they killed humans; some weren't. All of them liked to gather interesting trinkets. A magical sword would qualify.

"Go inside, Gene." I drew Chopper and pointed it toward his house. "Trouble is coming."

As I spoke, the birds came within range of my senses.

"I *can't* get rid of the crop," Gene whispered, his gaze still locked on the bog. "We need that money to pay the taxes on the farm. Are you sure the berries were affected?"

"Get inside *now*." I pushed him toward the door.

Two brown-and-black birds came into view, similar in appearance to eagles but much, *much* larger. They could pick up humans; reports of cattle found dropped from great heights and mutilated in their fields suggested they could also pick up cows.

Gene caught sight of them, cursed, and lifted his rifle. Rocs weren't as impervious to mundane weapons as dragons, but they were still hard to kill. This was a job for Fezzik.

"That won't do anything. I promise." I turned him around and manhandled him toward the door. "Wait inside."

He found out I was stronger than I looked and stopped struggling, especially after I kicked him in the back of the knee and almost threw him at the door.

Sindari crouched as the rocs flew over the bog. One screeched like the terrifying bird of prey that it was. Their beady yellow eyes were both focused on me.

Gene must have realized how large they were, because he finally allowed himself to be shoved into the house. I slammed the door shut and ran back to Sindari's side.

My phone buzzed again.

I ignored it and yanked out Fezzik to fire at the closest roc. The bullets, imbued with magic beyond what the pistol itself held, hummed to my senses.

The birds must have sensed the threat, for they tried to wheel away, but they weren't fast enough. Several rounds slammed into the chest of my target. It faltered, flapping its wings wildly.

The other roc screeched and dove for me. I backed away, not wanting to end up fighting in the water.

Sindari bunched his muscles and sprang into the air. He intercepted the great bird before it reached me, his claws raking its feathered sides as he sank his teeth into the side of its neck.

The one I'd shot bled red drops into the bog, but that didn't keep it from recovering and landing right in front of me. I fired twice more before it lunged in, its razor-sharp beak snapping toward my face.

I threw myself to the side in a roll. As I leaped up, I holstered Fezzik and gripped Chopper with both hands. The roc leaped into the air and flew at me.

This time, I held my ground. I crouched low to avoid the snapping beak, then lunged in to attack its breast. With a rapid thrust, Chopper dove through feather and into flesh.

An ear-piercing screech hammered my ears. Wings battered at me as the bird twisted, trying to rake me with its talons.

I yanked out my sword and rolled away again to avoid the wings, but not before the roc sliced through my sleeve and into flesh. Hot pain charged up my arm.

Cursing, I whirled to try to come in behind him before he could turn after me. But he was fast, and I slashed toward his beak rather than his butt. He jerked back, springing into the air before I connected.

Wind whipped at my braid as he flapped furiously to gain altitude. A splash came from the bog—Sindari and the other roc were wrestling in the water, the spray making it impossible to see details of the battle.

I was on the verge of running to help but sensed my roc banking to come back at me from above. Like an osprey diving for a fish, he plummeted toward me with his talons outstretched. They were targeting not me but my sword, though they would gouge the hell out of me in an attempt to snatch it.

I ran toward the house and leaped around the corner for cover. He altered his path and continued toward me, but I had time to bring out Fezzik again. I fired into his face this time, one of the bullets piercing his eye.

His feathered head jerked back, and he crashed into the house, knocking off siding and snapping wood. I leaped out from behind the corner and lunged in with Chopper. Before the roc could recover, I slashed down with a great blow and sliced through his neck.

The bird's head tumbled off, rolling to a stop in front of the door. Gene peeked out, looked at the bloody head, then leaned back inside and closed the door again.

A final splash came from the bog. Sindari strode out, gave me a baleful look, and shook himself vigorously. Water droplets flew in all directions.

"What was that look for? Don't you love it when I call you to Earth to engage in battle?"

Not in the water. Done shaking, he leveled another cool stare at me.

"You're the one who sprang out over the bog to attack it."

So I could bravely and nobly keep it from reaching you.

"I appreciate that, but I've seen videos of tigers swimming and frolicking in ponds. I don't think it's as bad as you say." I snapped my fingers. "I've even seen *you* swim. At my mother's house in Oregon before she moved up here."

That was on a hot day. This day is wet, damp, cold, and insipid. As is that footwear. He seemed to notice my giant rubber boots for the first time. *Why are you wearing those for battle?*

"I wasn't planning on a battle today." After making sure the second roc was as dead as the first—as promised, Sindari was an apex predator and had done the job as effectively as I had—I removed the clunky rubber boots.

You will have many more battles if you don't figure out how to remove the beacon from your sword. Is your mate not nearby?

"Zav went home to help his mother. Apparently, being the son of the queen of all of Dragondom involves a lot of political duties."

Hopefully, he shall return soon. Sindari shook himself off again. *I adore pitting myself in battle against enemies, but I fear that too many will come at once for us to survive against.*

"I'll head back to Seattle. Hopefully, Nin, Freysha, or one of Willard's book-loving agents will know how to make this stop." I cleaned and sheathed Chopper and headed for my Jeep. Willard should have already worked out the payment details with Gene and would give me my cut later. "It's good to know people with magical knowledge, right?"

Almost as good as knowing a powerful tiger willing to assist you in battle.

"Oh, I know that. I'm lucky to have such an ally." I patted him on the back.

Yes.

"And you're cheerful and appealing company too."

I am more cheerful when I am not wet.

"I've noticed."

Wind gusted, and heavy droplets of rain pelted down from the sky and onto the top of my head—and the top of Sindari's head.

His ears flattened. *Open the door to your conveyance. I will ride with you to warn you of further threats.*

Feeling like a chauffeur, I opened the back door. The seats were always down for him, though he barely fit inside, even with that concession.

Sindari climbed in, used a paw to swat some of my camping gear aside, and sat with his head pressed against the ceiling.

It smells in here again. He gave me another baleful look as I closed the door and went to the front.

"I got a new air freshener." I put my weapons in the passenger seat and flicked a brownish-purple cardboard tree acquired at the car wash. It dangled from the glove-compartment latch.

It's dreadful.

"It's a new scent. Blackberry Clove. I thought you might like it better than the others."

I do not. Your sword is still pulsing with energy.

"I know." I could feel it more than ever now that I'd removed the harness. Why did I have the feeling that this new effect wasn't going to fade away on its own? "The ride back could be fun."

Doubtful.

CHAPTER 3

RAIN HAMMERED THE WINDSHIELD AS we drove east toward Olympia. I no longer had the feeling that someone was watching me, so hopefully I'd left my possibly imaginary observer back on that farm.

That was good because I didn't want another fight. I'd made it through the roc attack unscathed, but the cut on my hand still throbbed. I'd bandaged it from the first-aid kit in my Jeep and was afraid to peel the wrap back to look at it. With my fast regeneration, a normal wound would have closed up and been well on its way to healed by now. Whatever this was, I doubted it was normal.

A familiar presence registered to my senses, and some of the tension seeped out of my shoulders. Zav.

There weren't too many enemies that could stand up to dragons, and I would be safer with my beacon sword if he was at my side. I hoped he could stay for a while.

Knowing his propensity for landing in the middle of the highway, I pulled over onto an unmarked road near the turnoff for Summit Lake.

Your mate approaches, Sindari stated. *You should not need my services further if he intends to stay.*

It amused me that Sindari called us mates. That summer, Zav had claimed me, in the way of dragons, and he used the term mate too. It seemed to be the equivalent of marriage on Earth, but I wasn't ready for that level of commitment. I simply told people we were dating.

"You don't want to stick around and say hi?" I stopped the Jeep on the shoulder.

Tall evergreens rose up to either side of the road and hemmed it in, until a hint of magic plucked at my senses, and the trunks leaned away from the pavement. In his native form, Zav landed in front of the Jeep, wings furled to his side, powerful muscles standing out under his sleek black scales. He lowered his head to peer through the windshield with violet eyes that weren't quite reptilian but were distinctively alien to someone who wasn't familiar with him.

The power emanating from him made the auras of the deceased rocs seem puny in comparison. The rain pounding down on the pavement all around him didn't land on his scales, as if weather wouldn't *dare* pester a dragon.

That is not necessary, Sindari replied. *You have a tendency to engage in mating foreplay when he is in the conveyance with you, and I believe you forget that I'm back here.*

"We're not going to have mating foreplay while I'm driving." I waved at Zav and grinned, happy to see him. It had been over a week, so I would have been happy regardless of my current predicament, but with his power, he might be able to flick a finger and remove the magical plague afflicting my sword.

You have done so before.

"Only once, and that was late at night in the long line for an extremely slow drive-thru restaurant. You could hardly count that as driving. And it's not like we had sex. We just kissed."

Admittedly with some vigor.

Being stuck back here while you did it was as unpleasant as that cardboard tree oozing noxious odors at me. As Sindari spoke, Zav shifted into his human form, a handsome olive-skinned man with short black hair and a short, neatly trimmed mustache and beard. *Summon me again if you are preparing to enter a battle.*

"I will. It would be a shame to miss your grumpiness."

Hmmph. Sindari turned into silver mist, then disappeared back to his own realm.

Zav opened the door, the crackling power of his aura engulfing me and making my nerves tingle, as it always did when we were close.

"What happened to your sword?" were his first words.

Usually, we greeted each other with a kiss—whether there were witnesses or not—so his focus on the sword attested to the gravity of the situation.

"I used it to destroy an artifact that was poisoning wildlife, and now it's pulsing with magic." I moved my pistol and sword harness out of the front seat to make room for him but left Chopper within reach in case he wanted to examine it.

"I felt the pulses of magical energy as soon as I arrived in your world." Zav sat down and picked up the sword.

"I'm hoping you arrived only a couple of miles from here and not a hundred miles away."

"I opened a portal over your domicile."

Oh, good. Only eighty miles.

"That's problematic. A couple of rocs already attacked me, presumably because they sensed its call and wanted it for themselves."

"That is likely. This is a desirable weapon, and now it is radiating its brilliance for all with magical ability to sense." He turned his gaze toward mine and rested a hand on my shoulder. "I am concerned you will be in danger."

"I have that concern too. Any chance you can make it stop?"

He started to turn his attention back to the sword, but he ended up focusing on the glove compartment. No, on the air freshener.

"What is that odor?"

"My air freshener. You don't like the scent either? Sindari isn't a fan."

"I do not. What is its purpose?"

"I've been taking Mom and Rocket on weekend hikes. He likes to fling himself in lakes. On the drive back, his wet-dogness permeates the Jeep and stays in the seats. My air freshener overrides that smell."

Zav squinted at me, as if he thought I was teasing him. "This odor is more unpleasant than the scent of a wet animal."

"That's debatable."

With a poof of flame, the air freshener went up in smoke. Tiny blackberry-clove scented ashes trickled to the floor.

"It is not." Zav returned his attention to the sword.

"Sindari may kiss you the next time he sees you."

"That is unacceptable. Only my mate may kiss me." Zav looked at me again, his lashes lowered and his gaze sultrier this time.

Before I could decide to lean in for that kiss, his attention returned to the sword.

"This is problematic. There is an overlay of magic atop the dwarven magic imbued in the blade. It may affect the sword's powers."

I hadn't wanted to hear that.

"I believe it is fae magic."

"Sindari found a fairy ring near the cranberry bog where someone had planted the artifact." Maybe I'd been wrong and the mushrooms *had* marked a doorway to another realm. The fae realm.

"It is *more* than an overlay." Zav rotated the sword, gazing at its length with his senses, not merely his eyes. "The strands of old and new magic are entwined. Interesting."

"Can you *unentwine* it?"

"Unentwine is not in your dictionary. Unentangle is the correct word."

"I know. I was using wordplay for humorous effect."

He didn't appear humored. He appeared… concerned. That worried me. Since dragons were so powerful, few things concerned them.

"Can the magic be *unentangled*?" I asked.

He studied the sword for a few more seconds, then noticed the bandage on my hand. "You are injured?"

"I cut myself on the artifact."

"You will let me heal it." He rested his hand lightly on mine.

I thought about pointing out that he needn't make things orders, but how could I object to being healed? "Gladly. Thanks."

The usual warm tingle of his healing magic flowed through me, but he frowned as he focused on my hand. "This is not a typical wound."

"I know."

He peeled back the bandage to reveal the gash as bad as it had been when I'd dressed it. "Something is driving away your white blood cells and not permitting them to repair the tissue. It is also forming a barrier against my own regenerative power. I don't sense fae magic tainting your blood, but there is *something*…" He kept scrutinizing my hand, making me feel like a science experiment in a Petri dish.

"I'm not going to turn into a zombie, am I?" I smiled, though fresh worry blossomed in my chest.

If Zav, the powerful dragon who could heal almost *anything*, couldn't fix it, who could? He had incinerated bullets lodged in my hip before, healed the damage within seconds, and left me without even a scar.

For some reason, I thought of the deer keeling over dead after a mere drink from the bog. What would happen if I couldn't figure out a way to heal this? Would it get worse and spread to the rest of my body?

"I may need to consult Zondia'qareshi, but I will come up with a way to heal it."

"Zondia? Your sister who hates me?"

"She is training to become a healer and has a great deal of aptitude and power despite her young age."

I thought of the lilac-scaled dragon in her human form, complete with black leather jacket and nose piercings, as she rolled her eyes at me. It was hard to imagine her handing me a Band-Aid, much less deigning to heal me.

Zav laid the bandage back in place and returned to contemplating the sword. "I believe I could remove all of the magic. I am uncertain if I can remove only the fae magic. I assume you wish the original enchantments that enhance the blade to remain."

"Damn straight I do. I can't be an assassin of magical bad guys if I don't have a weapon that can hurt them." Granted, Fezzik hurt *most* magical beings, and I'd done this job before acquiring Chopper, but it was *much* easier with the sword. I had some abilities that typical humans didn't have, but as full-blooded magical beings were fond of telling me, I was a mongrel and not as inherently powerful as they were. I needed every advantage I could get.

"Fae hide from dragons, so it may be difficult for me to find one to fix this. A dwarven master enchanter could perhaps put a protection spell on the native magic while removing the foreign magic."

"I don't think there are any dwarves left on Earth. I have Dimitri. He's a quarter dwarven, and he enchants yard art."

"That will not be sufficient."

"Well, he's my best bet, unless you want to take me to the dwarven home world, so I can hire a dwarven enchanter to look at it."

"That would be ideal, but I have recently learned from my cousin who rules over the dwarven home world that they have disappeared into their underground homes and closed up the entrances, enchanting them so well that even dragons have difficulty finding them."

"That's crappy timing. Why did they disappear?"

"We believe they worried there would be fallout from the confrontation between my clan and the Silverclaw Clan. It is possible that because they are hidden away, they do not yet know that my clan was victorious in that skirmish." He lifted his chin, his violet eyes blazing with pride. "As you know, since you were there and went into battle at my side." His gaze turned back to me, the blaze growing softer in a way that put bedroom thoughts in my mind. Too bad we were still many miles from my bedroom. "You vexed my enemies and then *slew* the treacherous Shaygorthian."

"Yes, I did." I smiled, always pleased when he thought highly of me, especially since we'd started our relationship with him calling me a mongrel and throwing my Jeep—my *previous* Jeep—into a tree. "With the help of my sword. If dwarven enchanters aren't available right now, I'm going to have to hope that Dimitri, or maybe the half-troll enchanter who's mentoring him, has a clue."

I did worry that if unentangling the magic was beyond Zav it would also be beyond those two. Or anyone else in the city.

"A powerful fae enchanter would also be able to remove the magic," he said, "but their people are also reclusive and shroud their realm in magic that makes it difficult to portal to. If someone I was familiar with were inside their realm, I could find entrance by using them as a beacon, but without that…"

I thought about mentioning my earlier feeling of being watched—if it had been the fae who planted the artifact, wouldn't he or she know how to remove its taint?—but that had been little more than a hunch. Even if someone had been there watching me, they would be gone by now.

"I could return to my world and consult with a powerful dragon enchanter," Zav said, his gaze still locked on mine, "but I am concerned about leaving you without protection. You are a capable warrior, but it is possible that too many enemies will come at you at once for you to fend off."

"I'm concerned about that too."

"I will stay here and protect you." His eyes remained intense, his tone almost fierce.

Usually, I liked handling my own problems, but as he'd said, I might be in over my head with this. Besides, it warmed my heart that he cared and *wanted* to protect me. And maybe it turned me on a bit too.

"I appreciate that," I whispered, transfixed by his aura, his gaze, and *him*.

We leaned together, our mouths meeting, and I decided it was good that Sindari had left. We weren't driving now, and even though having sex in the Jeep wasn't the most comfortable thing, as his aura crackled over me, every nerve in my body tingling with his power, I decided I didn't care.

Zav *never* cared. Neither witnesses, rain, nor inconveniently placed gear shifts could deter him from sex.

He caressed my cheek, then shifted his hand to the back of my head, fingers kneading my scalp through my hair. If he noticed a car whizzing past to get on the highway, he didn't show it.

Tingles of pleasure raced through my nerves, and I was on the verge of unbuckling my seatbelt, tossing the sword in the back, and climbing into his lap when I sensed more magical beings coming close. As with the rocs, they were heading straight toward me. No, toward my pulsing beacon of a sword.

Someone's coming, I thought telepathically, my lips too busy for talking.

Since his senses were far greater than mine, he had to already know, but maybe he had some notion of having sex before they got here. Or commanding them to wait until we were done—dragons thought nothing of commanding lesser species, as they called everyone who wasn't a dragon, and I could easily envision him doing that.

Eight werewolves, yes. Come to me, my mate.

My seatbelt unbuckled without being touched, and he slid his hand down to my back, apparently also wanting me in his lap.

I gripped his wrist. *We should deal with them first, my horny dragon.*

Damn, there *were* eight, and they were less than a quarter mile away now, running fast through the woods.

I will deal with them.

While we're kissing?

While we are mating. I have missed you. My world is my home and calls to me at times, but dealing with my kin and the enemies of my kin is stressful. Taking this form and mating with you is pleasing. Magic flowed from his fingers and into my body, lighting up my nerves even more.

Zav. I opened my eyes in time to see huge gray wolves lope out of the trees. *This needs to wait.*

The wolves stopped at the edge of the road, yellow eyes staring into the Jeep. The sword might be calling to them, but they also had to sense Zav. In his human form, his aura wasn't as noticeable as when he was in his native form, but it was still impossible for those with magical senses to miss.

He didn't release me, but he turned his head to glare out at the wolves, his violet eyes flaring with his inner power. *You dare approach a dragon when he is with his mate,* he boomed telepathically. *You think to take the sword of a dragon's mate? Leave now, or I will incinerate you.*

A cedar snag near the wolves burst into flames, and they sprang back into the shadows of the forest.

Usually, I would berate Zav for bullying people, but I had little doubt they'd come to steal my sword, so they didn't have my sympathy.

The big wolves' hackles were up, and they bared their fangs, but they also shared uneasy glances with each other. After contemplating us for a few more seconds, they backed slowly away. Too slowly.

Leave! Zav boomed again.

A magical compulsion accompanied the word, and they whirled and sped into the trees, sprinting back the way they had come.

We will continue. Zav looked at me again, not concerned that the dead tree was still burning. Someone would report that, and a fire engine would arrive soon. As much as I enjoyed having sex with Zav, I didn't want a firefighter to peer into the window and see my naked butt in the air.

I rested a hand on Zav's chest. "How about we save it for tonight?"

My phone buzzed, and I held up a finger to check it. "It's my boss. I have to take this."

Looking a touch petulant, Zav leaned back in his seat. He glared out the window, as if looking for more dead trees to light on fire.

"Hey, Willard," I answered, a little breathless from the kissing.

Hopefully, she wouldn't notice.

Zav's eyes were boring into the side of my head, and I had a feeling he was contemplating incinerating my phone. I reached over and rubbed his thigh through his robe, hoping a little fondling would mellow him out.

"How about sending an update after you finish a mission, Thorvald?" came Willard's Southern drawl. "I prefer to hear how it went from you, not the irritated farmer who's pissed because you said he couldn't harvest his berries and also left a giant decapitated bird on his front stoop."

She also sounded like she was in the mood to incinerate things. Everyone was grumpy today. It had to be the rain.

"There are dead animals all over his property," I said. "I fail to see how one more bird matters."

"The *size* is the problem. He can't drag it to his fire to burn."

"He's a farmer. He should have a tractor with some attachments. Look, it's been a rough day." I explained the artifact, my sword situation, and the fact that I'd been further delayed picking up alchemy supplies for the needy vampire living in the basement. Not to mention Dimitri's fudge.

"He can't get his own supplies?" Willard asked.

"I don't think vampires like going to the beach. Even if the Washington coast isn't known for its blazing sun, it does peek through the clouds from time to time." I picked up the keys—they'd tumbled to the floor during our hanky-panky—and stuck them in the ignition. It would be dark soon, and even with my mighty dragon warrior to fend off bad guys, I would rather not deal with attacks at night. "I did complete the mission, which was only to get rid of the artifact problem, as I recall. There was nothing about helping the client dispose of corpses. Nor professionally remediating tainted water—you may want to send someone out to check on that. Are you going to pay me?"

"Yeah, yeah. Prepare a thorough report when you get back, send it over, and I'll round up your funds and meet you at the usual spot at eight tomorrow morning."

"The Starbucks Reserve Roastery? Don't you want to support a local, independent coffee shop?"

"I've been to your place. It's full of goblins, and it's weird."

"You have a goblin secretary. How can you object to their kind?"

"I object to them en masse and amped up on caffeine. The last time I went, they were launching dice across the room with a trebuchet."

"That's for their board game. A roll doesn't count unless the dice bounce off at least two walls."

"One landed in my cup."

"I'm not sure how that affects the rules. Look, I'll buy you a cup of coffee if you come to our shop." It was a much closer drive than the Starbucks on Pike. If I was ambitious, and the rain stopped, I could walk. "You've had the goblin blend before and said it was good."

She grunted. "It's all right."

All right? When I'd brought her a thermos of it to sample that summer, she'd slurped half of it down in a minute flat.

"I'll buy you *two* cups," I said.

"Deal."

"You're cheap, Willard." I was a partial owner. I wasn't supposed to have to support my own local business.

"Don't make me dock you for leaving a bird corpse on the client's doorstep."

"Ha ha."

I started to hang up, but she added, "Are you going to be all right with werewolves and rocs and who knows what else coming to try to steal your sword? Do you want me to send a couple of men to your house to help?"

"Zav just got back to Earth. He's a good werewolf deterrent."

"I deter all lesser species who seek to molest my mate," Zav stated. "She is mine and not to be harmed. We will copulate soon."

My head thunked against the back of the seat when I rolled my eyes.

"I guess that explains why you were breathless," Willard said. "Meet you at eight."

She hung up before I could retort. Rude.

CHAPTER 4

MY ELVEN HALF-SISTER FREYSHA WAS sitting on the covered steps leading to the front porch of my Victorian house when I parked in the street out front. Night had fallen, it was still raining, and a chilly wind rattled the branches of the trees bordering the lawn. There was no reason for her to be sitting outside... unless she'd sensed my sword from halfway across the state and was worried about me.

"Val." Freysha sprang to her feet, her overalls clanking from gardening tools in the pockets. "What happened to your sword? I've been sensing its magic for hours."

"I was afraid of that."

Zav strode through the rain at my side, taking my hand and leading me to the steps. "Val and I will mate before she answers questions."

Freysha's lips parted, but she didn't seem to know what to say.

"My dragon returned to Earth horny." I pulled the artifact shard out of my pocket and handed it to Freysha. "Will you examine that and see if you can figure out anything more than that it's fae? And that it might have been stuck in a bog to poison the water for an unknown reason?"

Freysha turned it over in her hand. "Fae magic has some similarities to elven magic, but I have not encountered their kind often and do not recognize the enchantment on this. I will see if any of Colonel Willard's books have helpful entries. I still have them from when I researched your trinkets." She tilted her head, blonde hair falling away from one pointed ear. "Poisoning the water? Are you certain that was the intended result? The fae can be tricksters and are sometimes cruel to the other races, but they are not known to treat nature poorly."

"I'm not certain of anything, not even that fae were the ones who planted it. Sindari spotted a fairy mushroom ring with some old tracks, so it's as good a guess as any, but..." I shrugged. Now that the artifact was destroyed, I wouldn't normally care *who* had placed it, but I might have to solve that mystery before I could figure out how to make my sword stop pulsing magic.

"I will study it." Freysha looked at Zav. "In the kitchen downstairs. I will make sure not to go up to the second floor where my presence might disturb you, Lord Zavryd."

"Our rooms aren't that close," I said. "You don't need to stay away."

"In the kitchen," Freysha said diffidently and politely, "I will also not be disturbed by you."

"Ah." I pretended my cheeks didn't heat a few degrees as Zav tugged me into the house. "Show Zoltan the shard, too, when he gets back, will you?" I didn't sense his aura down in the basement and pretended he was off networking with business associates rather than drinking some neighbor's blood. "He may have some ideas. Oh, and tell him that his plants are in the back of my Jeep. So is Dimitri's fudge."

Maybe later, I would show my cut to Zoltan and see if he had any ideas. It still hurt but not so badly that I couldn't enjoy a couple of hours with Zav first. I'd missed him, and he'd been sending me seductive looks the whole drive back. Before I'd met him, I never would have guessed that a man in a black robe and elven slippers could get me excited. Funny how things changed.

"They will be pleased that you brought them gifts," Freysha said, trailing us up the steps.

"More like bribes. Zoltan promised to cut me a deal on my next invoice."

Zav led me across the living room toward the stairs. If I delayed by chatting further, he might sweep me over his shoulder and carry me up to the bedroom. Which wouldn't be awful. He had those nicely muscular shoulders.

My phone buzzed before we got to the stairs.

"Hang on." I checked it.

"Does that contraption never cease bothering you?" He again looked like he might incinerate my phone.

It was Amber, Amber who preferred texting to calling. Had something happened?

"It's my daughter. I have to take it." I patted Zav on the chest. "Wait for me in the bedroom, and I'll be right up."

I answered the phone, afraid it would drop to voice mail if I delayed.

"Very well." He looked over his shoulder as he ascended, sharing his flirtatious bedroom eyes with me. "I will wait for you naked and aroused, my mate."

"Oh, my God, ew," came a familiar voice from the phone.

"Hey, Amber." I decided not to say anything about Zav's comment. Maybe she would think it had been the TV. "What's up?"

"Your dragon lover, apparently. *Disgusting.*"

So much for the TV. I hadn't realized she'd met Zav enough times to know his voice.

"We're engaged in a consensual adult relationship," I said, hoping Thad had long ago had some version of The Talk with her. From what I'd gathered, she wasn't that into boys, but she had turned fifteen and was a sophomore in high school, so she was probably more worldly than I wanted to think. "My therapist promises me it's healthy and normal, not disgusting."

"Nothing you do is normal, Val."

I didn't know how to rebut that. She was right. "Did you call for a reason beyond reminding me of that? Did you change your mind about a weekend sparring session?"

"I have too much homework this weekend. I was hoping you could tell Dad to stop being stupid with women."

"As one of the women he was once stupid with, I probably can't advise him on that. But what's wrong? Isn't he dating Nin? She's nice."

Not only was Nin the maker of Fezzik, along with more magical ammunition and grenades than I could count, but I considered her a friend.

"He got a bunch of Tiffany and Cartier catalogs, and he's shopping for some ridiculously expensive bling as a gift for her. Is she another gold digger, Val? What the hell?"

"No, she's not. I highly doubt she asked for... Those are jewelry stores, right?"

"Yes, Val," Amber said in that tone one reserved for remedial students. "Expensive jewelry. Why can't he just get her flowers? Like a normal person? Are you *sure* she's not thirsty for earrings or bracelets and asked him for some? I don't like this."

"I've never even seen Nin wear jewelry. She holds her pigtails up with elastic hairbands."

"Pigtails. I forgot about that. She's practically younger than I am. This isn't working for me."

"She's thirty, and it's more important that it work for them." I didn't expect Amber to love the women her father dated, but her distaste bothered me more now that Thad was dating one of my friends, instead of that bitchy Shauna, who truly had been a gold digger.

"How can you say that? He's *my* dad. He hasn't even known her for two months. Did you know they're already *sleeping* together? I came out this morning, and she was *here*. In a *towel*. *Val*. He barely broke up with the *last* girlfriend. I have to do something about this."

"Ah, please don't."

"I don't trust her."

"If they're happy, you should be happy for him. I think he's been lonely."

"I can't believe you're saying that. I thought I could talk to you about this. Whatever." She hung up before I could come up with a response.

I stared at the phone, wondering if I should call her back. But what would I say? That she was being an immature brat about this? No, we'd finally gotten to the point where we had a modicum of a relationship. I didn't want to drive a wedge between us. Maybe I'd let her cool off and try calling later.

Or maybe I could come up with a way to let her get to know Nin without Thad in the picture. Would Amber agree to go someplace with me if it wasn't for a distinct purpose?

She'd helped me shop for dresses once, but that had been out of pity, since I had the fashion sense of a henchman in a dystopian novel. She'd agreed to the sword-fighting lessons, but only because she'd wanted a sword, and Thad had insisted I be the one to teach her to use it. Even though she spoke to me voluntarily from time to time, she still didn't seem to want to hang out with me. And I couldn't blame her for that when I'd stayed out of her life for more than ten years.

Maybe I would talk to Thad, if only to advise him on gifts that Nin might actually like. And that were monetarily appropriate after two months of dating. It wasn't as if Thad was Daddy Warbucks.

My mate, Zav's voice rumbled telepathically in my mind. *Why do you delay?*

Just dealing with some family matters. Hey, Zav. If you were going to give a woman a gift, you wouldn't buy something frivolous and expensive, right?

Do you wish frivolous and expensive baubles?

No. I'm asking for a friend.

Given the variety of horrific shoes he'd picked out for himself during his experiments with Earth footwear, I shuddered to think what kind of *baubles* he might select for a girl.

As a gift, I would allow my mate the honor of riding on my back as we soared over the ocean and witnessed sights that were magnificent and splendorous.

We've done that. You showed me a nest of recently hatched black oystercatchers tucked in a seaside cliff.

Was it not a fabulous gift? Far more appealing than baubles.

You're right. It was.

I had no idea how Thad could replicate such a gift, but I smiled and headed upstairs. I would figure out the sword—and how to bring peace to Thad and Amber's household—in the morning.

CHAPTER 5

ZAV AND I ARRIVED EARLY enough at the Sable Dragon to find open tables. It helped that Dimitri had rearranged the display cases of Zoltan's alchemical tinctures and creams to make room for more seating. The shelves of enchanted yard-art and house gadgets were relegated to the back walls—the last time we'd replenished our inventory, Dimitri had reluctantly agreed that his work sold the least and should take up the least space in our shop. That hadn't kept him from hanging the relatively flat pieces between the windows and on the wall behind the coffee kiosk.

Our barista, Tam, would occasionally give wary looks to the flywheel-and-mattress-spring *luck golem* leering down at her. Whether her primary concern was that it would fall off or put a curse on her, I didn't know.

Even though Tam was quick and efficient, the line stretched to the door. Most of the dozen-odd patrons waiting to order their coffee and eyeing tubs of strategically placed under-eye cream, muscle revitalizer, and stamina booster were half- or quarter-bloods, though like me, they looked more human than their troll, dwarf, elf, or orc ancestors.

At some point, Dimitri had put an enchantment on the facade so that those without magical blood were less likely to notice the shop. As much as he wanted those people for customers, it would have been hard to cater to both clienteles. Neither the police, military, nor any government institution acknowledged that magical beings existed, and the magical did their own part to hide themselves with glamours and illusions so normal people didn't notice them. They liked having a place they could come where they didn't have to worry about the mundanes.

Deciding to wait until the rush was over to order our drinks, I claimed one of the tables and pulled over an extra chair for Willard.

"The patrons of this establishment will notice your sword." Zav sat beside me, scooting his chair close.

I'd brought my weapons along, as I always did. Trouble liked to find me, so I had to be prepared, even when my sword wasn't acting like a lighthouse on a foggy night.

"I know. There's not much I can do about it. If I left it at home, someone would be along to steal it."

"That is likely. I might be able to craft an insulating vault that keeps the magical pulses from escaping." He gripped his chin thoughtfully.

"I'll keep that in mind as a possibility, but I'd be at a disadvantage in battle if I had to carry around a vault and stop to open it before engaging enemies." I imagined holding my hand up to an aggressive ogre as I slung a safe off my back and spun a combination lock to pull out my sword.

"This is true."

"I'm hoping we can figure out a way to make it *stop* pulsing. Soon." A new idea occurred to me, and I wasn't sure whether to laugh at it or take it seriously. "Are we sure the artifact caused this problem? You don't think it needs a new battery, do you?"

Zav's forehead creased. "What?"

Since he'd read the English dictionary, I suspected he knew what a battery was, just not the context. "Here on Earth, when a smoke detector is running low on its battery, it starts beeping to let you know it needs to be changed."

Maybe the artifact hadn't had anything to do with my sword's new pulsing. Maybe after ten thousand years, it had run out of magical juice and needed a fresh charge. Freysha had told me that the elves had to periodically reapply the magic that protected their cities and sanctuaries, so it seemed plausible.

"Could it be pulsing to let me know it needs to be recharged?" I added—Zav still looked puzzled.

"No. As I told you, I am able to sense the fae magic on it."

"Oh, right."

"Some enchanted artifacts and weapons do lose their potency over time, but that one will not. A dragon blade made by a master dwarf will remain powerful for all of eternity. Even if your hypothesis had some merit, I do not believe that it would emit *more* energy to alert its handler to the need for energy replenishing. That is illogical."

I could tell he'd never encountered a chirping smoke detector. Though, having found them irritating in the past, I wasn't sure his claim of illogic was wrong.

"I will continue to consider the problem while I protect you from those who sense the sword and wish to take it away from you." Zav gazed menacingly around the coffee shop—a few people in line *had* already peeked over at me—and rested a hand on my shoulder.

He'd already had an opportunity to protect me that morning. Before dawn, a pair of panther shifters had crept onto the lawn at the house. I'd woken to him scowling naked out the window at them and warning them that, should they come closer and attempt to steal my sword, he would incinerate them, then turn them over to the Dragon Justice Court for punishment and rehabilitation. The order of events hadn't made sense to me, but we'd just woken up, so it was possible he hadn't been at his best. He'd been at his best the night before, so I couldn't complain.

I smiled at the memory and patted his hand. "Thank you."

Dimitri came out of the back, carrying bottles of flavorings for the coffee kiosk, and frowned at me—no, at Chopper.

He bowed his head politely toward Zav, then asked, "What's wrong with your sword, Val?"

I sighed and gave him the story.

We'd left the house before Freysha had reported any news about the shard, so I didn't yet know anything more than I had the day before. My hand still throbbed under the bandage and showed no signs of healing itself.

"What are you going to do about it?" Dimitri asked when I finished my story. "I've been sensing it since before you even got back yesterday."

"I know. Everybody with an iota of magical blood is sensing it." As I spoke, a couple of troll-blooded men who'd purchased coffees gave me long speculative looks as they headed for the door.

"Maybe it's not a good idea for you to hang out here. I've finally gotten all the display cases accident-proofed, but I doubt they're *battle*-proofed." Dimitri frowned at his and Zoltan's wares—*breakable* wares.

"Zav is threatening to incinerate anyone who tries to steal Chopper from me. It'll be fine."

"I guess that's all right then."

Zav lifted his chin. "Do not doubt my abilities to protect my mate."

"Oh, I don't. Your abilities are great. That's why we named the shop after you."

Zav splayed his fingers on his chest. "After *me?*"

"You didn't see the new sign?" I waved toward the doorway. "The Sable Dragon. That's you."

"I am a black dragon."

"*See?*" I pointed at Dimitri, and he rolled his eyes.

"*Sable* is more exotic and literary than *black*," he said mulishly, the same argument he'd made when we'd discussed this previously.

"A sable is a mustelid mammal from this world," Zav said. "A dragon is nothing like a sable."

"Sable also means black," Dimitri said. "Noble and exotic black, not ordinary black."

"Sable mammals are in the weasel family. Weasels are considered unsavory in this culture, are they not? A dragon would not wish to be associated with an unsavory mammal."

"We didn't name the store after a *weasel*." Dimitri didn't dare direct his exasperated expression at Zav, so I got it.

Willard stepped into the shop, and I waved vigorously and pushed out her chair, hoping her arrival would save me from having to mediate this conversation. I'd *told* Dimitri to use the word black. Why did artists always have to have pretensions?

Willard paused to peer around for goblins and flying dice before walking toward us. Dimitri returned to stocking the coffee kiosk for the day.

"The goblins aren't early risers," I told Willard as she sat down across from me, nodding at Zav, whose expression suggested he was still debating the unsavoriness of weasels. "You're safe from dice until afternoon."

The line had dwindled, so I purchased black coffee for Willard, a can of sparkling mineral water for myself, and hot water and a tea bag for Zav. I hadn't yet found a beverage beyond water that he liked to drink, so I was experimenting. He'd expressed a distaste for coffee previously, and he wouldn't consume anything sweet, so I dropped the Earl Grey tea packet into the mug of steaming water and set it down in front of him. If it worked for Captain Picard, it ought to work for a dragon.

Even though Willard had probably consumed a cup of coffee within seconds of waking, she took a long swig from her mug before digging into her messenger bag to pull out a manila envelope.

"Is it acceptable?" I accepted the envelope, knowing I didn't need to count any money she gave me, and slid it into an inside pocket in my duster. "That's the goblin blend, slightly tweaked since you sampled it last. I understand it's even more potent now and can launch rockets into space."

"It's all right."

"We look forward to your Yelp review."

"Uh huh. What's wrong with your hand?" Willard pointed to my bandage.

"I cut myself on the artifact, and it's not healing. It's even got Zav flummoxed."

Zav was puzzling over the string and tag hanging out of his mug and didn't comment.

"Even Zav, huh?" Willard waved at it. "Want me to send Dr. Walker over?"

"I guess." I flexed my hand, wincing when that caused a stab of pain. It didn't bother me much when I wasn't moving it. "I haven't managed to catch Zoltan yet for a consultation. Have you two gone on a date yet?"

"Me and Zoltan? Vampires aren't my type."

"You and *Walker*. The sexy marsupial lion shifter with the thick tail."

I'd gone on a mission with Walker a couple of months earlier and knew he had a thing for Willard, but she wasn't reciprocating. She'd hinted before that she would like to meet someone, and he seemed like a good match for her somewhat abrasive always-in-charge attitude, but she refused to see it.

"No, we haven't dated. And we won't. I don't date ostentatious guys who are full of themselves."

"There is a string with paper dangling from my beverage," Zav said.

"It's attached to the tea bag." I pointed into his mug. "The tea is still steeping. Give it a couple of minutes to reach its full flavor."

I didn't like tea any more than I liked coffee—which made my investment in this place strange—but connoisseurs had explained the supposed appeal of both to me.

He read the tag. "Grey is spelled incorrectly."

"That's the British spelling. It's British tea. We also use grey here in the US when we want to be pretentious."

Willard glanced at the time on her phone. "Let me know when you're done educating your dragon and want to get to business."

"You gave me money. That's the only business I came for."

"I'm concerned that destroying that artifact isn't enough," Willard said. "Why was it placed there? Who placed it? And what did it do besides taint the water, if anything? Is it like that dark-elf pleasure orb that was one of many and part of a larger, more nefarious plot?"

I grimaced, not wanting to dwell on that mission. I was relieved I hadn't encountered another dark elf in the months since we'd stopped the eruption of Mt. Rainier.

After taking a sip, Zav set his mug down. "I do not like it."

"No need for you to leave a Yelp review," I told him.

He gave me a blank look.

"You're hard to please," I said.

He turned his head toward Tam. "Bring me water, human."

I waved an apologetic hand to her, went and got a bottle of water myself, and set a couple of dollars on the counter. "On Earth—" I placed the bottle in front of Zav and sat back down, "—it's appropriate to say *please* when you make a request of a person, though it's even better to lift your butt from the chair and get something yourself."

"Dragons do not say *please*. It is the honor of lesser species to serve us. Her day is improved from being in my presence."

"Oh, I'm sure." I looked warily at Willard, who probably had a meeting at the office coming up, expecting her to be annoyed by this further delay.

Her elbow was on the table, her thumb and forefinger forming an L to support her chin as she watched us, more in fascination than annoyance, I thought.

"Do you want me to go back out to the coast to investigate further?" I eyed the rain puddling on the sidewalks outside. The beach held no appeal right now, and I would prefer to solve my sword problem before taking another assignment, but Willard gave me more work than anyone else. If she wanted me to go somewhere, I would go.

"I already sent Lieutenant Dumas. You're good at destroying things, but tact isn't your strong suit."

"You say this like it's a character flaw."

"Odd."

Since I didn't disagree, I couldn't muster any disgruntlement over her assessment. "You know I prefer assassinations to dealing with clients."

"I do. I've got some of my guys researching fae and known entrances to their realm in the Seattle area—and at the coast. As far as I know, humans don't know how to get through their doors, but we're researching that too. If I get some good information or a fae contact, I want you to be ready to pay a visit. Even if the fae weren't responsible for the artifact, they may know who was."

Zav pointed at my can of sparkling water. "What are you consuming?"

He'd uncapped his bottle and drunk half of his plain water, which was his usual fare, so I was surprised that anything else would interest him.

"Carbonated mineral water—" I turned the can to read the back, "—bottled from a single source in the South of France."

"And you thought the tea was pretentious," Willard murmured.

"Shush. I can't help it Dimitri stocks the fancy stuff."

"I will sample it," Zav stated, forgetting the *please*. But as the mate of a dragon, it was, of course, my honor to serve him.

"Knock yourself out." I pushed it across to him.

Willard opened her mouth, probably to get back to the fae topic, but a handsome young man wearing a leather Harley jacket walked up to our table, a motorcycle helmet under his arm. He smiled politely at her before focusing on me. I braced myself for an attempt to get my sword. My senses told me he wasn't magical, so he shouldn't sense it, but something about him struck me as not quite mundane. The fact that he was model-in-a-swimsuit-magazine gorgeous might have been part of it.

"Good morning, ladies." He glanced at Zav, who was scrutinizing the back of my can, and didn't say anything to him. "I'm Dusty. I see you already have drinks." He looked specifically at me as he spoke and raised his eyebrows. "Could I buy you a scone?"

"No, thanks," I said. "We're having a business meeting."

"You probably don't want company then. Could I interest you in dinner later? Or maybe a ferry ride?"

Zav's head jerked up, and he clunked the can down on the table. I reached over and gripped his arm, hoping to keep him from threatening the guy. Unless he also sensed something not-quite-mundane about him and thought he was angling for my sword.

"No, thanks. I'm already dating someone."

"We are *mates*." Zav rose to his feet, ignoring my hand, and his eyes flared with inner light. "You will *not* proposition my mate."

"Ah, you're with her?" The man pointed at me. "Sorry, man. Nice trick with the eyes though." He snapped his fingers and pointed at Zav's face as if they were bros, then walked to the coffee kiosk.

I pulled Zav back into his seat before he could contemplate incinerating anything on the man—or the man himself.

Willard was still watching all of this with her chin in her hand. Her eyes gleamed with amusement. That was because she didn't know how irritated Zav got when men hit on me in his presence. And how dangerous an irritated dragon was.

"The males belonging to this verminous species are completely oblivious to my mark on you," he stated, eyes still blazing.

"We've discussed this," I said. "Humans can't sense your magical claim on me."

"You said we would acquire matching shirts with photographs of us together on the front, and this would inform the ignorant sense-dead of this race about our bond."

"Oh, I'd pay to see that." Willard snickered. Colonel tough-as-nails Willard never snickered, but her eyes were twinkling madly with delight now.

I glared at her. "That was a joke, Zav. I mean, if you want, we could get shirts like that, but I'm not wearing it every day."

The ogre and troll villains I confronted in my duties as an assassin would fall over laughing if I showed up to their lairs in a shirt like that.

"There must be a way to mark you for *them*." Zav glared at the man, who glanced back and winked at him.

Motorcycle Dude had a death wish and didn't even realize it.

"You have to put a ring on her," Willard said.

I shook my head and waved, trying to signal to her not to go down that road. I wasn't ready to marry Zav. We'd only been dating for a couple of months, and he wasn't even from Earth. How could a marriage with an extraterrestrial be legal?

"A ring?" Zav asked. "Finger jewelry?"

"Yup. An engagement ring." Willard smiled, looking at me but completely ignoring my imploring waves for her to drop the subject. "If you propose to her, and she says yes, you can get married in the human way. Then her ring would let others know that she's claimed."

"This is an excellent idea."

"You'd have to wear a ring too," Willard said, "so available women also know that *you're* claimed. You would be monogamous with Val, right? I don't want to push for this if dragons sleep around."

Zav's brow furrowed as he worked through what *sleep around* meant. "I have no need for another female. Val goes into battle with me and vexes my enemies. She is an excellent mate."

"I'm glad to hear it."

I lifted my hands. "Guys, could we change the subject back to our enemies and dealing with them? I'm not ready to get married."

"You're getting up there in years, Val," Willard said. "You can't be too picky or wait too long."

I shot her the dirty look that deserved. "You're single and older than me. You don't get to talk."

"Dragons do not typically wear jewelry." Zav looked at his hands. "But I could make an exception when I am in this form. Yes, I will get two rings, and we will wed." He shifted his gaze to me and grasped my hands, nodding intently.

"The girl gets a say in this, Zav. Marriage is forever, or at least as long as we're both alive." I decided not to explain divorce to him. Divorcing an extraterrestrial was probably as hard as legally marrying one. "We should spend more time together before taking that next step."

Especially given that he would live for centuries. Supposedly, my half-elven blood would allow me to live longer than the average human, but I had no delusions about living as long as a dragon. Given my dangerous job and my propensity for getting into trouble, the odds of seeing my next birthday weren't even that good.

"I please you, and we are excellent in battle together," Zav said. "There is no need to spend more time together. I have already claimed you as my mate. You are my mate, and I am your dragon. You have agreed to this."

I rubbed the back of my head and hoped the coffee drinkers at nearby tables weren't paying attention to this conversation. At least Motorcycle Dude had turned around to place his order.

"You *are* my dragon," I said, glancing at Willard and not appreciating her smirk. This had gotten serious, and I didn't want to continue the conversation in public. "Let's talk about it later, all right?"

"I am a powerful protector, among the greatest warriors of my kind," Zav said. "You would be foolish to wish another dragon as your mate."

"Oh, I know that."

"I also please you in the nest."

"I know that too."

"Is that dragon slang for the bedroom?" Willard asked. "Or is there an *actual* nest? I know he remodeled your house for you…"

"Don't you have a meeting?" I asked her.

She glanced at her phone. "I do. I'll let you know what I find out about the fae." She stood up but addressed Zav again before leaving. "Make sure you get the proposal right. That's the most important part. The ring needs to be perfect, and the proposal needs to be perfect. If you sweep her off her feet, she'll be yours forever."

"Stop giving him *advice*." I waved her toward the door. I was tempted to bodily push her out it.

"Don't forget my invitation, Thorvald." Willard smirked again and headed out but not without calling back, "I do enjoy a good wedding."

Zav looked far too contemplative.

CHAPTER 6

CHOPPER LAY ON THE MAGICAL anvil in the basement—a leftover artifact from the vampire smith who'd lived in the house before Zoltan had traded places with him—and Zoltan paced around it, his hands clasped behind his back. He wore a pinstripe suit with a red bow tie, stylish as always, though as far as I knew, he only left the house in the depths of the night to find promising veins. I pretended that didn't happen. So far, he'd left my veins alone.

"I sensed it yesterday like a lighthouse on a stormy night when you were still many miles from Seattle," Zoltan said.

"I know." I flexed my bandaged hand, intending to ask him if he had any alchemical creams that might help it. But the sword was my priority. "Everybody is telling me about that."

While Zoltan examined the blade, I dumped a couple of recently acquired Theo's apple-cider caramels out of a narrow box and into my hand. They were seasonal, so I had to stock up every fall. I'd stashed a couple dozen boxes in my bedroom, trusting that Zav, even though he did occasionally snoop around and examine my curious human belongings, wouldn't be interested in them. Dimitri was another story, but he didn't go in my bedroom, so they were safe there.

I popped one in my mouth and noshed the chewy chocolatey caramel goodness with delight. Given the way this week had started, and the throbbing pain in my hand, I needed some delight.

Val, Zav spoke into my mind from the dining room upstairs. I'd left him gnawing on several racks of ribs fresh out of the commercial smoker that I'd purchased—a kitchen item I never would have expected to need, but that had been before I started dating a dragon. *I sense that a portal has opened in the park nearby.*

Does it have to do with my sword? I hoped people couldn't feel these magical pulses all the way on other worlds.

It is possible. If you feel safe with the vampire, I will go investigate.
I'm his best client. He would be foolish to make a move on my veins.

"Any chance you can make it stop pulsing?" I asked Zoltan.

"I don't know. It's quite fascinating. I've not read of anything like this, and I am well educated, as you know." He waved toward a wall filled with bookcases—I had no idea how or when he'd gotten them all over here, since I had no memory of a moving van pulling up to the house. "May I?" He reached for the sword.

"Yup."

He picked it up, whistling as he walked to his lab counter and rearranged a few things so he could slide the blade under his microscope.

"That's not something I've seen before." I was tempted to take a picture.

"It's not ideal, but it's just slender enough to fit. It's not as if I can scrape off magic and put it on a slide." He leaned in to examine Chopper through the eyepiece.

"But magic is visible under a microscope?"

"Not ordinarily, but I have special lenses that I've made with my alchemy."

I paced as he examined the blade. Outside, night had fallen, and I thought about stepping into the yard for some fresh air, but he usually complained about light, no matter how minimal. When I'd opened the door to come in, he'd cursed the vileness of the solar-powered landscape lamps out back. Dimitri was in the process of building a "light lock," a windowless vestibule inspired by a submarine's airlock, that would allow us to enter the basement without letting in light that assailed His Highness's sensitive eyes.

The only things that didn't bother Zoltan were the red-light therapy lamps that he used for lab work and reading—as I knew from using my own night-vision charm, it was hard to read in the dark, even with magical assistance. As Zoltan had explained to me, they were a mix of infrared and red light, both of which were acceptable to vampire eyes. It amused me tremendously that he used lighting devices that were sold to people at a premium for rejuvenating their skin. Vampires had nothing to rejuvenate.

Are you investigating the portal? I noticed Zav had left the house and sensed him over at Green Lake.

Yes. It is open in the park, but I don't sense anyone magical nearby, nor is anyone coming out of it.

Can fae make portals?

It is possible that they can make them, but they are known to travel through the network of established doors that lead in and out of their realm instead.

Located in mushroom rings.

Yes. They are attuned with the natural world.

The natural world of fungi.

Plants and trees, as well. But they don't lend themselves to doorways. Zav's telepathic tone took on a suspicious mien. *I believe this portal was made by a dragon.*

Maybe your sister is coming for a visit. If she did, I would ask her to heal my hand, whether it involved eye-rolling on her part or not. *If Zoltan and Willard's people don't come up with anything to fix my sword, will you take me to the dwarven home world or somewhere I can find one of their master enchanters to question about my problem? I know you said they're in hiding, but maybe they'll come out of hiding to speak with me. I'm not nearly as scary as a dragon.*

You do not think you would vex them?

No, I'd be diplomatic. Despite what Willard thinks, I can hold my sharp tongue if I need to.

Interesting. I have not observed this.

Funny.

I sensed Freysha outside, and a moment later, she knocked. Zoltan grumbled something about the landscaping lights, but didn't scream when I opened the door to let her in, so maybe they weren't that much of an affront to his eyes after all.

My younger sister, who appeared no older than a teenager, thanks to her elven longevity, had bags under her eyes and looked like she hadn't slept.

"You didn't stay up all last night and today researching that for me, did you?" I pointed to the shard from the artifact that she held. "You didn't need to do that."

"I didn't intend to, but I have been sleeping poorly these past couple of weeks."

"Oh, hell, you *must* be my relative."

She tilted her head.

"I don't sleep that well anymore," I explained, though I didn't go into more detail. I'd been doing better since Zav had fixed up the house, helpfully using his power to utterly destroy the mold and must and mildew that had inhabited the second floor, but I still had nightmares of friends I'd lost over the years and of those I feared I would lose. It was why I kept seeing my therapist, Mary, even though I struggled to take some of the stuff she recommended to me seriously. My attempts at learning to meditate so far involved me sitting cross-legged while listening to woo-woo music and constructing to-do lists in my head.

"I believe my problem is the environment here. It is not ideal for elven physiology. I have grown many plants to help filter the air, but I may need to return home for a time to recover before returning to continue my engineering studies."

"The air on Earth bothers you?" I touched my chest, thinking of my own sensitive lungs.

"Yes. I believe that is the reason that elves left your world as your people became more numerous and invented more technologies that create pollution. The particulate matter in the air is difficult for our kind to filter. Also, our world's native air has differences from Earth's too, so that is a further impediment to living here for extended periods."

"Do you think that might be why I have some trouble with breathing? I didn't when I was younger, but..." I had admitted this to Zav and Mary, and Willard knew because the military knew everything about me, but I'd never opened up about it to Freysha. "I've had more trouble lately."

"It is possible. As a half-human, your physiology should be more adapted to this world, but your world has changed much since humans evolved."

"So I've heard."

I didn't know how this new information helped me, other than making me wonder if I should try to retire one day in Elf Land. That would be difficult, given how unwelcome I'd been the one time I'd visited. My father, King Eireth, had come out to meet with me in secret.

Freysha held out the shard to me. "I have researched the books I have and examined this to the best of my abilities. I still only know that it's fae and that it possesses what they call imbuing magic."

"Meaning?" I glanced toward my sword, my recently *imbued* sword.

"I don't think its purpose was to poison the water. That may have been a byproduct of the magic it was radiating. That magic was designed to imbue something with its essence. Its purpose is likely to mark what it touches, somewhat similar to the way Zav has marked you so others will know he's claimed you."

"You're saying that the whole point of that thing was to put its essence on my sword?"

"To put its essence on *something*. It's possible that your sword was simply the first viable option that came along."

"Why would someone put it in the middle of a cranberry farm miles from the nearest town if the purpose was to attract an appropriate sword or tool or whatever for marking? And why would such an artifact even exist?"

"In the early days of exploration between the Cosmic Realms, as the various magical races were learning how to make portals and how to travel to different places, all of the worlds were considered wild worlds. Artifacts like the one you destroyed could be carried along and used to create landmarks, transmitting magical energy for many miles around so that travelers could find their way back to them."

"Like leaving breadcrumbs in the forest?"

Her forehead wrinkled, so I gave her the CliffsNotes version of "Hansel and Gretel."

"More permanent than breadcrumbs," Freysha said. "The magic is designed to be sensed for hundreds of miles in all directions."

"I've noticed."

Freysha chewed on her lip as she gazed over at the sword. "I do not wish to alarm you, but I think it is possible that someone set that artifact there to draw you specifically to it."

"Why stick it outside of Long Beach if it was for me? They could have plopped it down in Green Lake." I waved in the direction of the water, though I was relieved that whoever had done this hadn't opted for a populated park in the middle of the city. People *swam* out there on nice days, and you couldn't skate the paved path without running into ducks and geese. Having flocks of them keeling over all across the busy park would have stirred up the whole city.

"I do not know, other than that a remote location might have had fewer variables to deal with. And someone who knew you might know that Colonel Willard would dispense you to investigate it."

"And that I'd also solve the problem by beating up the artifact with my sword?" Sadly, I *was* that predictable.

"Possibly. I only posit a hypothesis."

"I'll keep it in mind."

That Starsinger fop just flew out of the portal, Zav roared into my mind, making me wince. *If he has come for your sword, I will utterly destroy him.*

Uh. That dragon had sung to me in the past and tried to woo me away from Zav—not because of my irresistible hotness but because his clan found it pleasant to irk Zav's clan.

He flees! He saw me and leaped back through the portal.

You are *fearsome.*

He must have come for scheming and inimical reasons. When he saw me, he fled out of fear of being caught. I will follow him through the portal and question him. You are in no danger, correct? I do not believe this will take long, but I do not wish an enemy to attack you while I'm gone.

I almost said I needed him to stay and help me, if only to keep him from walloping on one of the few dragons who hadn't come across as an arrogant prick, but I didn't sense any enemies about, and it was possible that the dragon—Xilneth was his name—was up to something.

I'll be fine. I've got Freysha and Zoltan to help me defend the place.

That vampire is no help. He would be too busy complaining and grooming his attire to enter into battle.

I had seen Zoltan throw bears across a scientist's laboratory, so I knew that wasn't true, but it was easier to amend my statement than explain. *Very well. Then I have Freysha and Sindari to help. I know you believe him a capable warrior.*

Yes, the tigers of Del'noth fight well. I will return soon. After I have smote that weasel—that sable*!—Xilnethgarish.*

I thought you were going to question him.

If he resists my interrogation, I will smite him.

Zav's presence disappeared from my awareness, leaving me wondering if he was serious or simply having a grumpy evening. I had noticed that Xilneth's mere appearance could turn him grumpy.

"Val?" Freysha touched my arm. "Your mate has left this realm."

"I know. I was just talking to him. He's going to question a dragon who may be scheming inimical things."

"I hope that no trouble will come while he's away."

"Me too."

"It is good that you have been practicing your magic. You are more capable of defending yourself from enemies these days." Freysha smiled at me.

I was glad she believed I was making progress during our lessons. It didn't always feel that way to me. I'd learned to extend my range when it came to sensing magic and communicating telepathically with others, and I was better at resisting compulsion spells others tried to put on me, but I couldn't smite enemies, hurl fireballs, or knock assailants off cliffs with the power of my mind. Granted, Freysha, with her specialty in forest magic, hadn't tried to teach me any of those things.

"Let's hope." I set the shard next to Zoltan's microscope, in the hope that it would help him unravel the mystery of the sword.

"You do not believe so?"

"I appreciate what you've been teaching me. I'm just not sure it helps me in battles, other than as a means of defense."

"Is defense not important?"

"It is. But my specialty has always been *offense*. Strike them before they can strike you."

"Hm. Let me show you something new for you to work on while our esteemed alchemist studies your sword." Freysha opened the door, ignoring a dramatic sigh from Zoltan, and we stepped out into the dark misty night.

The rain had stopped, but the air was so thick with moisture that it created a halo around the patio lights. I pulled my duster tighter around me. Seattle never got very cold, with snow being a rarity, but the dampness had its own power to chill.

Freysha gestured toward the boulders at the back of the yard that formed a retaining wall for raised plant beds. "Please have a seat."

"This lesson requires that we be outside on wet rocks?"

"It does. All forest magic is best employed when close to nature."

"You may have noticed this is a suburban neighborhood."

"Fortunately with trees and some appealing ground." She sat on a boulder and waved at the moss that kept neutralizing Dimitri's attempts to grow grass in the shady backyard.

"Appealing. Exactly what I thought of it when I first walked back here." Admittedly, everything around the house looked much better since Dimitri had started working on the yard.

"I did."

I sat beside her. If she wanted to teach me, I had better pay attention, especially if she had *offensive* magic to show me. If Zav was gone longer than he expected, I might need it.

"What's the lesson tonight, Sensei?"

"You will learn to use the ground's natural materials to form roots that can grow up and entangle your enemies. You have seen me do this."

"I have. They looked more like vines than roots. I wondered how you turned the dirt into them."

"On all worlds, the basic building blocks of matter are the same. Magic may alter the arrangement of those blocks from soil into plant matter."

"Am I about to get a molecular science lesson?"

"Touch the earth. It will be easier for me to show you than explain."

Since Freysha's lessons regularly involved me sticking my fingers in dirt, I no longer found such requests strange.

She knelt down, resting her hand on the damp moss, and I followed suit. Her other hand settled on my shoulder, and she did the telepathic equivalent of a screen share.

I experienced her sending her magic into the ground and reforming the dirt into tendrils that seemed half-plant, half-root. Shoots formed and pushed up through the ground. They rose slowly, though I'd seen her create them almost instantly before, because she wanted me to witness what she was doing.

Envision it happening in your mind even as you slide your will into the earth.

I refrained from making sarcastic comments about sliding my will around and focused.

These tendrils can be used to entrap an enemy when you face multiple foes, she explained. *Or to keep a goblin from stealing your snacks in the conservatory while you are potting new plants.*

Is it possible that you speak from experience? I imagined vines wrapping around Gondo's legs to keep him from swiping cupcakes off a plate.

It is possible.

Though I tried several times, nothing happened until Freysha sent some of her own magic to blend with and guide mine. With her help, I coaxed a scrawny root out of the ground. It rose up four inches into the air before flopping over. I snorted. That wouldn't do much to entangle an enemy. It might trip a chipmunk.

Freysha withdrew her assistance and presence abruptly and leaned back. She squinted toward the house.

"Trouble?" I sensed Zoltan at work in the basement but nothing else in the house. Dimitri hadn't come home from work yet. I stretched out toward the park, searching for portals or other magic that might threaten us.

I detected something—*multiple* somethings—as Freysha said, "I fear so. Creatures of dark magic approach."

"Dark magic?"

The auras of these beings felt different from the shifters and rocs that had come looking for my sword, different from any of the magical refugees that lived here on Earth. They had a nebulous aspect, and there seemed to be a whole pack of them. They were coming from the lake, as if they had risen up out of its depths, and they were heading this way.

"They are crucible beasts, crafted from fire by a mage and molded into creatures." Freysha looked gravely at me. "Depending on the power of the mage, they can be very difficult to destroy."

"Are they coming for my sword?" I sensed them continuing in this direction and doubted there was any chance they were just in the neighborhood.

"Their master may have created them to kill you so he or she can take your sword."

"Fabulous."

"It will be better to face them outside. If they enter your house, it will catch fire."

"Oh, hell no. Zav just remodeled this place for me." I sprinted to the basement to grab Chopper. No way was anything burning my house down.

CHAPTER 7

"STAY BACK AND LEND WHATEVER help you can," I told Freysha from the walkway in front of the house. "I'll do the fighting, but if you can root them, I'd appreciate it."

"Fire magic can be devastating to forest magic, but I will try." Freysha stayed in the shadows by the porch. My secret weapon, I hoped.

Six four-legged fiery creatures had come into view, prowling up the street toward me. Shaped like huge wolves, they glowed orange like molten lava and sprouted flames instead of fur. The hollow black eyes in their lupine faces stared straight at me. Every detail of their bodies, from claws to fangs to tongues lolling from their mouths, was crafted from flame.

"I suppose talking to these guys and bargaining with them is out." I tapped my feline charm and summoned Sindari.

"They do not speak," Freysha said.

"What about their master? Do you sense anyone? Would he have to be nearby to command them?" I scanned the neighborhood, trying to sense such a controller hunkered between the parked cars or in the hedges in front of houses. Nobody was out walking their dog tonight, so there would be no witnesses for this battle. Unless someone heard it and came out to investigate.

But as I'd learned in past months, the neighbors tended to look the other way when strange occurrences happened at this house. Long before Dimitri and I had shown up, it had garnered quite the reputation. The few neighbors I'd talked to had peered at me as if I were nuts for moving into the "haunted vampire lair," as they called it. If anyone had thought it strange when Zav magically caused two massive dragon-shaped topiaries to grow at the corners of the lot in plain view of the sidewalk, they hadn't mentioned it to me.

I eyed those topiaries now, wondering if they could help with this battle. Their heads occasionally moved, and they growled like Rottweilers if intruders came close, but I hadn't witnessed any other home-security benefits.

"It is possible," Freysha said after a thoughtful pause. "I sense… No, nothing. For a moment, I thought I did. But if someone is here, they are cloaking themselves."

Sindari solidified in the mist beside me and immediately faced the approaching threat. The flame wolves were walking, not running, as if they had no reason to rush to engage us. They could take their time and savor the moment.

Or maybe they were investigating the defenses around the property. A few times, they lifted their snouts as if sniffing the air—or checking for magic. Dimitri had installed numerous alarms and deterrents around the yard, sculptures and pillars that were half art and half defense against intruders, but I doubted they would do much against these guys. It would have been better if he'd installed automatic sprinklers.

Crucible beasts, Sindari spoke into my mind. *They will be formidable foes and painful to touch. Do not let them bite you.*

"I wasn't planning on it." I touched Fezzik's handle, thinking of getting in a few preemptive strikes.

"Bullets will not slow them," Freysha warned.

"These are *magical* bullets." I drew the pistol.

Letting fire creatures get close enough for a sword fight seemed like a bad idea. Hopefully, the fire-resisting charm on my leather thong would help protect me, but it had never been enough to fully thwart flames.

I will have to be careful in turn with biting them. Sindari crouched, but he didn't rush out to greet them.

I didn't blame him. I wouldn't want to bite something made from fire either.

As I aimed Fezzik at the lead creature, waiting for it to come fully out from behind parked cars, an uneasy feeling came over me. It was the same feeling I'd had at the bog—that I was being watched. Damn it, had the same invisible stalker trailed me back to Seattle?

I glanced toward the roof of the house, some vague instinct telling me the observer might be up there, but I didn't see anyone. Nor did my senses detect anything except the creatures. They blazed to my senses, their auras stronger than elves or ogres or other full-blooded magical beings. They were pure magic, not creatures that had magic flowing through their blood.

As the lead creature came out from between the parked cars and stepped up onto the curb, a buzz rang out—one of Dimitri's alarms. Intruder alert. No kidding.

I aimed between the flame-beast's eyes. An eerie roar came from its fiery throat—it sounded like a forest fire growing in intensity—as it prowled across the sidewalk toward me. I fired, bullets streaking for its eyes, their magic leaving blue trails in the air. One of Dimitri's statues spat thorns at the creatures.

My bullets passed straight through the beast and thudded into a car and a telephone post on the far side of the street. Dimitri's thorns also passed uselessly through it.

"Shit." I jammed Fezzik into its holster as all six creatures shifted from walking to charging—straight at me.

Sindari sprang to intercept two of them, but the others rushed around him.

"*Keyk!*" I shouted, one of the handful of command words I knew for Chopper.

Its blade turned from a blue glow to an icy white one. I leaped to the side as the creatures rushed me, trying to position myself so I would face only one at a time. A tall order.

As I danced aside, the closest beast startled me by spewing a gout of flame from its molten throat. The stream of fire scorched my ear as it blasted past my head. My charm protected me somewhat—my hair didn't burst into flame—but the heat promised I'd be in trouble if the flames struck me full on.

With a fast swing, I whisked Chopper toward my attacker's neck. Was it possible to behead a fire creature? I would find out.

My blade met resistance as it bit into the side of the beast's thick neck—I'd been afraid it would sweep uselessly through like the bullets—but it didn't behead it.

The creature wheeled, fiery maw snapping for me. Intense heat blasted me like a crematorium door opening. Forced to cut my attack short, I skittered backward.

The injury on my hand stung, irritated by the heat and the hilt of my sword. Too bad.

Another flaming beast charged me. I waited until the last instant to dodge, striking with Chopper, then gliding out of its reach. My blade struck the side of its head, but the blow didn't seem to harm the creature.

As more of the beasts tried to surround me, I danced in and out and to the side, slashing and stabbing and doing my best not to let them flank me.

By the porch, Freysha called upon her magic, the flare of it tickling my senses. I dared not look in her direction to check on what she was doing.

Sindari yowled in pain. I glimpsed him releasing one of the beasts that he'd bitten and scampering back, shaking his scorched maw.

Silvery tendrils of energy flowed from the porch and wrapped around two of the creatures, keeping them from charging at me again. They spewed gouts of flame at Freysha, but she formed a barrier in the air, keeping the flames from torching her—and the porch posts.

"Thank you, Freysha," I called as two beasts backed me toward the shrubs at the side of the yard. Little fires burned in the grass, charred spots forming where they walked.

The two creatures charged. I ran to the left, putting one beast in the way of the other, then rushed back in to attack the closest.

Need more power, Chopper, I thought to it, though I doubted that would help.

Heat blasted my cheeks as I stabbed Chopper at the beast's skull. The icy blade drove in, the air crackling as its frost magic seemed to intensify. The blade met the molten flesh of the creature, and it flared white.

The beast didn't scream, but it jerked away from me and rolled on the ground like a dog. Finally, a blow that had hurt one of them.

With the first on the ground, the second creature had the opportunity to rush close to me. It snapped as I sprang away, but my back struck one of the hedges, and I didn't fully evade it. The beast's flaming fangs sank into my arm.

Blistering pain lanced through my body. I twisted and slammed a side kick into its chest as I jerked my arm away. Its teeth were as solid as any real creature's, and they raked through flesh and muscle as I shoved it back.

A surge of fury lent me extra speed and strength, and I rushed after it, slashing Chopper straight into its face. The beast tried to duck but not quickly enough. My sword hammered into it, again flaring with white energy.

My arm throbbed with agony, but I cut into the creature again and again. The sole of the boot I'd used to kick it burned, but I ignored it, only paying attention to destroying this enemy. Thankfully, there weren't others nearby to take advantage of my singular focus.

Freysha still had two immobilized with her silvery magical vines, though a glance at her bared teeth and the intense concentration on her face suggested she wouldn't be able to hold them indefinitely. Sindari was keeping the two others busy, much as I had, dancing in and out, raking with his claws. He'd learned not to bite them. I couldn't tell how much damage his claws did, but they were paying attention to him instead of me, so it had to be something.

The two creatures I'd dealt lethal blows to started to fade before me. Their molten flesh melted, then disappeared completely, leaving only patches of lawn burning where they had stood.

Realizing my boot was on fire, I stomped it on the grass until it went out.

As I rushed to help Sindari, Zoltan stepped out from around the corner of the house. He wore some black-tinted goggles and carried not a weapon but what looked like a perfume atomizer. Since one of Sindari's foes turned to attack me, I couldn't watch him closely, other than to glimpse him striding toward Freysha's captured beasts.

My new foe sprang for my face, orange jaws yawning open as it angled toward my throat. Instead of dodging, I stood my ground. I'd proven I could kill them, and I would do it again.

I struck before the beast could bite me, willing my own magic to flow down my arms and into Chopper's blade to add force to the blow. The sword lopped off its head as heat blasted me, and it sprayed flames like a mortal being would spray blood.

The flames struck my clothing, singeing my jeans and striking sparks of pain all over my body. I flung myself to the ground, rolling across the grass several times. I sprang up, whirling toward the creature in case it survived that blow and came after me. But without its head, it was done. Like the others had, it faded from existence.

Panting now and in pain from multiple wounds, I turned to look for another foe. Sindari roared and swiped mightily at the one remaining fighting him. He gouged it deeply in the flank. It spun to snap at him, but he snapped back, their fanged jaws locking. The flames had to hurt him like crazy, but his powerful chest and leg muscles flexed, and he hurled the foe across the yard.

Flames flew off it as it tumbled through the air and slammed into the side of my Jeep.

"*Sindari*," I groaned. "Please fling the Satanic flamethrower creatures at *other* people's cars."

Meanwhile, Zoltan was spraying his concoction all over the two immobilized beasts. Whatever it was, they dropped to the ground and writhed as the droplets struck them. One spat flames at him as it rolled, and he cursed, scrambling backward.

I rushed up in time to grab him and keep him from falling.

"Dreadful creatures!" he yelled and leaned back in, spraying them liberally.

"Give me that." I grabbed the bottle, pulled off the sprayer top, and doused them a lot *more* liberally.

I rushed across the yard and also dumped the liquid on the one that Sindari had thrown. The creatures writhed even more vigorously as the liquid poured over them.

Noxious smoke flowed into the air, smelling like burning tires. But Zoltan's concoction worked, and the rest of the creatures faded and disappeared, leaving only scorched earth behind. Our scorched *lawn*.

Freysha slumped against a porch post. Sweat glistened on her brow.

"*Really*, dear robber." Zoltan snatched his bottle back from me and picked up the top I'd let fall to the ground. "Do you have any idea how much the bark of the *Polylepis* shrub, the primary ingredient in my fire-destroyer formula, costs? It grows only at a specific altitude high in the Andes Mountains."

"I'll get you a fire extinguisher that you can use next time."

"That would do little against *magical* creatures. My formula was engineered specifically to thwart fire magic."

"I guess there's no point in helping Dimitri install sprinklers then."

Zoltan peered into the empty bottle and shook his head in disgust. "Now, I've nothing left should an irate dragon with smoking nostrils assail my stronghold."

That was why he had a fire potion on hand?

"You consider our basement your stronghold?" I removed my jacket so I could look at the wound on my arm, which now trumped the wound on my hand for pain. It was a mixture of a burn and two deep fang gouges that dug almost to the bone.

"I have fortified it. Had you run inside, we could have kept the beasts at bay with my powerful magic."

"I didn't want to chance them lighting the house on fire. The lawn is bad enough." I walked around and stomped out burning grass with my boots.

Sindari watched me blandly as he licked his gums—probably trying to quench the pain from biting those creatures. Poor guy. *Usually, I relish it when you call me to assist you with battle, Val, but that was a most unappealing enemy.*

I agree. Thanks for helping.

Where is your mate?

Another dragon lured him away so the creatures could attack me without him jumping in to help.

I paused. It had been a joke, but might it be true? It would be a large coincidence if the two events had happened at the same time, but why would Xilneth join forces with some mage after my sword? Maybe whoever was staking out my home had simply taken advantage when Zav left our world.

"Why did such creatures come here to attack?" Zoltan looked at Freysha.

"Because of Val's sword, I would guess," she said.

"They lacked fingers or thumbs. What would they do with a sword?"

"A mage would have conjured them into existence."

I looked toward the roof again. During the fight, I'd been too busy to worry about being watched, but now that everything except the throbbing in my arm was quieting down, the sensation of having a hidden watcher returned.

"You like the show?" I called to the roof, though I had no proof that anyone was up there. "We aim to entertain around here."

"Dear robber, was your head damaged during the battle?" Zoltan peered up at the empty roof. "Or are you speaking to the chimney?"

"Yes, the chimney was giving me sass."

"Odd. It doesn't sass me."

"That's because you're not the Chosen One."

"And you are?"

I lifted Chopper's pulsing blade. "My sword may be."

"I believe that's the Accidentally Marked One, not the Chosen One," Zoltan said.

"Not that accidental," I muttered, thinking of Freysha's earlier words about the artifact.

The feeling of being watched disappeared. Unfortunately, that didn't bring a sense of relief. I suspected that whoever had set this up would just try again.

CHAPTER 8

AS I STOMPED OUT THE rest of the flames on the lawn, an SUV turned onto our street, the headlights shining on the wet pavement. Hopefully, it wasn't a police vehicle that some concerned neighbor had called for after hearing gunshots. If I'd known how useless my bullets would be on the fire creatures, I wouldn't have fired even once.

That reminded me: I needed to leave a note on the car I'd shot and offer to pay for the damage. I could do that while I was repairing the blackened dents in the door of my Jeep.

"Never fight a battle on your own property if you can help it," I muttered.

Dimitri is not here. Sindari was licking his paws—they'd been scorched by the beasts too—on the charred lawn.

Nope. Are you disappointed that nobody's petting you?

Given that I was grievously wounded during the battle, I would not have minded having my head stroked by calm and appreciative hands.

I can rub your ears in a minute if you want.

Hm.

Why did I have a feeling Sindari felt Dimitri was better at petting tigers than I was?

The blocky SUV found parking around the corner and stopped. I sensed a magical being at the wheel—a familiar one. It had been a couple of months since I'd traveled to the gnomish home world with Dr. Daku Walker, but I remembered him well. Over the years, I'd met plenty of lion, tiger, and panther shifters, but a *marsupial* lion shifter was something new. Technically, something very old, since Thylacoleonidae lions had gone extinct during the Pleistocene era. Supposedly.

"I'm glad to see you, Doc." I waved as he walked up in an impeccable wool suit, his medical kit in hand, and winced because the movement prompted extra pain from my injuries.

Lucky for him, he would have even *more* wounds to examine on me. I hoped the gouges and singe-marks from the creatures weren't as difficult for my body to heal as the fae-tainted cut.

"I apologize for taking so long to get here. I was in surgery all day." Walker spoke with an Australian accent, which seemed right for a marsupial lion shifter. His nostrils twitched as he stopped in front of me. "Are you having a barbecue?"

"Not exactly."

His gaze settled on a still-smoking patch of lawn.

"Someone sent some fire beasts to attack me."

"Because of your sword?"

I'd sheathed Chopper, but he looked toward the hilt. Like everyone else with a magical heritage, he had no trouble sensing it.

"Come on inside. I'll tell you about it and give you food while you look at my hand and my arm." I waved toward the steps.

Freysha had been helping put out the fires—and sending some magic down into the ground that she said would assist the lawn in regenerating—but now she stood on the walkway, her eyes unfocused. She was gazing toward the rhododendrons under the window.

I started to ask if there was a problem, but magic tickled my senses. A moment later, a portal formed beyond the rhododendrons on the side of the house. Well, better than on the roof.

"Trouble?" I asked.

"It is one of my people," Freysha said before anyone came out of the silvery circle hanging perpendicular to the ground.

"That doesn't answer my question."

She smiled and walked toward the portal. A buckskin-clad, cloak-wearing elf with his long blond hair tied back by a twig headband hopped out, a bow in hand. His expression was stern as he frowned at me, so I resisted the urge to comment on his *Lord of the Rings* wardrobe.

He spoke to Freysha in their language, his voice as stern as his face. During their conversation, he glanced at me several more times, or maybe he was glancing at the hilt of my sword poking up over my shoulder. Had word of its throbbing magnificence made it all the way back to Elf Land?

"Do you know what he's saying?" Walker asked.

"I could." I pointed toward my translation charm. "But it doesn't sound flattering, so I'm choosing to remain in the dark."

Freysha turned to face me. "Our father is unexpectedly ill. I must go home to help care for him."

What did *that* mean? Was it common for an elf to be *expectedly* ill?

"Is it something bad?" I assumed a messenger wouldn't have been sent to retrieve Freysha if the king had a cold.

"I am not certain yet, but I will return when I can."

The male elf was frowning at me again. Suspiciously? Why would my tainted sword garner suspicion? Or was this about something else?

"Please practice your magic lessons while I'm gone," Freysha added. "And tell Gondo that I will help him complete his ambulatory windmill project as soon as I can."

"Okay." I decided not to ask *where* Gondo was building a windmill and why it needed to ambulate. It was also wise to remain in the dark when it came to goblin engineering projects. "If you know of any elves who can fix my sword, I'd appreciate it if you could send them my way. I'll take them to the all-you-can-eat salad bar at the Brazilian steakhouse."

A wonderful restaurant where I'd found I could satisfy Zav's and Freysha's dietary needs all in one place. Never mind that the manager had insisted on charging me for six people after Zav demanded that the waitstaff who came around with skewers of meat permanently station themselves next to our table.

"I will ask the prominent magic users in my city for their opinions on your problem."

I'd rather she ask them to *fix* my problem. Someone somewhere had to be able to, right?

"Thanks," was all I said. "Take care, and let me know if I can help with our—with the king."

If I hadn't had problems of my own to deal with, I would have offered to go along to see him, but we'd only met once, and I didn't know if he wanted to see me again. I also didn't know if they would *let* me come along. The male elf frowned over his shoulder at me again before they hopped into the portal, which disappeared after them.

"Have you irked the elves?" Walker asked.

"I hope not. I've already irked my vampire roommate this evening. He's retreated to his basement stronghold to make more formulas." I waved again for Walker to follow me up the stairs to the porch.

If you do not need me further, Sindari said, *I will return to my realm to heal more quickly.*

"I *hope* I won't need you further tonight."

Walker raised his eyebrows.

"Not you. I was talking to Sindari. Trust me. I need you." My arm was burning. I would have blown on the scorch marks if I'd thought that would work. With luck, Walker had something better than burn ointment.

"A man always likes to hear that. I haven't been able to get Willard to say those words yet."

"If a fire monster bites her in the arm, she'll come around." Once inside, I removed my jacket, sat at the dining room table, and laid my arm on it. The charred gouge marks were even more garish under the light.

"It would be impolite to wish that fate on her, right?"

"Probably so."

Walker eyed my arm. "That's not the wound she told me about."

I unwrapped the bandage on my hand. "No, that's this one, but if you wouldn't mind." I nodded toward the arm.

"Of course." After washing his hands in the kitchen, he withdrew a few magical tools from his kit and sat down beside me. He rested his hands to either side of my wound and closed his eyes.

I sensed Zav return to our world and let out a relieved sigh. Good. So far, he was my only proven deterrent to attacks.

"Your blood has been poisoned by magic." Walker pointed at my hand, not my arm. "I may need to take a sample."

"Sample away, Doctor. I love participating in science experiments."

"This other wound is simpler."

"Good. I'm glad *something* is."

My skin itched and burned as magic flowed into the gouges.

Did you learn anything from Xilneth? I asked telepathically as Zav flew from the park toward the house.

Lies.

If he told you that Stormforge dragons are a tad haughty and stuffy, then it might not have been a lie.

You speak ill of my clan?

Not you. Or your uncle. But the rest of them. Haughtiness abounds.

There was a battle in front of your house.

I know. I was in it.

Walker's eyes flew open. He must have sensed Zav flying in for a landing. "That's your ally dragon, right? Not an enemy?"

"He's my mate." I waved to myself, assuming Walker could sense Zav's mark on me.

"He won't be irked that we're alone in your house and I'm holding your hand, will he?"

"As long as you're not thinking lustful thoughts about me, probably not."

Zav had landed in the yard, but he didn't come in immediately. Maybe he was investigating the battleground instead of worrying about unfamiliar men in the house.

"I'll try to restrain myself, though the thought that he could read my mind is disturbing." Walker went back to channeling his healing magic into my arm.

What attacked you? Zav asked, and I explained it to him.

I mentioned the feeling of being watched and that Freysha had said a mage must have been responsible for summoning those creatures. In hindsight, I should have also told him I'd believed I'd been watched at the bog. He might have gone back and found something that my senses had been too weak to pick up on. But I hadn't been certain of my instincts yet then.

Now I suspect that Xilneth intentionally led me away from your world. He told me he wanted to warn you of danger, but I do not trust him.

What danger? The last thing I needed was more of that.

He heard from another dragon that had visited this world that a dragon blade located here is emitting a strong magical beacon.

That's not exactly news.

No, but it is troubling that word has traveled to other worlds. Dragons will not likely care, but many, many lesser species would covet such a blade. There are few of them left in the realms. The door opened, and Zav walked inside in his human form.

His eyes narrowed when he saw Walker, but he must have already sensed him.

"This is the man who healed my uncle in the Crying Caverns," he stated.

"Yes, it is."

"He heals you now?"

"I'm hoping so."

Still holding my arm, Walker did his best to stand and bow to Zav. "Good evening, Lord Zavryd."

"It is a displeasing evening."

"I concur," I said. "Zav, I think someone has been stalking me. More than that, I think this skulking spy is the mage who sent fire beasts to attack me. Can you think of any way I could set a trap for him or her? I assume the person has something like my cloaking charm."

"A trap?" Zav stroked his chin.

"Since I sleep here and spend a lot of time here, it seems like the natural place. Something like the traps in the Crying Caverns, maybe." I could ask Dimitri to make more devices for the yard, but judging by how little his thorn shooter and alarms had done to those fire creatures, having a dragon involved might be better. "We can't put explosives on the walkways—I'd like the mail lady to continue to be able to deliver packages—but what if something sprouted from the ground to ensnare intruders?"

I almost mentioned the new spell that Freysha had taught me, but it wasn't as if I could perform it well enough to help create a trap.

"The difficult part," Zav said, "would be building a trap that could detect intruders with camouflaging magic."

"Maybe they could register weight and go off if someone steps on them. Like a land mine. I don't think my cloaking charm camouflages my weight."

"This is a possibility, but where should I put such traps? Many people walk into and out of this house." Zav eyed Walker.

"This will sound crazy, but I thought I sensed someone up on the roof."

"Why is that crazy? Roofs are acceptable landing pads."

"Unless my stalker is a dragon, I wouldn't expect him to need to *land*." I didn't point out that the last time Zav had landed on the point- and nub-filled roof of our Victorian house, he'd knocked off the chimney. "Though people *have* opened portals up there."

"I will walk the grounds and consider traps while looking for signs that a mage-stalker was here." Before leaving the house, Zav pointed at Walker. "This shifter is having libidinous thoughts."

I blinked. "About me?"

"About your employer. She is not even here."

Walker's head jerked up. "I am *not*. I'm focused on healing Ms. Thorvald."

"Dragons know all." Zav walked out with his head up.

"Only dragons who snoop in other people's thoughts," I called after him. The door thumped closed without a response.

"Sorry, Doc," I said. "He gets huffy when other men talk to me, unless he's sure they're not interested, and he snoops in their thoughts to make *sure* they're not interested. It's something we need to work on. By *we* I mean him."

"My mind only wandered for a moment." Looking flustered, Walker drew a dark tincture in a bottle from his bag. Faint magic emanated from it. "This will further aid the healing of the burns."

"I'm sure that's true." I flexed my arm, pleased to see the fresh gouges sealed and the burned skin starting to heal. The wounds had shifted from hurting to itching, usually a good sign. I rubbed some of his potion over the area.

Walker removed antiseptic, a syringe, a scalpel, and two vials. "Who's going to get the bill for this? You or Colonel Willard?"

"Hm. I was on a mission for her when this all happened, but she didn't order me to cut myself with the evil artifact, so I guess you can invoice me."

"Are you sure? I enjoy taking bills to her office, so she can snark at me about my bachelor ways and ill-gotten wealth."

"I think it's the ostentatious display of your ill-gotten wealth rather than its existence. The giant Mercedes SUV that she says looks like a toaster, for example. Also, is snark a verb?"

"Certainly. Would she be less likely to snark at me if I showed up in a Honda?"

"Oh, I have no doubt. She drives a Honda herself, so she must approve of the brand."

He swabbed my skin, then slid the needle into my vein for the blood draw. "I'm not sure my building's HOA allows economy cars."

"I really hope you're joking."

"Yeah, but they do give you a crappy parking spot in the back of the garage if you drive something modest."

"It's hard being affluent, isn't it?"

"Didn't you get paid in gold bars for your last assignment? I want to take a tissue sample from around the wound too." He finished the blood draw and pointed the scalpel at the cut that wouldn't heal.

"Have at it. And yes, I did, but I spent the money on commercial kitchen equipment to properly feed an always-ravenous dragon."

"Now I hope *you're* joking." He smiled but his gaze drifted to the huge double-door restaurant refrigerator visible in the kitchen. We'd taken out some of the cabinets to make room for it.

"Only partially. The commercial smoker and chest freezer are in the conservatory. I had to get a Costco membership so I could buy ribs, burgers, turkey drumsticks, and sausages in bulk. I'm thinking of switching to a farm share, so the truck will wheel the sides of beef straight up to the house."

"Practical."

"That's me. I now know how mothers with families of six to feed feel." I winced as he applied antiseptic, then scraped away bloody flesh from the edge of my cut. "Though, technically, Zav eats more than a family of six could."

Zav was probably working up an appetite right now as he walked around on the roof. With two floors above me, I couldn't hear him, but I sensed him strolling about and doing his investigation.

"Does his family come over for the holidays?" Walker looked far more amused than sympathetic to my plight.

"No. At least they haven't *yet*." I imagined Zondia, the queen, Uncle Ston, and however many relatives Zav had showing up for the dragon version of Christmas and shuddered. There wasn't enough meat in all of Seattle to feed that family.

As Walker finished with my cut and rubbed his magical goo on my hand, I texted Willard to let her know about the attack and ask if her intelligence gatherers had learned anything more about the fae. A second after I sent it, my phone buzzed.

"Hey, Nin," I answered, glancing at the time. "What's up?"

"We must have a business meeting with all of the owners of the Sable Dragon."

"Uh, okay."

"Is tonight good for you?"

"Tonight? It's almost midnight."

"I can come to your house. I am with Dimitri. I was helping clean and close up the shop." No doubt after she'd worked all day at her own food-truck business. "He is having a crisis of faith."

"I just said I wanted to hire someone so I could spend more time working on my art," came Dimitri's voice from the background.

"This is important, Val," Nin said sternly. "We must speak."

A thunk-thunk sounded next in the background. Were the goblins playing their game there tonight? I wouldn't blame Dimitri if he was tired of being there full-time, since full-time tended to mean from six a.m. to midnight, every day of the week.

"That's fine," I said. "I'm here getting my arm fondled."

"We will come immediately. Please wait to mate with Lord Zavryd until after our meeting."

"That's not who's fondling my arm tonight, but okay."

She hung up without responding to my stab at humor. Clearly, Dimitri's crisis of faith had her concerned.

CHAPTER 9

D OCTOR WALKER LEFT WITH MY blood and tissue samples, promising he would call as soon as he got results back from his lab, and Nin and Dimitri arrived shortly after. Dimitri parked his orange camper van in the yard since there wasn't room for him to parallel park it in the street. A relic from the eighties, with the interior decorated with yellow curtains, a stained carpet, and *X-Files* paraphernalia, the vehicle had prompted more than a few neighbors to raise their eyebrows. There was no way it would get a parking spot in the hoity-toity garage where Walker lived.

Nin slid out of the passenger seat, a hoodie pulled up against the drizzle, so I couldn't tell what color her pigtails were this week. She worked as many hours as Dimitri, if not more, so I didn't know when she found time to dye her hair, but she'd told me that one of her roommates, who was in beauty school, practiced on her for her homework.

"Hey, Nin," I said from the covered porch, my bandaged hand in my pocket as she walked up.

I surveyed the damp street and empty sidewalks, wondering if my invisible stalker was still around, but with Zav back in the area, I no longer had that feeling of being watched.

Two pine cones tumbled off the roof and hit the sidewalk, making Nin jump and look up. "Good evening, Lord Zavryd," she called up.

Another pine cone tumbled down.

"Come on in." I waved to the open door. My arm already felt better, but the hand still hurt, and I tried not to think about what would happen if Walker couldn't find a way to heal the strange wound.

"Your lawn has been damaged," Nin observed. "And it smells like smoke."

"Yeah, have you ever encountered crucible beasts?"

"No."

"Good. Don't."

She gave me an odd look but stepped into the house.

Dimitri was slower walking in, pausing to frown at his yard statues and alarms. A few of them had been damaged in the battle. Amazingly, the two dragon topiaries that Zav had, with Freysha's assistance, caused to grow up and be shaped almost overnight were still standing healthy, green, and undisturbed at the corners of the front yard.

"There was a fight?" Dimitri asked as he tramped up the porch steps, the boards creaking under his six-and-a-half feet of solidness.

"Yup. Crucible beasts. Sorry the lawn took a few hits. I thought it was better to fight outside than let them burn down the house."

"We may need to get better insurance, Val."

"The house is covered in case of fire, theft, and vandalism."

"What about extreme mauling by monsters?"

"I already checked. That's not available in our area."

"Hm." Dimitri walked inside, a slump to his shoulders.

Why did I have a feeling the meeting was Nin's idea and not his?

The van's sliding door opened, and another visitor hopped out, a three-and-a-half-foot-tall green visitor with a nest of wild white hair. Gondo's vest pockets clattered as he trotted up, either because of tools or discarded junk he'd been gathering all day.

"Greetings, mate of the mighty dragon Lord Zavryd." He used his finger to draw a wrench in the air in front of his chest—the typical goblin greeting.

"Nin invited you to our meeting?" I asked.

"No, but I was at the shop when they closed, and I asked for a ride home."

"You don't live here." A burst of panic filled me as I worried whether Dimitri had offered him a room.

He wouldn't do that without consulting me first, would he? He couldn't.

"No, I don't, but I live *close* to here now." Gondo waved in the direction of Green Lake. What, had he claimed some bushes or one of the public bathrooms? "With some city goblins who've made a home in the park. But they always eat all the food they scrounge before I get home. Do you have food?"

"I guess. Come on in." I paused before stepping inside. "Do you know anything about fae visiting our state?"

Willard kept Gondo on her staff because he was a huge gossip and because everyone else in the magical community gossiped to goblins in turn. She claimed he knew the goings on of almost every ogre, troll, orc, and kobold in the western half of the state.

"I know where some of their mushroom rings are. And I know they're snippy and rude to goblins. Technically, they're snippy and rude to everyone except beautiful maidens and handsome… What is the term for virgin males in your world?"

"I don't think there is one. Historically, our society never went gaga over virgin guys."

"Fae ladies go gaga for them. Elven *hyleetha* too. Fae ladies find elven males particularly desirable, but they are dangerous to seduce. Humans are very easy. Goblins would also be easy, but nobody ever seduces goblins. It's strange."

"No doubt. I'm not worried about seduction schemes. I'm concerned about fae possibly being behind planting an artifact that marked my sword with a nasty energy beacon."

"Yes, I have sensed your sword since yesterday. It is oozing very enticing magic now that makes me wish to visit it and perhaps acquire it, and I do not even use weapons. Goblins prefer tools. Much more practical. What can you do with a sword that you can't do with a battery-operated drill?"

"Nothing. You should stick with drills. Do you know any fae I could speak with about my problem?" I thought of Willard's Corporal Clarke, who I'd always thought had some fae blood mixed with his Jamaican heritage. If nothing else came up, maybe I would have a chat with him.

"I have never seen a full-blooded fae male or female or even one of their doorways open," Gondo said. "They visit this and other worlds infrequently and do not stay. They reside in the magical realm they crafted long ago, and it is similar to the Del'nothian tigers' realm—it exists *between* worlds, rather than being *on* a world. It is difficult for all but the most powerful mages from other worlds to make portals to the fae realm. Most must be invited through their magical doorways."

"I don't suppose you know how to activate one?"

"There are keys that are sometimes given to friends of the fae, but that is rare, since they do not care for outsiders, other than using them for carnal pleasures. And, of course, the fae themselves can use their magic to open the doorways."

"So my best bet would be to find someone with a key?" Even though I'd interacted with numerous magical beings over the years, I couldn't remember anyone ever mentioning having such a key or having a relationship with the fae. Like Gondo, I'd never met a full-blooded fae, only those like Corporal Clarke who were perhaps a quarter fae.

"Or to make a key. A powerful enchanter with knowledge of their kind might be able to do that."

"Val?" came Nin's voice from inside the house. "Zoltan has joined us in the dining room, and we are ready for our business meeting."

"Do normal businesses have meetings after midnight?" I muttered.

"Goblins have meetings at all hours while enjoying coffee and good company."

Zav leaped down from the three-story roof and landed in the yard.

Gondo squawked and hid behind me.

"How's the trap-setting going?" I held a finger up toward Nin. "Do you need a goblin to help?"

That would keep Gondo from joining our meeting—or building anything out of our living room furniture.

"I do not." Zav looked over at us, and his violet eyes flared with inner light.

That was usually meant as a warning and hinted that he was irked. Gondo scurried into the house.

I detect that someone was here, Zav informed me telepathically. *By the signature of their magic, not any trail that could be followed.*

Someone fae?

Someone elven.

I sagged against the doorjamb. The last thing I needed was another race involved in orchestrating my problem.

You're sure it wasn't Freysha? We were making roots grow in the backyard earlier. I snapped my fingers. *Oh, and a male elf made a portal to pick her up. That may be what you're sensing.*

The portal was on the roof? Zav gazed around, nose in the air, though it wouldn't be his eyes or ears that he used to sense magic.

No.

I sensed the residue up there.

Damn.

Allow me to continue to investigate. Perhaps I can determine where he went.

It's a guy? How can you tell?

I can tell. Zav stalked off toward the side yard.

CHAPTER 10

"DIMITRI WISHES TO LEAVE THE business," Nin said as soon as I sat down.

"No, I don't. That's not what I said." Dimitri lifted his hands as if he worried I would beat him up. Or maybe that *Nin* would beat him up.

She wasn't scowling at him, but she did wear a concerned expression.

"You did not say anything to me about leaving the business," Zoltan said, sitting at the end of the table with a pair of tinted goggles on. "My tinctures and formulas are starting to sell regularly. This represents a small but pleasing diversification of my income. I will raise the prices soon, once a sufficient number of customers have realized how powerful my wares are."

"Yeah, yeah, your potions sell fine." Dimitri slouched down in his seat. "And the coffee sells outrageously well. Especially that high-octane goblin blend."

"That is naturally the case," Gondo called, not from the living room but from the kitchen. "I had a hand in its development. Perhaps I should be given free coffee for life."

I hoped he was rooting for food and not *building* anything. I could only see the top of his head over the counters.

"We cannot afford to give away free beverages. We are a start-up. A start-up that cannot lose its manager." Nin pinned Dimitri with her concerned gaze.

"I just said I'd like to hire another part-time person so I can work there fewer hours. With all the hours I'm there, selling tinctures and coffee and stocking shelves, not with *my* art—" Dimitri spread his hand on his chest, "—but with everybody else's stuff, I'm barely getting any time to learn from Inga and work on my projects."

"A business is strongest when an owner-operator is very involved," Nin said. "I understand that you wish to pursue and perfect your art, but can it not wait until we are more established? These early days are critical, and as you pointed out, few of your art pieces sell, so it is not imperative that more of them be created."

"It's imperative to *me*." Dimitri thunked his head onto the table.

Nin looked at me and Zoltan, as if we could solve this problem.

"Hiring another part-time employee doesn't sound like a bad idea," I said. "If the business can afford it."

Clattering noises came from the kitchen. Gondo's head was no longer visible.

"I am concerned that if Dimitri is not there as much and not as involved, the business will suffer," Nin said. "Part-time hourly-wage employees have little invested in the success of a business. Also, given our occasionally brutish clientele, I believe someone who appears large and menacing should always be on the premises." She looked at Dimitri *and* at me. "Tam has occasionally felt unsafe when she is there alone. She has some magical blood but no superhuman abilities."

"I didn't know that. I can come by and loom menacingly more often." But maybe I shouldn't volunteer for that until I fixed my sword. I didn't want Dimitri's shop to burn down or otherwise be destroyed by monsters trying to get at me. "Or maybe we could hire Inga away from her fence-enchanting gig. She's half-troll and decidedly fearsome—just look at how well she's keeping Reb in line. Besides, her other job doesn't pay well."

"She is large and menacing and keeps your young troll employee on task," Nin said, "but we do not need an enchanter unless that side of the business picks up."

Dimitri didn't speak but shook his head with his face still pressed to the table.

"Maybe we could figure out how to make that happen. If we want Dimitri to stay passionate and involved…" I spread my hand toward him.

Nin propped her elbow on the table and gripped her chin. "Yes, I see your point. Creating and enchanting are his passions, not coffee."

"Someone finally noticed," Dimitri muttered.

"It is difficult when the results of your passion are not desired by others."

Dimitri slumped lower. "My enchantments are getting better. Inga's lessons are helping. It's just hard to show off how the alarms and defense systems work until they're actually installed. I sell more of the yard statues that aren't enchanted, that are just art."

"Maybe you should make a list of what you've sold," I said. "Or survey the coffee customers and ask what they would buy. Then make more of that. No offense, Dimitri, but not many people want or need a bear-holding-a-fish wind spinner made from old pipes and hood ornaments."

Nin dropped her hand. "That is actually good advice, Val."

"You don't need to sound so surprised."

"You have not shown much interest in or knowledge of business practices in the past."

"Even a broken cuckoo clock is correct twice a day," Zoltan murmured.

I gave him the glare that comment deserved, but Nin wasn't done speaking.

"It would be wise to survey the customers and see what they would buy." She nodded to herself. "I will arrange this. And then Dimitri will make items that will sell."

Dimitri lifted his head, but he didn't look much happier about this proclamation. "I'm an artist, Nin. I have to make what calls to me when I touch the metal."

"You will be called by what the customers want." She nodded again and stood. "Meeting adjourned."

Dimitri's shoulders still had a slump to them as he pushed his chair back.

I grabbed his arm before he could slouch out to his van. "What if you alternate?"

"What?" He squinted at me.

"Make a thing that the customers like, and then make a thing that, uh, calls to you from the metal. Could you do that and be happy?"

"I… maybe."

"Your contagious enthusiasm makes me want to jump for joy. Or slit my wrists. It's one of those."

A whirring sound came from the kitchen. I decided not to look.

"I'm just worried the customers will want inane or boring stuff. Like tissue boxes and spoon holders."

"Have you *seen* our customers? If an ogre were to buy a tissue box, I'd fall over. Make things that cater to the magical. Those are most of our customers anyway."

"Like what?"

"I don't know, but no ogre lair I've been in has a wind spinner out front. They live in caves. Goblins and trolls build their homes in parks and forests. Think meat cleavers and cave organizers."

"Cave organizers? What would *that* be?"

"I don't know, but when you figure it out, you'll have customers."

He looked more thoughtful than depressed as he walked toward the door, but I didn't know if I'd cheered him up or only stymied him.

Zoltan disappeared back into the basement, and I caught Nin before she could head out. My first thought was to encourage her to take Gondo with her, but I realized she might be my best resource for keys to fae doorways.

"I know gnomish enchanting is what your grandfather taught you, but do you know anything about the fae?" I asked.

"Very little. My grandfather has traveled across many worlds, so he may have knowledge of their ways."

"Is he still in Seattle?"

"No, he returned to Thailand to visit my grandmother. She was very pleased at his return, and they are enjoying sweet and naughty times together once again."

I decided not to ask for details on that. "Can he break away for long enough for a phone call? I need a key that works on fae doorways, so I can visit their realm."

"They do not like uninvited visitors to their realm."

"Nobody likes it when I show up at their door, but they'll have to deal with it. And tell me why they planted that artifact that messed up my sword."

"I will call him and ask if he knows how to make such a key," Nin said.

"Thank you."

The whirring sound grew louder, and a self-propelling cart made from my cutting board, two rolling pins, a vegetable peeler, and more utensils I couldn't identify rolled out of the kitchen. Gondo ambled out after it and raised his arms.

"A gift for the Goblin Whisperer."

"Is that me?" I asked.

Nin nodded. "Gondo and the other goblins from Idaho have not forgotten that you helped them find a new home, and they remain impressed that you attracted a dragon as a mate."

"What is it?" I watched the cart whir around the dining room table. "And is that the lefse rolling pin my mother got me?"

"It is a meal-delivery cart for dragons," Gondo said. "Large enough to hold many racks of ribs."

"We were planning to make lefse together this winter." I hoped he hadn't damaged the rolling pin in making this creation.

"Which is still more than two months away. In the meantime, you can deliver many meals to your mate." Gondo bowed deeply, his pockets clanking. "You are most welcome. I have helped myself to your food."

He walked to the front door with boxes of Pop-Tarts and Froot Loops sticking out of a sack slung over his shoulder, looking like a burglar making off with a stash.

"That's Dimitri's food," I said, "and he's going to miss it in the morning."

"It's fortunate that you are wealthy now and can easily replace groceries," Nin said.

"That wealth is going to be temporary if I have to feed the entire magical community. I better look into some high-yielding investments."

"Yes." Nin clapped me on the shoulder. "I am so pleased that you are thinking more like an entrepreneur now. Perhaps later we can talk about value stocks versus growth stocks, and index funds and ETFs."

"Scintillating topics that will make me leap out of bed in the mornings."

"They will. Now, I must go. Dimitri is giving me a ride home."

"Hey, Nin?"

She paused and looked back.

"How do you feel about jewelry?" I asked.

Maybe it wasn't too late to nudge Thad in a different direction with his gift selecting.

"I do not have feelings about it."

"You don't own much that I've seen. If you could choose between a pretty necklace and a new deep fryer for your truck, which would excite you more?"

"I cook only healthy food. My truck does not need a deep fryer. I *have* been looking longingly at the 110-cup RiceMaster 57155." Nin clasped her hands in front of her chest like a little girl dreaming of a trip to Disneyland. "It cooks and warms *and* has a steamer attachment." She skipped to the front door, leaving me alone with the whirring goblin cart.

It was too late to text Thad, so I emailed him from my phone. *Nix the expensive jewelry; the RiceMaster 57155 is the way to Nin's heart.*

Hopefully, he would take my advice. I didn't know if Amber would be less irked by the idea of her dad buying his new girlfriend kitchen appliances, but a rice cooker couldn't possibly be as expensive as the jewelry in that catalog he'd been looking at.

I headed up to the bedroom, hoping Dimitri and Thad would take my advice and hoping it would be useful. A life coach, I was not. I had problems of my own that I couldn't solve.

Your existing magical defenses are inadequate for protecting your home against intruders, Zav spoke into my mind. *I will add power to the dragon-shaped topiaries to improve them. My mate must be safe in her own home.*

Just don't animate them or give them glowing eyes.

What is wrong with glowing eyes? My eyes can glow.

You're not a bush.

I will ensorcell them sufficiently to protect you.

Did that mean the topiaries were getting glowing eyes? At least Halloween was coming up. They would be appropriate for the month. After that… we'd be like that house that never took down their Christmas lights.

"So *many* problems of my own," I muttered.

Zav came in a few minutes later and opened his palm to reveal a round wooden token with a faint magical signature. An unfamiliar leaf was engraved on one side, the elegant design making me suspect it was elven. One edge of the token had been charred, maybe from one of the fire beasts walking next to it.

"I found this on the sidewalk at the corner of your property," Zav said. "It is an elven *syasha*."

"And what is that?"

"The tokens have a variety of uses, from keepsakes to granting luck. Sometimes, they are left behind to convey a message."

"What kind of message?"

"I believe the term in your world is *calling card*."

"Hm." I flipped the token over. There was a dagger on the back. "I'm guessing this one wasn't left to grant me luck. You think it was intentionally placed?" I eyed the sidewalk through the window. Why set it there instead of on my porch if I was meant to find it? Any dog walker passing by might have found it lying out there. "Or did it fall out of someone's pocket?"

"I would guess it was placed."

Too bad Freysha was gone. She might have recognized it or have been able to tell me more.

I was half-tempted to ask Zav to take me to the elven home world, but nobody there had been that welcoming or helpful the last time I'd visited, except for my father himself, and if he was ill, the pointy-eared brute squad might not let me in to see him.

I held it out, intending to give it back to Zav, but he'd already left the bedroom. He appeared in the front yard, clasped his hands behind his back, and considered the topiaries. There was no doubt; they would have glowing eyes by dawn.

CHAPTER 11

ZAV ACCOMPANIED ME TO WILLARD'S office in the morning. It was strange having a bodyguard. I was used to *being* a bodyguard. I was even more used to being an assassin of magical bad guys, but it would be impossible to sneak up on such a person right now. Chopper rode in my scabbard, continuing to pulse that tainted fae energy, as we parked and walked toward the blue-gray office building. The IRS sign out front said nothing of the army detachment that worked there, keeping an eye on the magical community in the Pacific Northwest.

"I received word from the queen this morning," Zav said as we walked.

"Your mother came to Earth?"

"No, my sister. She relayed the message. The queen wishes to have all of the escaped criminals on her lists captured and returned to our world for punishment and rehabilitation before *Yavnokar*."

"Which is what?"

"The Eyrie Launch Festival. It is in approximately two months. It is a time when the queen's position as leader of the Ruling Council—whether she will continue to reign over our kind or another will take her place—is determined. Our clan is now in a good position to continue to hold power, thanks to the return of so many of our kin that disappeared over the years." Zav nodded toward me, acknowledging the role I'd played in freeing them. "But since those criminals escaped during her rule, she would like them all returned before her position might possibly be contended. The Silverclaw Clan will point out our failure to keep criminals properly rehabilitated. Even though it was a plot of elven rogues, it happened under her wings."

"It makes sense that she'd want to take care of it."

"In order to make this deadline, I will need to return to collecting criminals that have fled to Earth."

"Meaning you can't stay here and be my bodyguard indefinitely?" I opened the door, and we turned down the hall toward Willard's office.

"You will have to accompany me so I can continue to protect you. It will not be unpleasant. You will ride on my back and know the glory of traveling to exotic lands with the wind caressing your scales."

"If I develop scales, I'm going to have to start paying for Zoltan's tinctures."

A passing soldier heard this, and his eyebrows flew up. He glanced at me, then at Zav, taking in his robe and the water sandals he was wearing today instead of his elven slippers. A couple of months ago, he'd adopted them as his preferred Earth footwear and wore them when we were out among humans. Thankfully, the soldier made no comment about the style. Over the months I'd known him, Zav had worn no fewer than six pairs of boots and shoes in his quest to find acceptable footwear to wear here in place of his slippers, which someone had called unmanly. These were hideous, but I wouldn't call them feminine.

"I need to figure out how to fix my sword before I can go with you, Zav. All I would do now is alert criminals that we're in the area."

He looked glumly over at me. "Yes, this is a problem."

"Willard said she has something for me. Maybe it'll help."

Early that morning, she'd responded to my text, asking me to come to the office. She hadn't commented on the fire creatures or my new elven stalker.

"I hope this will be the case," Zav said. "Alternatively, you could give it to me, and I could take it to a master dragon enchanter to see if she can unweave the two magics. However, it is still possible the sword would lose its dwarven magic in the process."

"I need to avoid that. Would a dwarf master enchanter be better to ask?"

"Possibly. If we can find one. When there is time, I will take you to their world, and perhaps a dwarf who would remain hidden from a dragon will come out to see you."

"They should. I'm lovely."

"Do not apply your sharp tongue to the dwarves."

"I wouldn't dream of it."

"If you are snippy with them the way you were with me this morning, they will not help you."

"I wasn't snippy this morning. I said no glowing eyes on the shrubs, and you made them glow *and* flame."

"To further protect your premises and as a deterrent to the riffraff."

"The riffraff will be there within the hour recording the bushes and putting them on social media."

"If they draw too close to the topiaries, fire will shoot out at them. This is for the protection of my mate and our domicile. It is for your own good."

"The last time you said that, you kidnapped me."

"Yes. For your own good."

The door to Willard's outer office was open, with Gondo standing on the desk and tinkering with a model windmill as well as a miniature steam truck that I'd seen before. In a corner of a junkyard somewhere, he was working on a full-sized one that he would be able to ride to and from the goblin sanctuary outside of the city.

The inner door was open, with Willard sitting at her desk, the surface stacked with so many books that I could barely see her. She didn't usually keep magical artifacts in her office, but I sensed something positioned under or inside her desk.

I walked in without asking for permission, removed my sword harness, flopped down in one of the two guest chairs, and flung my leg over the armrest.

"Make yourself at home," Willard said, infusing an impressive amount of sarcasm into her Southern drawl.

Zav considered my pose, walked to the second chair, and carefully arranged himself in an identical position. Assuming this was required for human meetings? Maybe I shouldn't be a bad influence.

"Men in robes shouldn't throw their legs up on things." Willard pointedly did not look at the shin hair now on display.

At least the robe was long enough that she wasn't in danger of seeing Zav's lack of underwear. That was one human custom I hadn't been able to convince him to adopt yet. Apparently, when elves wore robes, they didn't put anything on under them.

"It's too bad you're preoccupied with other problems, Thorvald. I have a job here that would be perfect for you." Willard tapped a folder atop a stack of books. "There's an orc motorcycle gang terrorizing people on the highway between Deming and Sedro-Woolley. They all bow to their leader, Doktail, who's the one corrupting the youths and turning them into murderers."

"Doktail?" Zav put his foot down. "That is one of the criminals on my list. I will hunt him down. Val will accompany me."

"Val may want to do her own thing." Willard spread a printout of a map of the Seattle area across the stacks of books. Numerous parks and houses were circled in red ink. "Per her request, I've been putting together all the fairy rings reported this fall. I also had one of my sergeants dig this out of the evidence room in the basement. I'd almost forgotten about it." She opened a desk drawer and withdrew the magical artifact I'd sensed.

It looked like a large ceramic toadstool—or maybe a Smurf house—that someone might put in their fairy garden. The bulbous cap was painted red with white dots, the thick stem was yellow, and a patch of textured green paint—grass—covered the round base. If not for the magic the thing emanated, I would have guessed she picked it up at a yard sale.

"A few of my research analysts and I came in early to work on your problem." She rested the toadstool on top of another stack of books. "You're welcome."

"Uh, thanks?" Was that toadstool an answer to one of my problems?

"I have seen those before," Zav stated.

"I haven't," I said.

"My analysts say they were historically distributed in Europe, perhaps by traveling gypsies sympathetic to the fae, to villages full of attractive young men and women. If one of them wished to have a fae lover, they were to activate the device near a fairy circle and wait naked in the moonlight."

"The fae seem overly interested in sex with other species," I said, thinking of my conversation with Gondo.

"That was my impression from the literature." Willard waved at a few of the books, translations in journals sitting on top. "My thinking is that you might be able to use that to set a trap and lure one of them out. But you'll probably need help. It's doubtful the fae will come out for you."

"Because I'm a half-blood mongrel?"

"Because you're not a virgin. I assume. Given that you have a daughter and that your dragon is sitting with his legs splayed and oozing testosterone at me."

"That's his dragonly aura, not testosterone."

"My mate is experienced in sexual matters and an expert in the ways of pleasing a male," Zav stated.

"Fantastic. I'll put that on her résumé." Willard waved at the artifact. "If you find a virgin to go with you, the literature says they have to be within twenty feet of the fairy ring and rub the cap there."

"She *is* fantastic," Zav said. "I was wise to claim her before another dragon saw how excellent she is in battle, how much she vexes enemies, and how loyal and faithful she is."

I reached over and patted his knee, appreciating his praise—even if I was still trying to figure out how to get him to be less forthcoming when it came to discussing sex in front of other people.

"It's not necessary for you to bring him to meetings," Willard said.

"Is his dragonly aura distracting you?"

"*Something* is." She waved toward his legs.

Maybe more was visible from her desk than I'd thought.

Zav stood up. "I will acquire the orc leader and halt the activities of the roving gang."

"I take it back," Willard told me. "Bring him any time you wish."

"He is a handy dragon," I said.

Zav lifted his chin. "Yes."

I rolled up the map and gingerly picked up the mushroom thingamajig, hoping it wasn't as fragile as it looked. "If I find a virgin to rub this, there's no chance of an army of fae coming through, is there? It would just be one guy?"

Since I didn't know many virgins, only one person came to mind. She would only help me if I paid her—or bought her an expensive item of clothing—but that seemed a reasonable tradeoff. Assuming she wouldn't be in any danger that I couldn't protect her from. And assuming she *was* a virgin. If she wasn't, Thad and I might have an awkward discussion coming up.

"None of the texts mentioned armies," Willard said, "just horny fae lovers."

I had no idea if whatever random fae showed up would know anything about the artifact and who had placed it, but one of their people would be more likely to know how to fix my sword than an enchanter from another race. And without a key, this was the only way I had of getting a fae visitor to come to our world.

"Thorvald?" Willard asked.

I paused in the doorway as Zav continued out.

"For future reference, even though Zav is extremely handy, please let him know that we have an underwear-required dress policy in this office."

"I'll mention it, but he's a free spirit."

"So I saw."

CHAPTER 12

SINCE ZAV REFUSED TO LEAVE me long enough to deal with the motorcycle orcs himself, I flew along with him, and we descended upon them together. Willard had texted me the locale of their hideout, so finding them wasn't difficult. Thanks to Zav's extreme competence as a warrior, I'd only gotten to beat up one while he'd flattened the other nine and captured the leader. We'd also freed three young women they'd captured and had caged in their den of iniquity, so that made me feel good about coming along, even if I was preoccupied by planning my mission to nab a fae.

Now, I was riding on Zav's back as we passed high above the Skagit River and perusing Willard's map. The salty wind blowing in from nearby Puget Sound tugged at my braid—not any scales, thank you, Zav.

The orc leader—the criminal on the queen's list—was riding in the extra-dimensional pocket Zav could make to store things in while he flew. That was fine with me. I didn't like carpooling—or dragon-pooling. Zav planned to drop him off at home while I visited with Thad and tried to recruit my daughter.

Being extremely careful not to drop my phone, I texted Amber and asked if she was home and if I could come by. It was Saturday, and I knew from her social-media posts that she'd had a swim meet last weekend and was staying in and doing homework—AKA "just chillin'"—this weekend.

To practice sword-fighting? she replied.

We can if you have time, but I have a job to offer you. I thought she would be less likely to say she was too busy if money was involved.

A paying job?

Yeah.

I'm in. But we can't tell Dad. He says I can't get a job until I'm sixteen. He started with eighteen, and I worked him down. He says that sports and good grades are my job. The pay on sports and grades is sucky, Val.

Is there any pay at all?

I get fifty dollars for every A that I get on my report card. That's hardly anything. My friend's mom got fifty dollars for A's when she was a kid thirty years ago. I can't believe Dad doesn't know about inflation.

If Amber didn't want to tell Thad about this, maybe sneaking her away for the afternoon would be easier than I thought. Normally, I wouldn't keep things from him, but taking one's daughter to use as bait to lure a fae perv with a virgin obsession seemed... difficult to explain.

"Maybe this is a bad idea," I announced, more to myself than Zav or the random seagull who'd spotted him through the clouds and was flying away at top speed.

If you do not wish to be separated from me while I deliver our criminal to the Dragon Justice Court, you may accompany me.

"That's not what I was talking about, and I think I'll be okay on Earth without you for a couple of hours."

Since you were integral in freeing so many of our clan members, my mother no longer loathes you. You do not need to avoid her.

"I'm glad to hear that, but I still don't want to visit her. No offense, but she's a grump."

Add to that Zav's description of their people holding their court from perches in towering mountains full of eyries, and I had a feeling it wouldn't be the most comfortable place for a legged being to visit.

She carries many responsibilities.

"Grumpily."

Sometimes this is true. Not all dragons have my sublime personality and even temper.

I telepathically sent him my memory of him throwing my Jeep up in a tree the day we met.

Mouthy half-elves can try the sublimeness of even the most even-tempered dragon.

"I'm going to assume you're using mouthy in its most affectionate sense."

Of course.

We were passing over Union Slough north of Everett. If I was going to change my mind, I didn't have much time. I called Willard to ask her opinion. She would want to know we'd captured her orc, regardless.

"Colonel Willard," she answered.

I summed up the results of the mission, then asked, "Are any of your younger soldiers virgins, by chance? Or older ones are fine too."

"That's not in their records, and I don't ask. Judging by comments made around the office on Monday mornings, no. I thought you had someone in mind when you left."

"Amber, but I'm having second thoughts. Zav and I *should* be able to protect her—given that Zav flattened nine orcs in under four minutes, he should be able to protect anyone from anything—but if something goes wrong… she's just a kid. My kid." And *Thad's* kid. My stomach twisted at the idea of explaining an injury or something even worse to him.

"She has a magical sword, and you've been teaching her how to use it. And she's six feet tall and as snarky and sarcastic as you. I don't think you're going to find a more capable virgin."

"Are sarcasm and snark useful in dealing with sex deviants?"

"I'm positive. It's up to you, Thorvald. I just provide the magical mushroom statues. I'll prepare your payment for capturing Doktail. Or should I give Zav the payment? It sounds like he did all the work."

"I'm the one who buys his meat, but I'll ask if he wants some US dollars to store in his extra dimensional pocket."

"You don't say things like that to normal people, do you?"

"I don't know any normal people anymore."

"Lucky you. I still have to interface with higher-ups that think we deal with the occasional *X-Files* situation. Willard out."

She hung up, leaving me staring down at my phone. "I guess she has a point. Amber is more capable than most young people."

Direct me to the location of your daughter. Zav didn't comment on the rest.

I started to give him the address, realized he didn't have a phone loaded with Google Maps, and did my best to telepathically share the location with him. "Do you want to be paid and have some Earth money? Willard is offering."

I collected the orc criminal for the queen, not for payment. Dragons do not work for currency. We work to further our missions in life and for the honor of the clan.

"Do you mind if I take the payment? My mission in life is getting paid so I can afford to buy my mate racks of ribs."

I will allow this.

"You're a good dragon." I patted his side.

One with a sublime personality. He banked as we neared Edmonds and descended toward the neighborhoods near the water.

"It's much improved these days."

Hm.

Thad's BMW was parked in the driveway. So much for my hope that he wouldn't be home.

Zav landed in the front yard, the breeze from his wings knocking a few soggy red leaves off the maples. A bicycler glanced our way, but didn't appear to notice his substantial black-scaled form or me sliding off his back.

"Thank you for the ride." I saluted him, assuming he would remain in his dragon form and open a portal to take his criminal home.

But as I walked up to the door, I sensed him shifting into his human form and striding after me.

"You're coming?" I tried not to grimace, but he hadn't made the best first impression on Thad.

"Only for a moment. It occurred to me that your former mate—your former inadequate and inferior-to-a-dragon mate—may be able to answer a question I have."

"I'd prefer it if you call him Thad instead of describing him. And I'm *positive* he would too."

"Very well."

"I don't think he's going to answer any of your questions."

"All lesser species should be eager to fulfill the needs of dragons."

"Yes, but as we've discussed, Earthlings aren't aware of what an honor that is."

"Perhaps you should speak to your world leaders and inform them so they can get the information out to their minions."

"I'll do that the next time I'm at the White House."

"Excellent."

I knocked on the door, still relieved that Thad had broken up with the girlfriend—the ex-girlfriend—who hated me. Amber might not agree, but I thought Nin was a *much* better option.

Thad answered, and I hurried to speak before he could object to Zav's presence. "Hey, Thad. Is Amber ready for her sword-fighting lesson?"

"She's on the patio, doing her nails and reading a textbook. I didn't think you were coming this weekend." Thad squinted at Zav, who stood with his chest puffed out and his head up, oozing his dragon aura.

"Change of plans. She texted to let me know she has time."

"Guess you can go back then. Is your assistant here to act as a practice dummy that you poke with your swords?" Thad looked hopeful.

"Dummy!" Zav looked at me. *I will take the information I need by mind-scouring him.*

I smiled at Thad and put a hand on Zav's chest. *Don't even think about it. If you want to know something, you'll have to talk to him like a civilized person.*

He is the one failing to be civilized and properly respectful of dragons.

"No," I told Thad. "He's only staying briefly. I believe he has a question for you."

"What is it?" Thad's squint remained suspicious.

"I actually don't know. You two can bond in a manly way while I spar with Amber." *Be nice, please,* I added telepathically as I walked through the house to the backyard. *I would be upset if you incinerated, mind-scoured, or otherwise threatened him.*

Hm.

I couldn't interpret that and paused at a corner to look back. Zav was peering down at a catalog lying on a console table by the door while Thad stood with his arms folded over his chest.

That wasn't the jewelry catalog that Amber had mentioned, was it? I hoped Zav wasn't contemplating getting earrings for me, especially since he had no money.

"What do you want to know?" Thad asked him.

Having a feeling I would hear the details of the conversation later, I went outside and found Amber sitting next to the gas fire pit with the flames dancing as she played on her phone. Her textbook was open with fresh highlights on the pages, so I assumed this represented a break and that she actually *was* doing homework this weekend.

"Hey, Val." She surprised me by standing up and sticking her phone in her pocket instead of ignoring me for five minutes. "What's the job and how much are you paying?"

"Strapped for cash, are you?"

"My allowance doesn't cover my weekly needs, and Dad says we already did all of our school shopping for the year. For the *year*, Val. I can't wear the same things in the winter and spring that I'm wearing in the fall." Amber looked me up and down from jeans to gray shirt to black duster and combat boots. Fortunately, she didn't point out that the only changes to my wardrobe were to switch from a short-sleeve T-shirt to a long-sleeve one with the passing seasons. "I need reserves for emergency clothing purchases."

"I think I'll only need you for a few hours today. What's minimum wage?"

"Fifty dollars an hour, and I'm worth way more than minimum wage."

"Fifty dollars an hour? Wow, I'm way underpaid."

"That's between you and your boss. You can have me for four hours today—I have a study group later this evening—for seventy-five dollars an hour."

I pulled out my phone.

"You're not using a calculator, are you?" Amber rolled her eyes. "That's three hundred dollars."

"Thanks for the demonstration that your math skills are up to par. I'm texting your father and asking what he pays you for extra chores."

"Dad underpays me. He's a slave driver. Only twenty dollars to wash his car this summer. I was out roasting in the hot sun like a migrant orchard picker for *hours*."

"Are you taking drama classes at school?"

"No, why?"

"You should. You're a natural."

"Ha ha. Okay, two hundred dollars, and I'll work with you for five hours. But no washing cars. I've seen the mud plastered to your Jeep. You'd need a chisel to clean that thing."

"All right, deal." I stuck out my hand. I'd paid orcs more than that to blab on their kin. It amused me that she didn't care what she would have to do.

She turned my knuckles over and gave me a fist-bump. "Does the job start now? We could skip the sword training."

"You might need the training for the job. We better do an hour."

After a few dramatic sighs, she went to her room and returned with the practice swords we usually used, as well as the magical short sword that Willard had allowed her to have. It was technically on loan, pending the discovery of the owner it had been stolen from, but that person likely lived on another world and wouldn't come looking for it.

"Have you been doing your katas?" I'd taught her a few series of exercises that she could do on her own to practice footwork and defense.

She shrugged. "Some."

"Is that code for none?"

"I've just been busy."

I decided not to nag further. That summer, after being scared by several encounters with dragons, she'd been eager to get a magical weapon and learn to defend herself, but months had passed without any further threats, and her fear had likely dwindled. Since I would prefer that she *wasn't* in danger on a regular basis, I couldn't regret that. It was always possible she would return more faithfully to practice the following summer when school was out again.

I would regret not getting to spend time with her every week, but maybe I just needed to come up with more paying gigs for her. Was it wrong to bribe your teenage daughter to spend time with you? Or was it typical? I needed more mother acquaintances to consult on these matters.

Fifteen minutes into our practice session, our jeans cuffs damp from the wet grass, Zav spoke into my mind.

I have learned what I wished to learn. He is a meager resource. I will leave to turn in the criminal now and return soon to protect you further.

Thank you.

Metal rang as Amber took the offensive, and I parried a combination of high-low-high blows. Chopper's hilt rubbed against the cut in my hand, making me wish Walker would call soon with news on it, but I kept going. I didn't want to give up a chance to work with Amber.

I am told that the rings in the human catalogs aren't magical.

I almost missed a parry. *Why are you looking for magical rings?*

For the proposal. I have been researching this human custom. There must be an engagement ring and then later matching wedding rings, which we will both wear. I refuse to wear an inferior ring, nor will my mate wear an inferior ring. They should not be simply decorative. They should have some value. I am considering going on a quest.

A quest? Did Thad suggest that? Zav, we're not ready to get married. You don't need to get a ring yet. We're still figuring each other out.

We will explore each other's nuances further after we are mated in the human way. You will wear the ring I acquire for you, and horny males will not ask you to go for walks with them while fantasizing about having copious amounts of sex with you.

"I got you," Amber blurted, as I scrambled to focus on defending while being overwhelmed by Zav's words.

"Yes." I acknowledged that she'd brushed my shoulder. "Good one."

Zav, as long as I'm with you, it doesn't matter what other men are fantasizing about. I'm not going to go off with them to have sex or anything else. You're my dragon, remember?

Yes, I know this, and I know you will not betray my trust, but I do not wish to have them drooling over you like drogdar *on the tundra anticipating a kill. Your employer said that a ring will stop this. You will have a ring, my mate. As soon as I locate a worthy one. The trinkets in this catalog are insufficient.*

The trinkets in that catalog probably ranged from ten- to a hundred-thousand dollars. If they weren't sufficient for a woman, I couldn't imagine what would be.

Zav...

I must deliver the orc before he runs out of air. I will return soon. Be vigilant, and do not place yourself in danger without me.

He disappeared from my senses. A couple of minutes later, Thad came out, his furrowed brow attesting to puzzlement or concern or both.

"Let's take a break." I held up a hand, though I was reluctant to stop when Amber, tongue stuck between her teeth, was more focused than usual. Almost hitting me must have excited her.

"Sure. If you're tired." She smirked at me.

"Val?" The odd note in Thad's voice made Amber turn toward him.

"Are you all right, Dad?"

"Just a little stunned. Flummoxed. Concerned."

Hah, I'd known concern had been in the mix.

"Are you going to marry that... *man*, Val?" Thad stared at me.

"He's a dragon, Dad."

"Are you going to marry that *dragon*?" Thad corrected, still staring at me.

"I don't know. Maybe someday. It's complicated. He's not from around here."

"No kidding," Amber said. "He's weird. But super powerful. All the dragons are, but he's even more..." She groped in the air while she looked for the word. "*More*," she settled on. "That makes him scary."

The look Amber directed at me also hinted of concern. I was touched that she cared, but it bothered me that Zav scared her. As far as I knew, he'd never done anything to her; he rarely spoke to or interacted with her at all. He just had that *aura*. The aura I found appealing and sexy but that alarmed others. Admittedly, the auras of all other dragons alarmed me too.

"He asked me to show him engagement rings and the procedures for proposing." Thad shook his head slowly, still looking like someone who'd been hit by a boxer's glove. Or maybe a train.

"Willard put some notions in his head."

"Your *boss* suggested he marry you?" Thad had met her once and probably couldn't imagine stern, iron-jawed Willard ever discussing romance or marriage with anyone.

I decided not to share that Willard had been joking about dragon weddings almost as long as I'd known Zav. "She pointed out that if I was wearing a ring, other people might not hit on me as often."

"You're not going to do it, are you?" Thad asked. "You can't marry someone that demanding and haughty and *strange*."

Something about Thad objecting to the idea made me want to defend it, even if I'd been dismissing it earlier. "He's already claimed me as his mate. We're more or less married as far as the rest of the Cosmic Realms are concerned. It's only humans that can't sense the magical mark he's left on me."

"Cosmic what? Wait, what do you mean he's *marked* you?" Thad looked me up and down, as if seeking a cattleman's brand seared into my flesh. "And *claimed* you. This doesn't sound like a healthy relationship."

"It's fine, Thad. I can take care of myself."

He shook his head. "I know you can, but… I don't like him."

"That's because he doesn't like you either. He only charms people he likes."

"*Are* there people like that?" Amber asked.

"Not a lot that I've noticed. He's charmed me though. He renovated my house, and we go into battle against enemies together." I realized others might not find those things charming, but they meant a lot to *me*. "And he regularly tells me that I please him."

"Gross," Amber said.

"Not in bed." Though I liked to think I did please him there. "I vex his enemies."

"You are *so* weird, Val."

"She tells me that regularly," I told Thad, who was pushing his hand through his short hair and still looked distressed.

"I know. I think she may be right."

"Funny."

Thad walked slowly back toward the house, bumping his shoulder against one of the covered patio posts and barely noticing.

"Are we doing this job today?" Amber asked when he was gone.

"Yes." I was relieved to change the subject. "Bring your new sword. It could be dangerous." There. I'd told her. I didn't want to bring her along without letting her know there was a possibility that things could go wrong. "We're going to summon a potentially bad guy. I'll protect you, but there could be a fight."

"Okay," she said, unfazed, "but we need to go soon if it's going to take hours."

I debated if I wanted to explain more—she didn't seem to care. It might be easier to explain once we were standing in front of the fairy ring. Besides, I had an inkling she might object to being used for her youth and innocence.

"We need to wait for Zav to return. My Jeep is back at the house, so he's our ride."

"Our *ride*?" she mouthed, horror in her eyes. "Can't we get an Uber? I don't want to ride a dragon. Besides, I have a study group I have to be back for tonight."

"We could do it tomorrow." I not only needed Zav to give us a ride; I wanted him nearby when we tried to pull this off. Amber would be much safer if he was there for backup, especially given that other sword-coveting beings might show up.

"I'll be working on a presentation with my lab partner all day. I'm super busy this year, Val."

"Well… maybe he'll be back by the time we get there." I pulled out my phone, deciding we could get a ride and do some preliminary scouting. The circles on Willard's map outlined entire city blocks. Given that lack of precision, it would probably take a while to find the fairy ring. We would wait until Zav returned to use the statue.

"Get a ride where? You didn't say where we're going."

"Magnuson Park." It had been the only public space on Willard's map of known and semi-permanent fairy rings. The others looked to be in people's yards. I didn't think we should summon a fae I might end up battling in front of someone's doorstep.

"Magnuson Park?" Amber curled a lip. "I thought you'd want me to take you shopping again. Your wardrobe needs a major overhaul."

"I know, but *you're* the one who's going to need to look good for this." That probably wasn't true. The fae shouldn't be able to see her until he actually arrived. I assumed.

"In that case, I need to shower and change and put on makeup. That's an extra fee. I'm raising my rate to two-fifty."

"I'm trying to decide if you're a shrewd businesswoman or a greedy teenager." Maybe I would ask Nin her opinion.

"I'm *totally* shrewd."

CHAPTER 13

THE DRIVER LET US OUT in one of Magnuson Park's many lots, and I gazed out at the grassy fields. I'd forgotten how big this place was. If this fairy ring was like the one by the bog, I wouldn't sense anything magical about it. It would just be a circle of mushrooms in the grass. In the grass somewhere among hundreds of acres of trees, fields, paths, and beaches.

I'd had the driver stop at my house so I could pick up the artifact, and I now carried it in a backpack slung over my shoulder. I had my weapons, of course, and touched Chopper as I surveyed the house-filled ridge to the west of the park and also the cars in the lot. It had been a couple of hours since Zav had left, and I hadn't had that feeling of being watched *yet*, but by now, I expected it.

"Are we doing something illegal?" Amber asked after the car pulled away, putting on the sword belt that she'd likely only worn once before.

Her short sword lacked the power of Chopper, but it emanated a serene rippling magic that reminded me of burbling streams. It was supposedly an elven blade.

"Nothing illegal. Why do you ask?" I waved toward the closest path but faltered as she came closer and I had a closer look at the sword belt. Willard had given it to me to give to her along with the blade. It was—or *had been*—simple brown leather without adornment. Now, it was dotted with symbols in forest-green and sea-blue sequins. "Did you bedazzle your weapons belt?"

"Yeah, it was super boring."

"Is that the Speedo logo? And… Lululemon?" My brain hurt at the idea of decorating a beautiful and powerful elven weapon with corporate crap. At least it was only the scabbard and belt.

"I put some brands I like on there. So?" Amber shrugged. "I'm asking because you haven't really said what we *are* doing, besides summoning a bad guy. I figured it was something you didn't want Dad to know about."

"That part is true. There's a small possibility that it will be dangerous, and I was afraid he wouldn't approve of me taking you into a dangerous situation."

"He wouldn't, but he's too busy being stricken by your dragon wanting to propose to have noticed."

"I doubt that's true."

"That he's stricken or that he wouldn't have noticed?"

"The latter. He did look stricken."

"Are you really going to *marry* him?" Amber eyed me as we headed up the trail into the park. Her expression had changed from concern to one that portrayed disbelief and pity that I had to go through life being so strange.

"I don't know. Maybe someday. It's complicated."

We walked in silence for a while, passing soccer players going at it on the wet fields. I wondered if I should be wandering across those fields, or if a fairy ring would more likely be in a remote untended snarl of thickets. If it were on a lawn, the mushrooms would be destroyed whenever the groundskeepers mowed, wouldn't they? Maybe the magic made them impervious to lawnmower blades.

We crested a hill, and Lake Washington should have been visible ahead of us, but fog obscured the water. It was creeping into the lowlands, hiding the park's beaches from view, and would make it hard to spot mushrooms from far off. Wonderful.

"I'm afraid Dad will get married again," Amber said, the naked honesty surprising me.

"To Nin?" I hadn't gotten the impression they were that serious yet.

"To anyone."

"That's not okay?"

She gave me a scathing look.

I hoped she wouldn't rag on Nin again. It was hard for me to take her side or even be a neutral third party when a friend was involved.

"He's so busy all the time with his work and business that I hardly see him that much anyway." Amber studied the path ahead. "I mean, I'm busy too, but I miss it when we hung out more. When he was with *the girlfriend*, she was always over for Sunday-night dinners. *Our* Sunday-night dinners. I have swim team every evening during the week, so we hardly ever eat together, and meets on the weekends, but we always had Sunday nights. It was super lame when *she* was there. And then she was gone, and I was so stoked, but now, he's just dating someone else again. I don't want your weird friend at our dinners."

This wasn't quite the rant I'd expected, but maybe it meant that Amber objected more to *anyone* taking Thad's time and not Nin in particular.

"Have you told him that Sunday-night dinners are important to you?" I asked.

She rolled her eyes. "He should know."

Of course. Parents were supposed to be mind readers.

Well, *I* would tell Thad if she wouldn't. And maybe I could suggest that he take a little more time off work. Not that I was a good example of having a healthy work-life balance. As my therapist would be quick to point out. I'd canceled our last appointment because of the job at the coast.

"If you ever need a place to hang out while he's on a date or something, you can come by," I said, though Thad had probably told her my house was off-limits. He and Amber had been there when one of Dimitri's barbecues had been crashed by orc mercenaries, and a killer magical creature had flown out of a portal on the roof. "Or if you need help with homework or something."

"Oh, please. You had to open a calculator app to multiply seventy-five by four."

"That *wasn't* why I took out my phone. But there's a vampire alchemist living in the basement. I'm sure he's good at math if you need more than my modest skills can provide."

"I can just imagine explaining a vampire tutor to my teachers."

A faint hint of familiar magic teased my senses, and I halted and turned toward the water. "This way."

I didn't know if it was a fairy ring or something else, but we would check it out. Letting my senses guide me, I strode through the damp grass and crossed another path, noting how close we were to another parking lot. If this ended up being the spot, we could have had a much shorter walk.

There weren't many cars in that lot. Even though it wasn't raining, dusk wasn't that far off, and it was chilly and damp. Here and there, trees shed yellow and orange leaves.

We walked into the fog, and I almost flinched in surprise when a gray triangular shape loomed up ahead of us. Taller than our heads, it looked like a giant shark's fin. I snorted when I realized where in the park we were. The Fin Project. Back in the nineties, someone had taken old submarine fins and embedded them in the ground here. They were supposed to simulate a pod of orca whales swimming through the Sound.

Amber didn't comment on them. She'd probably been to the spot before and recognized it before I had. The fog made everything look different than on a bright sunny day, and there was something eerie about the giant metal fins rising up out of the gray mist. Or maybe it was the faint magic that felt alien and unfriendly and grew stronger as we meandered between them. It had also grown quiet, save for the lapping of water against the nearby shoreline. I could no longer hear the shouts of the distant soccer players. Maybe they had called it a day and gone home.

My senses led me to a couple of fins near a tree. There among the roots bulging up from the grass was a ring of gray mushrooms more than ten feet in diameter. They were indeed undamaged by lawnmower blades despite rising up prominently.

The magic emanating from the spot surprised me, since I hadn't felt any from the mushrooms at the bog. Was this perhaps an older and more frequently used doorway into the fae realm?

"This is the spot." I waved, not sure if Amber's quarter-elven senses would allow her to sense the magic.

"The spot for *what*? Mushroom picking?"

"No, it's a fairy ring. A *real* fairy ring. Technically a fae ring. I don't think fairies exist, at least not in the Tinkerbell sense of the word. The rings are magical doorways to the fae realm. We're going to try to get one to open the door and come out." I slung off the backpack. "That's what I need your help with."

Hopefully, Zav would return soon. I wanted to finish this before it got dark. The fog made it seem later than it was, and it would only grow denser as night approached.

As I pulled the artifact out of the backpack, the sensation of being watched returned. Damn it.

I glowered at the fairy ring, though I didn't think my watcher was that close. My senses were useless in detecting him, but some ancient human—or elven—instinct told me he was atop a nearby hill, looking down upon us.

The urge to tap my cloaking charm came over me, but there was no point. In an earlier experiment with Dimitri, I'd learned that the sword's new beacon overrode the charm's magic. He'd had no trouble detecting me even with it activated.

It didn't matter. I couldn't have hidden and left Amber out in the open as a target.

Instead, I touched Sindari's charm and summoned him. If my stalker sent another pack of fire wolves, I didn't want to fight them by myself.

As he formed, I considered Amber, all my doubts returning that I'd done the wrong thing by bringing her here. She was poking around on her phone, with no inkling that we might be in danger.

Are we on a training mission? Sindari asked after he formed. *Your offspring is here and armed.*

Something like that. My stalker may be back, and we're about to summon a horny fae guy. We may need your help.

To defeat him, I trust. Not cure him of horniness.

No, but you standing on his chest and dripping saliva from your fangs might have a quelling effect on that.

My fangs are fear-inspiring.

I've noticed. Do you sense anyone out here?

Yes. Your mate approaches.

A second later, Zav's presence came on my radar. He was flying in this direction from the west.

Perfect timing, my handsome dragon, I spoke telepathically to him, not having to feign my delight—and relief—at his return.

Of course, Zav replied. *It did not take me long to drop off the criminal and inquire about possible rings I could quest for among dragons who pay attention to tales of magical treasures.*

Uh, good. I think. Will you park yourself up on that ridge somewhere? If you're right beside us when the fae guy comes out, he may turn around and flee before we can grab him.

I can grab him with my magic. My mate, you do not sound properly enthused about the ring I will find you. I will not quest for anything except a sublime ring that will be useful in our battles against enemies.

It's the marriage thing I'm not sure I'm ready for yet. Can we talk about it later? I've only got Amber for a couple more hours, so we need to do this.

We are already mated. Is not an Earth marriage only a matter of making it official for the humans of your world?

I don't know. It's a little more real to me. It implies forever. Or as long as we live.

"This article on fairy rings doesn't say anything about *fae*," Amber said, reading from her phone. "It says they're naturally occurring and detectable by fungal spore pods in rings or arcs with fungus mycelium present in the ground underneath. Popular in folklore, they're linked with witches and the devil."

"I hope you don't think you can get information on magical races and manifestations of magic in our world by searching on Wikipedia."

"*Everything* is on Wikipedia."

"Uh huh. You better call Willard's intelligence department if you want correct information. I've read the entry on dragons, and other than the part about them flying, having wings, and breathing fire… a lot was left out."

Amber spotted Sindari and almost dropped her phone. "Where'd he come from?"

"The realm of Del'noth."

"Is that near Oz?"

I doubted Sindari knew the reference, but his green eyes narrowed, as if he suspected being the butt of a joke.

"Behind it and a little to the left. Don't worry about Sindari. He'll help if there's a battle. And here comes Zav." I pointed toward the sky and Zav's dark, powerful form soaring toward us, wings outstretched as he glided the last half mile. "We have lots of backup now."

Maybe too *much* backup. I worried that the fae guy wouldn't show up if he sensed a trap.

Zav landed in the middle of the fairy ring, shifting into his human form in front of us. He was wearing a new pair of shoes. They were a ridiculously vibrant yellow with holes in them.

"Are those *Crocs*?" Amber asked, staring down at them.

They contrasted greatly with his silver-trimmed black robe, so they were hard to miss.

"Ugh, they *are*," she said. "My dad has a pair just like that. They were a gag gift from his co-workers before he quit his last job to start his own company."

I rubbed my hand across my face. "Where did you get those, Zav?"

"Your former mate gave them to me. He said they were lucky and that I would be more likely to get the answer I want when I propose to you if I wear lucky shoes."

"You weren't insulting him at the time, were you?" It was hard for me to imagine mild-mannered and easy-going Thad sabotaging someone's proposal plans, but Zav was a special case.

"I spoke to him as is appropriate for a dragon speaking to a menial being from a lesser species."

"So, insults."

Zav gazed blandly at me.

I pointed toward the hill where I'd sensed the watcher only to realize I no longer felt like I was being watched. Either I was going nuts, or Zav was an excellent deterrent to stalkers. Maybe the shoes had scared the guy away.

"Sindari, can you trot around the perimeter of the area and see if you catch the scent of any elves or suspicious people lingering around here? Especially up on that hill? And Zav, I think your presence may make fae unlikely to appear."

"You don't think they'll come just to see him in fluorescent Crocs?" Amber whispered.

Zav looked down at his feet.

"I think they're going to be more interested in you." I patted her on the shoulder. "Zav, will you either fly back up to the ridge or camouflage yourself? If we need you, I'll yell."

"You should let me remain and do the speaking," he said. "Fae are not known for being truthful, but they would not dare lie to a dragon."

"Didn't you say fae hide from dragons and do their best to avoid them?"

"Yes."

I had no idea if the fae could tell what was waiting for them outside of their realm before they walked through their doorway, but in case they could... "The ridge, please." I pointed.

Zav gazed at me, his jaw set mulishly for a few seconds, but then he turned and walked off across the damp grass. The Crocs squeaked until the fog enveloped him, and he disappeared from my senses.

"He can turn invisible?" Amber asked.

"Something like that." I held out the mushroom statue to her, then drew Chopper. "I need you to rub the top of that while I hide behind that tree. I promise I'll be right there."

"Uh." She stared at the statue without taking it. "I have questions."

I'd expected her to have them earlier, but I was glad she was asking now. I did a quick summary of my week so far and what I hoped to accomplish—with her help.

"You're using me as bait?" Amber asked.

"Yes."

"And you're just assuming I'm a virgin?"

"I've never seen a post about boys cross your social-media pages. I keep an eye on you."

Amber propped a fist on her hip. "Maybe I like *girls*."

"The virgin thing should still be in place then. Rub the mushroom, please." I offered it to her.

"Can I lop the balls off any guy who comes out and drools on me?"

"Yes, but not fatally. I need to question him."

"Non-fatal ball-lopping. Got it." She took the artifact and eyed it from all sides. "This looks like it came out of Smurf Village."

"That was my assessment too. I'll be behind the tree."

"Is there any point in hiding when your sword is radiating like Fukushima?"

"We'll see."

The tree wasn't far away. I could spring into the middle of the fairy ring in a second.

Amber sighed, set down the statue, drew her sword, and tapped the top of its cap. Like me, she faced the ring of mushrooms with her blade raised, her crouch promising she was ready for a fight.

A silly feeling of pride came over me. My daughter wasn't going to be some helpless maiden waiting to be victimized.

When nothing happened, Amber rubbed the top of the artifact, leaving her hand on it for longer. Its magic grew stronger, the little statue going from dormant to active. A faint green cloud emanated from it, and Amber jumped back. The cloud formed into a tendril that drifted toward the center of the fairy ring, and the magic inherent in the living mushrooms also increased. It had a discordant and unappealing nature, and gooseflesh rose on my arms.

A surge of power flowed from the statue along the tendril to the center of the ring, and it poofed into a large cloud that filled the air.

"Doorbell rung," I murmured, and crouched, ready to charge as soon as someone came out.

CHAPTER 14

MINUTES PASSED, AND THE MAGIC of the fairy ring and the artifact returned to their former dormant levels. I bit my lip, waiting for our intruder. Amber, with her sword still in hand, shifted from foot to foot.

"How long are we going to stand here before accepting this didn't work?" she asked.

"Longer than five minutes."

"You should have brought snacks."

"Sorry."

I wished I knew a previously fae-visited virgin that I could have consulted. It hadn't occurred to me that a summoner might have to wait for hours beside the ring for her would-be lover to arrive.

I do not sense any elves, Sindari said. *I did cross paths with Lord Zavryd. He's keeping his aura to a minimum.*

How did you find him then? The shoes?

My path happened to go close enough to him for me to detect him. Footwear does not emanate magic.

Good to know.

Amber sighed loudly and dramatically, looking pointedly in my direction. "I should have asked for more money."

"Because you're working so arduously?"

"It's hard work being tense and ready to fight."

I lowered my sword, worried that the fae had detected me and that was the reason he wasn't answering the door. Should I back farther away and ask Amber to try again? The idea of leaving her to fend for herself repelled me. I stayed where I was. And waited. It was growing darker.

Amber took out her phone and started texting friends or maybe playing a game. I practiced Freysha's root magic, envisioning making massive tendrils that could spring up from the earth and entangle my foes. Something the size of a worm rose up two inches from the ground and wiggled in the air. My powers were immense and would drive fear into my enemies' hearts.

I kept practicing. I'd managed to give the root more girth and a few more inches of height when the magic of the ring increased.

"Get ready." I released my own magic and crouched again as a green glow formed in the ring.

"You think?" Amber was already crouched with her sword raised.

To capture a fae, Sindari told me from wherever he was hiding himself, *you may need to get him to leave the ring. Otherwise, I believe he will easily jump back through the doorway at the first sign of trouble.*

Thanks.

The green glow shimmered, and something akin to a tunnel entrance appeared. Not one but two figures stood outlined inside of it.

I tensed. It hadn't occurred to me that more than one fae might come.

Two achingly handsome males stepped out of the doorway but not outside of the ring, so I held my position. They had green hair swept back into braids, chiseled jaws, perfectly straight noses, and prominent cheekbones. Their dark brown eyes scanned the area, and for a moment, they looked right at me—dismissively—before their gazes settled back onto Amber.

They checked her out brazenly, and I clenched Chopper tighter, fighting the impulse to leap into the ring and brain them both. Worry sparked in her eyes, but she stood her ground, her sword up as she faced them.

They nodded what might have been appreciation and murmured to each other in their tongue. I touched my translation charm. Were they discussing if they believed this was an ambush? They'd seen me with my sword. They had to think that.

"She is beautiful," one said. "I will take her first."

"You always get to go first."

"I am the eldest. It is my right. You may take the other."

They both wrinkled their noses in my direction. I clenched my jaw and willed them to step out of the ring so I could grab one.

"I'd rather take her sword. Its call is almost as erotic as a virgin. If we took it back to the queen, she would reward us."

"Strange. It bears the mark of our kind. Maybe the queen has already laid a claim on it."

I almost spoke out to ask them what they knew. I doubted they realized I could understand them and was loath to give up that advantage, but this was the information I'd come for. It didn't sound like they knew who had marked my sword, but maybe they had ways to find out. I just had to capture one...

"Pleasure first, brother," the oldest said, his gaze shifting back toward Amber. "Other rewards later."

"Precautions first." The other flicked his finger.

At first, I didn't sense anything, but the magic of the mushroom artifact grew less noticeable, and then it extinguished completely. Had he broken it for some reason?

Careful, Val, Sindari warned. *They're muting magic.*

What does that mean? All magic?

My sword's familiar powerful aura diminished, startling me. Then Sindari's presence disappeared, his charm growing cold where it dangled under my shirt. All of my charms grew cold, and the next time the brothers spoke, I couldn't understand them.

They sprang out of the fairy ring, one rushing for Amber and one rushing for me.

Worried about the loss of my magic, I was almost caught off guard. But by the time he reached me, I had Chopper up, ready to defend.

"Run back," I barked to Amber, though neither of the fae had weapons.

The one charging me lifted his hands. Bright green tendrils of power stretched toward me like vines.

I slashed Chopper at one and was relieved when my blade cut through, slicing off the end before it touched my face. But there were four more, growing and flexing toward me, and I had to duck and dodge sideways to avoid them. They grasped in the air like fingers, trying to entangle me. The magic was not unlike what Freysha had been teaching me with the roots but stronger and more dangerous.

Something gripped my boots, keeping me from moving farther away. Not expecting it, I almost pitched over, but I recovered as the fae male stretched his hand toward me, more tendrils shooting from his fingers.

Sword moving in a blur, I sliced through them even as the ones wrapping around my boots curled up around my ankles, further entwining me.

I could use your help, Zav, I reluctantly admitted.

I couldn't feel Sindari at all. Somehow he'd been banished. What if Zav had been too?

Amber screamed. Terrified for her, I lunged for the fae male, ignoring the tendrils in favor of slashing at him.

My attack startled him, and he jerked back too late to avoid a gash to his cheek. One of the magical vines around my ankle extended up to wrap around my waist, trapping me further. The fae scooted out of my range, a hand to his cheek, and I couldn't chase after him.

I bent and slashed at the entangling vines with Chopper. Even though the sword's power had been lessened by the fae spell, it wasn't gone entirely, and it cut through the magical tendrils. But they grew back as quickly as I could hack them away.

The fae male lowered his hand from his cheek, dark eyes blazing with anger, and his aura grew more intense—more powerful—to my senses. If I couldn't get away from the damn roots, I was dead. And so was Amber.

Even as I cut through the tendrils again, I accepted that they were regrowing too quickly. I had to armor myself somehow, keep them from wrapping around me. Could the elven magic I'd learned to shield myself from mental attacks work against physical ones?

The fae strode toward me, lifting a hand, an invisible power gathering in his palm—some energy ball he intended to throw at me.

As I'd done in other battles, I envisioned Freysha's fern fronds gathering around me, placing themselves between me and the tendrils, between me and the fae. I willed the magic in my blood to flow into the barrier and make it a reality.

A tendril tickled my calf, as if to taunt me and proclaim my magic ineffective.

To the side, Amber gasped in pain. Fury exploded within me, and I focused even harder to turn the fronds into a real shield. A shield that could beat the crap out of this magic.

Abruptly, everything released me. More than that, the tendrils were hurled back, smoking as they landed on the earth.

The ball of energy in the male's hand grew, blazing white. I willed all of the fronds to combine to form a thick wall in front of me. He released

SECRETS OF THE SWORD I

the ball of pure energy, and it blasted toward my face... only to halt a foot away, slamming into my magical barrier. It dissipated, the energy dispersing and disappearing, and the male's mouth opened in shock.

I sprang at him, slamming the flat of my blade into the side of his head before he recovered.

He stumbled into the tree, cracking the other side of his head on the trunk, and he collapsed on the ground. Not waiting to see if he was conscious, I spun and ran to help Amber.

But I only made it three steps before stopping. Zav stood at her side, and the other fae male floated in the air in front of them, yellow ropes of power pinning his arms against his sides. His feet twitched, and he cursed, but he could do no more.

"Thanks, Zav." I was relieved to see that Amber appeared unharmed, though bits of dead grass stuck to her clothes—had she been rolling around and wrestling with that jerk? Her eyes were wide, but she gripped her sword and looked ready for another fight if need be. "I was worried you'd been banished from our world along with Sindari."

"A dragon banished? By a lesser species? You have seen my vast power and know I would not permit this to happen. Do you wish me to question this prisoner? You appear to have knocked your fae out." He looked at the crumpled male by the tree, then gave me a pleased smile. "My mate is an excellent fighter."

I forced a return smile for him, but I didn't feel pleased with myself. If he hadn't been here, the fae he'd captured might have had time to drag Amber back to his realm. I hadn't expected to have Sindari dismissed before the fight even began.

"Yes. I would appreciate it if you question him. Will you see if he knows anything about the artifact from the bog or how to fix my sword?" I walked around his prisoner to stand beside Amber and put a hand on her shoulder.

I would have preferred to hug her, but she'd never indicated that she would be open to that, not since she'd been a toddler and I'd been a part of her daily life. Regrets for all the years I'd lost with her welled up inside of me, and I was glad Zav took over and that I didn't need my voice for a moment.

"I'm okay, Val." She didn't shrug away my hand. "I didn't expect him to be so fast. He tangled up my feet with something too." She stared at the ground, though nothing but grass and dead leaves were down there now.

"I know. Me too. This wasn't a good idea."

"Are you sure? You got your prisoner." She looked at the male, then looked away.

His head was thrown back, his entire body rigid. Zav hadn't moved, but he had to be doing that mind-scouring of his, digging into the fae's thoughts and probing for answers.

"He helped me," Amber admitted.

"Zav?"

"Yeah. I was on the ground and pinned. I couldn't do *anything*." She curled her lip in disgust and frustration. "Then he showed up, flung that guy away, and leaped over me to ooze his magic over him."

"He does that."

"I guess he's a good dragon."

"I've found him to be so." I smiled, glad that Amber now thought so too.

Our fae captive might disagree. His head fell forward, and his body went limp. If not for the magical bonds, he would have tumbled to the ground.

"I *am* a good dragon, and we will wed in the way of humans soon," Zav said, though he didn't look away from the fae. "After I find a proposal ring. It is difficult to seek such treasures when I must remain here on Earth due to this other threat, but soon I will find time to do so. My mate must have a ring at *least* equal to her other trinkets."

"That's not necessary," I murmured, wishing he'd focus on the current problem and stop planning the wedding I didn't know if I wanted to have.

"There were some cool panther rings in that catalog," Amber said. "Diamond panthers."

I elbowed her. "Don't *encourage* him."

Earlier, she'd sounded horrified at the thought of me marrying Zav.

"My mate does not need more felines adorning her. A *dragon* ring would be far more appropriate. Its eyes could glow, as with the topiaries."

I tried not to rock back in horror at the thought, but it was hard. It hadn't occurred to me that he would find something truly hideous and expect me to wear it, but as I looked at the backs of his yellow shoes, I realized it should have.

"Jewelry shouldn't *glow*," Amber said sternly. "That's tacky. And whatever is on it, panthers or dragons or unicorns, shouldn't be too large. Think elegant and understated."

Even though Zav wouldn't listen, I could have hugged her for trying.

He gazed over his shoulder at her. "Understated?"

"Yeah. Big gaudy rings are for people who crave attention. That's not Val. Elves are elegant, right?"

"Elves are elegant," Zav agreed, his expression thoughtful as he turned back to his task.

"Thanks," I whispered, hoping her advice helped.

Amber only shrugged. She was about as likely as a dragon to offer a you're-welcome.

"He has no knowledge of the artifact or who placed it in the bog," Zav said after a few more minutes, "but he believes the queen would know how to remove the taint from your sword."

"Good. How do I get on her calendar?"

Zav tilted his head in puzzlement. Maybe dragons didn't have calendars.

"How do we talk to her?" I clarified.

Before he could answer, the fairy ring flared with green light and its power surged. Even Zav appeared startled, for he scooted back, shielding Amber and me with his body.

Another door formed, a figure appearing in it, and two white beams shot out. As I scrambled to create another magical barrier, Zav instantly raised one of his own, protecting the three of us.

But we were not the targets. One beam struck the male on the ground and the other hit the bound one. Magic surged from the doorway, explosive light and power making me turn away. A shriek sounded, then was cut off.

The power from the fairy ring disappeared, leaving the area in darkness. Something splattered against my clothes and struck my cheek. I wiped it away from my face as I turned back, only to find the two males had been blown to pieces.

I wasn't usually squeamish, but my stomach churned at the bits of flesh and bone and organ scattered around the clearing. It was as if they'd been struck by grenades.

Amber stumbled away from me and threw up.

"Hm," Zav said.

"*Hm?* What happened?" I flung a hand toward the fairy ring. "Was that their *queen*?"

Could she have known that they'd been captured? Someone must have known. Someone who didn't want me making an appointment with her…

"Another fae acting on her behalf, perhaps," Zav said. "Or simply someone enacting a punishment on them for being caught."

"Can we go after whoever that was?"

"Even a dragon cannot force open the doorway in a fairy ring. Their magic is elusive, and they've spent millennia learning to hide their realm and its entrances from my kind. They did not wish dragons to rule over them."

"Odd."

"Indeed. Dragons are fair and superior rulers."

I shot him the sarcastic look that comment deserved, then went to Amber's side. "Sorry about that. This evening isn't going as expected."

She heaved again, fingers twined in the grass. I decided this wasn't the time to offer to take her for the snack she'd requested. Right now, she probably wanted nothing more than to go home and rest. And shower. I grimaced and wiped some gore off the back of her shirt.

"Did you get what you need?" she rasped, sinking back on her knees.

"I got a little bit of information, but not really."

Crunches came from the other side of the ring, Zav stepping on the ceramic shards that were all that remained of the artifact. I hadn't noticed it being struck, but it was as demolished as the two males. Unless Willard had a few more of those things stashed in her evidence room, I had no way to entice a fae to open a doorway to Earth again. Damn it. How was I supposed to get to their queen?

"Are you still going to pay me?" Amber dragged her sleeve over her mouth. "Because this was *way* worse than washing Dad's car."

"Worse than roasting in the hot sun like an orchard picker for hours? Are you sure?"

"*Positive*. Is your job always like this?"

"More or less." I didn't think I'd told her I was an assassin, just that I worked for the government and took care of bad guys. I rarely blew them up, but it was still grisly work.

"Maybe you should retire."

"I'm kind of young for that. And if I didn't take care of the bad guys, who would?"

"*He's* pretty good at it." Amber pointed at Zav, who'd wandered over to one of the larger pieces of dead fae. Most of the torso of the one he'd had bound. It had been thrown twenty feet in the explosion.

"This isn't his world," I said. "For the most part, dragons don't care about what happens on Earth, because this isn't one of the planets they rule. He's just here collecting some criminals that escaped from the Dragon Justice Court."

"Like those creeps?" Amber nodded toward the fairy ring.

"Actually, he only helped with them because of me. I don't remember any fae mentioned on his list of criminals."

"Oh. I guess you should reward him."

I would reward Zav well, once we both returned to the house and scrubbed ourselves clean, but I doubted Amber wanted to hear about my sex life.

"He's already got fluorescent yellow shoes," I pointed out. "Aren't those reward enough?"

"Try cash, Val. And don't forget mine."

Not mentioning that dragons preferred to be paid in meat, I dug into my pocket for the wad I used to bribe snitches. I counted out the twenties I'd promised her, plus a few more. Combat bonus.

"I didn't mean *real* cash. Don't you have Venmo?"

"I don't even know what that is."

"Cash App?"

"Nope." I pressed the bills into her hand.

"You're a fossil."

"Yup." I rose to my feet, and she let me help her up.

Zav walked toward us, something in his hand. It looked like a green skeleton key.

"This was in his pocket," he said. "There is a faint magical signature, but I believe it was damaged."

"Any chance that's a key to the door?" I waved to the fairy ring.

The mushrooms hadn't been damaged by the explosion—not so much as a cap knocked off—and the ring still emanated that baseline magic, implying it was still active. The idea of the fae needing keys to their own doors seemed silly. From what I'd experienced, they had plenty of magic.

"It does match the magic of the ring," Zav mused. "It's possible the males brought the key for the virgin."

"Could we *not* call me that, please?" Amber asked.

"Had she pleased them," Zav said, ignoring her, "they may have wished to allow her access to their realm for further trysts."

"*Pleased* them?" Amber looked at me. "Gross."

"Yes," I said. "I recommend avoiding trysts with magical guys with green hair. They're always trouble."

"I don't want to know why you know that."

Zav stepped into the fairy ring and held up the key.

Though I didn't want to deal with more fae tonight, I held my breath, hoping this was the answer. If I had a key, I could figure out how to call Sindari back, grab some reinforcements, and storm their realm to demand the queen fix my sword.

But nothing happened. Zav lowered the key and stepped back out of the ring.

"Damaged." He handed it to me. "But perhaps not irrevocably. If one of your enchanter acquaintances has knowledge of fae magic, they may be able to fix it."

I couldn't imagine Dimitri, Nin, or even Inga having learned fae magic, but maybe Nin's gnomish grandfather could help. He'd mentioned being a world-traveler—*worlds*-traveler—before being captured and imprisoned for twenty years.

"I'll find someone to fix it." I jammed the key into my pocket. "And then I'm going to go kick the queen's ass."

"Do you not merely wish her to remove the taint from your sword?" Zav asked.

"I want that, and then I want to kick her ass for tainting it in the first place."

"A more diplomatic approach might serve you," said Zav, the person who assumed lesser species were always honored to serve dragons and who was never diplomatic. That worried me a little. Were the fae truly that powerful that even dragons didn't try to boss them around? Tweedledee and Tweedledum had seemed more like young idiots than great fae sorcerers, but even they had given me trouble.

"She is the leader of all of their kind and very powerful," Zav added. "Ass-kicking could lead to repercussions for your people."

I wanted to mulishly say that I didn't care, but all I truly needed was my sword fixed. And, ideally, to know why they had planted that artifact to curse it in the first place. These two fae hadn't seemed to recognize me or the sword, so it wasn't as if all of their people were out to get me. Maybe just one was. That was who I needed to find. It wouldn't be enough to get my sword fixed if someone was still gunning for me.

I patted the key in my pocket. One step at a time.

CHAPTER 15

"HOW ARE YOUR RELATIONSHIPS PROGRESSING?"

"Are they supposed to progress? Like go on a journey up a mountain or something?" I sat in the chair in Mary Watanabe's office—my back to the wall as I kept the door, the window, and her desk in my line of sight. Coming here when I was actively in danger wasn't a good idea, but if I allowed that to affect when I came for my therapy appointments, I'd never make it in. Besides, this whole proposal-ring thing with Zav had me flustered, and I wouldn't mind hearing her opinion. My main hope at the moment was that it would take Zav three years to find an appropriate ring and that I would be ready for marriage by then.

"You tell me." Mary gave me that patient smile of hers, her fingers poised to take notes on her laptop if need be.

"Can't they exist and be fine without *progress*? Like if you start dating a guy, can't it just be because you enjoy spending time with him? Do you have to think of marriage as the end goal?"

"If both of you agree that marriage isn't the end goal, then there's no need to worry about it."

"What if *he* wants marriage, and you're not sure yet?" I didn't know why I used a hypothetical *he* and *you*, as if she didn't know exactly who I was talking about.

During the drive back to Thad's house, Amber had offered Zav more advice on what constituted quality jewelry. He'd listened attentively. After his timely help with the fae, Amber no longer seemed to be against the idea of me marrying him. She was even *helping* him. Or maybe her assistance was personally motivated: she didn't want to be seen in public with a mother wearing gaudy jewelry.

"Are you still seeing Mr. Zavryd?" Mary knew Zav was a dragon—or she at least knew I *believed* he was—and was fairly up-to-date on the whole being-claimed-and-now-living-together-part-time thing.

"Yeah."

"He wishes to get married? I thought he'd claimed you and that was something similar in his culture."

"It is, but he wants to marry me so I'll have a ring that will tell other guys not to ask me on dates."

Her eyebrows rose. "He's jealous of other men?"

"I'm not sure if it's quite jealousy, but he has notions about it being an insult to his honor if they approach his mate. He wants a way to let them know I'm taken."

"Does he trust you not to flirt with them or engage with them when he's not around? Or do you think he has feelings of insecurity that you might leave him?"

"I don't think that's it." It was difficult for me to imagine Zav being insecure or doubting his appeal and prowess in any circumstance. "I think it's bound up in humans not bowing and scraping to dragons like the other species do. He seems to genuinely find it an affront to *him*."

"It sounds like he has a few issues he may need to work through. Has Mr. Zavryd ever seen a therapist?"

I laughed. "No, but I'll be sure to recommend it to him."

"I'm serious, Val. My colleague across the way is an excellent couples therapist. Or you could bring him in, and we could have a dialogue if you're more comfortable with me."

I dropped my face in my hand, somewhere between amused and horrified. Though if Mary *met* Zav, she might understand him better. I had no idea if Zav would agree to such a meeting. He wasn't that far away, as he continued to be my bodyguard throughout this sword craziness. Technically, I *could* invite him...

"Should I bring him in today?" I glanced at the time on my phone. I still had more than half of my session left.

Mary raised her eyebrows. "Is he waiting in the car?"

"He's on one of the old tanks at Gasworks Park. Alternating between fishing and sunbathing."

The eyebrows climbed higher.

"He's enjoying that it's sunny today. His world is much warmer, and the Pacific Northwest weather hasn't won him over, especially now that it's fall."

"He sounds like a cat." Mary rose and went to the window, which had a view of Lake Union and Gasworks Park.

"You won't be able to see him. Dragons are usually camouflaged to mundane humans unless they wish to be seen. It's why there have only been sporadic sightings reported, even though dragons kept visiting Seattle this summer."

"I see." Her tone was neutral—*carefully* neutral—and I worried I'd surpassed her ability to suspend disbelief when it came to magical beings she couldn't see. She might even now be wondering if Zav truly existed or if I had an imaginary boyfriend.

"I'll see if he'll come. He's visible when he's in human form. If he wants to be." *Zav? My therapist would like to meet you.*

What is a therapist?

She helps me with my personal problems.

You may share your personal problems with me! You are my mate.

I'll keep that in mind. I refrained from pointing out that he was *one* of my personal problems. Or at least a concern that I needed to puzzle out. *Can you find me in this office building?*

I can find you anywhere. What a silly thing to ask.

I sensed him springing off the tank and flying in this direction. "He'll be here shortly."

Mary returned to her seat. "I'll pretend I don't find it puzzling that you invited him without using your phone."

"I told you my half-sister has been teaching me to use my inherent magic, right? That includes developing my ability for telepathy."

"That sounds... handy."

"It is. No need to worry about going over your limit on your cell plan." I smiled.

She looked concerned. I was getting that a lot lately.

A shadow fell across the window, and Mary jumped up, knocking over her chair. The frame squeaked open, and I dropped my face in my hand. I should have known Zav would take the most direct route.

At least he was in his human form by the time he landed on the tile floor. Mary gaped at him, taking in his tidy hair, trimmed beard and mustache, wrinkle-free robe, and… yes, he was still wearing the yellow Crocs. I would have to plot some revenge on Thad. Lucky shoes, my ass.

"I am Lord Zavryd'nokquetal. Val is my mate."

Mary recovered her ability to speak faster than I expected. "So she's told me. I'm Mary Watanabe. Val is my client. Let me get you a seat, Mr. Zavryd."

"*Lord* Zavryd'nokquetal. Or Lord Zavryd if you must."

"His mother is a queen," I explained.

"Wouldn't that make him a prince?" Mary dragged a chair over to set next to mine and extended a hand. "Please have a seat, ah, Lord."

He strode over, rested a hand on my shoulder, then scooted the chair closer and sat next to me, shoulder to shoulder.

"Thanks for coming," I told him. "Did you catch many fish?"

"A few, but the fish are extremely small on this world. Not at all satiating to a dragon. I will require meat later."

"You require meat every night."

"Yes. My new favorite is the meat cube. It is delicious. Will there be a meat cube tonight?"

"Meat *loaf*. And yes, I put four in the smoker this morning."

"Only four?"

"I ran out of bacon. That's the secret ingredient." One of very few ingredients. Zav had nixed the first version, in which I'd followed the recipe and foolishly included bread crumbs.

"An excellent ingredient. Bacon does not exist on my home world. I will be careful not to tell other dragons about it, or this world will be invaded."

"We don't want that. Tell them all we have here is asparagus." Aware of Mary watching us with a bemused expression, I explained. "Dragons are carnivores. Since Zav and I started dating, I've acquired a commercial refrigerator, freezer, smoker, and Costco membership. My most recent acquisition was a meat grinder. We're experimenting with patties and loaves."

"Val feeds me, and it is excellent," Zav stated, glancing at Mary, though he gave me his bedroom eyes, so I had a feeling he was ready to fast forward to dinner and after dinner.

"I wouldn't have guessed she was the type to cook for her man."

"Taking him out to dinner every night is cost prohibitive." I patted his arm and pointed to Mary. "I'm sharing details of my personal life with my therapist, and she's giving me advice. Since you're a big part of my personal life, we thought you should meet."

"It's an honor, Lord Zavryd." Mary managed to say that with a straight face.

"Yes," Zav stated. "Val is my mate. I have claimed her. She is fortunate to have been chosen by such a powerful and influential dragon."

"You think so?"

"I do. Now, I am seeking an appropriate ring for Val so that I may propose to her in the human way, and all people of your world will know that she is my mate and I am her dragon."

"*All* of them?"

"Yes. Among dragons, we mark our mates with magic, so that all others who can sense magic know they are claimed, but humans are sense-dumb and oblivious. I have been informed that a ring makes a couple's relationship clear in your world."

"Are you sure Val wants to get married? Did you ask her?"

"She wants to be mated with me. She has told me. I am a good protector and have status among my people. These are things that a mate desires. I also satisfy her in the nest. We have excellent and vigorous sex."

I was tempted to drop my face in my hand again, but by now, Zav talking about our sex life with near-strangers wasn't a surprise.

"*Did* you tell him that?" Mary asked curiously.

"He claimed me… to protect me. I wasn't initially consulted or enamored by the idea of being claimed, but I understood why he did it. I thought it was all a ruse at first…" I looked at Zav.

He didn't seem to object to me explaining this. He'd flung his arm over the back of his chair and was turned sideways to face me as well as Mary. His ankle was up on his knee, shin hair on display. Remembering that Willard had apparently gotten an eyeful of my underwear-eschewing dragon, I nudged his leg back down to the floor and patted his thigh.

"Well, it became not a ruse, and after a while, I didn't mind being Zav's mate." I realized that Mary would want more honesty than that—and Zav deserved honesty, too, though he probably knew the truth. "I started to fall in love with him."

"Yes," Zav said. "We go into battles together and hunt and fight well together. We are good mates."

"I *am* a little concerned…" I looked at him again. "That the main reason he wants to get married is so I'll wear a ring and other guys won't hit on me when we're together."

"It is intolerable when that happens, yes." Zav nodded. "It is a slight against my honor when a male attempts to *skylitha* my female, especially when she is right beside me. If a dragon did this, I would be within my rights to challenge him to a duel and slay him."

"Is that the only reason you want to marry Val?" Mary asked. "So other men know she's, ah, yours?"

Zav paused to consider this. "We are mated in the dragon way, so we should also be mated in the human way. The entire Cosmic Realms, including this backward planet, should know we are mated. In all senses of the word. As my mate, Val is due my protection. Others should not seek to harm her if they know she is mine. If they do—" his eyes narrowed, "—they will regret it."

This explanation made me realize he truly might want to get married for more reasons than jealousy of random guys hitting on me. If he wanted a wedding so we would be mated in the human way as well as the dragon way… that kind of made sense. I hadn't caught Zav in many lies—except when he'd said he wasn't attracted to me and later admitted he was—so I doubted he was prevaricating now.

"It's good that you're talking this through," Mary said. "Not surprisingly, you seem to have a few cultural differences to overcome—"

"A *few*," I said.

"—but that's typical with interracial marriages."

"What about interspecies marriages?" I asked.

"That's not usually allowed on Earth."

"A dragon marries whomever he wishes." Zav propped his ankle up on his knee again. "Species regardless."

I tugged the hem of his robe down in the hope that the family jewels wouldn't be revealed.

"You keep touching my leg," Zav said. "Do you wish to *tysliir*?"

"Not in my therapist's office, no. But your leg is difficult to resist."

"*I* am difficult to resist." He gave me his bedroom eyes again.

"Yes," I told Mary. "Cultural differences."

"I see that." She typed a few notes into her computer. "I believe our session is up for today. Thank you for coming by, Val. If you wish to speak further about this topic, please let me know. Also, don't forget your meditation and breathing exercises. They will help you remain calm during turbulent times."

At first I thought she meant being proposed to by Zav, but I remembered I'd started out explaining my sword and assassin woes.

"Thanks."

"It was good meeting you, Lord Zavryd," Mary said.

"Yes," he said simply.

"We will return to your domicile now?" Zav asked as we walked out—through the door this time.

"Not yet. I'm taking the fae key to Nin to see if she can figure out how to re-magic it. Do you have anything you need to do? I hate to drag you everywhere to protect me." I remembered that sense of being watched that I'd had again the night before and was glad my stalker hadn't summoned something to attack me while we'd been dealing with the fae. If Zav hadn't been there, would he have?

"I have more criminals to seek out, but until your sword ceases its transmissions, I will not leave you. This is unfortunate since I could perhaps search for someone talented enough to repair it if I could leave this world with it. You would need to come with me. I will not leave you again."

"Let me see if Nin can do something about this key, and if not, I'll go with you to see dragons or whoever you think is best." I tried not to cringe at the idea of visiting other dragons, but I would be curious to see his home world. "I assume everything will be easier—" I waved at my sword, "—if I don't have to deal with the fae."

Getting a key that worked would only open the door. I had no idea how far I would have to travel in their realm and what battles I might have to fight to find my way to the queen.

"Yes. The fae are difficult."

"And dragons aren't?"

"Dragons are also difficult."

"So what you're saying is I have a difficult path ahead."

"It will be a flight, not a path."

I clasped his hand as we stepped into the elevator. "Dragons are *definitely* difficult."

Chapter 16

THE TINY COMPARTMENT IN THE back of Nin's food truck where she crafted magical weapons was too small for pacing, but I bounced from foot to foot as she bent over the large green key with a loupe, studying both sides, both ends, and every nook and crevice in the decorative top.

The key itself was simple, and if it were mundane, I would be certain my lock-picking charm—or a hairpin—could thwart the door it was meant for. But it oozed the same type of fae magic I'd felt coming from the bog artifact, and I'd already tried my charm on a fairy ring, so I knew that wasn't the answer. I crossed my fingers that Nin could revive the doorway-opening magic within the key.

Every time her assistant knocked at the inner door, needing help with the lunch rush, I wanted to grab Nin and pull her back to her examination. Though impatient to make progress on my problems, I nobly refrained. It was bad enough that I was breathing down her neck, but if she wanted me to beat it, all she had to do was ask. Then I would switch from hovering inside to hovering outside.

A pack of thuggish troll teenagers had been loitering by my Jeep when Zav and I had walked out of Mary's building. He'd scared them off with a flaring of his eyes and flexing of his magical power, but they'd promised to return when he wasn't around and relieve me of my sword.

Though I could likely handle some teenage trolls, I was tired of the sword calling to everyone with the least hint of a greedy streak. I also hated that Zav felt he had to stick around and be my bodyguard. He had work to complete for his mother and likely other duties at home. Toddling along after me all day couldn't be that exciting.

He'd gone off to hunt and had offered to take my sword with him for a few hours, like an in-law offering to babysit for the evening. Maybe it hadn't been wise, but I'd given it to him. I would hate to bring hordes of trolls, werewolves, or anything else to Nin's food truck, and I suspected Fezzik and I could handle any mundane trouble that might crop up while Zav was gone. If we couldn't find a solution, I might have to give the sword to him permanently, but after Sindari's charm, Chopper was my most valuable and treasured belonging—and my greatest advantage in battle. We *had* to find a solution.

"I am familiar with fae magic, but I have not seen much of it." Nin set down her loupe. "I believe the magic in this key is dormant and need only be activated, perhaps with magic, perhaps merely with a word."

Too bad Freysha wasn't around to read some fae dictionaries for me. I hoped that whatever was wrong with our father was resolving itself.

"I thought—hoped—your grandfather might know how to activate it," I said.

"That is possible. He is far more experienced than I." Nin grabbed her phone. "Let me take some pictures to send him."

"Your gnomish grandfather who's only been back in this world for a couple of months has a smartphone? How does the credit check for a cell plan work when you're not from Earth?"

"My grandmother does. They are living together again. She will show him."

"Ah. I've been thinking of getting Zav a phone, so I was wondering. I suppose I could get a second phone and number and put him on my plan. But I'm not sure if he would actually use it since he can speak telepathically to me. There's also the possibility that he would use it all the time and send me photos and links to shoes when I'm in the bathtub."

"You say that as if it is not typical of most couples these days."

"I suppose that's true. I haven't been in a serious relationship since smartphones became a thing."

"It is fortunate you have found someone again."

I smiled. "Yeah."

A knock sounded, not at the inside door this time but at the exterior one. Since I was closest to it, I opened it.

Thad stood outside in a sweater and rain jacket, and I worried that Amber had told him everything and that he'd come in person to chew me out. But how had he known I was here?

Wait, he was holding a box wrapped in green paper with a fancy gold ribbon and bow. He must have come for Nin. Maybe Amber hadn't shared the previous evening's details with him.

His gift was small, more the size of a jewelry box than a rice cooker.

He almost dropped it when he saw me. "Oh, uh, Val."

"After all these years, you still remember my name. I'm touched."

"I was expecting Nin."

"She's here." I shifted so he could see inside.

"Hello, Thad." She smiled shyly and waved at him. "It is good to see you. Did you come for *suea rong hai*?"

"I always enjoy your food, but I came to give you something." He looked at me. "Uhm, Val. Would you mind, ah—doesn't your dragon mate need you to visit him?"

"Nope. He's flying up and down the coast with my sword to mystify the land-bound stalkers who have been after me because of it."

Thad gazed blankly at me. Amber probably wasn't the only one in the family who thought I was weird.

"He's lucky he's able to fly, given the holes in the shoes that someone lent him," I said. "Holey shoes can't be aerodynamic."

Thad's face grew a tad sheepish, but he didn't reply. He gave Nin a significant can-you-get-rid-of-her look.

"Allow me to give you a few minutes of privacy." I hopped out and moved to the corner of the truck to stand under the awning.

Since it was raining, I didn't go farther, which left me close enough to hear their conversation. Hey, I couldn't help it that half-elves had superior hearing.

"You brought me a gift?" Nin asked after Thad stepped inside. "That is very thoughtful."

"I hope you like it. I just wanted to say—" Thad lowered his voice—I didn't look back to see if he glanced outside to see if I was listening, "—I had a nice time the other night and hope you did too."

"I did enjoy spending the night with you. A gift is not necessary though."

"I know, but I wanted to get you something."

The rain slowed to a drizzle, and I could have moved farther away, but my feet were reluctant to move. Clearly, my feet were responsible for my eavesdropping tendencies. Faint rustling reached my ears as Nin opened her gift.

I fiddled with the bandage on my hand. Maybe I should leave these two their privacy and call Dr. Walker for an update.

"Earrings?" Nin asked. "From Cartier? Thad, are these not extremely expensive?"

"They're pink sapphires mounted in a gold frame. Remember how your hair was pink when we met? I thought you would like them."

I caught myself holding my breath, so I wouldn't miss her response. There was a long pause before it came. Nobly, I resisted the urge to peek back through the doorway to look at her expression.

"They are very pretty, Thad, but I cannot accept such an expensive gift. I thank you, but please return them."

Thad's pause was just as long and twice as awkward. "Oh, okay. No problem."

"I do appreciate you thinking of me. Will you stay? May I make you some food?"

I nodded, hoping he didn't take Nin's refusal as a personal rejection or slight against his ego.

"I should actually get back to work," Thad said. "I'll call you this weekend."

He hurried out of the food truck, walking rapidly and not looking in my direction.

I sighed and resisted the urge to yell "rice cooker" after him. He wouldn't appreciate my input and probably hated that I'd been in the vicinity for this setback.

Nin leaned through the doorway, frowning after him until he was out of sight, then said, "Please come back inside, Val."

I climbed into the truck. "Everything okay?"

"Yes." Nin hunched over the key again, and several minutes passed, making me think she didn't want to talk about it. Then, without looking up, she said, "Is it wrong to reject a gift from someone if you believe it is too expensive?"

"No."

"I did not mean to hurt his feelings. I..." Nin bit her lip and looked back at me. "I did not ask before we started... I mean, I did not plan to start seeing him. He came to the food truck several times, and he makes me laugh when he talks about his computer business, and he listens when I talk about marketing. He is a nice man, but maybe I should have asked you, since you were… married. Do you mind if I see him?"

"Nope."

"I think his—your—daughter does not like me."

"Yeah, but she's a teenager. She doesn't like anyone except for boy bands and movie stars. I'm hoping she'll grow out of that eventually. As for the gift thing, maybe you could tell him what you like and what price range is acceptable for you."

"I do not want him to believe he needs to get me gifts at all. Perhaps for a birthday present, it would be acceptable, but not because…"

"You slept with him?" I raised my eyebrows.

"Yes. Not because of that."

"Guys like it when you sleep with them. They want to encourage you to do it often. Hence gifts. Let him know what you like. And your price range. I know it's weird, but you don't have any trouble being blunt about money with everyone else."

"I am not dating everyone else."

"Just be yourself."

Nin turned back to the work table and picked up her phone to continue taking pictures. "I will consider your advice."

And *I* would consider sending Thad another email waxing poetic on the enjoyableness of rice cookers. Though it was possible Nin would also consider the RiceMaster that she dreamed of too expensive for a gift. Maybe he could get her some fancy chocolates from Theo's. They always had quirky stuff at the factory in Fremont.

"Do you like chocolate, Nin?"

"If it is not too sweet."

Dark chocolate, check. If Thad asked for advice, I would suggest that. Though I had a feeling he wouldn't bring up this moment with me. Ever.

While Nin called her grandmother, I texted Thad. He would have to get over any mortification he felt. I'd forgotten something I wanted to bring up.

Amber mentioned that she likes your Sunday-night dinners together and has been bummed that you haven't had as many of them lately— or that girlfriends have been present. I just thought I would pass that information along in case it's helpful. The last thing I wanted to do was come across as judging him for being busy. He was the one who'd been there for her these past ten years while I'd been fighting bad guys.

Okay, thanks. That was a terser response than I usually got from Thad, so I didn't add on my suggestion for dark chocolate and rice cookers.

My phone buzzed, startling me. It was Amber.

"Hey," I answered, stepping outside again. "Everything okay?"

"Yeah. I just wanted to see... Maybe we should get back to doing the sword-fighting lessons every weekend. I can make time."

Her encounter with the fae male must have rattled her. That hadn't been my intent, but if it made her want to redouble her practice efforts, I would count it a victory.

"Sure. Sundays?"

"That's fine. Did you talk to Dad?"

At first, I thought she meant about the Sunday-night dinners, but he couldn't have said anything about that to her yet. "I just saw him, but we didn't get a chance to talk. He came to talk to... someone else."

"The new girlfriend." Her voice conveyed her eye roll. "I know. He left with the jewelry he bought."

"Well, he's returning with it. Nin wouldn't accept expensive jewelry." Maybe I shouldn't have said anything. This wasn't any of my business—despite my eavesdropping.

"She didn't?" Amber sounded surprised, even shocked. "They're *beautiful*. I saw them."

"Maybe he'll give them to you."

"Yeah, right. She really didn't take the earrings?"

"Really."

"Wow. Huh."

I didn't know if that would change Amber's opinion of Nin—she shouldn't be able to label her a gold-digger going forward—or if she would think Nin was silly not to accept such a gift.

"Anyway," Amber said, "I called because Grandma called."

"Oh?" I supposed it was silly to be envious that Amber called my mom *Grandma* and me Val. It wasn't as if I'd been there to be a mom for her. And Grandma had kept in touch with her and Thad over the years.

"I missed her call, but she left a message asking if I want to go hiking with her again. Can you talk to her? I don't want to hurt her feelings, because she's old and stuff, but I really don't want to go tramping around in the mud for miles and miles. It's super boring, and I don't know what to talk to her about. Last time, she kept lecturing me on medicinal herbs of the Pacific Northwest and how to survive if I'm ever lost in the woods. Val, the only time I *go* to the woods is with her. I like my wilderness paved with easy access to Jamba Juice and Mod Pizza."

"One of the reasons she moved up here was to spend more time with you." And with me, I amended silently, feeling guilty that it had been a couple of weeks since I'd called. "I get that hiking isn't that entertaining…"

"It's a snooze-fest, and I get blisters. Seriously, walking for hours is pointless. What is the appeal?"

I decided not to try to convince her that being out in nature and getting exercise was healthy. Mom had given *me* that spiel when I'd been a kid, and I remember being bored on her hikes too. Those had been pre-cell-phone days, so there hadn't even been anything to listen to or tinker with. Once, I'd brought a book, and she'd given me a lecture when I tripped over a root while reading.

"Spending time with a family member is the appeal, I believe. Is there another activity you'd be willing to do with her?"

"I could take her shopping."

I stifled a laugh—barely. Mom was even less likely than me to wear a dress or buy something that didn't come from Goodwill. Her hiking boots were the only things she spent serious money on. She probably felt she could since she didn't wear shoes anywhere else if she could get away with it.

"She might go for REI," I suggested.

"I wasn't talking about shopping for dehydrated food and tents."

"They have clothes."

"Oh, please. Just tell her to come over to the house for Sunday-night dinners, will you?"

Another twinge of envy went through me. *I'd* never been invited to the Sunday-night dinners… Admittedly, that would be strange, since Thad was there and we weren't married anymore. It wasn't that I wanted to have family dinners with them, but Amber had admitted that was her special dinner night, and I couldn't help but feel wistful over the lack of an invitation. Still, she'd agreed to weekly sword lessons again. That was promising.

"I'll let her know. Anything else?"

"Nah."

"See you next weekend then."

"Good. I look forward to poking you in the ass again."

"It was the shoulder, and I was distracted."

"In my mind it was the ass. Bye."

I called Mom to tactfully let her know that Amber loathed hiking but that she was invited to weekly dinners, and she answered promptly.

"Oh, hello, Val. I was just thinking of you. I volunteered with the local park organization to help maintain the trails out here, and while I was trimming back foliage, I found an elven luck coin. I'm curious if it's real and if they once lived in this area, or if someone made a copy. It looks recent rather than the forty-plus years old a legitimate one left behind would be. A real one would be magical, but of course, I cannot tell if this one is. The next time you visit to hike, will you look at it and let me know if it has power?"

"An elven *luck* coin?" I thought of the one Zav had found—I'd left it under a flower urn in the backyard, feeling I should keep it but not wanting to risk carrying another mysterious trinket around on my person. I also hadn't wanted it inside the house. "Describe it."

"There's a leaf on one side and a dagger on the other."

I swore. "Someone left its mate outside my house after an attack the other night. Zav thought it might be a calling card or a message."

From someone who wanted me dead. I stared bleakly at the phone.

"That is possible," Mom said slowly. "From what I remember, some elves make a number of them and give them out for various reasons."

"Where did you find it? Near your house?"

She'd ended up moving out east of Duvall, near Moss Lake Natural Area and the old logging roads where I'd looked for a dragon cave that summer. I'd suggested she avoid the area due to goblins living around there, but she'd found a cabin for rent near the trails and had fallen in love with it. It had come with a pottery shed and working wheel, and she now had a new hobby.

"Yes. On the back trail that meets up with the official trails."

"Near your cabin?"

She hesitated. "Yes."

I swore again. "I think the same person who's been stalking me may have come to check you out." That filled my gut with anxiety. What if the guy tried to use my mother against me? Maybe he'd thought to kidnap her to trade for Chopper, and it was only luck that she hadn't been home when he had come by.

Either way, I couldn't let Mom be endangered. I had to put the faesword quest aside to deal with my elven stalker. Assuming Zav would give me a ride to the elven home world, I would ask Freysha or anyone else who might know who the coin belonged to and how to deal with him.

"Rocket hasn't alerted me to any trouble."

"This guy has a camouflage charm. It's good enough to fool me, so I'm sure it could fool Rocket."

"I'll point out that dogs have superior senses to humans and likely even half-elves, but I will accede to your point that elves might be able to sneak up on us."

"Thanks. Can you pack a bag and come to stay at my place in Green Lake for a few days? It'll be safer here." I knew Mom preferred her privacy and easy access to the woods, but she could dodge the bikers and joggers to hug the urban trees at the lake for a few days. "Zav has been adding security features to the yard that should be a lot more powerful than Dimitri's."

"Will you be there?"

"Yeah, but I am planning to take a trip first."

As soon as I checked in with Amber, to make sure nobody had left coins around *her* house, I would visit the elven home world and find out everything I could about this assassin. Whether the elves wanted to talk to me or not.

CHAPTER 17

"THANKS FOR BRINGING ME HERE, Zav." I patted his scaled flank as we soared over the forests of Veleshna Var.

The last time we'd visited, the foliage had been blue and purple; today, it was silver and pale green and dusted with snow. This was strange to me, since the trees appeared deciduous, and winter had clearly come, but Zav had said the elves used magic to change the colors of the leaves. Maybe that included keeping them on branches throughout the winter—or maybe trees on other planets didn't lose their leaves.

"I don't think I'm going to be welcome," I added, "but it's time to deal with my stalker, one way or another."

If he was from here, maybe I could show up on *his* mother's doorstep and leave a calling card.

The elves will not dare reject the mate of a dragon, Zav said telepathically.

"I think you said that last time, and they rejected me while inviting you inside for sex."

One elf did that. The males had no interest in having sex with me.

"That's surprising given your allure. I'd expect you to get passes from the other side too."

I will have sex with nobody but my mate. Prepare yourself. We will pass through their defensive barrier.

Remembering the unpleasant zing from last time, I braced myself and laid my chest against his back. Zav always promised his magic would keep me from falling off, but the lack of a saddle or a harness hadn't stopped making me nervous.

A painful buzz similar to electricity zapped my body, and I grimaced. I also braced myself for rejection from the elves, worrying they wouldn't let me in to see my father or send a message to Freysha that I had come to visit. Maybe my telepathic range would be great enough that I could reach out to her. But picking her out inside a city of tens of thousands of elves would be a challenge to my abilities.

As soon as we passed through the invisible barrier, squawks sounded, and I sat up. Huge birds were flying toward us, huge saddled birds with elven riders. They carried bows and swords, and their blond and silver braids flew behind them as their avian mounts flapped their powerful wings.

Since my father had ridden one of those birds the last time I'd been here, I searched the riders, hoping he had recovered and would be among them. He had been the only elf interested in talking to me. But not surprisingly, he wasn't there.

"Is this the welcoming committee, or are we about to get shot at?" I asked.

They would be incredibly foolish to shoot a dragon.

"What about the rider on the dragon's back?"

Also foolish.

One of the birds banked and flew alongside Zav, though the bird didn't look pleased at getting close. Its beady eyes watched him, and it kept trying to scoot farther away. The rider used magic—I could sense him applying it—to force his mount to stay close. Assuming he meant to speak, I tapped my translation charm.

"Noble dragon," the elf called over the wind of our flight, magic amplifying his voice, "it is always a blessing to be visited by one of your kind..." Why did that sound like buttering-up language rather than anything genuine? "But we have closed our city to outsiders at this time. We must ask that you respect our wishes and depart."

The king is still ill? Zav asked.

The elf hesitated, glancing toward the other riders. "He is not accepting visitors at this time."

Because he is ill. Val Thorvald is his daughter and has the right to see him, per your own rules and accordances.

Another hesitation. This time, the elf looked at me. His eyes held the same suspicion that the elf who'd picked up Freysha had expressed.

SECRETS OF THE SWORD I

What if she'd been taken home not because our father was sick but because they'd wanted to get her away from me?

I will not allow harm to happen to those nearby if an enemy shows up who seeks to acquire my mate's sword, Zav said, perhaps thinking that was the reason for the hesitation.

It *was* possible—though I doubted roving gangs of teenage trolls would be a problem here—but I suspected something else.

"You are correct, noble dragon, that the king is ill. Our healers are studying that which assails him, but it is a strange affliction that came upon him suddenly. We suspect it was delivered by an enemy too cowardly to show him or herself." The elf squinted at me.

Uh huh. I was a suspect. But *how*? It wasn't as if I could have mailed an envelope filled with anthrax to another planet.

What kind of infection? Zav asked, and the suspicion in his tone alerted me to what he was thinking about.

The bacteria that had been designed to infect dragons—and that we also knew worked on gnomes. It might work on elves too. But who would have bothered? We'd defeated the leaders of the dragon clan who'd been responsible for that scheme.

"I am not a healer and do not know the exact details, but those with medical expertise believe he was infected deliberately by someone who wished him ill—or to take the throne. Should that happen, his daughter is not yet old enough and educated enough to be considered a ruler. The king's passing would cause great instability among our people."

Neither Val nor I were responsible, Zav stated. *We will see him and check this infection ourselves. My clan has recently dealt with something that could be similar.*

The elf cleared his throat diffidently. "I'm sorry, noble dragon, but that will not be permitted. We are not allowing visitors to the city right now."

A dragon goes where a dragon wishes. Zav flapped his wings harder and pulled away from the giant birds.

I twisted to watch the elves, worried they would attack him. Their weapons and gear all emanated magic, so it was possible their arrows could harm Zav. They could absolutely harm me.

The birds picked up speed to try to keep up. A distant sound rolled across the treetops, coming from the opposite direction, the direction we were heading. A strange mix of a gong and a chime, it had to be the elven alarm bell.

"Maybe this isn't a good idea, Zav. I can find someone else to ask about the token. Maybe Greemaw the golem would recognize it." Despite my words, I hated the idea of leaving without knowing what was up. What if my father was dying? I'd barely gotten a chance to know him, and he hadn't yet had a chance to meet Amber. It seemed like he should before passing away.

Besides, if he had the same bacterial infection that we'd dealt with, we knew how to cure it. I could offer to get some of Zoltan's formula for the elves.

You will see your father. You are entitled to see him under their own laws.

Yeah, but they think I might be responsible. Though I don't know how. It's not like I can make portals and visit any time.

They may believe you infected him with something when you visited him last.

When I visited him two months ago? That would be the slowest reproducing bacteria in existence.

People make suspects of those they wish to believe are suspects.

"Tell me about it," I muttered.

The birds had fallen farther behind, not able to keep up with Zav's powerful wingbeats, but lights flashed up ahead.

Hold on, Zav told me. *They have activated their defenses.*

"What does that mean?" I flattened myself to his back again and flung my arms wide, doing my best to hug his broad form.

I will protect you, my mate.

Light flashed around us, and I sensed magic hammering a barrier that Zav had erected. No elves were in sight now. These seemed to be automated attacks. One looked like a grenade hitting his barrier, an explosion booming as we flew through smoke.

I was relieved that Zav kept flying and didn't raze the forest or light anything on fire. Maybe that would keep the elves from retaliating with even more force. I couldn't be the only one in the Cosmic Realms with a weapon capable of piercing a dragon's defensive barriers and cutting into their flesh.

Up ahead, the city in the trees came into view. Far more elves than last time stood out on the platforms, most of them armed and armored. So much magic emanated from the trees and from the weapons and artifacts the elves carried that it battered my senses, making me want to squint my eyes shut and cover my ears with my hands.

Thinking of Freysha's lessons, I formed the mental fern fronds around my mind. The battering lessened, and a calmness came over me.

Until a pompous female voice spoke into my mind. *You are not welcome here. Tell that dragon to take you back to your vile world.*

I want to see my father and ask someone a couple of questions about an elf that's been stalking me on my vile world. Who are you?

Queen Ytalina, wife of Eireth. You are not welcome.

I know, but that's true of most places I go. Is Freysha home? She might be able to answer my questions.

She will spend no more time with you. Had I known she was on your loathsome world instead of studying on the goblin home world, I would have forbidden it.

Erg. I had assumed that Eireth had told his wife where their daughter was going for months. Had he even mentioned that he'd met with me?

I dropped my forehead against Zav's scales as he descended toward the same platform we'd landed on last time. The elves raised their bows, but seeing a huge black dragon barreling down on them must have convinced them how foolish their plan was. They scattered and made room for him.

Despite his speed coming in, Zav spread his wings and alighted in a graceful landing.

Can you help me find Freysha, Zav? I searched for her aura among all the tens of thousands of elves in their aerial city. My ability to detect magic and magical beings had improved, but everything here was magic, and I struggled to pick out individual people. *She may be able to help us or vouch for me or something.*

A dragon needs no one to vouch for him.

I need someone to vouch for me. *I'm a scruffy mongrel, remember.*

You are my mate. I will vouch for you. Zav shifted into his human form, startling me since I hadn't slid off his back yet. I ended up on my feet behind him, gripping his shoulders.

Several grim-faced bowmen and women had weapons pointed at us—more at me than Zav, but he wasn't being ignored. They didn't yet speak. Maybe they were waiting for the queen to come out and officially shoo us away.

Zav used his mental powers to guide my mind into one of the massive trees, where levels and levels of rooms had been carved out—or opened up with magical manipulation. Freysha was inside the tree, several floors down and heading upward quickly. Did elves have elevators? My mind conjured a cartoon image of an elevator inside a tree trunk.

Hey, Freysha, I sent telepathically. *Zav and I have come to ask a couple of questions.*

Yes. Her response was dry. *The whole city knows you are here. I'm coming.*

Also, I'd like to see our father if it's possible. Can you vouch for us?

I don't know. I'm young, and my parents don't always listen to me. I'll try. She'd crossed to another tree, this one closer to us, and seemed to be hurrying. Good.

A door on a nearby trunk opened. Unfortunately, Freysha wasn't the one to walk out.

The beautiful woman who strode out in an elegant blue robe with silver trim—it looked like the female version of Zav's black robe—had perfect lips, exotic blue-silver hair, and looked to be about my age. That probably meant she was three hundred. The pompous way she held herself told me she was the queen before she spoke.

"We have closed our city to outsiders." She addressed Zav and ignored me, despite our chat. "Even to dragons. I apologize, Lord Zavryd'nokquetal, but this is a stressful time for us."

"My mate will see her elven father," Zav said. "She is concerned for his well-being."

"She is suspected of being the one who infected him," Ytalina said icily, managing to glare at me while maintaining her expression of haughty pomposity.

"Uh." I raised a finger. "How? I haven't been here for months."

"An illness may lie dormant and attack the body later during a time of stress. Our healers have agreed upon this. They also agree that this illness may have been custom-crafted."

"Do I look like someone who can genetically engineer or magically engineer anything? I can barely change my own oil."

Her brows drew together, but before she could ask what that meant, Zav spoke again.

"We *will* see the king." He strode forward, radiating power and forming a stronger barrier around himself—and I felt it wrap around me as well.

As the bowmen pulled back their strings, glancing at the queen for direction, Freysha burst out through the open door with her hands up.

"Zav and Val!" she blurted. "I'm so glad you were able to come." She patted in the air toward the bowmen and smiled at the queen. "Mother, I invited them. As a dragon, Lord Zavryd has great power, including great *healing* power. When I heard Father was mysteriously sick, I wanted to do everything I could to help him."

Freysha was the only one smiling. Somehow, she made it look authentic instead of tense and worried. She was also the only one wearing laboratory goggles over her brows and a tool belt. My half-sister looked like she fit in here about as well as Gondo would.

Her mother squinted at her for several long moments, and I had a feeling a telepathic conversation was going on between them.

Does your sibling seek to embroil us in a mistruth? Zav started his own telepathic conversation with me. *I do not approve of dishonesty.*

I think she's just trying to get us through the door without a few dozen arrows sticking out of our hides.

I could accomplish that. No elven arrows will pierce my barrier.

Good.

Whatever illness your father has contracted may be beyond my ability to heal. As you know, I can regenerate many wounds and cure simple diseases, but I am not a dedicated healer.

I flexed my hand, the wound that wouldn't heal sending a stab of pain up my arm. *You can stand at his bedside, grip your chin, and say, "Hm," and, "Ah," a few times.*

That is not an effective way to heal someone.

"Come with me, please, Val and Lord Zavryd." Freysha waved for us to follow her inside.

Zav didn't hesitate. That had been where he'd intended to go anyway.

I stayed close, glad he kept his barrier up, especially when the queen followed right behind me and ten of the bowmen followed right behind *her.*

An escort. How lovely.

We descended in an all-wood elevator, passed through more rooms than even the thick trunk should have been able to hold, and headed across a covered wooden bridge to another tree. They were all connected, either by bridges or the expansive platforms—most trees had at least three layers of them—and nothing had been nailed or screwed in. The bridges looked like they'd grown naturally out of the trees and were covered in bark as if they were branches.

We passed a few curious elves, but the way was mostly clear.

"Everything okay here?" I murmured to Freysha as we crossed a bridge wide enough for us to walk side by side.

She shook her head and replied in English. "It's believed that Father was infected or poisoned by an outsider because another faction of elves or another intelligent race wants us weak and without leadership so they can attack."

"Who's in charge while he's laid low?"

"*I* am in charge," came the queen's cool voice from behind us. She must have had the equivalent of my translation charm, or maybe her innate magic allowed her to understand other languages. "And I am a capable ruler, despite my daughter's implication otherwise."

Freysha paused to give her mother a bow-curtsy. "My apologies, Mother. You know it was not my intent to suggest otherwise. I am simply saying that others who do not know you might think you are not as formidable as Father."

"They should know I am capable. If anything, one wonders if they'll target me next." The queen gave me a pointed look. "And if they sent an assassin to do the job."

Zav had been walking ahead of me, but he halted to turn and glare at the queen. I barely kept from running into him.

He placed a hand on my shoulder. "My mate is honorable and plans nothing duplicitous toward her ancestral people."

This defense touched me, given that he'd considered me an ignorant vigilante when we first met. He probably still thought my methods unorthodox, and I knew he didn't approve of me killing criminals instead of handing them over for dragon rehabilitation, but at least he was standing up for me to others.

"If you cast aspersions upon her character, you cast aspersions upon me," he continued, "and I would be within my right to challenge you to a duel to clear my honor."

The queen clenched her jaw, and the bowmen once again fingered their weapons and exchanged looks with each other. She had to hate having some outsider come in and challenge her authority in front of her people, but in this case, I sided with Zav.

"Lord Zavryd," Freysha said. "Please come this way. Nobody will challenge you. We will be most appreciative if you can heal my father."

The queen nodded to her, and Freysha tried to lead Zav off, but she wouldn't grab him, so it wasn't effective. He was still staring at the queen, as if he expected her to challenge him to a duel any second.

"Come on, my mighty dragon." I wrapped an arm around his waist and turned him toward Freysha.

He didn't resist me, fortunately, or I couldn't have moved him. Head up, he followed after her.

Thank you for defending me, I told him silently as we entered another trunk, this one as thick as the Space Needle.

You are my mate. Your honor is my honor.

I squeezed his waist and released him as we trod up stairs—wooden, of course—and passed through a great arching doorway into a personal suite. It was almost startling that the furnishings weren't made of wood. Though on closer inspection, it was possible they were made from cork or some other bark tissue. The seats had bulbous shapes that reminded me of a cross between a stool and Dimitri's Gamersac—which was, as far as I could tell, a modern interpretation of a beanbag chair.

"Wait one moment." Ytalina lifted a hand toward our group and strode up three steps to open a door and go inside.

I imagined her stashing away dirty laundry draped over furniture and picking up empty ginger-ale cans, or whatever sick elves consumed. Though they probably had maids or this world's equivalent for tidying their rooms. Surely, kings and queens didn't pick up their own ginger-ale cans.

"He's awake and knows you're coming," Freysha said quietly.

"Will he mind seeing us?" I thought about pulling out the token and asking her about it, but all ten of the bowmen had trailed us into the suite, and I was hesitant to reveal it. Though it was unlikely that Eireth's sickness had anything to do with me being stalked on Earth, the timing was conspicuous. Elven oddness happening on two worlds at the same time? It might not be unrelated.

The door opened, and the queen beckoned us in.

I'd hoped that Freysha and Zav and I might be able to see Eireth alone, but she settled into a chair inside the bedroom. Worse, an elf I didn't know at all, this one in a gray robe, sat in a chair by the wall, his chin to his chest, his white hair down past his shoulders. Aside from the pointed ears, he looked like Father Time taking a nap.

"The healer," Freysha explained, waving for me to follow her to the side of Father's bed.

It was more like a wide hammock with four corners attached to trunk-like posts than the California-king poster bed I expected royal people to have. What I would call sheets looked to be made from soft, fuzzy moss, and I wondered what dryer setting those fell under. The blanket and pillows were almost normal, though they had a fuzzy surface as well.

Eireth didn't look like the strong, middle-aged elf male I'd met two months earlier. He was pale, with his cheekbones sunken, but most striking was a gray scaliness to his exposed skin. It made it look like, given enough time, he would turn into a lizard man.

"So much for it being the same bacteria that we dealt with this summer," I muttered, hopes of being able to cure him with a dose of Zoltan's formula dissipating.

I joined Freysha at his bedside, but I didn't know what to do, other than stand there awkwardly. His breathing was steady and regular, but his eyes were closed. Freysha had said he knew we were here, but he appeared to be sleeping. What would I do if he woke up? Pat him on the shoulder? We hadn't even touched the first time we'd met. He hadn't known what to make of me, and I'd been wary of him.

"I recognize this," Zav stated.

The queen rose to her feet, and the healer also stirred.

"You know the illness?" Ytalina asked. "Our best healers only know that its origins were not here on Veleshna Var and that it's not natural to our people."

"It came from an outsider," the healer said in a reedy voice. His faded-blue eyes widened when he saw me—and widened further when they locked onto my sword. "Is this the one we suspect of the crime? She carries a tainted blade."

"No," Freysha said firmly. "This is Val. My half-sister."

That news didn't seem to surprise the healer. I had a feeling my name and relation to Eireth had already been bandied about.

"This is a result of dragon magic." Zav waved at the king. "It has nothing to do with Val."

"Several experts have studied him." The healer touched his own chest. "We did detect magic, but it lacks the signature of dragon magic. We would have known if your kind had been responsible."

"It is dragon magic," Zav repeated. "An old magic that is not used frequently anymore, but many hatchlings are taught it as they are growing because it is so simple. It is believed to be the first magic we learned as we evolved into the superior beings we are today."

I managed not to snort. The elves were staring at him in enraptured silence. Even Eireth's weary eyes had opened and focused on Zav.

"There are those who use it today when they do not wish to leave the telltale signature of modern dragon magic on the items—or beings—they affect." Zav turned toward the room. "Your king was afflicted by a dragon."

CHAPTER 18

"WHEN DID THIS START?" ZAV asked the queen and the healer. "Have any dragons visited your city recently?"

"They come to hunt in the wilds, but they rarely come into our city." Ytalina came to stand on the other side of Eireth's hammock and took her husband's hand. She spoke quietly to him, asking if he'd met with any dragons in the past month.

"I have encountered two dragons in recent memory," Eireth rasped, his rough voice nothing like the smooth authoritative baritone I remembered.

"Including Zav?" I asked.

"Three dragons." Eireth smiled wanly. "One was Lord Quaresthee, several weeks ago, who warned us that there might be a war between the Silverclaws and the Stormforges." He paused to cough.

Ytalina and the healer exchanged long, knowing looks, which made me wonder if they believed Eireth could die from this. If that was a possibility, maybe we should be looking for someone to heal him rather than worrying about who caused it, at least for now.

"He is a regular messenger of the Dragon Ruling Council and Justice Court," Zav said, "and has allegiance to our queen and our clan."

"Yes," Eireth said. "He returned in surprisingly short order to let us know that a Silverclaw plan had been thwarted and that the Stormforges were solidifying their rule over the Dragon Ruling Council."

"That is correct," Zav said.

"He shifted into elven form and visited me in person to inform me of the news. I do not recall any magic being used, but it was a week or two after that when I started feeling ill."

"I cannot imagine why he would wish you harm, but I can question him."

"After that, also shortly before I started feeling ill, a Lord Xilnethgarish came, warning me that the remaining Silverclaws were not pleased that they had been thwarted and that allies of the Stormforges should be careful in the coming years."

"*Xilneth* was here?" I looked at Zav. "Isn't it funny how he keeps showing up?"

"Did you have any contact with him?" Zav asked Eireth sternly. "Or did he come close to you? Physical contact would not be necessary."

"No. He flew over the city during a religious ceremony—I was marrying two young elves." Eireth glanced between me and Zav.

My cheeks warmed as I remembered he'd offered to marry us the first time we met. Had that been before or after Zav promised me out loud and in front of Eireth that sex with him would be fabulous?

"He warned me telepathically," Eireth continued, "from miles away, and then flew out of my range. To hunt, he said."

"It is unlikely he could have used his power to infect you with this illness from that far away." Zav sounded grudging when he said that. He'd probably already been fantasizing about beating up Xilneth and dragging him before his Justice Court. "Is it possible he only claimed to hunt and then sneaked into the city and was close without your knowledge?"

"Our alarms would have informed us if a dragon breached our barriers," the queen said. "We have always sensed dragons flying close."

"Hm." Did Zav think he could sneak in if he wished? "Then only Lord Quaresthee was here in person in the past two months?"

"And yourself." The queen looked at him and at me, though there wasn't as much accusation in her eyes this time.

If she believed Zav about the dragon magic, she couldn't logically still suspect me.

"My clan ousted the old king who acted against our kind and ordered the assassinations of some of my relatives," Zav said. "You will recall that our queen *chose* Eireth among the elves you offered up as potential rulers. We would have no reason to make him ill."

"Nobody doubts you, Lord Zavryd," Eireth murmured, closing his eyes again.

Zav laid a hand on his forehead, and magic surged from him and flowed into Eireth. Freysha's brows rose in a hopeful expression. A soft sigh escaped Eireth's lips, and Zav withdrew his hand.

"I do not have the knowledge to eradicate the magical affliction," Zav said, and Freysha's shoulders slumped, "but I know of dragon healers who could. I will return to my people and find someone who can come help. I will also question Lord Quaresthee if I can locate him."

"Thank you, Lord Zavryd." Freysha bow-curtsied to him.

Zav met my eyes. *Do you wish to come with me or stay with your family?*

It still seemed strange to think of Freysha, and especially our father, as my family, but I would rather hang out with them than ride Zav all over Dragondom and back. Besides, I hadn't gotten a chance to ask about the token. That was the main reason I'd wanted to come.

How long will you be gone, and do you think I'll be safe here from sword-hunters?

Less than a day, and the only ones who could get to you would be elves.

Given that my stalker is elven, that's not that comforting.

I am certain they would not attack the king's daughter in his home.

I was less certain of that—the queen still looked like she would happily usher in the bowmen to perforate me soundly. *I'll stay if they'll let me.*

If I wish my mate to stay, they will allow it, and they will treat you respectfully.

You have a high opinion of yourself.

Of course. I am a dragon. Zav came over and hugged me—both Ytalina and the healer rocked back, as if this was a shocking gesture.

I decided not to truly stun them by wrapping my legs around him and kissing him like a sex-starved fiend—though the thought crossed my mind.

"My mate will stay here while I seek the perpetrator and a healer," Zav stated. "If she is harmed, I will be livid and vengeful."

"Do dragons have the expression *you attract more flies with honey than with vinegar*?" I asked him.

"Dragons incinerate flies. They are obnoxious."

"Never mind then."

"She will not be harmed," Ytalina said. "We will find a suitable dwelling for her."

Suitable dwelling? Why did a stable under the trees pop into my mind?

"She may wish to visit with her father," Zav said. "He should have a boost of strength from the vigor I gave him."

Eireth's eyes were open again, but if he felt any vigor, he was saving it for later.

Zav released me, strode out of the tree house, shifted forms, and sprang into the air to fly off and create a portal outside of the elven barrier.

"Is it all right if I ask Freysha something before you cart me off to a suitable dwelling?" I asked—Ytalina was already reaching for the door, probably to bring in an escort to drag me out.

"Freysha may go with you." Ytalina pointed toward the door.

"I would like to stay with Father for a while. Had I known before that he was so sick, I would have asked to leave Earth weeks ago." Freysha sat on a stool beside Eireth's hammock and took his hand.

Ytalina frowned at me, her arm still up and pointing out the door.

"I am feeling a little better." Eireth squeezed Freysha's hand, then nodded to me. "Let her stay, Ytalina."

"I will have someone come for her in five minutes." Ytalina strode out with the healer following after her.

Using a whisper of magic, Freysha closed the door.

I walked over to it, touched Sindari's charm, and summoned him. Freysha and Eireth watched curiously as the silver mist formed and he materialized.

"I need a favor," I told him.

Sindari gazed around, his senses no doubt helping him get his bearings. *We are in the middle of an elven city. You do not plan a battle, do you?*

Hopefully not, but can you sit right there? I pointed to the floor in front of the door.

Sindari squinted at me, suspicion in his green eyes, but he sat on his haunches in an ideal position to block it from being opened.

Perfect. Thank you. I stroked the back of his neck.

"Did you summon a mighty Del'nothian tiger to be… a doorstop?" Eireth asked.

"Also to deter whatever nanny the queen sends to collect me. He's very ferocious. His roar routinely prompts enemies to lose bladder control."

"I would prefer that not happen in my bedchamber."

"We'll save it for an emergency situation," I said, pleased that a hint of humor twinkled in Eireth's eyes.

He wasn't radiating vigor, but he did seem perkier since Zav applied his magic.

Is this truly the only reason you summoned me? Sindari's tail twitched and thumped against the door.

Zav left to hunt for some dragons, and even though I'm positive that Freysha and Eireth don't wish me any ill, I'm fairly certain every other elf in the city would be happy to see me fall off one of their platforms to my death. If you could keep an eye out for potential enemies, I would appreciate it.

If the door opens and hits me, I will bite the foot off the responsible party.

If they're fantasizing about throwing me off a platform while they open the door, that'll be perfect. I pulled up a poofy chair, sat beside Freysha, and dug out the token. "I'm sure Zav will find someone good to heal you," I offered, feeling I should say something about Eireth's illness before switching topics.

"His sister, perhaps," Eireth said. "I believe she is studying to be a healer."

"Zav mentioned that," I said, "but I hope he gets someone less lippy for you."

"I care little about lips, only about being well again. Had I known a dragon was responsible and might be able to cure me, I would have sent someone to their world myself. I do wonder why I was targeted."

"You haven't come across any tokens like this around, have you?" I held it up to show him, though I couldn't imagine that it had anything to do with a dragon poisoning him.

Freysha shook her head, but Eireth sucked in a startled breath.

I offered it in case he wanted to look closer, though I was encouraged that he recognized it.

"Where did you get it?" He reached for it but paused halfway, as if afraid it would zap him.

"Someone left it on the sidewalk in front of my house after siccing six fire dogs—crucible beasts—on me. Zav found it. I've also had the feeling of someone watching me lately. Zav hasn't been able to hunt down whoever it is, but we think it's an elf."

Eireth finally took the token—was that a tremor to his hand? From the sickness? Or something else?

"I don't recognize it," Freysha said.

Eireth eyed both sides of the token, his gaze lingering on the engraved dagger. "I have two coins exactly like these. The assassin who killed my cousin, the famous orator and diplomat Persylvar, left them over the eyes of his victim. He always leaves at least one behind after he makes a kill, thus to ensure he gets credit."

"Assassin?" My stalker was a professional hitman? That couldn't be good. "An elven assassin?"

"Yes."

"I didn't know that was a career here."

Eireth closed his eyes. Maybe he had been close to the cousin—or the assassination had been recent.

"It's not encouraged," Freysha murmured.

"I was expecting a mage, to be honest." I waved at Freysha. "You said it would take a magic user to summon those beasts, right?"

"He is both," Eireth said. "His elven name is Varlesh Sarrlevi, but most of the races call him their version of Night Avenger. He is known to attack in the dark of night, and he rarely takes political or passionless assignments, as the stories say. He always hunts down victims that someone loathes and wants revenge on. Someone who is willing to pay well. Unlike most of our people, Varlesh covets wealth and is rumored to have investments and great mansions on many worlds." Eireth handed the coin back to me. "These are stories, mind you. I have not met him. I researched him after my cousin's death, having some notion of hunting him down and slaying him, but our justice fetchers found the bitter rival who'd hired the assassin. They arrested him. That had to be enough for my desire for justice. Had I gone after the assassin himself, he would have likely killed me. He was trained by mages and masters of combat from several different races, and he's reputed to be *extremely* formidable."

I held up the coin. "So, why didn't he kill me? Why'd he leave the coin outside? And why'd he leave one on a trail by my mother's new place?"

"Sometimes, he warns his victims before—" Eireth sat up, alarm flashing in his eyes. "He threatened Sigrid?" He leaned out of bed and gripped my wrist, the tremor gone and replaced by worried strength. "Is she all right?"

"She's fine. She never saw anyone, but I was concerned, so I had her move in to my house. She's staying there for a few days until I figure everything out with my sword—and this assassin."

An assassin who was *extremely* formidable, apparently. If that was true, I was in trouble, but why hadn't he confronted me directly? Was he studying me before attacking personally? Testing me?

I grimaced as that struck me as very plausible. Thanks to the dwarf I'd rescued from the panther-shifter brothers, my reputation had spread beyond Earth. According to Nin's grandfather, I was now known to be a slayer of dragons. He'd thought me some mighty warrior. I was all right, but I had a feeling my supposed greatness had grown with each iteration of the tale. Who knew what this assassin had heard?

"I am concerned," Eireth said. "Why would he even be aware of Sigrid?"

"Me, I'm sure. Maybe he was letting me know that he's checking out my family." I rocked back on the seat, abruptly wishing I'd warned Amber and Thad. What I would have said, I don't know. Watch out for elven stalkers leaving wooden coins? "I need to get back home."

"Lord Zavryd will return soon," Freysha said.

"Isn't there someone here who can send me back?" I asked. "You can let him know where I went."

"You should not go anywhere without him," she said. "His presence is probably the reason the assassin hasn't tried again."

"If my mother and daughter are in danger, I can't stay here." I clenched a fist. "Who hired this guy, anyway? It doesn't sound like he's from Earth or would have come to my world if he weren't hunting me."

"That is likely true," Eireth said. "He's not known to speak with his victims before he kills them, nor give out information on who hired him. It took our investigators some time to hunt down the culprit—after my cousin was dead and it was too late for it to truly matter."

"Wonderful," I muttered.

Someone comes, Sindari told me.

A menacing assassin?

Someone carrying towels and sheets.

The door opened a couple of inches before thumping against Sindari's haunch.

An uncertain male voice called, "Is Ms. Ruin Bringer ready to be seen to the room that has been prepared?"

"No, she's not," I said, "and the name is Val."

Hadn't the queen or anyone else been given my real name?

"I've been asked to escort you to your room."

Sindari leaned on the door, and it thudded shut. *There is also a dragon in my range.*

"I sense a dragon that is not Lord Zavryd." Freysha frowned at her father. "Is this one of the dragons that visited you? That may have infected you?"

Eireth closed his eyes. I tried to stretch out with my more meager senses.

It is Xilneth, Sindari said.

Hell.

CHAPTER 19

I SENSED XILNETH FLYING HIGH OVER the city. Above the barrier that Zav and I had flown through? Or had he entered elven territory, as unfazed by their defenses as Zav?

Greetings, Ruin Bringer, slayer of bullying Silverclaw dragons and mate to an unworthy and extremely stuffy Stormforge dragon.

Uh. What was I supposed to say to that? *Zav is worthy.*

But he is stuffy. I see you agree.

What do you want, Xilneth?

Eireth and Freysha were both looking upward, as if they could see the large green dragon soaring above their tree homes. Sindari remained blocking the door, but his tail was twitching. The servant with the towels had stopped knocking and trying to get me to come out, but low voices from the sitting room reached my ears. I heard "dragon" and "Xilnethgarish" among the words.

I have come to deliver my warning. I did not trust that Lord Stuffy would share it with you. He chased me off your world as soon as I entered. As if I am some rat to be driven out of the cave before it can eat the cheese!

Dragons have cheese?

No, but humans do. It's delightful. If you bring me some, I'll tell you more about your sword.

This was, if memory served, my third conversation with Xilneth, and they had all been odd. If he wasn't a suspect in Eireth's illness, I wouldn't have minded talking to him—especially about my sword—but this might be a trap. Did he want to lure me out into the woods to bop me on the head and steal Chopper? Before, he'd wanted to have sex with me—to irk Zav, primarily, I gathered—but that might have changed.

Xilneth... how old are you?

I will be one hundred years old soon!

Is that young for a dragon?

He sounded young. Maybe like Zondia, he was their equivalent of a teenager.

I am young and virile, yes. Do you wish to receive my warning?

Yeah. I'll get you whatever kind of cheese you want once I'm back on Earth.

Excellent! Where can we meet? The elves are forbidding me from landing in their city. Something has them in a tizzy.

I eyed Eireth. Something. *Just give me your warning telepathically, please.*

That is so impersonal! Would you not like to meet in person so that I may sing to you again? His telepathic tone turned sly. *I see that your mate is not on this world. Perhaps you would like me to shift into my elven form. After I deliver my warning, you will be so pleased with me that you will wish to frolic naked under the branches. Once you have been with Xilnethgarish, you will never wish to return to a stuffy, arrogant, haughty dragon. That will irk him so much! It will be fabulous.*

"He's flying around our city," Eireth reported. "Our people are warning him that dragons aren't welcome at this time. He's staying right outside of our barriers."

"I know." I sighed. "He's hitting on me."

"Hitting... on?" Eireth's eyebrows drew together, and he looked at Freysha.

"My mother never used that expression when you were on Earth?" I asked. "He's trying to get me to come out, meet him, and have sex with him. And he says he has a warning for me."

"You are mated, and he knows this. Such activity would be frowned upon by dragons. By all species with scruples. I will speak with him." Eireth closed his eyes.

"Feel free to tell him to beat it," I said.

If this was the same warning about my sword that Zav had already shared with me, there wasn't much point in speaking further with Xilneth. I doubted Zav had withheld anything from me, unless he'd deemed it frivolous and not worth mentioning.

While Eireth distracted Xilneth, I turned the token over in my hand. Were there any more questions I should ask him before leaving? Was there any way this token could lead back to whoever had hired the assassin? It would be useful to know who wanted me dead. The fae queen or some other fae? I couldn't imagine why. Before this week, I hadn't had any dealings with them.

Ruin Bringer! Xilneth cried in my mind. *The elven king is lecturing me!*

That's what kings do.

He is asking me to leave this world, but I have not given you my warning. Will you not meet me in the forest?

Nope. Tell me what you've got to say, and I'll buy you whatever kind of cheese that you like.

I like the moldy kind.

Gross.

It's pungent and tickles my taste buds!

I sighed again. "Is a hundred years old very young for a dragon?"

"Yes. Even younger than thirty-seven for an elf." Freysha smiled—that was her age. She was immensely more mature than Xilneth. "He is barely out of his adolescence."

Very well, Ruin Bringer. I do not wish to be chased off—or lectured into senescence—before I can deliver my warning. As I told the Stuffy One, it is now known far and wide that one of the legendary dragon blades is emanating fae magic that can be sensed from a thousand miles away.

A thousand miles? That was even worse than I'd thought.

There is more that I didn't tell Zavryd'nokquetal, Xilneth added, his voice a whisper in my mind.

What?

I did not wish to admit weakness to a Stormforge dragon.

"I've told him to leave and am sending the riders out to shoo him away," Eireth said.

I held up a finger. "He may be telling me something useful."

"If we believe he is the one who afflicted our father with this illness," Freysha said, "nothing he says can be trusted."

"If he *is* the one who did it," Eireth said, "I will ask the riders to do more than *shoo* him."

You can admit weakness to me, I told Xilneth. *I have weaknesses of my own. It's no big deal.*

To a dragon it is *a big deal. We are supposed to be supreme hunters and warriors, but I am a lover, not a fighter. That is a human saying, yes? Maybe you understand.*

Nobody would call me a lover instead of a fighter, but I said, *Sure. Tell me.*

The Silverclaw dragons were very angry after you helped the stuffy one free his kin.

I was rather hoping we'd killed all the angry ones.

No. Their clan is large, and the ones that were killed had time to warn their kin before their end. Some of the Silverclaws wished to attack back in some sneaky guerrilla way, to deliver a blow to the Stormforges. But they did not believe they would be successful. Not only are the Stormforge numbers once again more substantial, but they expect retaliation and are prepared. The only one they could take revenge upon is not a dragon and does not live on their world and under their protection.

Why do I have a feeling that's me?

Yes. It is you. Mythrarion Silverclaw hired an assassin to hunt you down.

I groaned and sank to the floor.

Problem, Val? Sindari abandoned his spot by the door and padded over to peer at me with his green eyes.

"So many problems."

Everyone was looking at me now.

"Well, technically only two problems, but it seems like more." I pushed my braid over my shoulder. Hell, maybe it was only one problem and all tied together. Could the assassin be working with the fae? Or was this whole sword thing just a coincidence?

How do you know all this, Xilneth?

Was he the dragon equivalent of Gondo? Someone who hung out at all the coffee gatherings and heard all the gossip?

I regret to admit to you that I delivered the message from Mythrarion to the assassin. Varlesh Sarrlevi is his name. I did not wish to, but the brutish Mythrarion is stronger than I am and threatened to kill me if I didn't do this for him. He tortured me! Had you met me, I could have shown you my dreadful wounds. I promise that I resisted him, but he is very strong, and I do not like pain. Or death.

Why did he need you to be the intermediary?

So that if his plan failed, if the assassin rejected the job and reported to the Stormforges, Mythrarion would not be discovered. He forbade me from telling the assassin who was hiring him. I delivered the message and a bag of gems as a partial payment and said nothing of the origins, though I believe the assassin knew. Everyone knows the Silverclaws are angry and vengeful right now. The only question might have been which of them was behind this.

So you haven't told anyone... except me? Why *are you telling me, Xilneth?*

I do not wish you to be slain by an assassin! We have not yet frolicked naked under the trees. Also, you retrieved our queen's egg from those who stole it. The Starsinger Clan owes you a debt. That hatchling has come out and is now a new little sister for me.

The Starsinger queen is your mother?

She is.

No wonder he'd been the one sent for the dragon equivalent of pickles and ice cream.

I did not wish to betray you, Ruin Bringer. Look. He shared a telepathic image of himself, his flanks charred and scales broken with great gouges sliced into his side. *The fiend even bit my tail!* Another image came of a long tail with a bite taken out of one side.

The wounds did look painful. If he was showing me the truth. I would check later with Zav. I assumed Zav had seen Xilneth at the portal.

I thought if we met in person you would see my wounds and believe my story. And also you would wish to commiserate with me.

While frolicking naked?

Exactly! The wounds would not affect my ability to pleasure you. They are healing now.

I'm so glad. I rubbed my forehead. *If Zav spoke to this Mythrarion Silverclaw and convinced him, diplomatically or forcefully, to un-hire the assassin, would Sarrlevi leave me alone?*

I believe that is possible, but please do not let Zavryd'nokquetal know that I was the one to inform you of this. The odious Mythrarion will come after me and kill me. Or he may harm others in my clan. I cannot permit this. If it had been any other elf or human than you, I would not have defied him. But I have great guilt. And I am now hoping for pungent cheese.

I'll get you some. If I survive the week.

Excellent. You will survive now that you are forewarned. You are crafty for a non-dragon.

I hope so.

His presence faded from my senses, and I explained his message to the others.

"I do not believe he can be trusted." Freysha glanced at our father. "I *do* believe a Silverclaw dragon may have hired the assassin as a way to avoid dealing with Lord Zavryd and possibly incurring his wrath, but it is strange that Xilnethgarish would tell you about it and risk incurring wrath himself."

"I wonder if the attack on me is tied in." Eireth rested a hand on his chest. "As Lord Zavryd'nokquetal said, it was the Stormforges who chose me as king, and we have been aligned with them these past decades."

"Who would rule if you died?" I asked.

Freysha winced at the bluntness.

"Freysha is too young. The court would have to put forward options, and there would be a vote." Eireth scratched his cheek. "I do not think any of the choices would be friendly to the Silverclaws though. Few have any love for them. Even the rebel elven factions—those who would be happy to see my reign end—aren't allies to them. They loathe all dragons."

"What if it's not about dragon and elven politics? What if the assassin has just been trying to deprive me of allies? And *tools*?" I touched Chopper's hilt. "Your people suspected me of poisoning you, right? And this resulted in Freysha being taken from Earth. Freysha, who has been living in my house and teaching me, and could be helpful if an assassin showed up. And if someone manages to take Chopper from me, then I'd have a hard time fighting off an assassin alone."

"It's a possibility," Eireth said slowly, "but I would remember if a known assassin had come and infected me. Besides, Lord Zavryd'nokquetal said it was dragon magic."

I shrugged, not married to the idea. "It was just a thought."

"We will have to see what your mate learns." Freysha offered me a hand. "Do you wish to rest until he returns? I gather there's a room for you. Or you could rest in my room if you wish."

I still wanted to go home and check on Amber and Mom, but I let her pull me up. "Let's see your room. I'm curious how an elven princess lives."

"Not how you think, I suspect," Eireth murmured, his eyes closed again.

Some of his palpable weariness had returned, and Freysha watched him with concern, even as she led me out.

Maybe Zav's spell was already wearing off. I hoped he found someone who could help. I also hoped that Eireth's illness wasn't in some roundabout way my fault.

CHAPTER 20

FREYSHA'S ROOM WAS NOTHING LIKE any princess suite that any fairy tale had ever described, but as soon as I walked in and smelled the mix of foliage and flowers and wood glue and tool oil, I said, "Of course."

Vines twined up lattices built onto the walls, the plants sprouting from wooden loam-filled pots that appeared to grow out of the floor itself. Tools from pliers to wrenches to sketching kits hung from nubby branches sticking out of the plants like pegs on a pegboard. Worktables filled most of the available floorspace, with blueprints sprawled across some and half-completed projects on others. Artwork of interestingly engineered cities on other worlds was pinned to the ceiling, foliage stretching out from the walls to half cover some of them. A bed barely large enough for Freysha hunkered in a back corner. It was raised up with bookcases underneath it, tomes and scrolls filling the cubbies.

It occurred to me that I might not have gotten all my *weirdness*, as Amber repeatedly called it, from my mother's side of the family.

Sindari, who'd padded in after me, walked up to a planter and sniffed the contents. Some intriguing relative of catnip, perhaps.

"This is my first time seeing plants used as tool organizers." I tapped what looked like wire crimpers dangling from a branch, a green tendril around the handle holding it in place.

"The perfect solution for an elf engineer." Freysha smiled a little wistfully. "My family thinks I'm strange, but Father supports me in my endeavors."

"And your mother?"

"She lectures me if I bring in axes, awls, saws, or anything that cuts wood. That's not the elven way. So I have to hide edged tools." Freysha lifted a leaf like a lily pad, revealing a hammer and awl underneath.

"Sort of like hiding the pot in the underwear drawer, huh?"

"Pot?" She touched the edge of one of the planters.

"Never mind. If it helps, my mom thinks I'm odd too. She doesn't realize that *she's* the odd one. She doesn't even wear shoes."

"Many elves do not wear shoes unless they're on a trip." Freysha smiled. "We don't have nails or broken glass littering our cities."

"Maybe that's where she gets the tendency." I spotted a chair, but I was too agitated to sit down and paced around the room instead. "You can go back and sit with Eireth—our father—if you want. I'm worried about everything and will be lousy company."

You did ask me to work as a doorstop. Sindari hopped onto the bed, which promptly looked even smaller with his huge tiger self on it. *That is certainly not the act of good company.*

I called you to let me know when strange adolescent dragons were in the area.

Which I did.

Yes. Thank you. I supposed I should dismiss him. I wouldn't likely be in trouble until I got back home again. But since Sarrlevi was an *elven* assassin, wasn't it possible that he could follow me here? I assumed he had the ability to create portals if he was a great mage as well as a fighter.

"I will return to your world to help you with the assassin," Freysha said. "And to protect you from Xilneth if he has been lying and is scheming against you in some way."

"Thanks, but you should stay and make sure our father is safe. If someone tried to kill him once, they could try again, assuming Zav finds someone who can heal him."

Maybe Freysha hadn't considered that, for her face turned grim. She walked past the bed, saying nothing about the giant silver tiger reclining on it, and stopped in front of a worktable facing an oval window that looked out into the treetops. Fresh dirt littered the surface of the table, a few unidentifiable moist gray bits mingled in, and four glowing orbs hummed softly along the back. The entire table radiated magic, not only the orbs. She pulled a terracotta box off a shelf and removed a lid.

"I have been working on something that may be useful to you." Freysha scooped dirt mixed with the gray bits into the box, grabbed a watering can, and sprinkled water inside.

"Oh?" I wondered if there were tiny holes in the lid of the box that would allow something to sprout. Visions of Chia Pets formed in my mind.

"I was able to locate books on fae magic in our library here. Even though the different races usually aren't able to use or copy each other's specific type of magic, the fae do a great deal with plants and the earth, so I thought I might be able to emulate something of theirs using my own forest magic."

"Something?" I decided it was unlikely she had seen Chia Pets and would get the reference.

"Have you been practicing making the roots?" Freysha pulled a pouch off another shelf, grabbed a pinch of some kind of reddish dust, and sprinkled it on top of the concoction inside the box.

"A little bit, yeah." I thought about sharing how I'd practiced at the park before the fae guys had come out to beat me up.

"I believe that if you plant these spore plugs in the ground along with a suitable substrate—" Freysha waved at what I'd been considering dirt in the box, "—they will grow swiftly and form a fairy ring. Normally, it would take many days, but you may be able to coax them to grow more quickly using the same magic that draws out the roots." Freysha put the lid on the box, brought it over, and handed it to me. "If I have created these correctly, through the magic of the interdimensional mycelium, the ring will automatically connect with the other fairy ring doorways in their network."

Interdimensional *what*? I needed Willard with her science books for a translation.

All I asked was, "You mean this can make a door into the fae realm?"

"It can make the framework for a doorway, yes. You will still need a key to open the way."

"Uh, not to sound ungrateful, but what's the point then? I thought I'd just go back to Magnuson Park if Nin gets my key working." Or maybe to another ring on Willard's map. The exploded fae body parts might not have been cleaned up yet at the park, and walking through that sounded unappealing.

Freysha smiled knowingly. "The rings the fae have made have the equivalent of your world's door chimes on them—many are monitored directly. Strangers are not permitted in."

"What happens if fae that go out get captured?" I thought of the two males who'd been killed by some unknown being lurking in their magical passageway.

"The fae do not allow their people to be captured. I have heard of them taking their own lives—or others taking their lives for them—if they are. It is feared that they would be tortured and give away the secrets of their realm and their magic. When they leave their land, they know the risk."

Someone must have been monitoring the fae doorway in Magnuson Park. By calling and capturing those guys, I'd condemned them to their deaths.

"Using an existing doorway would be dangerous," Freysha continued, "but it would be some time before a new doorway was discovered and added to the monitoring system—or closed down. Also, you could plant this fairy ring right in your own yard."

"Because who wouldn't want a doorway to Fae Land in their backyard?"

"I suggest the front yard. The earth is loamier."

"Even better."

I considered the box. The idea of being able to sneak into the fae realm was appealing, and if I *did* grow the mushrooms in the front yard, I would be protected by Zav's defenses around the borders of our property. Assuming Nin could bring the key out of dormancy, it might take me a while to figure out how to use it to open a doorway. During which time, if I was at the park, I would be vulnerable to attack.

"Okay, I can see how this would be useful." I hefted the box. "Thank you. Do I just dump the contents on the ground and use my mind to will the mushrooms to grow?"

"Bury the plugs in a circle, making sure no cement or other obstacles will break the ring. There is a *sileysa* inside. Place it in the ring last and tap it to activate it. It will prompt the mushrooms to grow mycelial tendrils to each other."

"Got it."

"Please be careful. Once you breach their borders, it will not take them long to sense you. I almost suggested that you leave your sword with Lord Zavryd, but..." She tilted her palm upward.

"I need to take it since the whole point is getting this fae queen to remove the magic."

"Yes. Any of their more powerful mages may be able to do that."

"I'll start my search at Diagon Alley then."

Her forehead crinkled.

"You know, where wizards shop in *Harry Potter*. Never mind." I patted her on the shoulder. "Thanks for making this for me."

"Of course. Sitting with Father has not been very stimulating. This project gave my mind something to do." Freysha turned toward Sindari, who was rubbing his cheek on the pillow. Scratching an itch, not scent-marking the bed, I hoped. "You and Sindari will want to wait and make sure nobody follows you through the doorway. The idea that someone has ordered an infamous and dreadful assassin to kill you concerns me."

"Ditto."

Sindari lifted his head. *Are we going on this adventure now?*

As soon as I can figure out how to magically grow a ring of mushrooms in the lawn.

So... not soon?

Your confidence is delightful.

All of me is delightful.

There's a piece of moss dangling from your ear.

Elven pillows are filled with moss. Sindari flopped his head back down onto said pillow. *They are springy and smell like the forest. Much more appealing than your strange synthetic fluff pillows.*

I had no idea mighty apex predators were pillow connoisseurs. Also, when were you on my bed checking out my pillows?

Tigers didn't smile, but Sindari managed to convey something similar. I wasn't that surprised. I'd caught him lounging on Dimitri's Gamersac before.

"Sorry about the tiger fur on your bed," I told Freysha, who was watching his pillow appreciation with a hard-to-read expression. "He likes pillows that smell like the forest."

"As do elves. When I return to further your training, I may have to bring my own pillows."

"I could get some goose-down pillows. Those ought to be equally interesting to tigers. I don't know about elves."

"Hm," she said noncommittally. "Regarding your other problem, I will ask my family to try to find enough gold to offer to pay the assassin not to hurt you, but our people do not typically hoard jewels or gold or what many of the other races consider valuable, so we do not have much of it."

"Moss pillows won't work as an enticement, huh?"

It was an *elven* assassin, after all.

"Likely not. The gold and jewels may also fail. I believe the code of assassins—such as I have heard it described—will forbid anyone except he who hired the assassin to rescind the contract. He should not be bribable."

"Yeah, I would never let the guy I was hired to kill pay me off to leave him alone." Strange that I was now being hunted by the elven version of myself. Except that *I* only killed murderers and rapists, not hard-working half-elves just trying to get by. "And don't worry about it. It's my problem. I'll deal with it." I hefted the box. "If I can get the fae to nix the beacon magic on my sword, we'll be on level ground. I can sneak around just as easily as he can then."

Would that truly be level ground? It sounded like this guy with his wizarding skills—and who knew how many centuries of master sword training—could kick my ass.

"You will be less disadvantaged then, yes." Freysha nodded.

Less disadvantaged. Why did that sound like a polite way of saying I'd still get my ass kicked?

"Any chance I'll be *advantaged*?"

"You are a capable warrior, Val, and you are learning some magic, but you still have much to learn to become a master. You are not very old by elven standards. I am surprised that he is testing you and did not simply attack you outright the first night. But he has lived a long time and fought many foes, so perhaps patience and caution are some of his strengths."

Val's reputation has grown as tales of her exploits have gone beyond her own world, Sindari said. *Not long ago, a tiger in my own realm shared a story he had heard of the Ruin Bringer and the talented and incredible Del'nothian warrior who walks at her side.*

"Incredible, yet modest and very regal," I said.

Indeed.

I decided to peek inside the box in case anything inside was mystifying and I needed clarification. Like what was that s*ileysa* she'd mentioned?

A swirly green-and-yellow marble lay nestled among the dirt and little cylinders—spore plugs, she'd called them. It flashed at me a couple of times.

"I assume this isn't a jawbreaker."

"What is a jawbreaker?"

SECRETS OF THE SWORD I

"A hard candy that you suck on. If you try to bite it, it breaks your jaw. Not really, but that's the inspiration for the name."

"I would not recommend biting this. It is made from earth and fungi and magic. But do not lose it, as it's key to activating the fairy ring."

"I won't. And these are the plugs?" I prodded one of them. "Do I need to water them?"

"You can. Let them settle overnight and then apply your growth magic, as with the roots. That is all. Very simple."

Very simple for the woman who could take a dying houseplant and turn it into a Jurassic jungle covering the walls in two days.

Lord Zavryd has returned, Sindari announced. *And his sister.*

Ugh, I'd been hoping he would find another dragon healer. One who's older and nicer. It was hard for me to imagine Zondia sitting beside Eireth and holding his hand.

I have not noticed that there are many nice *dragons.*

"Tell me about it."

Freysha had an abstracted look and did not comment on only being able to hear half of my conversation.

"The dragons are here." She waved for me to follow her out. "Let's meet them in Father's room."

Zav and Zondia in their human forms—no, wait, Zondia had altered her appearance slightly to add pointed elf ears—were already inside Eireth's room with the queen and the healer standing by.

Freysha and I slipped inside and stood out of the way, but everyone noticed us anyway. Perhaps because Zav strode to me and took my hand and kissed it.

Eireth looked at us, and I sheepishly hoped Zav wouldn't talk about sex. But he merely shifted to a handclasp and stood at my side. He looked at the new box I gripped in my other hand while Zondia walked to Eireth's bedside and closed her eyes.

"A gift from your sister?" Zav asked.

"Yes. A kit to make fairy rings. They're the trendy new thing, better than Chia Pets."

He considered me for a moment but must have decided he wasn't curious about Chia Pets. "You will enter the fae world as soon as you are able?"

"To take care of my sword problem, yes. I'll better be able to handle the assassin then."

"Assassin?" Zav asked.

Ah, right. He had missed that part.

"Silence for the concentration of Lady Zondia'qareshi," the healer ordered. The queen was glaring over at us as if we'd been speaking scandalously loudly. Apparently, healing ceremonies were like libraries.

I switched to telepathy to explain what I'd learned from my father. More reluctantly, I shared my conversation with Xilneth. I expected ire from Zav about him coming here while he was gone, even though I left out the mentions of nude frolicking.

Zav's eyes did indeed flare with inner light, but all he said about Xilneth was that he'd told the fop he was only to speak to *him* about me, not seek me out behind his back. It was the dragon who'd hired the assassin who incensed Zav.

That coward! I will challenge him to a duel and slay him for his conniving underhanded weaselly ways. No dragon would ever *hire an assassin from a lesser species.*

Except this one. I squeezed his hand and patted his arm, afraid the anger he was radiating would distract Zondia. Even I could feel the change to his aura, the fury crackling tangibly around him. Had this Mythrarion Silverclaw been in the room, Zav would have torn his head off without bothering with dragon-dueling protocol.

He will rue that choice, Zav said. *I swear it.*

Eireth sighed, a faint release, as Zondia's magic brought some lessening of pain. Zav straightened and turned to face the procedure, but his eyes were still glowing. The queen gave him a concerned look. The healer kept glancing at the door. Yup, everyone could feel him radiating that anger.

Did you learn who infected Eireth? I asked, in part because I wanted to know and in part to distract him. Maybe I shouldn't have shared the Silverclaw dragon's name. What if Zav insisted on dragging me off to confront him? I had to go back to Earth to check on Amber and Mom. If the assassin kidnapped them or hurt them because I'd disappeared...

I have no proof, no. Lord Quaresthee disappeared. According to the queen, he's been gone for three days. That is suspicious, but I cannot condemn him without more evidence than that. Sometimes, dragons go off to hunt and seek solitude on their own.

He wasn't bitten and scarred up before he left, was he?

Zav looked sharply at me. *One of my brothers* did *mention that he looked like he'd been in a fight recently. Why?*

I explained Xilneth's wounds, including the tail bite, though I admitted I hadn't seen them in person. He could have been showing me whatever he thought would win sympathy from me.

My brother mentioned a noticeable tail bite on Quaresthee. Mythrarion's signature torture move?

Zav scowled at the floor. *Quaresthee is older and was never known as a supreme combatant, so it is possible he could be bullied by a stronger dragon. And it is* highly *plausible that someone like Xilnethgarish could have been easily cowed with a few superficial injuries.*

I thought about pointing out that *anyone* might have been cowed by having half his tail bitten off, but I supposed that wasn't true. Zav had been gravely injured in battle many times in only the few months that I'd known him. It was unlikely that anyone could force him into action through torture.

When you saw Xilneth, I asked, *was he injured?*

Yes, he did have fresh wounds.

Huh, he'd been telling me the truth. At least about the injuries.

I must confront Mythrarion as soon as possible. Zav met my eyes. *You will come with me. It is not safe for you to return to your world without me.*

I'd been afraid he would feel that way. *I need to check on my family before I go anywhere else with you.* I showed him the assassin's token. *The bastard left one like this at my mother's house too. She might be in danger right now.*

If we stop Mythrarion, we can stop the assassin.

Do you know where Mythrarion is?

If Zav could open a portal on top of the dragon's house—cave—and the whole trip could be completed in twenty minutes, I wouldn't object to going with him.

But Zav hesitated. *No. Most of the Silverclaws have grown scarce since we uncovered their foul scheme and slew several. It will take time to find him.*

I need to go home first. I thought about pointing out that he wouldn't want me and my beacon of a sword flying on his back if he wanted to hunt down a dragon who didn't want to be found. We would never get anywhere close to Mythrarion if he could sense us coming from a thousand miles away.

Maybe I didn't need to say it. Zav's gaze drifted toward Chopper's hilt, as if he were thinking the same thing.

He frowned down at the floor again. I was surprised his glowing eyes didn't bore holes through the wood.

The sooner I find him and confront him, the sooner I can force him to call off his assassin, Zav reasoned. *If I take you back home, will you stay in your domicile that I have enhanced with protections? I believe even an elite elven assassin would hesitate to breach its borders now.* He reached out and took the token, and his eyes flared brighter, more with triumph than anger this time, I thought. *The assassin's essence remains on this. I can tune the traps to be even more effective against him.*

I don't mind staying at the house as long as I can have Mom stay with me. Maybe I can talk Amber into spending a couple of nights too. I could lure her down with the promise that she can use my laptop to shop online all night.

That would only work if it wasn't in the middle of the school week, so it was probably wishful thinking. I hoped the assassin didn't know she existed. An elf could have learned about Mom and her relationship with Eireth, but why would he think I had a daughter? Hopefully, he only knew me by the Ruin Bringer stories and wouldn't think a notorious dragon-slaying individual would have kids.

That is acceptable. All who stay in the house should be safe. The wards will protect against those who may seek the sword as well. Zav nodded. *I will worry about you, but that will give me more incentive to find Mythrarion and deal with him swiftly.*

I squeezed his hand again, touched to have him admit that he would worry. I didn't want to make him worry, but I didn't see a better solution. Since I didn't have any gigs from Willard right now, there was no reason I couldn't stay at the house. The whole time, I would feel guilty that he was out there fighting my battle for me, but I had only gotten involved in the dragon world because of him, so I wouldn't feel *too* guilty.

I'll worry about you too. Please be careful with this Silverclaw dragon. I smiled to lighten the mood. *Don't let him bite half your tail off. You would look funny.*

I am a superior warrior. My tail will not be in danger. He lifted his chin. *But even if I were horribly maimed, I would not look* funny. *Dragons are always magnificent, even battle-scarred dragons.*

What if the missing tail made you fly lopsidedly? I shared an image of him flying in wobbly circles like a drunken bird.

He squinted at me. *Are you* teasing *me?*
Maybe a little.
Have we not discussed that lesser species do not tease *dragons?*
We have discussed that, but if you really want to get married, you should know that human wives tease their husbands all *the time. It's a cultural imperative.*

That is because they are not married to dragons. *Dragons are not to be teased except by other dragons and then only clan members.*

If you say so. I squeezed his hand, but I also shared the image of him engaged in lopsided flying again. Maybe the thought would inspire him to be careful in battle with his enemy.

Human matings must be very strange.
You sure you still want to get married?
Yes. When I bring Mythrarion to you, battered and mauled, you will tease *him. And I will allow this.*
Considerate.
Yes.

CHAPTER 21

IT WAS AFTER NINE P.M. when Zav's portal returned me to the house's front yard. He didn't come with me; he was already heading off to hunt for the Silverclaw dragon who'd hired my assassin.

I couldn't help but look toward both streets in view from our corner lot and out toward Green Lake, the distant lights along the paved path glowing yellow, a few people out despite the later hour. They were joggers and walkers, not, as far as I could tell, assassins.

For the moment, I didn't have the feeling of being watched. Good. I'd been afraid I would find the guy staking out the house like movie cops hoping to break up a drug deal. Though an elven assassin probably wouldn't sit in an old Ford, sucking down coffee and crullers.

Dimitri's van was parked out front, and so was Mom's SUV. I hoped that meant they were both home and safe and hadn't been approached by trouble while I'd been in Elf Land. The eyes of the dragon topiaries glowed orange, promising they were on the job. And was that smoke wafting from their shrubby nostrils? Maybe they'd recently chased off a dog-walker who'd wandered too close.

Shaking my head, I tramped up the porch steps. Zoltan was in the basement and Dimitri the kitchen, but since Mom didn't have magical blood, I couldn't sense her. There weren't any messages with dire news on my phone, so that was reassuring.

My hand throbbed, reminding me of the cut. Before leaving, I'd asked Zondia to look at it. She'd said she would need to see the artifact that inflicted the wound to figure out how to deconstruct the fae spell and had rolled her eyes when I hadn't been able to pull it out of my pocket. At least it sounded like she *could* heal the wound. I would get the shard back from Zoltan so Zav could give it to his sister to study the next time they crossed paths.

I found Dimitri at the dining room table with a bunch of his tools, recycled junk, and something that looked like a giant door knocker in the shape of a T-Rex. He was manipulating metal wire to add length to the tail.

"We have to talk, Val," he said as soon as I walked in.

Assuming he didn't want to discuss our no-yard-art-projects-on-the-dining-room-table rule, I asked, "Is Mom here and okay?"

Dimitri set down his pliers. "That's what we have to talk about."

"She's not okay?" I was about to surge up the stairs to check the room we'd given her, but he spoke first.

"She threw out all of my *food*."

I paused. "What?"

"My Cheetos, my Hot Pockets, my frozen pizzas, my *Pop-Tarts*. *Val!*" He gave me the most anguished look I'd seen from him.

"Why would she do that? They weren't expired, were they?"

"She said they were junk and poisoning my organs. She replaced them with *weird* food." Dimitri stalked into the kitchen, flung open the pantry door, grabbed a box, and thrust it toward me.

"Vegan organic toaster pastries," I read.

"The first ingredient is *amaranth*. What the hell is amaranth?"

"A grain?"

"The next ingredient is tigernut flour. Tiger nuts, Val! Sindari will be outraged."

"I'm sure you'll survive eating some healthier alternatives to your usual swill. If you don't mind, I have more pressing matters on my mind. Do you want to help me plant mushrooms later?"

He lowered the box and glared at me. "She got rid of your frozen burritos too."

"I'll talk to her."

"*Good.*" He put the box away, almost flinging it back in the pantry as if it were plague-ridden. "And you don't plant mushrooms. You prepare a substrate and then inoculate it with a spore syringe."

"I don't think we're talking about the same kinds of mushrooms, but you can help me if you want to lend your expertise."

"I need to finish my prototype." He waved to the table.

"I'll buy you a cart of groceries." I headed for the stairs, so I could check on Mom, though it sounded like she was not only fine but was also bored.

"From Costco? Not the hippie store?"

"Whatever you want." I shouldn't have said that; the Costco shopping carts were ridiculously large. And Mom would be affronted if her tigernut toaster pastries were replaced with a 64-pack of Pop-Tarts.

"I'll help," Dimitri said.

"Thanks. Meet me in the front yard in twenty minutes. The soil is loamiest up there."

"I wasn't going to ask."

I knocked on my mother's door, waited for her invitation, and found her inside reading in bed, with Rocket stretched out across the bottom. She was using him for a footrest, and he didn't seem to mind. Mom wore a floral flannel nightgown that extended to her ankles and looked like it had stepped out of the fifties.

"Don't let Amber see that." I waved to the garment. "She'll insist on taking you shopping."

Rocket opened his eyes without lifting his head and flapped his tail on the comforter, either acknowledging my presence or agreeing that the nightgown was dreadful.

"Is it not the trendiest fashion?" Mom asked.

"I don't think that qualifies as a fashion at all."

"*You're* judging my fashion tastes?" She looked me up and down from duster to jeans to combat boots.

"Strange, isn't it?"

"Yes."

"You doing okay?"

"I am, but where have you been?"

I hesitated. "The elven home world. I wanted to get some information about the tokens and thought they might know."

"You traveled there?" Her eyes grew hungry and wistful. "Did you see… anyone you know?"

"Yeah. Freysha, of course. And Eireth. He was sick—poisoned by a dragon, apparently—and Zav's sister was able to heal him."

Her gray eyebrows rose. "He's all right now?"

"I think so. Freysha is staying there with him while he recovers. And, ah, the rest of his family."

"His wife." She didn't sound pissed. The opposite. Flat and devoid of emotion.

"Yeah. She's a pill, if it helps. Freysha mentioned that it was an arranged marriage and that she was bummed because they—her parents—never seemed to fall in love with each other."

"Ah. You don't have to tell me the details. Or try to make me feel better. It was… a long time ago." She gazed toward one of the wainscoted walls.

"I know, but I'm sorry you didn't get to have your happily-ever-after."

"Few people do. I had a wonderful summer that year, and I have my memories. And you, of course." Now, she sounded like she was on the verge of tears.

Damn it, maybe I should have lied about where I'd been. I sat on the edge of her bed and clumsily put an arm around her shoulders. We'd so rarely hugged when I'd been growing up—it didn't seem to be in our DNA—and I wasn't sure if this was the right action now.

"Your gun is poking me in the ribs," she said.

"Sorry." I drew back.

"Thank you." She smiled at me, and I thought she meant for more than moving Fezzik.

"Has anything weird happened while I've been gone?"

"Dimitri had a hissy fit because I threw out his junk food."

"That's not weird, Mom. That's a normal reaction to losing a hundred dollars' worth of food."

Her nose wrinkled. "That wasn't *food*."

"I'm not sure amaranth and tigernuts count as food either."

"They're high in protein and fiber."

"Dimitri's not even twenty-five yet. I don't think he cares about his fiber intake."

"His colon will thank me later."

"Gross." I stood up and headed for the door. "Let me know if you see anyone strange skulking around the house."

Her eyes narrowed. "What did you find out about the tokens?"

If she hadn't asked, I wouldn't have told her, since I didn't want her to worry. She was already upset from learning that Eireth had been ill. But maybe the information would convince her of the importance of staying in the house. I explained what I'd learned and also filled her in on the problem with my sword.

"Zav is trying to find the Silverclaw dragon who hired the assassin, and he wants me to stay hunkered down here until he's done. We're hoping the assassin can be un-hired before he succeeds at killing me." Inadvertently, I glanced toward her window. She hadn't pulled the curtains, and I half-expected to spot my stalker out there hanging from the tree branches. "Have you heard from Amber?"

"Since you informed me that she has no wish to hike with me?"

"Yeah."

That had been another awkward conversation I'd wished partway through that I'd made Amber have with Mom herself.

"She invited me for Sunday-night dinner at their house," Mom said. "I said yes, but that was before I knew about the assassin."

"That will be resolved by then." I tried to sound confident. And I was. I had faith in Zav. "Hopefully, before she's in any danger."

Mom looked sharply at me. "You think the assassin knows about her?"

"I hope not. But I haven't… avoided her—avoided all of you—the way I used to, so it would be easier for him to find out."

I still didn't know why he'd left a coin where Mom could find it but hadn't harmed her. Just to make a statement to me? I hoped he showed up, so I could make a statement to him. If not with my sword, then at least with my middle finger.

CHAPTER 22

"ARE YOU SURE YOU'RE SUPPOSED to *bury* them?" Dimitri asked from his knees in the grass.

We'd cleared a ring of little spots for the mushroom plugs.

"That's what she said. We stick the plugs in the ground and then sprinkle them with the magic dirt." I snorted at how silly that sounded, but Dimitri had seen the box—and presumably sensed the magic of the dirt inside—so he didn't tease me about it.

"And it's best that we do this in the dark?" He shined his phone's flashlight over the ground.

"I don't think that was a requirement, but Freysha said they needed to settle in overnight. Maybe they sprout by moonlight." I eyed the cloudy sky and hoped a moon wasn't required.

"I've grown mushrooms before. They usually take more than one night to grow."

"These are magic mushrooms."

Dimitri quirked an eyebrow in my direction. Right, why had I been thinking he'd been growing shiitakes?

"*Real* magic mushrooms. I'm going to use my elite elven powers to make them sprout."

"Really? Can I watch?"

"No."

"Because it's sacred and you have to have snooty elf blood to attend the ceremony?"

"No, because I'm sure I'll screw up a bunch, and it'll take twenty tries." I shook my head, remembering the meager roots I'd conjured.

"Well, I knew *that*."

"Given the mess on the dining room table, I don't think you get to tease me about my abilities to create things." I dug out another little hole, stuck a plug in, and sprinkled the elven dirt over it.

"The mess is going to be fabulous, and everybody's going to buy one."

"A T-Rex door knocker?"

"A *dragon* door knocker." He scowled at me and opened his mouth to say more, but a *thwump* sounded, followed by the shriek of an animal.

I sprang to my feet as orange light blazed out by the sidewalk. No, not light. *Fire*. The topiary's eyes were glowing brightly as a gout of flame shot out of its mouth, angling down to bathe the cement. A raccoon scampered off across the street at top speed.

"I'm going to have to talk to Zav about the sensitivity settings," I muttered.

"I came back to the house for lunch today, and that thing was going off the whole hour. Kids were leaping in, activating it, and jumping back while their buddies took pictures of them."

"It's a good thing there's not a homeowners' association here." I wondered if the police would show up at some point.

Zav had promised that only magical intruders would be attacked in force and not by the topiaries. The real defenses were more deftly hidden. The topiaries were supposed to be for warning purposes only and shouldn't torch anyone. I was fairly certain the raccoon had been scared but not scorched.

"For so many reasons," Dimitri said. "But, believe it or not, they inspired me."

"Our new dragon bushes?"

"Yeah. That's why I'm making a version out of recycled metal."

"Will yours spout fire?"

"If I can make it do so without a propane tank. Inga said she would show me a way to enchant it. They won't be real flames, but that's probably better for legal ramifications."

"If you're planning to sell them, yes." I glanced at him, wondering if he'd done that survey of our clientele. "Did you ask anyone if they wanted one?"

"Yes." He looked glumly at me. "I surveyed people, the way you suggested. Handed them coffees and asked them what they would actually buy. The answers were varied and odd, but everyone either wanted something made for their race—it's hard for ogres to find vegetable peelers that fit their hands—or defensive systems. There are rumors that the city has gotten more dangerous of late, what with dragons flying around and vampires murdering people."

"We put a stop to those things. Well, I guess Zav is still flying around." I wondered if someone with magical blood and the ability to see him had noticed him fishing in Lake Union and sunning himself on the tanks at Gas Works the other day.

"Yes. The number one request, after size-appropriate kitchen gadgets, was a dragon deterrent. At that point, Gondo hopped up on one of the tables and described our topiaries in great detail. This changed into everyone jumping up and down and agreeing that their dragon deterrents should *look* like dragons and breathe fire out of their snouts."

"Why so glum? You like building stuff like that."

"Sure, I don't mind making one. Or even a couple, but..." His shoulders slumped. "Val, I took orders for twenty-eight today. And that was just from the people at the coffee shop that minute."

"That's good news, not bad news. You seem confused on entrepreneurship. I'll have Nin talk to you."

"I know it's good to have orders, but they're all going to be of the *same thing*. Val, I'm an artist, not an assembly line. Even worse, some people ordered them in different colors. A troll girl wants a pink dragon."

"They could exist. You've seen Zav's lilac sister. Though I understand that's not her natural scale color."

"A pink dragon would be garish and unnatural. Dragons are sea blue or forest green or *sable*."

"Oh, don't start that again. If you show me what to do, *I'll* come in and make the pink one as soon as I get this assassin off my back and my sword sorted out. At the least, I can hold your glue gun for you."

"I don't use glue." His glum expression turned to an affronted one. "I'm not an amateur."

A faint pinging came from the roof, one of Zav's alarms sounding. The air twenty feet above the house shimmered, revealing the protective dome of energy he'd installed over the property.

High above, a dark winged shape soared past the house. By night, it was hard to identify the species—all my senses told me was that it was magical—but it was the size of a man. Another roc or maybe a wyvern. Beady eyes glared down at me.

The bird continued past, disappearing behind tall evergreens rising up from a neighbor's yard. I sensed more of them out there, at least three others.

"Is it safe to leave the grounds and go to work in the morning?" Dimitri asked.

"For you, probably. I'm on house arrest until Zav gets back to protect me." I grimaced, hating that I had to hide behind his tail, but these were extenuating circumstances.

"Does that mean you're not going to visit the fae if you get the ring to work?"

"I'd be foolish to visit them by myself, given how much trouble two of them gave me and Sindari the other day."

Dimitri arched his eyebrows, as if to say that hadn't answered his question.

"I don't have a working key yet." Which was a good thing. Otherwise, I might have been tempted to try to deal with my sword without Zav's help. But for now, that wasn't an option. "All we're making is the doorway."

The side gate creaked open, and I sensed Zoltan heading our way. He hardly ever left the basement. Was he on the way out to find a vein to perforate?

"Greetings, dear robber and dear associate. Are you engaged in midnight gardening?"

"Yeah." I scooted dirt over the last of the plugs and the magical doohickey I'd buried in the middle, then stood up and wiped off my hands. "October is the season for that, isn't it?"

"I believe it's appropriate in any season when you need to bury your treasures."

"Treasures? I'm planting mushrooms plugs."

He stepped out of the shadows by the rhododendrons. "Midnight gardening is a term used to describe burying one's precious metals and other valuables so they won't be discovered in the house, should a burglar—or the government—intrude. It was not uncommon in my homeland before the war."

World War Two? Or One? Despite his Hungarian accent and vampire status, I sometimes forgot he'd been around a lot longer than the rest of us.

"Didn't they have banks and safe deposit boxes back then?" Dimitri asked.

"A service you have to pay for, and what happens if the government confiscates your gold? The yard is much safer, providing you remember where you buried your goods. And don't die without telling your family. That happened more often than you'd think."

"Actually, I'd expect that to happen *all* the time." My phone buzzed, and I dug it out of my pocket. "There's a reason metal detectors were invented."

"Perhaps so," Zoltan said. "I am off on an errand, providing it is safe. Menacing magical creatures have been circling the house since you returned."

"I know. Sorry if they inconvenience your feeding schedule." I answered the phone. "Hey, Nin."

"Good evening, Val. I hope it is not too late to call."

Zoltan lifted a hand toward Dimitri, then headed out of the yard, not denying that feeding was indeed on his mind. Better someone else's neck than mine, I supposed, though I wished he were like those special fantasy-novel vampires who could subsist on rats.

"It's never too late for you," I told Nin. "Do you have good news?"

"News? I am running a buy-three-get-one-free special at my food truck. It has kept me very busy."

"Isn't it usually buy-one-get-one-free?" I should have been more specific about what news I was interested in.

"That would cause me to lose money. Right now, if you bring three paying friends, you get a free meal. It is a popular deal with construction workers in the area."

"Does your busyness mean you haven't made any progress with the key?"

"It does not. I spoke with my grandfather, and he instructed me in fairy rings and fae magic. I am not able to precisely replicate fae magic, but I believe I have been able to use gnomish magic to do something similar. Do you wish me to go to a fairy ring with you to try it?"

"I'm on house arrest." I eyed my recently planted mushrooms. "But I'm trying to grow a fairy ring here. Freysha made me a kit."

"How long will that take?"

"Overnight, I hope."

"That kit sounds virile."

"Elves are good at growing things."

"I will bring the key in the morning on the way to work."

She lived in Queen Anne, and her food truck was in Pioneer Square. Our place wasn't even remotely on the way.

"Are you sure you don't want me to come by and get it?" I would risk leaving the protection of Zav's defenses to get one step closer to solving my sword problem.

"I will bring it in the morning. Goodnight, Val."

I put the phone away, ignoring another large magical bird flying overhead—the fact that they weren't testing the boundaries suggested Zav's magic was effective and would keep them out.

"I'm getting the key tomorrow," I told Dimitri. "What are the odds that these mushrooms really will grow overnight?" I was prepared to try my magic but figured they needed to settle in first. And possibly for a miracle to happen.

Dimitri was gazing toward the side yard and didn't respond.

I poked him in the shoulder.

"What?"

I repeated my question.

"Oh. Better odds if you water them, I'm guessing." He pointed toward the gate. "Do you think Zoltan has buried treasures in the backyard?"

"If he has, I don't want to know about it. A vampire alchemist is more likely to bury disgusting ingredients than gold, I think. Remember his old lab? He had all those organs and fetuses in jars of formaldehyde on the shelves. You better be careful with any more landscaping projects you take on."

"No kidding." He shuddered and went back into the house.

I started for the garden hose but paused, a thought occurring to me. If this worked and I *did* get an opportunity to visit the fae world, what could I offer to trade them for fixing my sword? If they blamed Zav and me for the deaths of the two fae guys who'd come virgin hunting, they wouldn't want to deal with me. *We* hadn't been responsible for the deaths, but I had tricked the males into coming to Earth. Would the fae shoot me on sight for that? Or was there something I could offer them that would entice them to deal?

Virgins were off the table. What else did they like?

I dug out my phone again and called Willard.

"Thorvald," she answered in a groggy voice, "I love it when you call me at midnight."

"I know you do. I waited until the appropriate hour."

"Is the city burning down?"

"Not that I know of. I have a question for you."

"Do I have to get out of bed and turn on the light for it?"

"It may involve some research unless you're already an expert on fae."

Going by her sigh, she wanted to hang up and stuff her head back under the pillow. That made me regret calling this late. I'd just assumed everyone spent their Friday nights midnight gardening.

"You can get back to me in the morning with an answer," I offered.

"Your generosity gives me warm fuzzies. What's the question?"

"What are the fae into? Like something I could find here on Earth to trade them. Something they can't easily get and would really like. I want to entice them to fix my sword and preferably not kill me."

"What are they into? Sins and vices, by all accounts."

"So I should offer them what? A hooker and a slot machine?"

"If you have those things in your house, I'm going to be concerned."

"I don't, and I doubt I can acquire them. I'm stuck at home, waiting for Zav."

Willard yawned. "I don't know what specific sins and vices they like. The other races just say the fae are hedonistic. You could offer to have sex with them."

"I'm sure Zav would agree to that."

"Zav is your only objection to having sex with strangers from another species?"

"Well, the ones that came out of the fairy ring weren't bad looking." I remembered them blown to bits, and my mood for humor disappeared. I went through the seven deadly sins in my mind, though the fae probably didn't know about Christianity or take cues from its teachings. "Are they into gluttony? I could bring them some of Zav's smoked ribs."

"I don't know, Thorvald. You figure it out while I sleep." Willard hung up.

She was a much better brainstorming partner during daylight hours.

After putting away my phone, I grabbed the hose and sprayed water over my future fairy ring. It had been raining most of the day and would rain again that night, so it seemed redundant, but one never knew. I attempted to channel some of my magic into the earth to will the plugs to grow, but Freysha hadn't taught me how to germinate mushrooms, so it was wishful thinking that it did anything.

As I put away the hose, the sense of being watched came over me. It wasn't a bird this time.

I picked out a cloaked and hooded form in the shadows between arbor vitae in the yard of the house kitty-corner to ours. The hilts of not one but two swords poked up over his shoulders. I couldn't sense him—and I could barely see him—but I knew without a doubt that it was the elven assassin.

It hadn't taken him long to figure out I was back on Earth. Had he come to check out the house's defenses?

His head tilted back as he gazed toward the roof—or maybe Zav's barrier up there. A few more big birds flapped past, making it visible against the night sky again. What birds wanted with a magical sword, I couldn't even guess, but the rocs at the bog had made it clear that they would swipe Chopper if they could. Or maybe the assassin had orchestrated that, the same way he had the attack of the crucible beasts.

Would he fight me if I charged across the street to him?

I was positive he would. Only the certainty that he would kick my ass kept me from striding out to settle things with him. It grated on me to hide, but what choice did I have? I was in this predicament because of dragons, and it was better to let dragons get me out of it. Zav would fix things. I knew he would.

I gave the assassin the middle finger, hoping the gesture translated sufficiently.

He didn't start or give any indication that he was surprised that I'd spotted him. Maybe he'd expected me to. Instead, he lifted his arm, not to return the middle finger but to offer what looked more like a salute. Then he bowed and stepped back, seeming to melt into the bushes and disappear.

"Guess that means Zav hasn't found the asshole who hired him yet." I sighed, turned off the water, went inside, and crossed my fingers that the defenses around the property were as powerful as Zav believed.

CHAPTER 23

MORNING FOUND ME HOLDING NOT a glue gun but a soldering iron and pliers for Dimitri as he worked on his project. It still looked more like a T-Rex than a dragon, but he promised that would change once he had the wings on.

I didn't mind the distraction. Since I'd woken up, my hand had been hurting more than ever. I'd changed the bandage, grimacing when I'd found the skin all around it turning an unhealthy greenish blue. The infection—or fae taint—was creeping up toward my wrist now. What if this turned into the magical equivalent of gangrene and I lost my arm?

"Breakfast will be ready soon." In the kitchen, Mom was making oatmeal, which Dimitri and I would be stuck eating, since she'd gotten rid of the frozen breakfast burritos. I needed this assassin out of my hair, so she could go back to her home, and we could stock up on the necessities again here.

My phone beeped with a text from Nin saying she was on the way. I'd already checked outside to make sure the assassin wasn't lurking about, but it was raining hard enough to deter even supernatural visitors. It was also raining hard enough that I hadn't been willing to spend much time trying to use the root magic to coax mushrooms out of the ground. I'd also spent a half hour willing them to grow right at dawn, but my magic was either too weak, or it had to be done from the lawn and not from a lawn-adjacent position on the covered porch. Later, I would give it another shot.

When I opened the door for Nin, she hurried up the steps onto the porch and shook off her umbrella and her jacket before stepping inside. Despite the weather, she wore a big grin as she flourished the key.

"Proud of your accomplishment?"

"Yes, but that is not why I am smiling. Thad got me a RiceMaster 57155. It is fabulous. Do you want to see it? It is in my car."

"I'll take your word for its fabulousness." I was far more interested in the key. As soon as I accepted it, I could tell its magical aura had changed.

"It is very nice. I will put it to use today."

"I'm glad he got you something functional."

"Yes. Function is more important than frivolousness."

"I have a feeling you've flummoxed a lot of guys you've dated." Not that I disagreed with her. I much preferred my magical charms that protected me in battle to purely decorative jewelry. Though I wouldn't have minded if the charm that protected me from mind manipulation were aesthetically pleasing. Instead, the goblin-made doohickey had been crafted from recycled junk and what looked suspiciously like used chewing gum.

"I do not know why. I am a simple woman."

I set the key on a stack of boxes of apple-cider caramels I'd brought down from my bedroom. They were the most sinful things in the house—especially after Mom had cleared out the pantry of Dimitri's stuff—and since it was fall, I could always get more if my idea worked.

"Are you going to start selling chocolates at the shop?" Nin asked.

"No, those are to bribe gluttonous fae."

That earned me a puzzled look.

"Willard says they're into sin and vice. Chocolate-covered caramels are sinful."

The puzzled look turned skeptical.

"I didn't have any hookers or slot machines." I shrugged, feeling silly. The chocolates were good—and expensive by my food-purchasing standards—but they would probably work better to bribe a goblin than fae royalty. Oh, well. If nothing else, I would have rations for my trip to Fae Land.

"Breakfast is ready," Mom called from the kitchen, followed by mutterings about how Dimitri needed to move his junk off the table.

"Do you want to stay for oatmeal?" I waved to the rain pouring down outside the window. "I doubt you'll have a lot of early arrivals standing in line at your food truck today."

"You would be surprised. Seattle foodies venture out in any weather for quality beef and rice. But I can stay for a few minutes. I left early since I had to drive down from Edmonds." Her smile threatened to come back.

"Ah. Rewarded him for his thoughtful gift, did you?"

"He gave me the gift afterward."

I envisioned Thad pulling a rice cooker with a red bow around it out from under the bed, then decided to put my imagination away. "I hope it serves you well."

"Yes." Nin hefted a hiking backpack that she'd taken out of the car. "I also brought you a fresh batch of my specialty magical grenades. I assumed you would need them if you use that key. My grandfather warned me that the fae do not like visitors from other worlds."

"They sound anti-social."

"Yes. We will not invite them to the coffee shop."

"You don't think they want one of Dimitri's dragon door knockers?" I'd toyed with taking one of those along with the chocolates, but he still hadn't finished the prototype.

"Door knockers?"

"Door knockers that shoot flames. He surveyed our coffee-shop clientele and that's the kind of *yard art* they would buy. If you knock and don't know the password, you're a flambé."

Nin frowned. "That device does not sound legal."

"It's what our customers want."

"There could be repercussions for selling something that harms people."

"You sell magical guns and ammunition."

"That is true, but guns are legal."

"Then fire-throwing door knockers must be too. You can't fault my logic, Nin."

"I… am not certain you should be allowed to attend business meetings anymore."

"You say that like it would be a punishment to me. If it helps, the police are never going to visit troll and ogre caves anyway." I clapped her on the shoulder and led her toward the smell of warm brown sugar and oatmeal.

"How does one affix a door knocker to a cave?" Nin wondered.

"I'm going to include an optional staking system," Dimitri said.

He and Mom were in the dining room with a pot of oatmeal—she'd cooked it on the stovetop instead of in the microwave. Maybe organic, all-natural oats couldn't be zapped with radiation. I stuck a finger in the bowl set for me for a sample. She'd mixed in raisins, apple chunks, and brown sugar, so it smelled and tasted better than I expected. It might even be up to my frozen-burrito standards.

"Thanks for making breakfast, Mom." I grinned at her as we sat down—Dimitri's project was off to one side of the table, the tools piled out of the way. "Just like old times, eh?"

Except when I'd been a kid, she'd made most of our meals over a campfire or the portable burner in the converted school bus we'd lived in. I trusted our recently remodeled kitchen was better for food preparation than that.

"Similar, but you didn't thank me then. You complained and then ran outside to play with your imaginary friends."

This made Dimitri and Nin smirk.

"I was an only child," I explained. "And we lived in the boonies. It was either imaginary friends or squirrels."

The doorbell rang. Since I wasn't expecting anyone, I grabbed my weapons on the way to answer it.

The elven assassin had been cocky enough to salute me from across the street; he might stroll up and ring the doorbell.

But Amber was the one standing there, wet and miserable in a thin hoodie, her arms folded across her chest. Rain poured off the overflowing gutters to the side of her.

She wore a backpack and had the weapons belt that Willard had loaned her, complete with magical short sword in the scabbard. If I wasn't certain she had a swim meet the following weekend and a math test on Monday, I would have guessed she was running away from home.

"Are you okay?" I looked toward the street, expecting Thad's BMW, but I didn't recognize the car driving off.

"I had a fight with Dad, and Jamie and Myung-sook aren't home this weekend. Can I stay here for a while?"

"Uh, sure." I waved her inside, though as soon as I did, I realized what the fight had likely been about, given how rarely Thad lost his temper or poked hornets' nests.

Nin peered through the doorway from the dining room.

Amber froze, her back going stiffer than a sword.

"Never mind." She spun and tried to stalk out again.

I caught her arm. "She won't be here long. We can talk if you want."

Amber jerked her arm away. "I don't want to talk about anything."

I was debating between letting her go and tying her to the couch when the hair rose on the back of my neck. I spun, expecting to see the assassin lurking again. But if he was there, he wasn't showing himself today.

"Let me out, Val. I don't want to stay here."

Shaking my head, I gripped her arm and blocked the doorway.

Wind swept through, battering the wet trees between the houses, and I sensed magic being used. It whispered all around the house, almost a tangible thing. It felt like a probe testing the boundaries.

"We've got trouble. You guys stay inside." I drew Chopper, stepped onto the porch, and closed the door firmly behind me.

Wind whipped at my braid as I descended to the yard. Though I thought—*hoped*—I was safe inside Zav's defenses, I touched the feline charm on my thong.

"Need some help, Sindari," I whispered to summon him.

The sky was gray overhead, almost black, but the rain lessened as the wind swirled around the yard, tearing leaves from the trees. Not a soul was visible on the street or even farther down at the park. Green Lake was always busy with people jogging or walking along the path, rain or shine, so that made me feel like I'd stepped into an alternate reality.

The sensation of being watched returned, though I couldn't pinpoint the location of the assassin this time. Rain kept pattering down onto the street even though it had stopped in the yard. I eyed the trees to either side of our grassy lawn. He could be anywhere just beyond Zav's border.

The patch of grass where we'd planted the plugs caught my eye. The mushrooms had sprouted. I swore they hadn't been there an hour ago when I'd been trying to use the root magic, but now, they rose higher than the grass, their gray caps stretching three or four inches wide.

We are going to battle the assassin? Sindari asked after he formed at my side.

I wrenched my attention back to surveying the area. The fairy ring could wait. "I'm not sure. In theory, he shouldn't be able to reach us in here."

I glanced over my shoulder to make sure Amber had obeyed my order.

She and Nin had opened the front door and were poking their heads out, six-foot-tall Amber above Nin. I scowled fiercely and waved for them to shut the door. They complied, only to press their noses against the window.

The assassin approaches, Sindari stated.

I whirled back to face the street.

Wearing the same dark cloak and hood as the night before, the assassin strode toward our corner, two long swords drawn. If he was equally talented with both hands, a sword fight with him would be a royal pain in the ass. Not to mention the mage powers he had.

I drew Fezzik and pointed it at his chest.

His face was still in shadow, the gray sky keeping the daylight from more than hinting at angular elven features, but when he reached our sidewalk, he shook his head. The hood fell back, revealing short blond hair shorn close to his skull—it made his pointed ears extremely prominent. His face was cold and stern as his blue eyes met mine. Had he been human, he would have been about thirty, but from what my father had said, he had to be closer to three hundred.

"Are we going to do more than make rude gestures at each other this time?" I kept my pistol pointed at his chest, though I doubted any bullets would reach him if I fired.

Magic emanated not only from his swords but from his body, as if he wore some armor under his brown and green clothing.

Are you ready for a fight if we can't escape it, Sindari?

Of course. I will attempt to circle him and spring onto his back.

"I am Varlesh Sarrlevi, traveler, mage, warrior, and accomplished assassin on more than twelve worlds," he called in accented English. "Come forth and face me in battle. When I slay you, I will tell your enemies and he who hired me that you died bravely."

"That'll be a dream come true," I muttered, then raised my voice to say, "I don't care what you tell Mythrarion Silverclaw about me, but I hope you told him he was a sniveling coward for hiring a famous elf assassin to come after me, a mere half-elf."

"I did tell him that," Sarrlevi surprised me by saying. "But I took the job anyway. It is not often anymore that I get to pit myself against a slayer of dragons. I look forward to besting you in battle."

"What a pill." I fired.

As I feared, my bullet bounced off his chest. Damn it, I didn't want to enter into a sword fight with this guy.

His eyebrow twitched—funny since he hadn't reacted at all to the bullet ricocheting off his chest. "Noble warriors face off with blades."

"Thanks for the tip." *I hope you bite him in the ass, Sindari.*

I shall endeavor to do so. He looked up at me. *Will we go out from this protection to face him?*

Do you think I can win? I was tempted, but Zav would kick my butt if I died doing something stupid. Of course, I'd be dead, so the butt kicking probably wouldn't hurt.

Alone? No. But you have me.

"Do you fear me, Ruin Bringer?" Sarrlevi called.

"The name is Val, and you've had three hundred years longer than I have to practice with swords, so I might be a touch wary."

"I thought your dragon blade and experience slaying dragons would make you too formidable a foe, but perhaps I overestimated you."

"Are you the one who planted that artifact and messed up my sword?" I asked, hoping Zav would show up if I kept Sarrlevi chatting for long enough, and tell the assassin he was off the job. "Because you were afraid to face me with it?"

"You have many allies, considering you are an assassin yourself. How did you find such a powerful sword?"

"It was a Blue Light Special at Kmart. You *were* the one to sabotage it, weren't you?"

"The fae owed me a favor. It is logical to use all the tools at one's disposal to even the odds before entering battle."

"No kidding." I jammed Fezzik into my thigh holster since there was no point in shooting him again.

"The dragon is gone. Your elven sister is gone."

I squinted at him. "Are you responsible for my father being poisoned?"

Had he wanted to get rid of Freysha because she was an ally who might help me? I could understand not wanting to run into me with Zav at my side, but was Freysha truly worth worrying about for someone like this?

"Fair battles are fought one on one."

Was that a *yes*?

His gaze shifted to Sindari. I glared at him. He had better not have a way to send him back to his realm. I couldn't lose him for *another* fight.

Sindari crouched, as if to spring across the barrier to attack Sarrlevi before he could do so.

The assassin tilted his head back and lifted his swords to the sky. Wind swirled around him, tugging at his damp coat. It battered at my side and whipped my braid around. There was nothing natural about it. The amount of magic emanating from the elf intensified, his aura growing brighter, as if he were building up to an explosion. An explosion of power?

The air hummed with electricity. Concern swept through me.

I believe he is attacking Lord Zavryd's protections, Sindari warned.

That's what I'm afraid of.

Dimitri, I spoke telepathically to him. *Get my mom and Amber and Nin, and go out the back door, please. Take them to the shop. Or anywhere. Just not here.*

Are you going to fight that guy? He was standing at the living room window and looking out at us now too.

I might not have a choice. Just get them out of here.

The air shivered, and power twanged at my senses like a tuning fork. With a great ripping sound, the topiary dragons were torn from the ground. Their eyes glowed and they spat fire, but that didn't keep them from flying over parked cars to land in the street.

More power assailed the barrier protecting the property. The assassin's eyes were closed. Hoping he was distracted, I drew Fezzik and fired again. But even if he *was* distracted, his armor protected him. The bastard wasn't even concerned enough to open his eyes.

I fired at one of those closed eyes. The bullet ricocheted off an invisible barrier instead of hitting him and whizzed up to the roof, blasting a brick off the chimney.

"No more shooting," I muttered.

In the house behind me, I sensed Dimitri leaving the window, hopefully guiding my mother and the others out the back door. The assassin should be focused on me, but he might tear the house apart with his power.

I will attack now. Sindari sprinted toward the elf.

As soon as I started after him, magical explosions battered at my senses from above and all around. The defenses were down.

Sarrlevi pointed a sword at Sindari as he sprang. A blast of magic came from it like a lightning bolt. Sindari twisted in the air, but it still caught him. With a burst of light, he disappeared from my senses—and this realm.

Swearing, I stopped a few feet away from the elf. I'd hoped to attack him while Sindari distracted him.

"Now," he said, pointing his sword at me. "We will battle one on one and see who the greater assassin is."

CHAPTER 24

SARRLEVI RUSHED ME SO QUICKLY, his twin swords slashing toward either side of my neck, that he almost caught me in the first second of our battle.

I sprang to the side, dodging one blade and deflecting the other. He spun after me, turning slashes to thrusts, metal screeching over the wind and rain as our swords met.

Right away, I knew I was outmatched. He had unearthly speed, and I could barely track his movements. When Chopper successfully parried, it was far more luck and reflexes than conscious thought, and in the opening seconds, he nicked me twice as he drove me back.

I scrambled between two parked cars, wanting to put space between us to buy time to think, to come up with an attack—or even a better defense—that might save me.

But he charged relentlessly after me, leaping as if off a trampoline. He flew over my Jeep to land next to me in the street. Before he even touched down, he was attacking me again.

I willed my magic to aid me, to make my speed as great as his, and maybe it helped a smidgen, but not enough to matter. His two swords seemed like two dozen, slashing toward my face, then my torso, then my leg, then all of my body at once.

As fast as I scrambled back, he was faster, and through it all, I sensed that he was testing me, that he hadn't committed himself fully yet. His eyes were narrowed as he launched blow after blow, watching my reactions. Somehow, I sensed that he couldn't quite believe that I wasn't better than this. Did he think I was luring him into complacency and that I would turn on the thrusters and kick his ass as soon as he grew less vigilant? If only.

I backed around the cars again, almost catching my heel on the curb, and scrambled back to the sidewalk. Were any of Zav's defenses left, or had Sarrlevi nullified them all? Too bad he'd taken the bushes out first—I would have loved luring him in to be torched.

A wave of power washed over me, willing me to drop Chopper and surrender the blade. Though the assassin spoke no words into my mind, he conveyed that he would make my death swift once I dropped it. He really wanted Chopper out of my hands.

Why? Did he think Chopper would summon some massive power that would roast him alive and save me? If it could do that, I sure wished I knew how to make it happen.

My mind-manipulation charm allowed me to resist the urge to surrender—barely. Glowering, I willed *him* to surrender, to toss his blades down and give up.

My mental magic was amateur, but maybe my desperation would lend it strength. Unfortunately, there seemed to be a steel vault around his mind. Freysha had taught me to create barriers with fern fronds. This guy created barriers with impervious metal alloys.

Sarrlevi's eyes narrowed further as he pressed me back yet again. I struggled to keep up with his pace, to keep my breathing steady.

Usually, my training kept me fit, and I could go a long time before gasping for air, but usually, I didn't have to whip my blade around at insane speeds to keep from being skewered.

He seemed to realize that I wasn't luring him in or faking anything. A glint of triumph lit in his blue elven eyes, and he picked up his already impossible pace, swords blurring as they struck in a never-ending flurry of blows.

Hot sweat streamed down the sides of my face. I tried again to summon my magic, to block him with arcane power as my ability to block him with my sword faded. But his stronger magic poured from him, batting my feeble efforts aside.

Before, I'd had luck using my magic to drill through the defenses of my foes, even dragons, long enough to strike, but even if I could somehow get past his magic, I couldn't get past his blades. I hadn't yet managed to launch an attack of my own. All I could do was defend as he pursued me with the tireless energy of a machine.

Fresh power swelled from the yard behind me. Another attack on Zav's defenses? Some monster the assassin was summoning to spring at my back? It wasn't as if he needed the help.

"Val!" came Nin's voice from behind me.

I swore. Why hadn't she gone with Dimitri?

Though taking my eyes from my foe could be suicidal, I couldn't help but glance back—and groan. Nin stood in front of the fairy ring, a green shimmering doorway visible inside the mushroom borders. She brandished a grenade in one hand and the key in the other. Amber was at her side with her short sword at the ready, her eyes fierce, as if she meant to spring in and help me.

"Get out of here!" I yelled at them as I parried a barrage of fresh blows and retreated from the sidewalk and into the yard.

"Enter the doorway," Nin called. "I will lock it after you so he cannot come in."

Amber grabbed one of the grenades from her pack. "Get down, Val!"

She hefted it to throw right at us.

I wanted to object, but there was no time. I blocked a swipe that would have taken my head off, then turned, ran across the grass, and sprinted for them as the grenade sailed over my head toward the elf.

My only thought was to knock Nin and Amber to the ground so they wouldn't be hurt in the explosion, but Amber sprang through the doorway. Nin waved the key and pointed for me to follow.

"You can't stay here," I yelled. "He'll kill you!"

The grenade went off with a shuddering boom that threw Nin and me toward the doorway. Just before I passed through, I glanced back and saw the elf fly backward. He hit the sidewalk and rolled toward the street.

The fae doorway enveloped me before I could tell if he got up. I spun through interdimensional space and lost all awareness.

CHAPTER 25

MY AWARENESS RETURNED IN TIME for me to feel myself land hard, my shoulder striking the ground as if I'd fallen from a three-story building. Pain blasted me as I rolled helplessly, bashing into a wall.

A groan came from my side. Amber?

I blinked my eyes, willing the stars to clear from my vision. A sickly green light glowed from dirt walls covered in vines. We were in a large tunnel, the ceiling and floor also covered in vines. They slithered and shifted, and I jumped up, thinking I'd been wrong and that they were snakes instead of plants.

But they didn't have heads, and they didn't wrap around me and try to squeeze me to death. Nin and Amber lay crumpled at my feet, only Amber stirring, and not very much. That had been one hell of a doorway to walk through.

I knelt, Chopper still in my hand, to check on them. Nin was out cold—I touched two fingers to her throat to make *sure* she was only unconscious and not dead.

She still had a pulse. Her fist was clenched around something. The key.

"Amber," I whispered, looking left and right down the tunnel, afraid the assassin could follow us through and would show up any second. "Are you all right?"

"Wha-da-hell-wassat?" she muttered, grabbing her head with her hands. Maybe we'd all crashed into the wall—the side of the tunnel.

"We took the exit ramp at top speed," I said, though I had no idea what had happened. None of my previous portal travel had been like that.

"Huh?"

"Aren't you studying for your learner's permit now?"

Amber sat up, blonde hair dangling in her eyes, and looked blearily at me.

"Never mind. Nin, I can carry you over my shoulder, but with my sword harness on, it wouldn't be a comfortable ride. You might want to wake up."

Only then did I realize that there was no sign of the doorway we'd come through. Had it, like one of Zav's portals, disappeared as soon as we'd used it? Or had Nin succeeded in locking it behind us?

Because it had taken the fairy ring to open it, I'd assumed it would be a semi-permanent passageway and that there would be another ring on this side. But the strange vine-covered floor was devoid of mushrooms, as far as I could tell.

"Also, I'm not carrying your bag for you." I nudged her backpack.

"You'll want it. It's full of grenades." Amber touched her temple and winced. "I hit my head."

"Did you guys intentionally come out to open the gate and escape with me?" I'd assumed it had been accidental, or a desperate action they'd undertaken when they'd seen I was losing the fight, but they both had their gear with them.

"We came to *save* you." Amber rolled her eyes, as if this should have been obvious, and I should be grateful.

Mostly, I was worried. "I wanted you to go with Dimitri and get out of there. Mom went with him, right?"

"Yeah. She's old. She can't fight. Not like me." Amber put a hand on the side of the tunnel and started to push herself to her feet, but the vine moved under her palm, and she shrieked and jerked it back.

"Ssh." I glanced left and right.

Freysha had thought that we'd be able to sneak into their realm undetected by making a new fairy ring, but I had no idea if we'd come out a hundred miles from their nearest doorway or a hundred yards. My sword was sending out its magical beacon as strongly as ever, so the odds of us staying undetected for long were poor.

"What are they?" Amber scowled down at other vines rustling under her boots. She lifted one foot and looked like she wished she could levitate so she wouldn't have to touch them.

Thus far, the vines hadn't wrapped around us and choked us, so I didn't mind them. "Fae decor."

I touched Sindari's charm, hoping I could summon him again now that the assassin wasn't around. Running into opponents who had the ability to dismiss him was getting damn inconvenient.

"Can the creepy elf guy follow us here?" Amber gripped the hilt of her short sword and peered in both directions. "Wherever *here* is."

"I don't know. Probably. We should get moving."

Assuming Nin woke up and could walk. I truly might have to sling her over my shoulder. Even as light as she was, I couldn't imagine walking very far that way. We might be miles from anything.

"Moving where?" Amber asked.

"I heard the fae queen would have the magic to fix my sword."

"I don't see a map to her hideout."

"She's probably got a castle, not a hideout. Queens are important, you know."

"Funny, Val." Amber took out her phone, as if that would work here. She seemed to realize right away that Earth's wireless coverage didn't extend to Fae Land, for she sighed and pocketed it.

Sindari's mist was slow to form, but I let out a relieved breath when it appeared, and he slowly solidified.

Nin finally stirred.

I squeezed her shoulder. "Are you irrevocably broken?"

"Maybe?" she rasped, wincing as she lifted her head.

She unfurled her fist and looked at the key. It still emanated magic.

"Can you use that to open a doorway back home when we need it?" I had no idea if the assassin would stake out the house or follow us through the fairy ring, but the urge to get moving made me antsy.

"I…" Nin pushed herself to her hands and knees and looked around. "I think we need another fairy ring."

"I was afraid of that."

Val. Sindari gazed at me. *I regret that I was so easily dismissed. Again. I wanted to sink my fangs into that assassin's torso and eviscerate him.*

Yeah, I replied telepathically. *Me too.*

Your human teeth would barely break skin. They are insufficient for evisceration.

We're a meager species.

Yes.

"Let's go for a hike." I helped Nin to her feet. "I understand Amber loves hiking."

Amber grimaced down at the vines. "This place is sick."

"It might make you appreciate the woods back home."

"It's making me appreciate my *room* back home."

I decided not to point out that she wouldn't be here if she hadn't fled her house in a huff. We had bigger problems to worry about.

"Let's find a door," she said.

"I'll do my best." I led the way with Sindari at my side, though I had no idea which direction would take us to a door. Nor did I want to leave, even if we found a way back to Earth. The assassin was waiting for me there. I couldn't face him again, not if I wanted to live.

***

As Sindari, Amber, Nin, and I walked down the vine-draped tunnels, avoiding forks and side passages in favor of continuing in the same direction, we didn't speak much. Nin and Amber would probably never be chitchat buddies, and I was busy reliving my fight with the assassin.

The sweat had cooled on my body, and the cuts he'd given me had stopped bleeding, but the memories were hot and fresh as I tried to figure out what I could have done better. If he followed us here and tracked us down, how could I win against him?

As far as I'd noticed, he had no weaknesses. He'd used both swords equally effectively, and that had been a big part of what made him so impossible to beat. Most people who carried a second sword used it more like a shield for parrying and defending, but he'd been an ambidextrous freak.

I would never be able to beat him with Chopper alone, unless I could figure out how to activate whatever Sarrlevi had been expecting from me, to draw upon my sword's power to use against him. If only I knew how. The only magical words I knew for Chopper caused it to glow to light the way at night, to turn cold, or to turn hot. There were times when such powers were useful, but not in a battle against an assassin. It wasn't as if I'd gotten close enough to touch him with my blade.

If I faced him again, my sword-fighting ability wouldn't allow me to win. I had to figure out something I could do with my meager magic to beat him. Or at least to distract him long enough that I could slip past his defenses.

Trying to shield myself from him hadn't worked. Trying to compel him to surrender hadn't worked. Maybe an indirect attack? I hadn't tried that. If I could master Freysha's roots, could I grow them up to snatch his feet? The idea of trying to do that while defending myself against swords moving at a hundred miles an hour was daunting, but maybe if I practiced a little…

I stopped at a three-way intersection with a patch of bare earth visible between the vines and probed down into the ground with my magic. The packed dirt was different here than back home, but I was able to shape it into tendrils and urge them up through the surface. They poked up more quickly than they had before. Either I was getting better, or something was different about this place.

"Are we taking a rest break?" Nin slumped against the side of the tunnel, ignoring the vines that protested her weight by undulating under her shoulder. "Or deciding on which direction?"

"I'm practicing something." One of the roots grew up more than a foot and waved in the air. I felt a hint of triumph.

Could I convince it to grab something? Like an assassin's ankle?

I pointed the tip of my sword above it, but something green sprouted out of a nearby vine on the ground, startling me into springing back. That wasn't my work.

Sindari crouched and growled as long green tendrils grew out of the vine. They smacked down upon my roots, batting them to the ground. Then my roots burst into flames and disappeared. The tendrils that had sprouted retracted and disappeared until only the original vine remained.

"I guess this is a no-practice zone," I muttered.

"This place is weird as hell," Amber said. "I want to go home."

"The assassin may be waiting there."

"*My* home." She planted her hand on her chest. "I shouldn't have left to start with." She glanced at Nin.

"Why did you?" I asked.

"Never mind."

Nin gave me a sad look and didn't say anything. I wanted to hug her. It wasn't her fault that Thad came with a surly teenager.

I picked one of the tunnels at random and tried not to think about how thirsty I was. Nin had grenades, and Amber had whatever clothes and chargers and devices she'd packed for her weekend escape, but I hadn't had a chance to grab anything, and I doubted any of us had food or water. Unfortunately, battling assassins was dehydrating.

Do you sense any people or signs of a settlement? I asked Sindari. So far, my senses hadn't detected anything like that, only a low level of magic that came from the vines.

I have not sensed other beings yet.

What about water that would be safe to drink?

Sindari stopped and looked back. *I did smell water back at the intersection, coming from the tunnel we chose not to go down.*

I halted, and Amber almost crashed into me. "We're trying the other tunnel. Sindari says there's water that way, and I'm thirsty."

"I have a couple of drinks," Amber said.

"That you'll share?" I couldn't imagine that she had much in her pack. Black with silver leopard print and fuzzy zipper tassels, it looked to have been chosen for fashion rather than carrying capacity.

"For five bucks."

"You're a lovely hiking buddy."

"Hey, it's not my fault you didn't come prepared."

"I didn't come prepared because I didn't expect to *go* anywhere."

"I will pay for a beverage for myself and Val." Nin pulled a cute sequined purse out of her pack and opened a pouch.

Amber eyed it. My sense of fashion was nonexistent, and I had no idea if she would also find the purse cute or deride it as some horrific design faux pas. Nin handed her a twenty-dollar bill.

"I don't have change." Amber pulled out two blue-and-black soda cans that I didn't recognize, probably something that had been invented in the last ten years.

"Perhaps you can pay me the change later," Nin suggested.

"Perhaps you can call it a tip." Amber smiled and put one can in Nin's hand and one in mine. She reached for the twenty in Nin's fingers.

Nin started to pull her hand back but must have decided that a hundred-percent tip, however poor a monetary-management decision that might be, was worth it if it bought peace with Amber.

I was debating whether I should put a stop to that, though I'd let myself be led down that same path before, when one of the vines rustled against my boot and distracted me. Maybe the things were thirsty as well. I didn't know if—I eyed the can to read the label—Berry Burst Game Fuel would be to their taste.

"Why is this can textured?" Nin was also eyeing the label. She didn't look any more familiar with it than I did.

Hopefully, this wasn't one of those things with enough caffeine to send an adult's heart into cardiac arrest.

"For enhanced grip. You know, in case you're sweaty." Amber looked at me and wrinkled her nose.

"I was in a battle," I pointed out.

"I know. You were super fast, but you were still getting your ass kicked."

"You noticed that, too, huh?" I opened the can, sniffed the syrupy sweet stuff, and wondered if it would be better to go hunt for Sindari's water.

That smells abysmal. Sindari's nostrils twitched.

Worse than my car air fresheners?

No. Nothing is worse than those.

I took a swig and grimaced as it hit my taste buds—it might have been more palatable cold. Too thirsty to care, I chugged the can anyway.

Nin, probably less desperate than I, read the ingredients. "What is glycerol ester of rosin?"

"Something good," Amber said. "You should start selling it at your food truck."

Judging by Nin's expression, she wanted her twenty dollars back.

Amber popped her can and started drinking, but one of the vines on the ground shifted and startled her. She flinched, and a few drops flew out. They spattered onto some of the vines.

"Creepy things," Amber muttered and took another drink.

I didn't expect anything to happen, so I wasn't prepared when several of the vines sprouted shoots that zoomed upward toward her. She shrieked and dropped the can. I lunged and caught it as I pulled her back. One of the tendrils had shot all the way up to her face level.

"Get back," I barked needlessly, tearing Chopper from its scabbard.

Its magical blue light flared as Nin and Amber scrambled farther down the tunnel. One of the tendrils tried to wrap around my arm. I slashed it in half—thankfully, Chopper sliced easily through it—but others went for me. No, they were going for the *can*.

I threw it down the tunnel. More tendrils sprouted up where it landed, descending upon it like vultures on roadkill. But the closer vines kept going after me. One whipped up, trying to get in my mouth. I slashed it and everything else around me, swinging Chopper like a scythe.

Sindari stayed at my side, swiping at the tendrils with his claws and snapping at them with his teeth. We devastated the plants, but even cutting them in half didn't kill them. The tips grew back within seconds. One wrapped around my leg while I was chopping at others.

"Look out, Val!" Amber yelled.

"No, do not use that," Nin called from behind me.

As I sliced through the tendril and scooted back, something sailed over my shoulder. One of the grenades.

"Shit!" I turned and ran, ushering Nin and Amber ahead of me as tendrils snatched for my back.

Sindari snapped at them with his jaws, keeping them from finding anchor spots. Then he sprinted after me. We hadn't made it far when the explosion rocked the tunnel, white light flaring like a sun.

The shockwave sent us tumbling farther, knocking us into each other. The ground quaked, rocking us all. I kept Chopper up, afraid I would accidentally cut someone. Wet bits of plant splatted against my back and exposed skin.

Nin and Amber went down in a pile. Feeling like I was surfing, I barely kept my footing. Images of the tunnel ceiling collapsing on us filled my head, and I lunged over and tried to protect Nin and Amber.

Thankfully, the quaking ceased, the vines around us stopped sprouting new tendrils, and the ceiling didn't collapse on us. Had this been a normal underground passage, I was positive it would have, but magic emanated from more than the strange vines.

I glanced back, grimacing at the carnage of dead plants spattering the ceiling, sides, and floor of the tunnel. The vines had all stopped moving. I hoped we hadn't killed them completely, especially since I'd come to this world looking for a favor. Or a trade might be more likely. Either way, I would prefer not to do any more damage to their people, especially now that I suspected Sarrlevi had been responsible for placing the artifact.

"New rule." I wiped moist plant bits off my clothing. "No more drinking."

Nin sat up, clawing pieces of the vine from her face. "Also, no more grenades."

"Are you kidding?" Amber pushed herself to her knees, grinning. "That was awesome."

"You could have brought the roof down on us." I dug out my kerchief to clean Chopper of plant grime.

"Hey, I was just helping. They were trying to kill you. I saved your life." Amber slapped the back of her hand against Nin's shoulders. "Your grenades are *tope*."

"Yes," Nin said, as if she knew exactly what that meant.

Since they were bonding—or at least talking—I decided not to point out that I hadn't needed Amber to save my life, nor had it been in any particular danger until she'd thrown the grenade.

Fae are coming, Sindari stated.

I swore. I couldn't sense them yet, but I didn't doubt him. *From which direction?*

Sindari faced down the tunnel in the direction we'd been heading but then turned back the other way. *Both.*

A lot of them?

Yes.

CHAPTER 26

TWO PARTIES OF FAE SCOUTS converged on our little group at the same time. I stood with my back to the tunnel wall, so I could look in both directions, with Fezzik in one hand and Chopper in the other. Amber had assumed a similar pose opposite me, with her sword in one hand and a grenade in the other. Nin stood between us holding two grenades. Sindari crouched several feet to one side, facing one of the parties and using his stealth. I could see him, but hopefully, the fae couldn't yet, and he could surprise them if they attacked.

But if we had to fight, we could be in trouble. Each group had ten fae males in armor made from some hard brown material, and each carried weapons that ranged from bows to spears to rope-based projectile launchers that I couldn't name. But the *ropes* were the same green as the vines. Maybe they *were* vines.

I'd already tapped my translation charm, but the fae weren't saying anything yet. It was possible they were communicating telepathically because both groups stopped twenty feet away from us, weapons pointed in our direction. Actually, their weapons were all pointed at me. More than a few of the fae eyed Chopper.

"My name is Val." I decided to try being friendly instead of opening fire—especially since I sensed magic coming from the armor they wore, and I feared Fezzik wouldn't work on it. "These are my friends." I didn't want to identify Amber as my daughter, lest they decide to use her to manipulate me. "*This* is Chopper." I hefted the sword. "You can probably sense that it's got a little fae-magic problem. Any chance that your queen or some other magically inclined person is available to remove the—" calling it a taint might be offensive, "—beacon that's been placed on it? I can pay. In gold, US dollars, or Game Fuel. The plants were into that."

Amber was in her fighting stance and appeared ready to save my life again, but that didn't keep her from rolling her eyes at me.

"I also have your chocolate." Nin pointed one of her grenades at her backpack.

"Oh?" I asked.

"I grabbed them when I took the key."

"Let's hope that means we're in a better bargaining position now."

"I doubt it," Amber muttered.

"That's because you haven't tried the chocolates." I thought about asking Nin to pull them out, but these were just the peons. We needed to talk to the queen or some high-level mage who could fix my sword.

"She is marked by a dragon," one of the fae holding a bow observed to another.

"Yes, I am," I said. "He'll be along any minute, by the way."

Nin lifted her eyebrows and whispered, "Do they understand English?"

"No idea. You want to try Thai?"

One of the fae with a spear and more ornate armor than the rest of his group stepped forward. "You have entered our realm without an invitation, and you have damaged the *uwayari*." The charm neglected to translate that. "The punishment for both crimes is death."

"I'm just here to get my sword fixed, and we were defending ourselves from the plant. If you try to hurt us, we'll defend ourselves from you too." My finger tightened on Fezzik's trigger, and I shifted the weapon and aimed toward his chest.

He didn't appear fazed. He also didn't appear to understand me, though the pistol probably made my intentions clear.

"If you are the mate of a dragon, there may be political ramifications for killing you, so we are capturing you and will take you to see our political leader."

"How about the queen?" I imagined being dragged before some lowly ambassador. "Or anyone with a translation charm would be handy too."

"You will drop your weapons." He pointed at the ground.

"Uh." I didn't like that idea, but they had us outnumbered and surrounded. And if I opened fire on them, the chances of bribing someone later would be nil.

I will help you retrieve your weapons later if necessary, Sindari said. *I do not believe they have noticed my presence yet.*

I didn't know if he would be able to *stay* unnoticed in the tight confines of the tunnel—people tended to see through his stealth magic if they got close enough—but we didn't have a lot of options here. *Okay, thanks.*

Careful not to make abrupt movements, I set down Chopper and Fezzik. Amber put down her sword, and Nin laid her two grenades on the ground. She didn't remove her backpack to relinquish the rest. Chances were they would demand it and search it, but I didn't blame her for trying to keep it. I hoped I could get away with keeping my charm necklace.

The vines shifted, sprouting again, and I tensed, expecting another attack. But they wrapped their new tendrils around the weapons and flicked them toward the fae patrollers. The males caught them without comment, only Chopper drawing any extra interest.

"A beautiful blade," one whispered.

"How did a mongrel from the wild worlds obtain it?" another asked.

"Theft. It could only have been theft."

"Maybe she raided a tomb of a famous warrior."

The looks they gave me were hard. Maybe theft wasn't a sin that the fae approved of.

"The queen will question her and find out."

"Then she will give her to us to enjoy." One of the younger fae in the back leered and looked me up and down, then gave Nin and Amber similar leers. "And the others too. Three exotic foreign females. *Delicious.*"

Fury flashed into me, and I stepped in front of Nin and Amber to block them from his pervy consideration.

"Keep your pants on," the fae leader said. "One belongs to a dragon."

"The others don't."

"No. They may be available for us. The queen will let us know."

"Does anyone know what they're saying?" Amber glowered at the one who'd been scoping her out.

"Yes," I said.

"Are you going to tell us?"

"You don't want to know."

Magic pricked at my senses, and a shifting and grinding sound came from behind me. I spun in time to see a hole open in what had appeared to be a solid wall. The earth melted away, forming a passage that in seconds went from nothing but earth to a green-lit tunnel similar to the one we stood in. Vines near my feet split in half, and new shoots formed and shot down the new tunnel, growing at impossible speed.

"Did I mention this place is a freak show?" Amber asked.

"Yes," Nin said.

"Good."

I kept myself from once more pointing out that she should have gone with Mom and Dimitri. She'd thought she was coming to help me, and it was hard not to be appreciative of that. I wished she weren't here, so she wouldn't be in danger, but it touched me that she'd cared enough to come.

"We are going along with them?" Nin asked as the males came forward, gesturing with their weapons for us to walk into the new tunnel.

Sindari was already trotting down it, taking advantage of the new space to stay far enough away from the fae to remain unnoticed.

"Yeah." I waved for Amber and Nin to go ahead of me. I didn't want Mr. Perv watching their butts as they walked. "They're taking us to the queen."

"Is that what we want?" Amber asked.

"I hope so."

CHAPTER 27

THE TREK WAS NOT A short one, and as the first hour bled into the second, I wished I'd taken that side passage to find some water. The fae hadn't taken Amber's or Nin's backpacks, and I didn't want to draw attention to them by asking for another canned drink. Besides, I didn't have twenty dollars to pay my daughter's outrageous rates.

At least the air here didn't bother my sensitive lungs. The scents of dirt and plant matter were heady, like walking into a greenhouse warmed by the sun, but there must not have been any mold, dust, pollen, cockroaches, pet dander, or the dozen-odd other things I reacted to these days. I thought of Freysha's comments about Earth's pollution affecting her. Maybe *that* was missing here. Judging by our long trek-on-foot, burning fossil fuels wasn't a fae pastime.

Our tunnel widened, with side tunnels branching off and large chambers opening up. Sindari kept padding along ahead of us, and I started to wonder if I should dismiss him and call him back later, when I needed him for a possible battle. But we appeared to be getting closer to a population center. Now and then, voices came from the side tunnels, and we started passing curious fae males, females, and children en route to their destinations.

The tunnel widened further, altering into something like an underground park, with walking paths around ponds and statues, fountains gurgling water that made me thirsty, and trees that didn't mind the lack of sunlight. Here and there, alcoves with hanging purple and green lights emanating magic were perched over benches the size of beds.

Some of those bed-benches were occupied by couples or groups in the middle of having sex, and I debated whether to pretend nothing was happening or tell Amber—I caught her gaping—not to look. Hopefully, she wouldn't tell Thad about this. Even though I hadn't invited her on this adventure, I felt responsible for her innocence.

"Those fae are feasting while they have sex." Nin pointed to one alcove where a fae server was delivering platters of foods I couldn't identify. A wall overlooking the park also held balconies where people ate and drank while watching the festivities. *Some* of them ate and drank. Some of them were distracted by their own festivities. "Maybe your chocolates will be useful in barter after all."

"They are interested in the Den of Carnal Pleasures," one of our captors said—it was the horny young one that had been talking about having sex with us. "We will bring them back here later."

"Yes. I look forward to it," another male said. "Remember the time a dragon joined us here? Perhaps that one's mate would enjoy an orgy."

"Newcomers make things so interesting."

"I think the chocolates are going to be too tame for these people," I muttered to Nin, glad we were approaching another tunnel—the exit out of the *den*.

"That's because this place is a freak show," Amber said.

The fae are known to enjoy carnal pleasures without shame, Sindari said, padding along indifferently.

So I've heard. I spotted a few people simply lounging in hammocks. Sloth, gluttony, and lust were covered. *I wish they'd enjoy them less with my fifteen-year-old daughter present.*

I am several centuries old, and I also do not need to see fae mating.

Not enough fur to interest you, huh?

No.

"I hope Zav can find me here." I wished I knew how his hunt was going. Would it take him days to track down that other dragon? Or months? "I don't know if these guys are going to show us a doorway out of here when we're done with our chat."

Amber glanced at Nin. "Can you slip me some grenades later?"

"I will attempt to do so," Nin said.

"Good."

I decided not to mention that grenades were unlikely to help with magical doorways. Amber and Nin were making eye contact and talking to each other. That was an improvement over that morning.

The new tunnel we entered glowed silver instead of green and sported a different type of plant. As with the others, tendrils or vines connected them, but they grew up in columns at regular points along the walls, with leaves giving them a bushy aspect. Magic radiated from those columns, though I couldn't tell what it did. Defenses? Maybe we'd entered the queen's palace.

The floor changed from earth to stone tiles, and the vines ended, leaving my boots clacking on the hard surface. Up ahead, the light that emanated from the walls grew brighter, and silver gates opened for us.

We entered another park full of fountains and trees and ponds, and bird chatter came from branches high above. As with the last chamber, there was a ceiling, but it had to be a hundred feet up. Insects that reminded me of cicadas also chirped in the branches.

A blue-scaled avian creature about three feet from beak to tail sprang from a perch near the gate and flapped across the chamber ahead of us. It veered around a copse of trees and flew toward another perch, singing a raspy song almost as awful as Xilneth's when he'd attempted to woo me with his vocal abilities.

Gongs sounded in that direction, and a stream of fae in green-and-silver robes and sandals walked out, looking curiously over at us. They carried gnarled staffs that clacked on the floor tiles. As we approached, they sat on stumps—or were those mushrooms?—that formed a circle reminiscent of the fairy rings, though more than twenty-five yards across. A giant gray mushroom chair much larger than the others arose on one side—a throne?—and the blue creature alighted on the back of it.

After the staff-carrying males and females seated themselves, our armed escort spread out at points around the circle. Several stayed with us, including the one carrying Amber's sword and my weapons. I didn't let myself get too far from him—in case this turned ugly.

A door behind the throne opened, and a buxom female with green-tinted white hair swept back in a coif floated out on a magical seat. She radiated power, her aura almost as striking as a dragon's. Her eyes were emerald green and bright with interest as she gazed at our group. Her cheeks were pink, but I couldn't tell if that indicated recent exertion—maybe she'd been getting randy in the den before this—or was her natural color.

As she switched from the floating seat to the throne, the scaled avian issued a series of noises somewhere between a chirp and a frog's croak. I checked to make sure my translation charm was still active, but if it was speaking a language, my charm was stumped.

"Yes, yes," she—the queen?—crooned and scratched its belly. "I will feed you later."

I stepped forward, hoping she would focus on me and ignore Nin and Amber. I would prefer it if everyone forgot they were here.

One of our guards lifted a hand and glared sternly at me. The one with my weapons, at a nod from the queen, trotted over and knelt before her. He lifted my sword in both of his hands, holding it out as if in offering.

I growled and stepped farther forward, ignoring my captor. Nobody was going to offer *my* sword to someone else.

"I'm Val Thorvald, and that's mine," I called, hoping the queen had some translation magic. "I came to see if you or one of your people could remove the beacon from it. That was an accident. Someone left a fae artifact on our world, and it was killing animals, so I was ordered to destroy it."

The queen had been paying more attention to her pet than the sword or me, but she lowered her hand and faced me now. "I am Queen Dithara. You are the Ruin Bringer."

"I see you're all caught up. I guess that's good."

At least she wasn't eyeing me with the raging hatred that so many magical beings who knew my name did. And she hadn't yet brought up the two fae males that had died in Magnuson Park. Maybe I would luck out, and she wouldn't have heard about that.

"I was asked," she continued, apparently able to understand my English, "to lend the artifact to be planted to attract you, so that your sword would be marked and all could sense it, and someone would take it from you. I'm surprised you have retained it."

"Yeah, I've met Sarrlevi and got the gist. What did he pay you to help him? I might be able to trade something of equal or greater value for assistance in removing the mark on my sword."

"What did he pay me?" Her smile grew impish as she extended her hand toward the doorway she'd exited from. "That which he always pays me for favors."

Sarrlevi strode out of the passageway, and I groaned. I should have sensed him back there, but this place was bursting with magic. A dragon could have been lurking in the tunnel, and I might have missed it.

His face was stern and stoic, the same as before, but sweat moistened his brow, and his cheeks were pink too. Hell, was he sexing up the queen for favors? How was I supposed to top that? If she was into pretty male elven assassins, I doubted I was her type.

Sarrlevi walked to the throne and stood beside it, facing me from the queen's side. She barely acknowledged him, instead giving her pet another scratch. Maybe his performance hadn't been stellar, or maybe it had been rushed. He wore the same clothing, armor, and swords he had for our battle, so it was unlikely he'd stopped at home first for a shower and cologne.

"Guess we didn't need to worry about him following us through the doorway," Amber muttered to Nin.

"He must have his own way to access this realm," Nin muttered back.

"If you're willing to give a guy a powerful artifact in exchange for sex, then wait until you see what I have to trade you." I waved for Nin to hand me her backpack. It was time to take a shot. "It's *way* better than elf bed-bouncing."

Nin slung the pack off her shoulder as she stepped up beside me—the guards looked on curiously but didn't try to stop her. Maybe gifts were common.

"In business and negotiations," Nin murmured, "it is better to under promise and over deliver rather than the other way around."

"Have you tasted the caramels? Trust me, they over deliver."

Amber strolled forward while I withdrew the caramels. I had a feeling she meant to sneak out a couple of grenades.

"Don't do anything with them," I whispered. "There's no way out of here except by negotiations."

"Are you good at negotiations?" she asked.

"No."

I straightened with several boxes of caramels in hand and approached the queen. She was watching me—so was Sarrlevi. I didn't know if that was better or worse than if they'd been engaged in hanky-panky.

"We will resume the battle from which you fled," Sarrlevi said in English.

"Yeah, I can't wait. Let me do my deal first, huh?" I held up a box, turning it about and highlighting the prize like Vanna White. "Queen Dithara, these are delicacies from my world. I've got several boxes of them that I'll give you if you can remove your magic from my sword. And several more boxes if you then return it to me and point us to the nearest doorway home. Preferably giving us a head start on your loyal bed friend there."

Sarrlevi squinted dangerously at me. Maybe I shouldn't go out of my way to irk him. If Zav managed to get the assassination assignment called off, I didn't want Sarrlevi deciding to take on the project just for fun.

Two guards stepped forward to block me from getting too close to the queen. I wondered if they'd stood guard while she and Sarrlevi cavorted under the covers.

"You like sweets?" I opened a box slowly, encouraged when she watched. Her nostrils twitched as the first chocolate-covered caramel came out. The pet also sat up straighter and sniffed liberally. "The first one is free. An overture of friendship."

The assassin snorted. I placed the chocolate in one of the guard's hands.

He sniffed it, then looked at his queen. "There is no magic about it, but it may be poisoned. Shall I taste it?"

"Do so."

He nibbled off a corner and chewed thoughtfully. He didn't spit it out. Zav would have. Hopefully, that meant fae were into sweets.

The queen leaned forward in her throne, nostrils quivering again.

Sarrlevi frowned and said, "We have a deal, remember," to her in her language.

"I gave you the artifact, as promised, and I said I would not interfere with your hunt." The queen held out her palm and nodded at the guard, not glancing at Sarrlevi as she spoke. "Your pretty face and agility will win you no more favors from me."

His eyes narrowed. "I do not ask for more favors, as you call them. Only that you allow me to finish dealing with her. You will not assist her in escaping."

"I will not, but *you*—" this time, she looked at him, her emerald eyes hard, "—will not presume to give me orders, elven outcast."

I didn't like this talk about being dealt with and not being allowed to escape, but if I could arrange for Nin and Amber to be taken back home, that would be a partial victory. The idea of my kid watching me get slain disturbed me more than the thought of *being* slain. And if I wasn't here to watch out for Amber and Nin, who knew what the creepy guards would do?

As the guard delivered the half-nibbled caramel to the queen, I crossed my fingers that she liked it enough to deal. She popped it in her mouth whole, without waiting however long the recommended time was to see if her taster keeled over. She chewed slowly and thoughtfully with her eyes closed. Was that an expression of bliss on her face? I hoped so.

Sarrlevi's face soured. Good.

"Yes." The queen nodded after she swallowed. "Yes, this is excellent. I will have more of them."

"Sure. Just remove the fae magic on my sword while leaving the original magic intact." I waved to the guard who was still on his knees before her throne, holding the blade horizontally above the floor.

The queen tapped her chocolate-smudged finger on her chin and considered me. Why did I have the feeling she was thinking of ordering me killed and *taking* the caramels?

I held up the boxes. "You'll find that you want more than this. Trust me. I can get you more back in my world. It's tricky, but I know where they're made and how to acquire them."

"Is Val bartering for our lives with chocolate?" Amber whispered to Nin.

"Yes, shh," Nin whispered back.

"Give me the sword." The queen waved the guard to his feet.

He rested it in her lap, and she placed her hands on it, but before wriggling her fingers and pouring any magic into it, she pointed to the armrest of her throne.

"The sweets. Place them here."

I shrugged, walked up, and did so. Sarrlevi watched me, his arms folded over his chest. I couldn't tell if he thought he was going to get screwed. I sure hoped so.

The queen noticed my bandage but didn't say anything about it. I thought about asking if she could also heal the wound, but the sword was my priority.

She extracted another caramel, popped it in her mouth, and considered the sword. She looked along its length from hilt to tip.

"I can remove our magic, but I have given the assassin my word that I will not impede his quest to slay you," she told me.

"Yeah, I got that." I kept myself from looking to where Sindari lurked to the side of the ring, but I hoped the assassin hadn't sensed him and wasn't expecting him. If he was busy swinging his blades at me, Sindari might be able to sneak in and take a bite before Sarrlevi used his magic to cast him out of this realm.

"You will have your battle here." The queen pointed to the empty ground in the middle of the ring of occupied seats. "In our arena for our entertainment."

Sarrlevi looked sharply at her. "I do not kill for entertainment."

"The battle *will* commence here. The victor, if not fatally injured, will join us in the den afterward. There will be a feast, and I will consume more of these brown squares."

"Not going to share them with your people?" I asked.

"No."

"I will not kill for entertainment," Sarrlevi said, stiffer than a tree trunk, "nor will I have sex in one of your libidinous group orgies."

She slapped him in the chest. "Don't be so stodgy and self-important."

His fingers twitched—I could tell he'd wanted to block that slap—but he forced himself to remain still and merely fumed, the tips of his ears turning as red as his cheeks. As much as I would have liked to feel smug, I hadn't figured out a way to beat him yet, so the odds were against me surviving the hour. How could I appreciate my sword being fixed if I was dead?

"I need you to send my friends home before the battle. They're not into orgies." I didn't even like anyone *talking* about orgies in front of my kid and was glad she couldn't understand the fae. Walking through their den had been torture enough. If I somehow survived this, I knew I would hear about it from Thad.

You're not allowed to take our daughter off Earth anymore...

"How many boxes more will you trade for their transport back to your world?" the queen asked.

"How many are left, Nin?" I hadn't rooted around in the backpack, not wanting the guards to notice the grenades, and searched for them all.

"I believe there are four more boxes," Nin said.

"Very well. They will be sent safely back to your world after the battle."

"Uh." I lifted a finger. "How about before?"

"All will witness this event and determine whether the Ruin Bringer, carrier of a great dragon blade, can defeat the famous assassin Varlesh Sarrlevi." The corners of the queen's eyes crinkled. "Also, they will attest, should you be slain and should your dragon mate come seeking vengeance, that *my* people had nothing to do with it."

She closed her eyes and drew upon her magic, a yellow light flaring all around Chopper. End of the conversation, that seemed to say.

Sarrlevi didn't appear worried by the idea of Zav's vengeance. He should have been. Zav would not only be irked to find me slain, but he had fond feelings for those dragon topiaries. Sarrlevi's career—and life—would be over.

Since the overlay of fae magic had flummoxed everyone from elves to dragons, I expected it to take the queen a while to fix my sword, but within moments, the magic appeared to flow upward from the blade and into her fingers. The glow intensified, and she cupped her hands to hold the energy in the air in front of her, then lifted her arms and flung it into the air. The yellow dispersed and dissipated.

Chopper still glowed in her lap, but it was the familiar blue glow, not a yellow taint, and I could no longer sense it sending magic out like a beacon to all within a thousand miles.

The queen opened her eyes and held the sword out toward me, hilt first. Even though we'd made a deal, it surprised me that she was giving it back. Everyone from goblins to rocs to magical toads wanted the sword, and with all her people surrounding her, it wasn't as if I could have kept her from taking it.

"If you manage to survive this battle—" she tilted her head toward Sarrlevi, "—I suggest you endeavor to learn more about your sword's capabilities."

"It's on my to-do list."

The knowing gleam in her eyes made me wonder if she had learned something about Chopper while she'd been removing the taint. Maybe that it had a self-cleaning mode and could have removed the magic by itself if only I'd known the appropriate ancient dwarven word to utter?

"It is time for your battle." The queen drew another caramel from the box.

"Wait," Sarrlevi said, and I hoped he'd received a text and his mom needed him to come home and take out the trash. "She is injured by your magic." He pointed to my bandaged hand. "Will you heal her before we fight?" He locked gazes with me. "I wish this battle to be *fair*."

I didn't. I wished to have an advantage.

"You will pay later?" The queen smirked at him.

He sighed. "Yes."

It had to be onerous work servicing a queen in bed.

"Very well." She crooked a finger for me to approach.

I rested my hand on the arm of her throne, and her magic flowed into me like a waterfall pouring off a thousand-foot cliff. I gasped at the pure power surging into me. Pain burst from my wound, and I would have jerked my hand back, but her magic held me in place. I feared that this had been a trap and that I would die at her hand, but after a few seconds, the pain faded, replaced by intense itching. It was almost as bad, but then that too faded.

The queen's power released me. "You are healed."

I rocked back. Having the power withdraw so quickly left my legs weak, but I locked my knees so I wouldn't fall. That would be more embarrassing than being defeated by an assassin.

Fortunately, the feeling passed quickly, and my hand felt normal for the first time in days. I peeled back the bandage to investigate. Only a faint scar remained.

It occurred to me that I was close enough that I might be able to grab her, press my sword to her throat, and try to force her people to let us all go—sans the assassin. But after feeling her power flow into me, I couldn't imagine that working. Her magic was too great. And did I truly want to threaten her when she'd fixed my sword and healed my hand? *Sarrlevi* was my enemy here. He was the one I had to deal with.

And he knew it. He nodded after my hand was healed, then strode out into the center of the circle, drawing his twin swords.

"Since you fight for your life," the queen said, pointing for me to join him, "you may use all magic and abilities at your disposal, but if your Del'nothian ally interferes, I will banish him from this realm." She looked straight at Sindari.

Ugh. So much for my belief that Sindari had managed to remain hidden from everyone.

"No problem." I suspected Sarrlevi would have detected him and banished Sindari again anyway. "He's only here to advise me."

I advise you not to engage in a battle with that assassin again. Sindari had been poised to spring into action, but now, he moved to sit beside Amber and Nin, just another spectator.

Unfortunately, I don't have a choice.

He sighed into my mind. *I fear that's true.*

The queen lifted her hands, fingers smudged with chocolate. "Let the battle begin."

CHAPTER 28

THE FAE SPECTATORS CHEERED AND jeered and placed bets with each other as I retrieved Fezzik from the guard who'd taken it, then walked slowly into the circle to face Sarrlevi. I wasn't going to get out of this, so I had to figure out how to win. One way or another.

"Piece of cake," I muttered.

"Val?" Amber asked, uncertainty tingeing her voice. Without translation charms of their own, she and Nin couldn't know what we'd been discussing, but as I stopped several feet from Sarrlevi and faced him, both of our weapons drawn, there couldn't be much doubt about what would transpire next. "Mom? What's going on?"

Mom. It was the first time she'd called me that since she'd been a toddler, since before I left her and Thad. She almost sounded like that toddler now, worried and afraid instead of sarcastic and jaded. It probably didn't help that several of the fae males had crowded close to them, weapons drawn, to make sure they didn't interfere.

I held up a hand toward Sarrlevi, hoping he would give me a second to explain. "This guy's been hired to kill me. The fae will let you and Nin go after we fight, but they're insisting that we entertain them by having our grand showdown here."

"Showdown to the death?" Nin asked quietly.

She and Amber stood shoulder to shoulder now, both with the same concerned expressions. Maybe they would get along better after this adventure together. I smiled bleakly. It would be nice if at least *some* good came out of this.

"That's usually the goal of assassins." I holstered Fezzik since Sarrlevi had already proven capable of deflecting its bullets. It would be me and Chopper for this, that was it.

"Who hired him to kill you?" Amber asked. "Can't you pay him to get out of it?"

"It was a dragon, and that's not how it works. Zav went to look for him to try to get him to call it off, but..." I spread a hand. It was going to be too late to matter.

Sarrlevi waited patiently, watching me with his swords in his hands, the tips toward the ground. Now that he'd cornered me, he wasn't in a hurry.

I drew a deep breath, wishing I could think of a way to delay this, to buy time for Zav to find me. But I had no idea if he was even looking for me. It could be weeks before he finished his hunt and returned to Earth, only to find his defenses decimated and me missing.

Zav, I thought into the void, *if there's any way you can hear me and sense that I'm in trouble... it would be an opportune moment for you to show up and help me.*

Unfortunately, my telepathic range only extended a few miles, and I'd never heard of any magical beings, even dragons, communicating between worlds. There was no chance that he would hear me.

"You are ready?" Sarrlevi lifted his swords and arched his eyebrows.

"No. Will that keep you from killing me?"

"I never fail to complete a contract."

"Guess that's a no." I lifted Chopper and willed my fledgling magical power into the blade, requesting the sword help me defend myself against the assassin's dual weapons and lightning speed. Maybe Chopper would be pleased that I'd arranged to have the taint removed and would be extra exuberant to help.

As Sarrlevi advanced, Chopper flared a more intense blue than I'd ever seen. The assassin paused, squinting at it and squinting at me, but whatever he thought about the illumination, it didn't deter him for long. He sprang.

Even faster than I reacted, Chopper reacted. The blade whipped up, knocking aside two thrusts from the assassin's longswords. It was the same parry I would have made, but Chopper was guiding my movements rather than the other way around.

SECRETS OF THE SWORD I

The assassin wasn't fazed by my defense and pressed the attack even as I was still trying to process my sword's unexpected new ability. I willed Chopper to keep defending me, and it did, even sending some of its magic through my body, helping my feet dart about in sync with the sword maneuvers. Again, they were all the moves I would have chosen, just faster and without conscious effort.

As we circled, I glimpsed Sindari straining against the magic that held him, his chest muscles taut as he tried to spring in to help.

Chopper's helping me, I told him telepathically, blocking a slash toward my face. *Just watch Amber and Nin, please.*

Your sword is assisting you in battle?

Yeah. I parried a pair of thrusts in rapid succession. *I'm not sure how or why, but it's helping.*

The assassin picked up the speed of his attacks. Chopper flared brightly, matching him, directing my arms to zip about so quickly I felt perpetually off balance. But the sword's guidance kept me alive, kept Sarrlevi's blades from darting in close enough to cut.

A faint furrow creased the assassin's brow as he methodically tested me, failing to slip his blades inside my defenses, as he had in our last encounter.

Chopper's assistance didn't keep me from feeling the strain of moving my limbs so quickly, nor the battering of Sarrlevi's blades against mine that jarred my joints. With my feet darting around the circle, keeping me out of reach, I knew I would be breathing heavily before long. I had to figure out a way to attack, not just defend.

It may have the inherent ability to do so, Sindari suggested after watching a few more of our exchanges. *And you've either accidentally called upon it, or this place, being more magical than Earth, is amplifying its usual powers.*

Guess I'll put it on my list of places to visit for vacations. I danced back far enough to give myself time to dash sweat from my eyes.

Surprisingly, Sarrlevi didn't spring to take advantage of my split-second pause in battle. He waited for me to realize I needed a collection of tennis sweatbands if I was going to let Chopper drive me this hard. As soon as my hand lowered, he lunged in again with a fresh barrage of attacks, his face tight with concentration.

We have to attack, buddy, I thought to Chopper, though I didn't usually chat with my sword. Maybe I should. *Not just defend.*

Abandoning words, I again willed Chopper to get the message. Its magic zipped through me like sentient caffeine. My arms and legs moved so quickly I thought I would trip over my own feet. Chopper launched an offensive combination of thrusts, aimed to get past the assassin's whirring blades, but if my shift to attacking surprised Sarrlevi, he didn't show it. Metal rang, echoing through the chamber, as he easily parried every thrust. Even with Chopper's help, I couldn't breach his defenses, not with a sword alone.

But maybe with Chopper taking charge of my bladework, I could concentrate on doing something with my meager magic. The entangling roots? Could I create them here?

Sarrlevi's eyes narrowed as he failed to breach my defenses. Then I sensed him calling upon magical power of his own. As he lunged in, trying to outsmart me by swinging one blade for my head and thrusting one toward my groin, he hurled a wave of energy at me.

Chopper whipped high and low faster than lightning branching to deflect the blows, but it couldn't assist me against the magic. Too late, I channeled my power into forming a barrier. His magic shredded it and knocked me twenty feet backward through the air.

I twisted in a sloppy somersault, trying to land on my feet. Several of the fae observers skittered out of the way.

"Mom!" Amber shouted in warning as I came down, finding my feet but flailing for balance. "Knife!"

I barely saw the glint of metal as something like a throwing star sped toward my heart. Chopper whipped up, again guiding my hands as I dodged. A *tink* sounded as the projectile ricocheted off my blade.

One of the fae yelped as it sped past, slicing through his clothing—and maybe his flesh. Nothing I could do about that. Sarrlevi charged in again, as relentless as the stormy sea.

Hot sweat dribbled down the side of my face and moistened my palms as Chopper and I defended once again. Sarrlevi's brow wasn't even damp. The bastard.

Chopper continued to guide my defenses, leaving me the concentration to use my magic, but it was hard with blades clanging inches from my face, metal screeching in my ears. Further, those fae guards were all too menacing as they loomed next to Amber and Nin. Was that one gripping Amber's shoulder? Presuming to *touch* her?

I snarled, tempted to pull out Fezzik and shoot the fae—maybe *he* wouldn't have magical armor that could knock aside bullets—but Sarrlevi pressed in close again. Even with Chopper guiding my arms, I dared not let myself become too distracted. I needed to use the brain space his guidance bought me and find a way to end this fight.

I funneled my magic into the ground under the assassin's feet, willing roots to come up and entangle his feet. To my surprise, tendrils much larger than any I'd ever created burst from the earth. But it wasn't instantaneous, and Sarrlevi had already moved on from the spot. He circled me, trying to get to my side or around to my back.

Spinning, I met his attack, leaving the roots to flail two feet in the air, useless as we danced around the circle. My breathing sounded in my ears, growing heavier. Not yet ragged and desperate, but my arms and legs were also growing heavier. I wouldn't be able to keep up this pace much longer.

Somehow, Chopper channeled more magic into me, giving me a second wind.

We're going to have a chat about your abilities later, I told it. *And the fact that you've been holding out on me.*

Fresh magic buzzed at my senses—Sarrlevi drawing upon his power again.

This time, I acted quickly enough, building the mental defenses that Freysha had taught me, imagining a wall of fern fronds between us. His power railed at them, and the leaves shuddered and swayed, like palm trees in a hurricane gale, but it didn't get through and hurl me across the circle again.

One tiny victory…

Or maybe not. As he kept thrusting and slashing with his swords, the magical attack went on and on, sapping my strength. My wall of fronds weakened and wavered, and some of his power crept through, a magical wind blasting me in the chest, slowing my movements, my ability to defend myself.

Sarrlevi's eyes lit in triumph.

Sindari roared so loudly that it startled me. It startled Sarrlevi too. The magical attack disappeared, and he half-turned to face Sindari, readying himself in case the tiger sprang for his throat.

But the fae magic continued to hold Sindari in place. He was just voicing his disgruntlement—and buying me a tiny distraction.

Once again, I willed the entangling roots to rise up and grab the assassin's legs. Thanks to Sindari, Sarrlevi was standing still for the first time. He glanced down, spotted the danger, and crouched to spring away.

I attempted to use my magic to keep him in place with the same kind of wind power he'd used on me. Chopper, of its own volition again, swung toward his face. Another distraction.

The roots rose up several feet, wrapping around his shins and calves. With a surge of euphoria—it was working!—I funneled more of my magic into the ground, wanting an entire forest of roots to ensnare him.

He slashed at several of the tendrils, trying to escape, but dozens more rose up, obeying my wishes. Sindari was right. This place had more inherent magic. It was much easier to call upon my abilities here.

Before I'd done more than start to believe I might defeat this guy, he glowered at me and hurled his greatest blast of power at me yet. My breath whooshed out as invisible energy slammed into my solar plexus. I flew backward again, and this time, what seemed like boxers' gloves rained down at me from all sides as I tumbled through the air and across our arena. One blow landed on my knee, another on my hip, and agony burst from both spots. The power spun me in the air, so I lost my bearings and didn't know up from down.

Through the pain and disorientation, I focused on only one thing: keeping those roots growing from the ground and further ensnaring Sarrlevi. I willed them to pin his arms and legs and entire body to the earth so he couldn't cut himself free.

I landed, not on my feet but skidding on my back across the floor. The assassin's power released me, but it didn't matter. The momentum sent me careening, the ground pummeling me as his magical attacks had.

Two fae chairs impeded my wild tumble, and I flopped to a stop, too winded and in too much pain to spring to my feet again. But I had to. The roots entangling Sarrlevi writhed and tightened around him as he tried to hack them away with his blades, and I had no doubt that he would find a way to free himself. I had to get up and finish him off before he could recover and finish *me* off.

As I rolled to my hands and knees, gasping for air and fighting against the pain assaulting my entire body, a surge of magical power erupted only a few feet away from me. A silvery glow preceded a portal forming in the middle of the fae circle.

Zav?

Hope surged through my battered body, but I rose to one knee with Chopper in hand, wariness mingling with the hope. What if it was the dragon who'd hired Sarrlevi? What if he'd killed Zav and had come to finish me off?

CHAPTER 29

IT WASN'T AN ENEMY BUT a familiar figure that strode through the portal to stand beside me. Zav's hair was mussed, pain tightened the corners of his eyes, soot smeared his cheek, and blood ran from cuts that gouged his temple and jaw. His silver-trimmed black robe was uncharacteristically rumpled with a long tear in the side, a deep puncture wound visible through the hole. Emotion made my eyes water as I realized he'd had as bad a day as I'd had.

Even though he was battered, the power of his aura flowed into the chamber, dangerous and deadly. For me, it was also familiar and comforting, but I doubted anyone else felt that way.

The fae sprang off their perches and backed away from the circle, some reaching for weapons, others raising their staffs like shields. Only the queen did not appear alarmed. Dithara rose up, her hands on her hips, as if she were only annoyed that the battle had been interrupted, but she did jerk her chin, summoning her guards to stand in front of her throne.

My mate, Zav spoke into my mind. *I have been victorious and defeated the ignoble coward who paid the assassin to target you.* He rested a hand atop my head as he looked around, his gaze catching on the assassin.

Still entangled, Sarrlevi slumped onto his back. Giving up? Good.

I looked over to make sure Amber was all right. The guards still surrounded her and Nin, keeping them from running into the circle, but nobody was manhandling them, and they appeared rattled but unharmed. Also good.

Sindari padded over to stand by the assassin, guarding him to ensure he didn't find a way to get out of the vines and skulk off.

I'm glad. Thank you. I wanted to spring to my feet and hug Zav, but I'd clobbered my knee, and it shot pain through me when I tried. Instead, I leaned into Zav and hugged his thighs. It was good enough for now. *I'm relieved to see you.*

He wasn't wearing the hole-filled yellow Crocs. Maybe he hadn't thought them intimidating enough for facing a room full of fae warriors and mages.

Zav lifted me to my feet, as solid as a mountain even though he appeared even more wounded than I. His arms wrapped around me to support my wobbly legs, and I leaned gratefully into him, careful not to touch that puncture.

As he hugged me, his healing magic flowed into me, and the tears that had already been threatening spilled from my eyes. Even though I wanted him to take care of himself, it always touched me when he was injured, yet used his energy to heal me first. Blood dripped from his wounds and mingled with my own. He must have come immediately here from his battle with Mythrarion.

You have defeated the assassin. Zav was staring over my shoulder at the entangled elf. *This is excellent. I am most proud of you, my mate.*

Thanks. I'm pretty tickled with myself too. I still didn't know exactly why Chopper's power was greater here—or was it simply easier to access?—but after this mess, I vowed to take some time off work to research the blade and learn everything I could about it. I was tired of being in the dark—and tired of being hunted down by people who wanted it when I didn't even fully know its value.

Tickled? Zav stroked the back of my head.

Yeah, tickled. I'll show you with a feather later.

I know the meaning of the word, but I do not know this saying. Zav's hand paused mid-stroke as he shifted his thoughtful gaze to my face. *I also do not know what role a feather would play in the activity.*

Foreplay. I can see I need to educate you.

In the nest? His eyes shifted from thoughtful to intrigued—maybe a touch randy. He always got excited when I defeated my enemies.

In bed, yes. I smiled and patted his chest.

Thumps on the ground startled me. Zav gazed around again, this time at the fae observers and the queen instead of the assassin. They were thumping their sandals on the ground in unison.

Nin and Amber eyed them warily, but it didn't seem to be an ominous gesture. More like the equivalent of clapping. Their guards had backed away, leaving them free to come into the circle if they wished. I waved Amber over, wanting her close. With Zav here, the fae shouldn't try anything else—and so far, the queen hadn't gone back on her word—but I didn't want to take chances.

Nin came with her, the backpack slung over one shoulder. Amber gripped two grenades that she must have sneaked out—or been given by Nin—during my fight. I was glad she hadn't hurled them but pleased she'd wanted to help.

I will speak with the assassin, Zav said. *Later, after we have healed our injuries, you will show me what is done with a feather.*

Sounds like a plan.

Zav released me and walked toward Sarrlevi, but he paused and looked back. *You will also tell me why you allowed my topiaries to be destroyed.*

Don't look at me. It's not like I was out there gardening too vigorously. I pointed at the assassin. *There's your culprit.*

I may slay him.

Because he's been trying to kill me or because of the shrubs? Usually, I'd tell Zav not to be a bully and to let enemies live, but I wouldn't cry if he killed this guy. The thought that another dragon irritated with me might hire Sarrlevi again came to mind.

Both are equally vexing.

Equally? Zav, you're not mated to the topiaries.

He looked back, his violet eyes glinting, and I decided his humor was on display. How he could tell jokes when he was leaving blood on the ground as he walked, I didn't know.

"Val?" Amber poked my shoulder. "Do you need to go to the ER? You look like hell."

"Probably, but I don't think 911 is going to respond to a call from here."

"Does *he* need to go?" Amber pointed at Zav's back—he looked like he was trying to hide a limp in addition to the other wounds.

"He should be able to heal himself once he has some time to rest. He beat up another dragon for me, you know."

"You sound smug," Nin said.

"That's because I am. He's a good boyfriend."

I expected Amber to say he was weird, but she nodded instead. "Yeah."

Progress.

Zav stopped in front of Sarrlevi and waved a hand. My roots went up in a puff of smoke as easily as he'd destroyed my car air freshener earlier in the week.

Sarrlevi rose warily. None of the fae, not even his queenly lover, came forward to stand at his side. They had stopped stomping but were watching curiously. I took that to mean they wouldn't interfere, but we were still the entertainment. My life as a Netflix special.

"Your service is no longer required." Zav poofed a parchment scroll into existence, the bottom rolling open by itself as he held the top. "Mythrarion of the Silverclaw Clan has been defeated in a fair duel and, following the protocol of all three of the assassins' guilds in the Cosmic Realms, has signed this document to officially cancel your contract. Furthermore, he has been taken to the Dragon Justice Court for crimes against my family. By the time he completes his punishment and rehabilitation, he will not remember that you exist."

Sarrlevi read through the form with his mouth twisted in displeasure. "This is unorthodox."

"You will agree that the contract is canceled and that you will never threaten my mate again, or I will slay you." Zav lifted his chin, his violet eyes flaring with light. "By the laws of my people, I am within my rights to slay any who threaten my mate." His eyes narrowed, though a pleased smile—actually, that looked more like a sinister smile—stretched his lips. "But perhaps I would simply put the entangling roots back and allow her to slay you herself."

"There is a fifty-percent cancellation fee," Sarrlevi stated like a businessman negotiating a deal, not at all concerned by the threats of slaying. "Will Mythrarion be paying me, or will you cover it?"

"You agree that you will leave my mate alone and threaten her no more? Even if another tries to hire you?"

"I agree. She'll be deadly if she ever learns how to use all the powers within that sword." Sarrlevi inclined his head toward me, as if he were paying me a compliment.

"I'm already deadly, asshole."

He didn't appear affronted.

"How much is the fifty-percent cancellation fee?" Zav asked.

I gripped my chin, watching this negotiation with fascination, mostly because Zav did not, as far as I knew, have any money.

"Eighteen hundred gnomish phlanks or one thousand elvish yerv."

"Dragons do not carry currency," Zav said.

"Mythrarion was going to pay me with the equivalent in treasure. His cave was mounded high with it."

"I *knew* there were dragons out there with caves of treasure," I whispered to Nin and Amber. "All those fantasy authors *couldn't* be wrong."

"This is true," Zav said. "After I defeated him fairly in battle, I informed him that I would take some of his treasures as payment for the vexation he has caused myself and my mate."

That was surprising. Since when did Zav care about treasures of any kind? He snubbed money every time I mentioned it.

"Did he object?" Sarrlevi asked.

"No."

"Was he conscious at the time?"

"Insensate."

Sarrlevi snorted.

Zav waved a hand in the air, and I detected a hint of magic. Then his fingers disappeared from sight.

Amber gaped. Nin, perhaps more familiar with interdimensional pockets, did not find this as startling. The fae were still watching everything, the queen back in her throne, her scaled pet watching over her shoulder as she noshed caramels. I wondered if I should inform her about serving sizes. Did fae have to worry about calories?

Zav rummaged around inside his pocket, finally pulling out a large fistful of what looked like jewelry. He spread his stash on the ground, then surprised me by waving me over. They were all rings, some garish—was that a snake eating its own tail?—and some beautiful, gold or silver with exotic gems. Most of them emanated a little magic and likely had an enchantment or some power like my charms.

Did he want to know which might be worth the eighteen hundred gnomish phlanks? How would I know? I didn't even know the current exchange rate between Canadian and US dollars, despite crossing the border to chase down bad guys regularly.

The assassin waited with his hands clasped behind his back, his swords back in their scabbards.

Which ring do you like most? Zav pointed at more than twenty offerings.

Did he want me to pick the one to give the guy? Sarrlevi wasn't wearing any jewelry, so I assumed he would pawn whatever he got. What did it matter?

But Zav watched me intently, as if this mattered a lot more than I thought it should.

Uhm, those two are nice. I pointed to a couple of elegant ones, though they looked like they had been designed more for a woman's finger than a man's. Presumably, male assassins preferred manly jewelry.

Only nice? Zav asked. *Do none call to you in a passion-inspiring way?*

"Oh my God!" Amber blurted, startling me. She ran over and pointed at the jewelry. "Is this for the wedding? Are you picking an *engagement* ring, Val?"

"No." I shook my head, realizing Zav and I had been speaking telepathically so she couldn't have followed along. "I don't think so."

Zav raised his eyebrows.

"Wait." I stared at him. "*Am* I?"

The queen popped another caramel into her mouth.

"I have searched for many days on many worlds to find the vile dragon who hired an assassin to slay you. Then I fought him on land and in the sky in a ferocious battle that lasted many hours." Zav touched a hand to the puncture wound in his side. "Then I thwarted the magical illusions and traps that hid and protected his ill-gotten hoard of treasures so that I could find a ring worthy of your finger. This was a noble quest and sufficient to proclaim to the Cosmic Realms—and the idiot vermin on your planet—that we are eternal partners and to be wed in the way of humans so that you will be my mate, and I will be your dragon. Always."

"Wow," Amber whispered. "I may cry."

I was already tearing up. This whole month, I hadn't been certain I was ready to get married again—and to such a quirky strange being from another world—but now, I couldn't imagine anything else. I leaned into Zav and flung my arms around him. My first thought was that I didn't want to kiss him in front of all these people, but he kissed me, and it was perfect, and I realized I didn't care about the audience.

The assassin sighed. Maybe he had somewhere else to be. I ignored him and kissed Zav back.

"*I'll* pick out the ring," Amber said, surprising me by *not* sighing or saying that this public display was gross.

Sindari padded over and put a paw on one. *This one is appealing.*

"I think that's made of ivory." Did she understand him?

It is made of bone, likely the bone of a great predator that the jewel crafter slew him or herself.

SECRETS OF THE SWORD I

"Disgusting." Amber picked up a gold ring with a diamond framed by emeralds that matched my eyes. "*This* is a wedding ring. Or maybe an engagement ring. Definitely one of the two." She held it up to Zav, slapping his arm to get him to stop kissing me.

Zav didn't release me, but he drew his mouth back enough to frown at her, frown at me, and say, "Your offspring is impudent."

"How shocking," I said.

"Let me pick out the other one." Amber must have gotten over her fear of Zav and his mighty aura, or maybe the array of jewelry laid out was distracting her. "And he'll need a wedding ring too."

Nin came out and crouched beside Amber as they sifted through the options and picked out two more rings. It looked like I was getting a gold band to go with the diamond-and-emerald ring, and Zav was getting a thicker gold band with leaves engraved around the outside. It oozed elven magic. All three of the rings did. Hopefully, they didn't do anything strange. Like turn dragon lovers into toads. Amber was going on aesthetics rather than magical power, so who knew what I would end up with?

Once the selections were made, Zav flicked a finger, and the rest of the rings floated up and into his hands. He strode to the assassin and held out the dubiously acquired bounty.

Sarrlevi gazed at him impassively, and I thought he might reject the offer, but he held his hands out. Zav dumped the rings into them, and Sarrlevi tucked them into a pocket and buttoned it shut.

"If you break your word and come after my mate again," Zav stated, "I will slay you ruthlessly."

"I'll keep that in mind." Sarrlevi waved his arm, and a portal formed a few feet from where Zav's portal had faded. He strode toward it but paused to look at me before entering. "You are not the great warrior that I expected. Had I not overestimated you, plotted to have your blade stolen, and worked to remove your allies from your presence, I could have killed you and completed my mission as soon as I first located you."

I was super broken up that he'd failed. "I guess you learned a lesson, huh?"

His elegant eyebrows shifted upward minutely.

"We've got a saying on Earth. Any fool can make something complex; it takes a genius to make something simple."

"I see," he said stiffly.

I supposed I shouldn't vex him, now that he was defeated and leaving, but he'd been vexing *me* all week. Besides, what did he expect after insulting me?

"Does it also take a *genius* to learn the abilities of the sword one carries?" he asked.

"I'm guessing it takes someone with a lot of free time on their hands. I've got cleaning the lint behind the dryer and scraping leaves out of the gutters next on my to-do list, but I'll add sword research to the end."

"You are strange, mongrel." Despite the words, he bowed to me before springing through his portal, rings clanking in his pocket.

"I really don't think *I'm* the strange one here," I said as the magic of the portal faded, the fae queen and her minions still watching.

"Yeah, you are, Val." Amber clapped me on the shoulder. "Nin agrees." She looked at Nin.

"Val is one of my best clients," Nin said. "She always needs more grenades and ammunition, and she pays my prices without haggling."

"Nin agrees that you're strange." Amber nodded.

"We will return to your world." Zav looked toward our audience. "And the fae will not bother my mate or her offspring again."

"*We* didn't bother anyone, Lord Dragon," the queen said, chocolate smudged on the side of her mouth. "She intruded upon *our* realm."

"She will not do so again, providing that you do not send artifacts meant to ensorcell her sword again."

"That will depend on whether handsome elven assassins with excellent bedroom skills come requesting them again." The queen winked.

Amber couldn't have understood the fae words, but maybe the wink conveyed enough. She glanced at Nin. "You'll at least agree that *this* place is strange, right?"

"Yes," Nin said. "I will agree with that."

Zav didn't seem to know how to respond to the queen. He strode back to my side, wrapped an arm around me, and his dragon's aura intensified, seeming to crackle in the air. His powerful magic streaked along my nerves, making me tingle all over.

"You're not marking me again, are you?" I whispered.

Sindari sat on his haunches, gazing at me. *You now glow with an intense dragon aura to those with magical senses.*

Didn't I already do that before? I replied silently.

You glowed with a faint dragon aura before. Now you are resplendent in dragonness.

Oh, fabulous.

"I am replenishing the magic that shows you are mine—and reminds others how disastrous it would be for them to attempt to harm you." Zav was glaring at the queen as he spoke. "Soon, you will wear my ring, we will be wed, and there will be no confusion that you are my mate, and I am your dragon. In *any* realm."

I doubted the queen was confused about that. She just didn't care. Maybe she had enough magical defenses here in her home that she wasn't worried about Zav being able to do anything to her. Or maybe she was powerful enough in her own right to deal with a dragon.

With a surge of magic, Zav re-formed his portal. He waved for Amber and Nin to go first. They hopped through together, shoulder to shoulder again, and I dared hope this little experience had bonded them enough that Amber wouldn't be tempted to run away from home simply because Nin spent the night with Thad.

"Because you have entertained me this day," the queen said as Zav and I were about to step through, "and provided an intriguing new sweet to tantalize my taste buds, I will offer you some information."

"Oh?" I asked warily.

"The power that enchants your blade has a distinctive flare that I have sensed once before, long ago. On a weapon that originated in the dwarven home world, its magic charged by a lightning bolt from one of the frequent storms that assault Mount Crenel. There are ancient dwarven caves and temples within that mountain. Perhaps there, you will learn more about your blade." Her lips quirked, and she caressed the remaining boxes of caramels. "Leave your dragon lover behind when you visit, for the dwarven masters who made the ancient dragon blades crafted them to slay their kind, and there are rumored to be traps and danger aplenty for the winged and scaled who seek the ancient holds."

Zav sniffed disdainfully, but his eyes were sharp as he filed away the information. He probably wanted me to figure out the powers of my sword as much as I wanted it.

"Until you learn to master that blade, you will be at risk of losing it to anyone more powerful and more wily than you." The queen looked toward a knot of young fae males—several were from the escort that had brought us here—but they cast their gazes downward, avoiding her eyes.

Had they telepathically asked her if they could snatch Chopper from me when they'd been escorting me in?

"You're probably right," I said. "I'll move sword research up above the gutters and dryer lint."

"A good idea." She waved a hand in dismissal.

"Oh, wait. I thought of one more thing." As long as she was in a good mood, I ought to make as many requests as I could. "Do you have anything that could un-taint the water that your artifact contaminated on Earth? It was killing the local wildlife."

Her eyes narrowed. "I may have a potion that could be used to such an end. What do you offer in trade?"

"Uhm." I started to propose more boxes of caramels but then remembered Dimitri's request from the beach. "How do you feel about cranberry fudge?"

An eyebrow lifted. "What is *fudge*?"

"You'll love it. I'll have whoever applies the potion pick you up some and leave it at a fairy ring for your people to collect." I imagined a white box of fudge with a pink ribbon around it nestled in the grass inside a circle of mushrooms. Nothing odd about that.

"It is excellent? Like the brown squares?"

"It's excellent." I was sure Dimitri wouldn't have made me bring him some if it wasn't.

"Very well. I will have a potion prepared."

"Thank you." I bowed, hugged Zav, then patted Sindari on the back, relieved we'd all survived the day.

We will travel to the dwarven home world soon? Sindari asked.

If I can talk Zav into taking me.

You will be able to. He cares a great deal about you.

He told you that?

He marked you with his aura, even more flamboyantly than before.

A sign of true love, huh?

He also risked his life traveling hither and yon to get an assassin off your back.

That is true. He's pretty special. I squeezed Zav's hand.

"What is dryer lint?" Zav asked.

"I'll show you when we get home."

"It is titillating? As with the feather?"

"On second thought, we'll skip the lint."

"Very well."

I dismissed Sindari back to his realm, and Zav and I sprang through the portal to go home.

CHAPTER 30

ONCE WE WERE IN THE front yard back home, it seeming like days since we'd left, I considered dropping to the grass and kissing the damp ground. If those ugly mushrooms hadn't been all over the place, I might have. Instead, I turned and hugged and kissed Zav soundly, glad he'd shown up in time to defuse the assassin situation.

Out of the corner of my eye, I glimpsed the curtains being drawn shut. Amber and Nin must have made it inside—and objected to the displays of smooching on the lawn. I hoped Amber was calling Thad. Even if she'd said she was spending the night at a friend's house, he would have worried if she hadn't responded to whatever texts he had doubtless sent since she left.

"Ah, excellent," Zav said, returning the hug, but only for a moment before he stepped back and raised a finger. "I must consult with a human expert."

"An expert on what?"

"Weddings and marriage proposals. One moment." Zav tilted his head, eyes half closing. Was he contacting someone telepathically?

"I'm pleased that you still want to marry me, but there's no hurry with the proposal or anything. We might want to heal your wounds, change clothes, shower…" I looked at the dark sky, hardly able to believe it was still the same night. "Go to bed."

But Zav remained in that head-tilted pose of concentration. Several seconds passed, and he frowned.

"She has refused to communicate with me telepathically." He gave me a stern look. "Telepathy is convenient and practical, not *creepy*."

"It's a little creepy if you're not used to it." Or if it caught you during a moment you'd considered private and personal. I'd had him contact me out of the blue when I was in the bath before.

"I require the use of your communications device." He pointed to the pocket where I kept my phone.

"It's late. Whoever you're talking to—" I had a suspicion—it wasn't as if he knew that many humans, "—will appreciate it if you wait until the sun comes up."

He held out his hand, palm up. "I have acquired suitable rings, so it is time for the proposal."

My phone buzzed. I answered it instead of giving it to him. It wasn't as if he knew how to make a call anyway.

"Hey, Willard. How'd you know I was back from Fae Land? With my sword fixed and the assassin off my back."

"Your dragon told me. Do you know how startling it is to be woken by a dragon speaking telepathically into your mind?"

"Actually, yes."

"Asking about *proposal* etiquette?"

"He's not contacted me about that before."

"I will speak with your employer and my human expert." He waved his extended hand.

"You think Willard is an expert on weddings? Willard, how many weddings have you been to?"

"More than your dragon."

"I will speak with her about this important matter," Zav said.

"Suit yourself." I gave him the phone.

Poor Willard.

"I have acquired a ring worthy of my mate and her increasing power and prowess in battle," Zav stated.

"Fantastic," came Willard's dry response.

"What is the procedure for the proposal ritual? I wish to go forward so that we will officially be mated in the way of humans so that all male humans know she is my mate, and I am her dragon."

"Is it okay if female humans know it too?"

"*All* will know. We are mates. Always. I have gone into battle against another dragon to protect her." Zav touched his chest, hopefully not planning to yank his robe off and show the phone his wounds—it wasn't a video call. "He dared hire an assassin to harm her. Now he is before the Dragon Justice Court."

"Look, it's the middle of the night. I'm sure it's a great story, but I don't want to hear it now. If you want to marry her, take her someplace romantic, drop to one knee, hold up the ring, and ask her if she'll marry you. *Ask*, don't tell. Good luck."

Zav opened his mouth, but Willard hung up before he could speak. He glared down at the phone.

Afraid his eyes would glow and he'd incinerate it, I plucked it out of his grasp. "Why don't we go shower, get the blood and plant bits off, and go to bed?"

Maybe if I kept suggesting that, he would get the picture.

Zav forgot his ire and gazed around, his eyes growing thoughtful. "This is the yard of your domicile. Do you find it romantic?"

"Uh." I eyed the destroyed bushes—someone had driven over one of the charred topiaries in the street—scorched remains of the lawn, and the giant mushrooms that I'd grown. They leered at me now, even larger than they had been hours earlier. Could a flamethrower destroy magical mushrooms? I had no need of a fairy doorway on my lawn now. "Not in its present state."

"Because the topiaries were destroyed." Zav nodded.

"Among other things."

"They were magnificent. I will plant new ones and craft them again into dragon likenesses."

"I'm sure the neighborhood will be thrilled."

"Yes." Zav clasped my hands. "How do you feel about the *backyard*? It was not damaged by odious assassins."

"It's all right, but look." I squeezed his hands. "There's no need to rush things. I'm glad that you want to marry me in the human way but—"

"Are you?" He gazed intently into my eyes. "I have sensed reticence in you when we have discussed this matter. Do you not wish to be my mate in the human way?" The power of his aura wrapped around me, surprisingly gentle and patient.

"I…" I looked at his torn robe, the deep gouges in his flesh visible by the illumination of the corner streetlamp, and thought of the days he'd been gone, hunting down another dragon—a *dangerous* dragon— entirely on my behalf. "Yeah. I do."

"Excellent. We will go to a romantic spot for the proposal." He released my hand so he could point toward the gate beside the house that led to the backyard. "No, wait. I know of an even better place." His pointing finger shifted toward the rooftop. "The view is excellent."

"You want to propose to me on the roof?"

"Yes. You will love it." He stepped back several paces and shifted into his dragon form, turning so that his violet eyes still held mine. *Climb onto my back,* he spoke into my mind.

"You needed to turn into a dragon to fly to the roof? You've levitated me places before."

In fact, he'd levitated me up to his back numerous times.

We shall take—what is the human expression?—the scenic route. His eyes flared with violet light. *It will be romantic.*

I wasn't positive he knew what romantic meant, but I climbed onto his back and refrained from making comments about saddles. His powerful haunches bunched, and he sprang into the air. When he flapped his wings, they took us not toward the roof but over the neighboring houses and toward Green Lake. He soared over the grassy lawns, empty bike path, and the water.

At this hour of the night—actually, my phone informed me that it was four a.m. now—nobody was out, and few cars traveled the streets as he banked and soared toward the Ballard Locks. Lake Union, where we'd once battled a kraken, lay quiet, no lights on in the houseboats docked along its shores. The Space Needle was lit up against the skyscraper-filled skyline, and Zav flew south to bank lazily around it and over toward Lake Washington.

The damp breeze that washed over us smelled of the sea and wood-burning stoves, and I decided that the flight was indeed romantic. He glided over the yacht club where he'd pestered me when I'd been working for the now-deceased Weber, and I tried to pick out the remains of his estate to the north.

Zav flew across Lake Washington and to the northeast, over Kirkland and Woodinville and out toward Duvall. As the water treatment plant where we'd battled Dobsaurin came into view, barely lit among the forest surrounding it, I realized Zav was taking me over places where we'd battled bad guys together.

He didn't go so far as to fly to Idaho, though I knew that house with the hot tub was a warm, fuzzy spot in his mind, instead turning back to fly over Bothell and the manufactured home park where we'd fought and finally defeated Dob. New homes had already been brought into the neighborhood to replace the ones that had been burned down, and only stumps remained of the trees that had been destroyed by dragon fire.

It pleases me to visit the places where we did battle and you vexed my enemies, Zav informed me. *It is romantic.*

I patted his cool scales. *You're right. It is.*

You vexed the assassin before he left. Zav's tone sounded pleased, even smug. *You called him a fool.*

Do you think that was a bad idea?

For most beings, yes, it would be unwise to vex an assassin, but you are the mate of a mighty dragon, and he will not dare go back on his word to me. Also, with those rings, I gave him the monetary equivalent of much more than he asked for, so he should not feel cheated. He should know that it is wise to please dragons, not vex them.

I think he's kind of honorable anyway and probably wouldn't kill someone just because they insulted him. I remembered how he hadn't taken advantage when I'd been wiping sweat out of my eyes.

His reputation is one of honor, yes. But also, it is wise to please dragons.

I've heard this.

Excellent.

Zav flapped his powerful wings and took us back toward my house in the Green Lake neighborhood. As he soared low, he startled a flock of seagulls snoozing on telephone wires. They took off with uproarious squawks, as if the mighty dragon might chase them down and eat them. No, he preferred barbecued ribs these days.

Zav alighted on the roof, avoiding the pointed tip of the turret. It had a weathervane on the top, which I assumed would not feel good poking into a dragon's butt. Of course, he had enjoyed crunching down on patio chairs, so what did I know? Maybe it was a delight.

I slid off his back, a hint of magic guiding me so that I came down lightly onto the sloped roof. Thanks to the park lights, I could make out the lake beyond the rooftops of the neighboring houses. The view *was* nice.

Zav shifted into human form and faced me. He cleared his throat like a soprano getting ready for a solo. Was he *nervous*? If so, that amused me vastly.

But it also made me think of the gravity of what he was about to ask. I wiped my hands on my jeans. They were damp. Maybe I was nervous too.

Zav patted his robe, as if he'd forgotten which hidden pocket he'd stored the rings in.

"It's dark up here," I observed inanely, for the silence seemed awkward.

"Is being in the dark with a sexy dragon not romantic?" Zav was probably giving me his half-slitted bedroom eyes, but I couldn't see them.

"Candles are even more romantic. So one can see one's sexy dragon."

He didn't poof candles into existence, but he did stop patting his robe and, with a whisper of magic, produced soft yellow light around us. It illuminated his handsome face, his perfectly trimmed mustache and beard, and his slightly curly black hair. He'd recovered from the wounds that had marred his face an hour earlier. The impressive healing power of a dragon.

"Val Thorvald," he said, producing one of the rings—presumably the one Amber had dubbed the engagement ring—and holding it aloft. "I wish to ask you—wait." He jerked the ring down and stared at it, as if ants had started crawling out of it. He stared so long that I grew concerned.

"Problem?" I asked.

"I do not know what this does."

It took me a moment to realize he must mean the magic imbuing it. *All* of the rings he'd pilfered from the defeated dragon's hoard had held magic.

He clenched his fist around the ring. "Wait here."

"Here?" I pointed to the roof under my feet as a portal formed behind him.

"Yes. Right there. I will return." He spun, robe flapping around him, and sprang through the portal.

"What if I have to pee?" I called after him.

But Zav and the portal vanished. So did the light.

"Wonderful." I debated on climbing down from the roof and taking a nap in my bedroom while waiting for him to return. Now that I wasn't battling assassins or fae magical vines, my body was making me aware that I hadn't slept at all that night.

Fortunately, I'd no sooner sat down than another portal formed and Zav emerged. He'd changed out of his elven slippers and into the "lucky" yellow Crocs.

I groaned and pointed to them. "*That's* why you left?"

He gazed down at the footwear that somehow managed to be brilliantly yellow even in the dark. "It is not, but I decided that they would be appropriate for this occasion, as the father of your offspring informed me."

"Someone who wants nothing but success for our wedded future, I'm sure." I doubted Thad minded if I got married, but he *did* mind Zav. Even if I found him lovably pompous, others swapped in another adverb. Obnoxiously pompous, perhaps.

"I am sure. He has stopped lusting after you. This pleases me. He knows that we are mates now and that to covet you would be in vain."

"Uh, that's good." I had a feeling that had more to do with Thad finding Nin than anything to do with Zav, but I was glad. "And possibly, you should stop reading people's minds."

"Lesser beings frequently plot against dragons. It is wise to comb through their thoughts in search of schemes."

"And lust."

"Yes." Zav produced the ring again, shaking out the voluminous sleeves of his black elven robe, and extended it toward me, both palms upward. "I have researched and learned what the elven magic imbued in these rings does."

"Is *that* why you left?"

"It is. I had hunches, but I wanted to ensure there was no possible way that someone might have tricked your offspring into choosing rings with powers that would harm us. Or that would work against our union. You will find it difficult to believe, but there are magical trinkets designed to keep away dragons."

"Yes, that's very difficult to believe. Who would want to keep away dragons?"

"Individuals with nefarious plots. This ring—" Zav touched the simple gold band, "—will assist you with gardening."

"Gardening? Like growing tomatoes?"

"Growing anything. Its magic is designed to bless the soil."

"That's going to help me in battles." I supposed all that mattered was that the ring wasn't unlucky and didn't allow others to control my mind from a distance.

"It could. Did you not defeat the assassin by sprouting roots from the ground?"

"You think that ring will help with that?"

"You may experiment once we are wed and it is on your finger." He pointed to the diamond-and-emerald one Amber had dubbed the engagement ring, then smiled slyly at me and gave me his bedroom eyes. "This one should enhance your cooking skills. The meat that you smoke will be even *more* moist and succulent."

"That couldn't have worked out better for you if you'd chosen it yourself."

"I was pleased to learn of its magical enhancement."

"What does the one you'll wear do?"

"The elven princess was not certain but thought it might have something to do with hair growth enhancement. She assured me that it is a very minor enchantment and would not overpower me even if it did something unappealing."

"You went to see Freysha?"

"And the king, yes. They are knowledgeable about elven magic."

"Is Eireth recovering? Did you ever find out who was responsible?"

"He is recovering, and Lord Quaresthee was responsible for the affliction. He was strong-winged by Mythrarion Silverclaw, the same as the cowardly Xilnethgarish."

"The assassin admitted he wanted all of my allies out of the picture."

"That is perhaps true, but Mythrarion thought it would be easier to get an elven assassin to kill you if you were believed responsible for the king's death, so he planted that seed. But the truth is now known, and I informed the king about the forthcoming wedding. He is happy for you and agrees that your life is blessed and it is a great honor to be chosen by a dragon."

"I'm sure. But you're supposed to wait until I say yes to the proposal before telling my parents about the wedding."

"That is a human custom?"

"It is."

"Then let us make it official." Zav held the engagement ring out to me and awkwardly dropped to one knee, concentration on his face as if he'd never gotten on his knees in front of anyone before and had no idea how to do it. "Valmeyjar Thorvald, great warrioress and overcomer of the weaknesses of her mongrel heritage, will you marry me, Lord Zavryd'nokquetal the great and noble dragon, and mate with me vigorously every night after making me meat?"

"*Every* night?" I didn't point out that he hadn't quite gotten the line right—he'd done better than I expected and made it a question and not a demand.

"Every night that we are not busy battling enemies."

"Okay, but sometimes, you have to bring me food too. Perhaps some exotic delicacies from the elven home world. Or scones from the bakery down the street."

"Yes. I will do this. And I will make you shudder and scream with pleasure in the nest before I take my own pleasure."

I blushed even though there was nobody else on the roof to hear that. "Something my roommates adore," I murmured.

"*You* adore it. That is what is important." His smile grew a touch wicked, and his eyes flared briefly with violet light.

"I guess it is. I accept your proposal, and I will marry you." I held my hand out to him.

He considered it, then clasped it and kissed my fingers.

"You're supposed to put the ring on it."

Willard must have hung up before going over that part. I wiggled my ring finger.

"Ah." The ring slid on with a perfect fit.

That boded well. I'd worried that elven fingers were more petite than mine. Maybe Zav had applied a little magic to it, being careful not to damage the imbuement that would improve my rib-smoking skills.

He rose up and hugged me and kissed me, gestures which I happily returned, trusting that he would use his magic to keep me from falling off the roof if we grew too arduous and I misstepped.

But he broke the kiss sooner than I expected, leaning back to gaze in my eyes. "We will wed soon, yes?"

"Soon," I agreed.

"Today?"

"Not that soon."

"Tomorrow?"

"A wedding is a big ceremony here on Earth. We're supposed to plan it in advance and invite all our friends and family." I choked a little on the idea that he might invite *his* family. Would Zondia show up? His uncle Ston? The *queen*? Maybe I would get lucky, and they would scoff at the idea of attending some silly human ceremony. "We don't have to have a huge wedding—it's not like I'm friends with that many people—but it would be nice to arrange it somewhere scenic, during a season where good weather is likely, with music and a nice meal."

I wasn't a girlie girl, but even I liked a good wedding.

"A meal? Like a *feast*?" There was that gleam in his eyes again.

"Yes, a feast. With lots of kinds of meat."

"Excellent. I approve. You will start planning immediately. You will tell me how to assist. Do you wish me to hunt down a *deradayk* and bring the carcass for preparation for the feast day? Will one be enough? Perhaps I'll take my brothers and cousins, and we'll hunt down *many deradayk*."

Visions of piles of dead animals on the lawn filled my mind.

"I'll, uhm, let you know once the planning gets underway."

"Excellent. Dragons are mighty hunters. We can provide sustenance for all who attend this glorious occasion."

I had always imagined a carcass-free wedding, but when one married a dragon, one had to expect the unexpected.

EPILOGUE

IN THE OFFICE IN THE back of the coffee shop, sitting shoulder to shoulder with Nin and young Reb, I used a pair of pliers to twist and attach one of the wire wings for the dragon door knocker I was working on. If anyone asked me, Dimitri's door knockers still looked more like T-Rexes than the mighty predators I was now intimately familiar with, but Dimitri was being careful not to ask me.

Reb was attaching legs to a purple door knocker. Nin was working on a pink one. Next to her, Inga, who'd also been pressed into work on our assembly line, was imbuing a completed door knocker with the magic that would allow it to spew fire from its snout at intruders or any hapless visitor who didn't utter the password in time.

Dimitri strolled in with a pen tucked behind his ear and a receipt in his hand. A big grin sprawled across his usually dour face.

"I have more orders." He waved the paper cheerfully.

Inga eyed him darkly. "We haven't finished the last orders."

When she'd agreed to tutor him in the ways of enchanting magic, she likely hadn't envisioned being put to work making dozens of door knockers. At least she and Reb were being paid. Nin and I were helping out because we were co-owners in the business, and attaching wings to T-Rexes was what good business partners did. Or so Nin had informed me when she'd talked me into coming down before dawn this morning.

"I also sold two bicycle-bear defender statues," Dimitri added, grinning even wider.

"Are those bears on bicycles or bears made from bicycles?" I asked.

"They're made from bicycle parts and spit tarry bits made from tires and other doodads. Zoltan made an allergenic coating to go on them. Trespassers tend to leave the premises swiftly to deal with itchy, sticky goo attached to their faces. My whole line of yard-art defenses is getting more attention now. The door knockers are luring people in, and I'm upselling them on other merchandise." He waved at Nin. "Thank you for teaching me that term and how it works."

"You are welcome," Nin said.

"You will thank me for teaching you how to use your magic to create materials that transform their state from solid to semi-solid when in the air," Inga said, lifting her chin.

"Uh, yes. Thank you. I would thank you more if you didn't rap my knuckles with a wrench when you're teaching me."

"You lack focus, just as with young Reb here." She reached over and *thwapped* him on the shoulder with a mesh wing—he'd stopped working and was perusing a LEGO catalog while munching on what looked like chocolate-covered raisins with fuzzy pieces of pocket lint dangling from them. "Boys need to learn to focus."

She squinted at me. I'd paused my work when Dimitri came in, but I hurried to finish attaching the wing, lest she *thwap* me too. From what I'd noticed of trolls, they considered what humans would call physical abuse to be a healthy part of a relationship. Maybe it was because *thwaps* rarely fazed them. They tended to be built like refrigerators. Tall, green refrigerators. Inga was only half-troll, but she still had refrigerator status.

"I'll take your spot, Val." Dimitri waved to my seat. "Your boss is out front and asked for you."

"Willard?" It was early, so I hadn't had a chance to let her know about the wedding yet. I wondered if I could press her into helping me arrange things. When I'd told my mother and asked her if she wanted to help, she'd suggested eloping to Las Vegas. A sentimentalist, she was not.

"Do you have other bosses I don't know about?" Dimitri asked. "I assume you don't let Zav push you around."

"I don't, but Sindari is out there, and he takes pride in strongly advising me on various matters."

We'd come from the house together, Sindari hoping that enemies would ambush me so that he could engage in a good battle. He'd been disappointed that the fae and the assassin had bound him with magic that kept him from joining in my *last* battle.

"Like petting him?" Dimitri lifted an arm, revealing silver tiger hairs on his dark sleeve.

"More like not irking dragons and removing the air fresheners from my Jeep."

"How demanding."

I gave Dimitri my seat and headed to the main room. The chatter of dozens of conversations in almost as many languages mingled with the hiss of the milk frother and the whir of the bean grinder. The scent of coffee hung in the air. I hadn't yet talked Dimitri into getting a liquor license so he could legally serve my preferred drink of hard cider.

To my surprise, Willard was sitting at a table across from Walker, coffee mugs in front of them. As I headed over, a green hand reached out and thumped my arm.

"Congratulations on your engagement," a goblin I didn't recognize said. "To be claimed as the mate of a dragon is a prestigious thing. Will we be invited to the wedding?" He waved around the table, which was packed with five more goblins, including the smirking Gondo, and covered in no fewer than fifteen espresso cups, most already empty. Centered among the collection was a contraption that looked like a miniature rocket launcher with glider wings. Hopefully, it didn't fire anything more dangerous than dice—or fly around the coffee shop.

"How'd you find out?" I directed that at Gondo rather than the one I didn't know, assuming he'd been the one to blab. So far, I'd only told my mother, Nin, and Amber.

"Lord Zavryd told me." Gondo hefted an espresso cup in the air and gave me what I gathered were congratulations in his language, though he finished with a wink and a leer, so something about sex was probably baked in.

Sometimes, it was better *not* to activate my translation charm.

"Thanks."

One of the goblins stood on his chair so that we were eye to eye. Somberly, he said, "It is a goblin tradition that the engaged couple buy drinks for friends, relatives, and coffee-shop customers. It is for good luck."

Gondo dropped his face in his hand.

"Nice try," I told his buddy. "You're welcome to ask Zav to pick up your tab. He's coming by later."

The goblin plopped back into his seat. "Never mind."

"Hello, Willard," I said, walking up to their table. "Dr. Walker."

"Thorvald." Willard lifted a mug—had she decided our coffee was worth buying after all?

"I regret that it's taken me so long," Walker said, pulling something out of his pocket, "but my lab people isolated the fae infection and came up with a magical antibiotic that will heal it." He held up a bottle of pills, but frowned when he noticed my hand no longer had a bandage.

"Thanks, but the fae queen healed it for me. In exchange for chocolate." I showed him the scar that was all that remained.

"Had I known there was a reward of chocolate, I would have had my people work more quickly."

"Sorry."

He started to return the pill container to his pocket, but Willard took it from him and placed it on the table in front of me.

"It's only a matter of time before she uses her sword to break some other artifact," she said. "She's got the subtlety of a typhoon."

"Really." I thought the odds of me cutting myself on another fae artifact were slim, but I took the pills. One never knew.

"Really," Willard said.

Walker noticed my ring and pointed at it. "That's a beaut. Tiffany? Cartier?"

Willard rolled her eyes, probably at his familiarity with luxury brands.

"Dragon lair," I said, showing it off. Not exactly a luxury brand, but I was proud that Zav had defeated another dragon to get it for me. Not just a random dragon but the one who'd tried to get me killed.

"I haven't heard of them," Walker said. "Local jeweler?"

"Something like that." I waved at the two of them. "Am I interrupting a date?"

"No." Willard pulled a manila envelope out of her briefcase and slid it across the table. "I'm paying him for services rendered."

"Oh?" I couldn't keep my eyes from twinkling madly.

She glared, not missing my insinuation. "For my *unit*."

"The whole unit? You must have excellent stamina, Walker."

"Yes." His eyes were twinkling too.

Willard rolled her own eyes. "The maturity level in your coffee shop equals that of a preschool jamboree."

A *twang* came from the goblin table, and something whizzed behind Willard's head, stirring her wiry hair, and clanked off a window. A twenty-sided die tumbled to the floorboards.

"Sorry," one of the goblins called, waving as Willard turned her glare on them. She'd had her sidearm halfway out of its holster.

"I won't argue with your assessment of our establishment," I said. "I'm surprised you're here. You've mentioned how odious you find it. Though I notice that your coffee mug is more than half empty."

"That's her second mug," Walker pointed out helpfully.

The glare landed on him—if Willard were capable of shooting daggers out of her eyes, half of the coffee shop would be dead by now.

"How long have you been here?" I would have come out earlier if I'd known she was waiting.

"Not long. I was thirsty."

"Thirsty? Or is it just that the coffee is tasty?" Since I wasn't a fan of the drink, I hadn't tried any of ours, but I kept hearing that the goblin blend was amazing, if higher octane than race-car fuel.

"It's all right," she said grudgingly. "I only came because I want to hire you. And to congratulate you on your upcoming nuptials." Her glare finally receded, replaced by a smirk.

"Yes, thank you for advising Zav on the proposal. He was certain to choose a romantic place."

"Candlelit dinner at the Space Needle?"

"The rooftop of our house."

"I hope it has a nice view."

"What greater view do I need than of my magnificent dragon lover?"

"Crikey, mate," Walker muttered, his Australian coming out.

"I'll take that as a no to the view," Willard said dryly.

"It was dark. What do you need me to do?"

"If you've solved the problem with your sword..." Willard looked at Walker.

He nodded. "Her sword is no longer vibrating like the ground during a kangaroo stampede."

"That's good. I think." Willard drew another folder from her briefcase and handed it to me. "We've got some thefts happening."

"Orcs holding up cashiers at the 7-Eleven on 15th again?" I groped for a polite way to say I needed to figure out the mysteries revolving around my sword before getting back to work.

"Not as far as I know," Willard said. "One of my agents managed to get photos of the thief. She's human, maybe part dwarf or elf or something else, but mostly human. She keeps stealing magical artifacts, rare books and art, and other extremely valuable items and—we just figured this part out—escaping to another world. Our team had her surrounded at a warehouse where they'd laid a trap, but she's acquired what we are dubbing a portal generator. There are photos of it in action in the file. Her ability to create a portal was unexpected."

"I'll bet." I flipped open the folder to look at the photographs. She was solid and muscular, so more likely part dwarf than elf. The portal wasn't quite like any I'd seen before. The silvery circle appeared to have been formed by a beam shooting out of a dome-shaped device with runes on it. It looked like a holographic projector, not a magical artifact. "I've never heard of a portal generator."

"Nor had I, but those are dwarven runes on the side. You can see them in the photos where we zoomed in. They translate to *the way home*. We're surmising that the portal may only go to one place, somewhere on the dwarven home world. And since you're the only agent I have with the ability to go after her—presuming you can talk your fiancé into taking you—I thought of you for the assignment. The usual pay."

If this thief was traveling to the dwarven home world, the same home world I needed to visit anyway, I was more interested in that assignment. That didn't mean I wouldn't barter—Nin would have approved.

"The usual pay?" I asked. "Isn't there anything in the Army handbook about paying operatives more if they have to portal across the solar system to another planet?"

"Interstellar travel isn't covered in my operations manual, no."

"Maybe it's time for an update."

"No doubt." Willard squinted at me. "Aren't you independently wealthy now? What do you care what I pay you?"

"It's the principle of the thing. But how about this?" I smiled, realizing I'd been given an opportunity. "I'll do the assignment for *free* in exchange for a favor."

"I'd rather pay."

"I haven't told you the favor yet."

"It doesn't matter."

"I'll talk Zav into taking me to the dwarven home world—" no need to mention that we already had plans to follow the fae queen's lead on Chopper and visit, "—and collect your thief, if you help me organize and schedule things for our wedding."

"I knew I'd rather pay."

"All you have to do is sit in your office and call people. Florists and caterers and such. That's what you do anyway, isn't it?"

"Yes, I can't tell you how often I call the florist with Army business. Don't you have relatives that can help?"

"Amber said her assistance would end at picking out dresses for me and the bridesmaids. Do you want to be one, by the way? Nin said yes, but if I can't drum up another female friend, Dimitri will have to stand in. Or maybe Thad."

"One's parents traditionally help out with wedding planning."

"My mother suggested we elope. She doesn't like crowds or ceremonies. She suggested that if I *did* have a ceremony, it should be in a forest clearing with everyone barefoot and wearing elven luck beads." I pantomimed a long necklace on my chest, in case she hadn't seen such beads before.

"All right. I'll help, if only to keep you from having a hippy wedding in the woods with your hulking male roommate in a dress."

"Excellent. I'll catch your thief." I was about to add more, but I sensed Zav flying into range.

He'd left early that morning without explaining where he was going, saying only that he would surprise me. I hoped he'd gone for scones, but I doubted it.

"Ruin Bringer," a gruff voice said, and a huge hand with the warmth of a meat cleaver dropped onto my shoulder.

I almost reached for Chopper, but the ogre gripping me wore a surprisingly affable smile. I recognized Trogg, the hulk who'd challenged me to a fight during the early days of the coffee shop.

"Yes?" I asked warily.

"Trogg and the clan look forward to your wedding. We will bring *ogdok*, a liver-stew specialty."

"Uhm. You're coming?" What I should have said was, *There's no way you're coming.*

"Lord Dragon invited everyone at the shop when he flew past this morning. He promised many *deradayk* carcasses to be smoked and roasted there. That is a delicacy from another world. Ogres love this meat." He patted my shoulder, then trundled to the back of the room where Dimitri was standing with one of his door knockers—this one painted black.

Trogg handed him a fistful of dollars and accepted it.

"On second thought," Willard said as Zav alighted in the alley behind the building, "a forest clearing may be the ideal venue."

"I think so." There was no way I could have my wedding in a church or anywhere indoors and civilized if ogres were coming. What had Zav been thinking?

"It might be hard to find someone to cater such a remote locale, but if everyone is bringing carcasses and liver-stew, then who needs a caterer?" Now Willard's eyes were twinkling.

I'd liked it better when she'd been glaring.

The door flew open with a gust of wind and Zav strode in, looking vastly pleased as he gazed around at the coffee shop before focusing on me. With his powerful dragon aura crackling magnificently, he strode toward me, pulled me from my chair, wrapped me in his arms, and kissed me.

Though I wasn't one for public displays of smooching, it was always hard to resist the titillating electricity of his aura—and of him. Returning the kiss *almost* kept me from noticing the claps, hoots, and jeers from the patrons.

That is almost as unseemly as when your mother's hound jumps, wags, and slobbers on himself at the same time, Sindari informed me from the back of the room.

Only almost? I replied telepathically, squeezing Zav's shoulders to let him know we were done. At least until we could find somewhere private. At which point, instead of kissing, I would be more interested in asking him why he was inviting ogres to our wedding.

Zav broke the kiss, but he didn't let me go. "I have news."

"Are those Crocs?" Willard had been sitting back with her elbow on the table as she observed us, but now she was pointedly observing Zav's feet.

"They're his new lucky footwear." I patted Zav on the chest.

"They are most comfortable," Zav said. "Almost as comfortable as my elven slippers. The holes keep my feet aerated."

"Which is important, I imagine," Willard said.

Walker nodded his agreement. "They're very bright too. I bet he'll never be hit by a car on a dark night."

Zav lifted his chin and glared at them. "Woe to the vermin who presumes to drive a conveyance into a dragon."

I patted him on the chest again to draw his attention back. "What's the news?"

"Your sister, the princess, has agreed to return and continue your magical tutelage. Also, your father has agreed to preside over the wedding and marry us in the elven way."

My father would come to Earth? To the place where my mother would be? Would she like that? Or be horrified to see that he hadn't changed at all while she'd aged more than forty years?

I forced a smile—Zav looked so pleased to have arranged this for me, and it *would* be nice to have my father at my wedding—but I could already envision awkwardness. He would get a chance to meet Amber, something I wanted to see, but she might call him a pointy-eared weirdo. Should I warn him about her? Were elven youths sarcastic and prone to cheating adults out of money?

"You'll have to have a priest marry you in the *human* way too," Willard said.

"It is a greater honor to be married by an elven king," Zav stated.

Willard shrugged. "You can do both, assuming you can find a human priest who isn't weirded out by the whole arrangement." She arched an eyebrow at me.

I tapped the folder, reminding her of the assignment I'd accepted and the deal that she'd… well, she hadn't exactly agreed to it, but she also hadn't vehemently said no. "It's a good thing you're handling that for me."

"I thought I was handling the florist and caterer."

"As you just pointed out, we won't need a caterer."

She snorted. "I'll see what I can figure out. You just find that thief for me."

"Thief?" Zav asked.

"We have a new mission," I told him. "Are you ready for a trip to the dwarven homeland?"

"You know I am." His eyelids drooped as he gave me his bedroom eyes. "By the time of our wedding, you will know all there is to know about your sword, and you will be an even *greater* warrior."

"Which will make me even better at vexing your enemies?"

"I do hope so." He smiled and kissed me again.

THE END

Made in United States
Orlando, FL
01 December 2023